GOTHIC MĒTIS

SERIES PREFACE

Gothic Literary Studies is dedicated to publishing groundbreaking scholarship on Gothic in literature and film. The Gothic, which has been subjected to a variety of critical and theoretical approaches, is a form which plays an important role in our understanding of literary, intellectual and cultural histories. The series seeks to promote challenging and innovative approaches to Gothic which question any aspect of the Gothic tradition or perceived critical orthodoxy. Volumes in the series explore how issues such as gender, religion, nation and sexuality have shaped our view of the Gothic tradition. Both academically rigorous and informed by the latest developments in critical theory, the series provides an important focus for scholarly developments in Gothic studies, literary studies, cultural studies and critical theory. The series will be of interest to students of all levels and to scholars and teachers of the Gothic and literary and cultural histories.

For all titles in the Gothic Literary Studies series
visit *www.uwp.co.uk*

Gothic Mētis

Cunning Monstrosity, Shapeshifting and Subversion linking the Nineteenth Century to the Present

Natasha Rebry Coulthard

UNIVERSITY OF WALES PRESS
2025

www.uwp.co.uk

British Library Cataloguing-in-Publication Data
A catalogue record for this book is available from the British Library.

ISBN 978-1-83772-213-6
eISBN 978-1-83772-214-3

For GPSR enquiries please contact:
Easy Access System Europe Oü, 16879218. Mustamäe tee 50, 10621, Tallinn, Estonia. *gpsr.requests@easproject.com*

FSC www.fsc.org MIX Paper | Supporting responsible forestry FSC® C013604

Typeset by Marie Doherty
Printed and bound by CPI Group (UK) Ltd, Croydon, CR0 4YY

Dedicated to the Carolinian forest
and the Rocky Mountains

CONTENTS

Acknowledgements

This book presents over a decade of thinking and research, some of which began with my dissertation at the University of British Columbia, Okanagan, in 2013. Firstly, I want to acknowledge that most of this research was conducted on Blackfoot Confederacy Territory in Lethbridge, Alberta, with the rest begun on unceded Okanagan Nation Territory in Kelowna, British Columbia. These lands have inspired my thinking and my being, for which I am forever grateful.

Thank you to my former supervisor and longtime mentor, Jodey Castricano, for too many things to name. I'm sure you'll see your inspiration laced throughout these pages. Thank you to my colleagues in the Academic Writing Program and English department at the University of Lethbridge. Thanks especially to Jacob Bachinger, David Hobbs, Noa Reich, David Kootnikoff, Jay Gamble and Adam Carter for reading some of my nascent work on Gothic Mētis and giving me insights and encouragement when needed. Thank you to my students in English, writing, and discourse studies for reading weird things with me in recent years and sharing your insights. My classes offered me a fruitful space to share my ideas, and my students continuously inspire me. I hope they will be the driving force in decolonising Western universities.

I am grateful to colleagues in the International Gothic Association, the North American Victorian Studies Association and the Victorian Studies Association of Western Canada for helpful comments and insights on work presented in conference papers over recent years. I am especially grateful to Sarah Lewis from the University of Wales Press, whose patience and support was crucial to my success as a novice book writer. Thank you also to Stephanie

Laine Hamilton for reviewing my Greek and giving me insights on how to apply it.

Thank you to my husband and partner, Clayton, for supporting me and encouraging me on this journey and for reading my work along the way. Thank you to my mom, Darlene, for doing so much for me in this life. Although she is not here to read these acknowledgements, thank you also to my Nana, my forever cheerleader. Thank you to my besties, Chantal Chubaty and Kelly Doyle, for your encouragement and love. Thank you to Mittens and Dotey, my feline companions along the way, and to the corvids who have become friends: Brandon, Brenda, Harald, Carol and Maggie.

Chapter 1 is based on work from my dissertation, *Disintegrated Subjects: Gothic Fiction, Mental Science and the fin-de-siècle Discourse of Dissociation* (2013), especially my chapter on *Strange Case of Jekyll and Hyde*. Everything else here is original work.

Glossary of Greek Terms

Biē brute force; strength.

Kairos nonlinear time; timely rhetoric; an opening; opportunity.

Metis Athena's mother; Greek goddess of cunning; daughter of Tethys and Oceanus.

Mētis cunning, adaptive intelligence; embodied cunning.

Phanes-Metis Metis in the Orphic tradition; an androgynous god swallowed by Zeus to recreate the world and ascend to supreme god; Phanes is also referred to as Erikepaios, Metis and Eros.

Poikilos variegated; many-coloured sheen; shimmering; iridescent.

Polumētis/Polymētis of many wiles; those with *mētis*; one of Odysseus's epithets in Homer's *The Odyssey*.

Polymēchanos of many contrivances; resourceful; of many resources; one of Odysseus's epithets in Homer's *The Odyssey*.

Poluplokos/Polyplokos complex; twisted; tangled.

Polutropos/Polytropos full of twists and turns; of many turns; versatile; one of Odysseus's epithets in Homer's *The Odyssey*.

Poros way; pathway; means.

Pontos shifting, chaotic, and/or mysterious space; an unplotted route or passage; a path or passage closed as it is opened; a path or route that is eliminated.

Technē art; artful practice; skill; knowledge or art as or in production; technology.

Preface: Opening Lines on Liminal Times

Like many writers before me, I wish that I could surreptitiously slip into my topic while shirking the responsibility to introduce it.[1] It is difficult to know where to begin with a topic like *mētis*. Both little known and hard to define, *mētis* has been studied as much by its absence as its presence in Western philosophy and myth.[2] Although *mētis* was central to Classical Greek thought, today it is better recognised by critical variants like Michel de Certeau's 'tactics' or Donna Haraway's 'tentacularity', concepts evoking creative play, transformation, subversion, entanglement and multiplicity.[3] Simply, *mētis* is cunning, adaptive intelligence. It is a defining attribute of tricksters and their paradox, ambivalence and generative chaos. In Greek myth, Metis was a trickster. The 'wisest among gods and men'[4] who could '[turn] into many shapes',[5] she was the shapeshifting goddess of cunning and wise counsel who helped Zeus overthrow the Titans only to be consumed by him in his quest for absolute power. Her eponymous *mētis* is a wiliness used to move between categories and disrupt stable power relations. Associated with braiding, weaving, coiling and twisting, *mētis* was also found in objects like traps and nets, the skills of weavers and hunters and cunning animals like foxes and octopuses. Those with *mētis* (*polymētis*) are also *polytropos* ('full of twists and turns') and *polymechanos* (of many contrivances).[6] The term may look familiar to Canadian readers as the Métis, a Canadian Indigenous group of mixed Indigenous and European ancestry. Métis scholar Gary Lowan-Trudeau explains that *mētis* originally 'meant "no one" or "no man"'[7] and thus describes 'someone who [does] not fit perfectly into any one category, but [is] skilled at blending in everywhere'.[8]

Working with these connotations and others, *Gothic Mētis* embraces the trickery of *mētis*, especially its hybrid, shapeshifting and subversive properties. A twisted, twisting transdisciplinary study, the book brings the ancient into conversation with the modern as it brings Gothic studies into conversation with rhetorical criticism and critical posthuman theory. My aim is not only to probe the theoretical and expressive traits uniting these domains but also, and more importantly, to craft a 'fuzzy logic'[9] that resists 'black-and-white reasoning'[10] and the tyranny of binaristic discrete categories that separate and elevate self from Other, mind from matter, human from non, subject from object, etc. Fuzziness acknowledges that 'everything is a matter of degree', therefore fundamentally connected, and that 'Everything is in flux. Everything flows': even seemingly stable matter is in constant motion.[11] Such a 'fuzzy logic' seems necessary for the present.

I was captivated by *mētis* in part because of its relevance for the early twenty-first century. A time of paradox, transition and liminality, our present moment models the shifting terrain (called *pontos* in classical Greek texts)[12] that necessitates the use of *mētis*. *Mētis* is a cunning that helps one to find a pathway, a poros, through unstable and precarious territory. It is also a reminder of our porosity: the ways we are open to others both virtually and materially. These connotations of *mētis* make it appealing for a study that attempts to chart some paths into a fuzzy logic that unsettles the lingering colonial and patriarchal attitudes, narratives and practices informing our current juncture. Defined by some as the Anthropocene, the early twenty-first century is a time of uncertainty, a paradoxical blend of 'high technological mediation [and] ecological disaster'[13] made even more disorienting by the accelerated pace of industrialisation, technification, population growth, globalisation and species extinction. The Anthropocene denotes an era of human dominance reshaping the planet not just for us but for all other lifeforms. While the Anthropocene seems to highlight the Anthropos ('man') as central to the planet, it reminds us of our imbrication in the geological and ecological cycles of the Earth and our entanglements with fellow creatures, the environment and the world. It is also an imperative to acknowledge how profoundly human activities have altered these cycles and relationships at a 'planetary scale'.[14] The precise start of the Anthropocene is debated, but most scholars agree that industrialisation and colonisation, and the capitalist greed that underpins them, were its driving forces. The Anthropocene, however dated and defined, thus illuminates the harmful effects of attitudes and practices that separate self from Other, human from nonhuman and mind from matter, rendering some forms of life exploitable.

This book began during the COVID-19 pandemic, which illustrated interspecies, global interconnections while at the same, facilitated greater division within and between communities, local and global. I finished it as wildfires raged across my home country of Canada, coming seemingly earlier and fiercer than previous seasons, which for many symbolise concerning changes in climate. These extreme events are among several that illustrate the interdependencies of humans and the more-than-human world in a time of flux. Post-pandemic and posthuman, our current moment is a time of liminality, wherein we find ourselves 'betwixt and between' times, states and identities. These shifting times require new modes of being and relating. This is where *mētis* comes in. Despite the complex history and meanings underpinning *mētis* that this study will tease out, fundamentally it is a cunning that allows one to be crafty, multiplex, shifting and ambiguous while navigating contexts or 'situations which are transient, shifting, disconcerting and ambiguous' and which defy 'precise measurement, exact calculation or rigorous logic'[15] – situations like the Anthropocene.

Liminal times require liminal (or fuzzy) modes of thinking and being. Liminality resists extremes, challenges binaries and embraces hybridity, bringing the self into contact with alterity. Anthropologist Victor Turner is credited with popularising the term and concept of the liminal in his study of rites of passage. For Turner, the liminal involves a movement 'betwixt and between' states of ecological, physical, mental or emotional conditions as 'a process, a becoming'.[16] *Gothic Mētis* explores such liminal being and thinking via the overlapping domains of *mētis*, the art of cunning and polymorphy, and Gothic, the mode of the uncanny, the abject and the monstrous.

Emerging as a popular literary genre in mid to late eighteenth-century England, Gothic has been associated with liminality and hybridity, doubleness and duplicity. Horace Walpole's *The Castle of Otranto* (1764), commonly cited as the first Gothic novel, was first purported to be a translation of a recently discovered Italian manuscript; however, in his preface to the second edition, Walpole admitted his ruse and described his text as an 'attempt to blend . . . two kinds of romance, the ancient and the modern'.[17] Complete with walking portraits, skeletal monks and subterranean crypts, Walpole's story established the popular formula for the Eighteenth-century Gothic novel: mysterious events take place in a gloomy medieval castle, a heroine is trapped and pursued by a villain through hidden labyrinthine passageways, characters are doubled and duplicitous, boundaries of reality, decorum and law are transgressed and much of the action occurs at night, involving supernatural events, prophecies or liminal states of dreams, hauntings and madness. Located in the remote past, in isolated settings and amidst ancient ruins, the traditional Gothic of writers like Walpole, Matthew Lewis, Ann Radcliffe and Clara Reeve focused on 'the archaic, the pagan, that which was prior to, or was opposed to, or resisted the establishment of civilised values and a well-regulated society'.[18] Gothic is associated with extreme emotion, excessive and hyperbolic language and confusing, fragmented narratives designed to stimulate as much pleasure as they do anxiety, terror or fear. In its over 250-year history, the Gothic mode has continued to thrive, taking on new forms and inflections while remaining characterised by excess, darkness and transgression; superstition, madness and emotion; the supernatural, the liminal, the abject and the uncanny; monstrosity, mystery, magic and perversion.[19]

Yet, as I hope to unpack in the pages ahead, Gothic does more than depict the macabre and strange for pleasing horror; its etymological and conceptual associations entwined with its eighteenth-century emergence against the grain of reason and realism have made it a mode primarily geared towards unsettling, perverting and subverting dominant orders of being and representing. Gothic exceeds the limits of realism and showcases a world of sentient matter, more-than-human subjects and posthuman subjectivities. Its excessive style and disorienting narratives undo demarcations between past and present, subject and object, alive and dead, animate and inanimate, highlighting instead the porosity and ambiguity of such categories. The transgressive, liminal and hybrid modes of being and writing displayed by Gothic can be described as *mētic*, and by pairing Gothic with *mētis* conceptually and methodologically, I aim to emphasise the applications of Gothic *mētis* for critical posthumanism. Broadly speaking, individually and collectively, Gothic and *mētis* align with critical posthuman thought. More specifically, in their theoretical and rhetorical challenges to unity, fixed ontologies and linearity, the Gothic mode and '*mētic* intelligence'[20] support the posthumanist quest to trouble European humanist binary models of self and environment, through which 'Man' is elevated above and separated from the-more-than-human world, mind is separated from and elevated above matter and plurality is rendered deviant, pathological and perverse. In the introduction that follows, I outline these domains further as I interweave them, ultimately moving towards a view a distinctly 'Gothic' *mētis* – a cunning liminality that operates in multiples, metamorphosis, monstrosity and transgression. By cunning liminality, I mean that which is ingeniously heterogenous, cleverly resistant to fixed ontologies and artfully malleable. The stuff of tricksters and monsters, liminality underpins the 'fuzzy logic' of decolonial thinking and efforts.

Gothic Mētis will inevitably be difficult to categorise, to summarise or to define; it is not a study that fits neatly into any discipline or period. This is intentional and welcome. After all, *mētis*, as I will explain, is not and cannot be the foundation for an empire: it is too tricky, too slippery and too ambiguous: 'Whatever [*mētis*] wins, it does not keep.'[21] It is for these reasons that I embrace it in as part of my quest to decolonise mind, research and expression. My hope in offering up this study is that others may find *mētis* as critically and personally stimulating as I have.

Notes

1 Michel Foucault, 'The Order of Discourse', in Robert Young (ed.), *Uniting the Text: A Post-Structuralist Reader* (Boston, London and Henley: Routledge & Kegan Paul, 1981), pp. 51–78.

2 Marcel Detienne and Jean-Pierre Vernant, *Cunning Intelligence in Greek Culture and Society*, trans. Janet Lloyd (New Jersey: Humanities Press, 1978).

3 See Michel de Certeau, *The Practice of Everyday Life*, trans. Steven F. Rendall (Berkeley, Los Angeles, and London: University of California

Press, 1984) and Donna Haraway, *Staying with the Trouble: Making Kin in the Chthulucene* (Durham: Duke University Press, 2016).

4 Hesiod, *Theogony*, 929a (c. 730–700 BCE), *https://www.theoi.com/Text/HesiodTheogony.html*, accessed 1 June 2022.

5 Apollodorus, *The Library* or *Bibliotheca*, 1.3.6 and 1.2.1. (c. 101–200 CE), *https://www.theoi.com/Text/Apollodorus1.html*, accessed 1 June 2022.

6 In reference to Homer's *Odyssey*. Lisa Raphals, *Knowing Words: Wisdom and Cunning in the Classical Traditions of China and Greece* (Ithaca and London: Cornell University Press, 1992), p. 211.

7 A reference to Homer's Odysseus and his skills in deception and disguise.

8 Gary Lowan-Trudeau, 'Methodological Métissage: An Interpretive Indigenous Approach to Environmental Education Research', *Canadian Journal of Environmental Education* 17 (2012), pp. 113–30, at pp. 114–15.

9 Bernd Reiter, *Decolonizing The Social Sciences and Humanities: An Anti-Elitism Manifesto* (New York: Routledge, 2021).

10 Bart Kosko, *Fuzzy Thinking: The New Science of Fuzzy Logic* (New York: Hyperion, 1993), p. 93.

11 Kosko, *Fuzzy Thinking*, p. 1, p. 5.

12 *Póntos* can refer to an uncharted path or the voyage one takes across 'an unknown and hostile region'. Detienne and Vernant, *Cunning Intelligence in Greek Culture and Society*, p. 152.

13 Rosi Braidotti, *Posthuman Knowledge* (Cambridge: Polity Press, 2019), p. 3.

14 Wendy Parkins and Peter Adkins, 'Introduction: Victorian Ecology and the Anthropocene', *19: Interdisciplinary Studies in the Long Nineteenth Century* 26 (2018), pp. 1–15, at p. 6.

15 Detienne and Vernant, *Cunning Intelligence in Greek Culture and Society*, at pp. 3–4.

16 Victor Turner, *The Forest of Symbols: Aspects of Ndembu Ritual* (Ithaca: Cornell University Press, 1967), at p. 93, p. 94.

17 Horace Walpole, *The Castle of Otranto*, ed. Frederick S. Frank (Peterborough: Broadview Press, 2011) [1764 1st edn; 1765 2nd edn], p. 65.

18 David Punter, *The Literature of Terror, Vol. I: The Gothic Tradition*, 2nd edn (London: Longman, 1996), p. 5.

19 Fred Botting, *Gothic*, 2nd edn (London; New York: Routledge, 2014), p. 2.

20 Raphals, *Knowing Words*, p. xii.

21 De Certeau, *The Practice of Everyday Life*, p. xix.

Introduction *Gothic* Mētis*: Cunning Monstrosity*

Inspired by unstable times and driven by a decolonial impulse, this is a book about a mode of cunning, adaptive intelligence long gestated within dominant Western culture and ready to propagate in the posthuman present. I invoke this cunning, named *mētis* in Greek,[1] to call upon and conjure forth a mode of thought, being and communication associated with the hybrid and liminal, one that has been hidden in the shadows, or perhaps belly, of Western philosophy since antiquity. Metis was the Greek goddess of cunning, a shapeshifting trickster who helped Zeus overthrow the Titans. While pregnant with Athena, she was consumed by Zeus so that he could absorb her cleverness and stifle her power. Too tricky and too fluid to be destroyed, however, Metis lived on within the belly of the patriarch, and her eponymous cunning denotes an intelligence that can be used to contaminate and unsettle structures and systems that seem otherwise unassailable. Popularised by Michel de Certeau as 'tactics', *mētis* is a cunning that can be subversive and creative, 'poetic as well as warlike'.[2] Such 'ways of operating' showcase a non-anthropocentric logic of creative adaptability that has been obscured by dominant Western culture's adherence to rationalism[3] and the associated colonial impulse to treat nonhumans as materials for exploitation and consumption. *Mētis* is an intelligence shared by gods, humans, animals and objects as well as a cunning way to transgress the boundaries between them. Much like the mythic Metis was consumed by Zeus, *mētis* has been swallowed by dominant Western philosophy prising logos over pathos, masculinity over femininity, mind over body, human over nonhuman and normalcy over aberration. Recent philosophers, feminists and rhetoricians have revived *mētis* in what Jay Dolmage calls an 'intellectual and material movement against normativity' that embraces the 'double and divergent',[4] the nonlinear, the nonhuman, the uncanny and the abject. To this critical mix, I add Gothic studies as an approach to exhume and reanimate *mētis* as a posthuman and decolonial practice and perspective.

While at first glance, a popular style of supernatural literature emerging in eighteenth-century England and a mode of wily intelligence rarely discussed since antiquity make strange bedfellows, as the following book outlines, the Gothic mode and '*mētic* intelligence'[5] similarly illustrate and inspire critical posthuman thought. Posthumanism encourages critique of European humanist Man as a universalising model for humankind and the ways this model has prioritised traits like masculinity, straightness and whiteness as the markers of human being. This critique stresses both the inadequacy of a singular model to 'accommodate human difference'[6] and the complex colonial and patriarchal baggage attached to the model, which has been circulating through Western institutions and discourses from antiquity. Wrapped up in civilising initiatives and ideals of human perfectibility, humanism has fuelled imperialism, sexism, ableism and other biases that reduce some subjects to 'disposable bodies' or objects.[7] I am especially interested in the post-anthropocentric strands of posthuman criticism, which ultimately emphasise the centrality of the human/nonhuman dichotomy in typical definitions of 'Man' and his demarcation from other lifeforms. Post-anthropocentrism primarily critiques the denigration of nonhuman or more-than-human subjects in the elevation of Man over other creatures and objects as well as mind over matter. Such critiques generally encourage an expanded view of self, subjectivity and consciousness while fostering an appreciation for the non-binary, the non-normative and the nonhuman.

Gothic literature began in opposition to eighteenth-century aesthetic and political principles demanding unity, verifiability and realism in the service of Enlightenment ideals. As the first section of the introduction elaborates, in labelling his experimental blend of the 'ancient and the modern' a 'Gothic Story', Horace Walpole's *The Castle of Otranto*, commonly cited as the first Gothic novel, initiated a challenge to literary, aesthetic, philosophical and political standards, specifically the 'order, symmetry, and classification'[8] of Neoclassical aesthetics and their constraint on the sensuous and the fanciful. Since the eighteenth century, 'Gothic' has become, as Frederick Frank explains in relation to Walpole's novel, a 'password'[9] to 'inhuman', nonhuman and more-than-human worlds; its characteristic hybridity and confusion unsettle boundaries between subject and object, mind and matter, human and nonhuman. Gothic and *mētis* are thus united in their emphasis on transgression, liminality and hybridity. On the surface, these traits manifest in liminal figures like monsters and tricksters, who defy categorisation and quantification, and various conceptual and structural models of hybridity, twisting and ambivalence. On a deeper level, however, the overlaps between Gothic and *mētis* reflect ways of thinking, writing and identifying that challenge and counter European humanist modes and their demand for a unified, coherent, hermetic and sovereign self. *Mētis* enables transgression and transformation, as seen by Metis's shapeshifting and subversion, and facilitates lateral or divergent movement, as illustrated by the crafty blacksmith Hephaestus, whose sideways facing feet embody his *mētis*.[10] For the purposes of this study, I treat *mētis* as a concept and a practice – a mode of hybridising, twisting or braiding that embraces multiplicity, fragmentation and divergence against the grain of linearity, unity and conformity.

To illustrate the conceptual interweaving of Gothic, *mētis* and critical posthumanism, I turn briefly to Mary Shelley's *Frankenstein* (1818). A patchworked text about a patchworked creature, the Gothic classic illustrates the modes of hybridity and liminality under study along with their posthumanist orientation. Centrally, Shelley's novel asks what makes a man *Man*, and the unclear, uneasy answers it provides have made the text a compelling modern myth of posthumanity. Shelley's novel is highly intertextual, stitching together multiple perspectives as it unravels the story of Victor Frankenstein and his 'creature'[11] via letters and journals woven into the frame narrative of captain Robert Walton's Arctic adventures. Frankenstein's

Creature is equally hybrid and complex. With parts drawn from charnel houses and slaughterhouses and a technologically mediated birth, the Creature is an impossible blend of living-dead, human-nonhuman and natural-artificial. His unnaturally large form, yellow skin and black lips signal his visible racially-coded difference, while his paradoxical mixes of brutality and sensitivity, masculinity and femininity, yield a 'bifurcated' gender[12] or perhaps trans-gender identity.[13] Frankenstein's Creature is thus the paradigm for both the Gothic monster and all that European humanism denies from its model of subjectivity: he is too artificial, racialised, animalised, feminised, hybridised and queer to fit the mould. More than simply a visualisation of the posthuman, though, Shelley's novel interrogates the underlying assumptions about humanity underpinning European humanism. Self-educated, literate and eloquent, the Creature models the treasured traits of *logos* so central to Man's alleged superiority over other creatures and things.[14] Those with *logos* possess speech, reason and civility in contrast to those who do not, like animals and barbarians. The Creature's ability to reason and to persuade illuminates the tenuousness of those traits most often used to demarcate Man from his others. Shelley's 'monstrous progeny'[15] thus raises important questions about who or what counts (and does not count) as a subject along with the modes of expression available to those outside the bounds of Man.

Shelley's text also offers a helpful pathway to understanding *mētis* – the art of cunning. A reference to Immanuel Kant's 1755 essay,[16] the subtitle links Victor Frankenstein to Prometheus, a Greek god who embodies the wiliness, foresight and duplicity associated with the intelligence called *mētis*.[17] Like the mythic Prometheus, Frankenstein uses his craftiness to subvert the standard order of things and bestow new knowledge upon humankind for which he famously suffers. The story of Frankenstein seizing the powers of life also resembles the Metis myths, especially those outlined in Hesiod's *Theogony* (*c.* 730–700 BCE), where a pregnant Metis is consumed by Zeus lest she bear him a son destined to become a more powerful king. In swallowing the then pregnant Metis, Zeus, 'the father of men and gods', gives birth to the goddess Athena 'by way of his head' while Metis 'remained hidden beneath [his] inward parts' as his advisor and unacknowledged mother of Athena.[18] Shelley's own creative powers laid enveloped by masculine authority, with claims that Percy Shelley had refined her story to become a masterpiece. In her famous introduction to the 1831 edition, Shelley used her *mētis* to secure her status as *Frankenstein*'s rightful author,[19] distancing her work from her husband's influence while ruminating on the nature of invention. She describes her process of 'seizing on the capabilities of a subject', the 'power of moulding and fashioning ideas suggested to it' and her efforts to 'describe the spectre which had haunted [her] midnight pillow' as she worked to fashion a ghost story from a dream. Without denying Percy Shelley's 'incitement' to develop her story 'to greater length' or his authorship of the first edition preface, Shelley claims that 'I certainly did not owe the suggestion of one incident, nor scarcely of one train of feeling, to my husband'. Much like the Greek trickster after whom her novel takes its subtitle, Shelley demonstrates foresight, bidding her now world-famous 'monstrous progeny [to] go forth'.[20]

Frankenstein exemplifies the cunning, liminality and multiplicity that define Gothic *mētis* along with its posthuman, post-anthropocentric inflections. Broadly speaking, *Gothic Mētis* weaves together the three domains of Gothic, *mētis* and critical posthuman theory. Such a model reflects the twisted, sideways movements of *mētis* and the associated skills of weaving or braiding[21] as well as a method/methodology known as métissage – a theory and praxis based in 'the ability to transform' and the 'properties of mixing'.[22] Métissage is necessarily interdisciplinary, using bricolage, or the 'conscious blending'[23] of distinctive theories and methods; it 'engages the world as dialogic and heteroglossic', inviting readers, writers and researchers to not only notice the intertextuality of texts but also 'to imagine and create plural selves and communities that thrive on ambiguity and multiplicity'.[24] In 'The Politics and Aesthetics of Métissage', Françoise Lionnet promotes métissage for its value in nonhierarchical or lateral relations that embrace indeterminacy and mixing. She characterises métissage as flexible, fluid and rebellious, relating it to Creolization and other forms of racial, cultural, linguistic and theoretical mixing[25] while aligning it with feminist and postcolonial thought. I follow Lionnet and view métissage as a concept and practice that resists 'essentialist glorifications of unitary origins, be they racial, sexual, geographic, or cultural'.[26]

Cynthia Chambers, Erika Hasebe-Ludt and Carl Leggo describe métissage as a practice emerging from 'the interval between different cultures and languages' and a *technē* (artful praxis) for blending space with place, the 'familiar with strange' and all manner of binaries, such as past with present, self with Other, 'local with global, East with West, North with South, particular with universal, feminine with masculine . . . and theory with practice.'[27] At its core, métissage involves the braiding and blurring cultures, genres and traditions to affirm difference, to resist polarisation and to challenge fixed ontologies.[28]

Métissage perhaps carries weight in the context of Canadian scholarship. Canada has been described as a 'Métis' nation,[29] 'built on intercultural cooperation and mutual influence between European and Indigenous cultures'.[30] Indigenous cultures, of course, have not been given prominence in Canada, given its colonial legacy and fraught history of the residential school system. Yet, as Blackfoot scholar Leroy Little Bear prompts, all Canadians, whether Indigenous or not, are affected by colonial legacies and have a role to play in decolonising the present.[31] Métissage, like *mētis* more generally, promotes what political scientist Bernd Reiter calls the 'fuzzy logic' of decolonisation, through which the binary, exclusionary 'rigid epistemologies and ontologies' of European colonial thought are supplanted by the 'fuzzy realities of life and the world', which Reiter suggests are best illuminated through Indigenous and non-European theories.[32] Canadian Métis scholars, including Dwayne Donald and Greg Lowan-Trudeau, have promoted and applied métissage in their research, linking it to decolonisation, Indigenisation and ecological thinking in which 'human beings are seen as intimately enmeshed in webs of relationships with each other and with the other entities that inhabit the world'.[33] Métissage thus connotes Indigenous theories in a way that I find both helpful and necessary to my research as a Canadian scholar. Although Indigenous theories are not my focus, *Gothic Mētis* promotes the ecological awareness and ethical relationality endorsed by Donald and consonant with many Indigenous theories. Such models of thinking, being and relating also inform theories like critical posthumanism and post-anthropocentric theory, which seek to shift perspectives away from European humanism and anthropocentrism for the ways these worldviews have separated humans from nonhumans and prioritised mind over matter.

In uniting *mētis* and posthumanism with Gothic, I aim to emphasise the ways in which Gothic has helped to articulate a multiplex, polymorphic and porous model of self along with a 'fuzzy logic' that unsettles distinctions between self and Other, mind and body, subject and object. My focus is especially on nineteenth-century Gothic for the ways it speaks to the rise and demise of the Anthropocene and offers a site for unsettling Man. The confluence of nineteenth-century sciences like geology, evolutionary theory, ecology and psychology collectively redefined human being and the place of Man in the cosmos, a redefinition spectacularly rendered in the period's Gothic. *Gothic Mētis* blends, braids and blurs the ancient with the nineteenth century and the contemporary to yield fresh insights about the Gothic mode's relevance and application in posthuman, liminal times. In the first braid of my methodological tapestry, I explore the Gothic – the broad domain of the uncanny, monstrous, and liminal – before turning to critical posthuman theory and finally back to *mētis*, the art of cunning and polymorphy. The introduction moves somewhat obliquely through eighteenth- and nineteenth-century England, our global post-anthropocentric present and the myths of ancient Greece. Each section offers a braid that will ultimately be woven into a more comprehensive vision of how 'Gothic *mētis*' can be understood and applied. Readers wanting to experience this text nonlinearly in the spirit of *mētis* may wish to read the following braids in a new order, beginning with either the second or the third braid before circling back and returning to the first braid.

The First Braid: Gothic's Twisted Domain

Untangling the Gothic Mode

Gothic is a notoriously tricky term to define. The term's conceptual and etymological capaciousness stem from its varied history as an adjective describing the Germanic Ostrogoth and Visigoth tribes, an ornate style of European architecture, Whig politics and a genre of popular eighteenth-century fiction, which showcased the supernatural and the irrational. As it came into widespread use in the eighteenth century, 'Gothic' stood for unenlightened, superstitious, 'old-fashioned', 'barbaric' and crude as opposed to rational, 'modern', 'civilised' and elegant.[34] 'Gothic' also captured an aesthetic of ornateness and miscellany, as seen in Gothic Revival architecture, and the political ideology of the Whig Party, which was hostile to 'tyranny and absolutism', particularly the 'autocratic forms of political order associated with the Romans' and the 'monarchical, crypto-Catholic despotism of Tory Royalists'.[35] All these meanings are entangled in Horace Walpole's *The Castle of Otranto* (1764). In crafting his 'Gothic Story', Walpole aimed to capture the excessive, baroque nature of Gothic Revival architecture along with the rebelliousness of Gothic politics.[36] Gothic architecture displays many of the aesthetic traits that would later come to define the Gothic novel: 'monstrous', 'confused and disordered' with lines 'twisted like corkscrews'[37] and excessive embellishment. Walpole's famous Gothic Revival villa, Strawberry Hill, was 'deliberately miscellaneous: a heterogeneous jumble' not easily classified.[38] This was the setting that inspired his 'Gothic Story', which he described as 'an attempt to blend the two kinds of romance, the ancient and the modern', or the fantastical and the realistic, and to release the 'great resources of fancy' that had been 'dammed up' by modernity.[39]

Gothic's emergence during the rise of the Enlightenment 'as the dominant way of ordering the world'[40] is noteworthy. Its rise in popularity was facilitated by what Robert Miles describes as 'the growing gap between world and thing'[41] and represents, as Jodey Castricano posits in her recent *Gothic Metaphysics*, 'not solely . . . a genre but rather . . . a significant metaphysical outlier to a worldview' that privileges reason, rationalism and verifiability.[42] More specifically, Castricano links the Gothic mode to 'an order of reality or worldview' in which 'matter and nature are accorded consciousness or sentience and seen as not only alive but *purposive*' and responsive.[43] Frederick Frank links Walpole's project to a larger Romantic desire to engage with 'inhuman and superhuman things' and recover what 'had been ignored or suppressed by the decorous standards of the Enlightenment'[44] in the disenchantment of the world. Although he does not mention it specifically, Frank's discussion points to Gothic as 'a password to'[45] the more-than-human along with the 'inhuman and superhuman'. As Frank's introduction to Walpole's novel outlines, the Gothic mode engages 'an outrageous new first law of motion' whereby '*the deader or more inanimate an object is supposed to be, the more likely it is to move, to feel, to think*'. Walpole's magical objects, like giant armour and an animate portrait, reveal what Frank describes as the '*sentience of space and place*',[46] which he claims is the foundation for the Gothic more generally and which Castricano links to a worldview 'not only reminiscent of alchemical thought and the Hermetic tradition but also stands as an ally to Indigenous thought' and the Romantic's claim that world is imbued with Mind.[47] The Gothic mode unsettles, as Cynthia Sugars and Gerry Turcotte claim of its Canadian variant,[48] and it unsettles not only Enlightenment and humanist values, but also the very views of subjectivity and reality they predicate.

Gothic protagonists are notoriously prone to madness, to fantasy, to extreme trance and dream states, and ultimately to breakdowns, challenges and questions to reality. However, if Gothic subjects are 'fragmented',[49] 'alienated, [and] divided from themselves',[50] then this might be because they find themselves faced with 'an order of reality or worldview long disparaged but not eradicated'[51] – a reality in which matter is sentient, purposeful and responsive and selves are porous, plural and pliable. Since the eighteenth century, Gothic has participated in what Robert Miles describes as 'the discursive construction of the human subject' and with this, its ability to be creatively, 'imaginatively disassembled, re-assembled, and generally re-figured'.[52] J. Halberstam makes a similar point when they claim, 'Gothic fiction is a technology of subjectivity', which generates 'deviant subjectivities' against 'the normal, the healthy, and the pure'.[53] Despite its heterogeneous, multiplex and manifold nature (or perhaps because of it), Gothic offers a 'coherent code' for the representation of fragmented subjectivity, for the representation of the subject 'in a state of deracination, . . . finding itself dispossessed in its own house, in a condition of rupture, disjunction, fragmentation'[54] – of a subject estranged from Enlightenment models of self, demanding unity, coherence and exceptionality. Indeed, Gothic may offer narrative and rhetorical strategies to render modes of intelligence, subjectivity and embodiment beyond and outside *the human* as it is defined in the European humanist tradition.

Gothic's Twisted Forms

Fred Botting positions Gothic fiction in the 'shadow'[55] of the Enlightenment, offering artists a 'negative aesthetics'[56] with which to counter and/or contaminate the dominant order of lightness, straightness, unity and reason. If Gothic emerges as part of a series of oppositions, though, it rarely respects its place in the binary; in its negative aesthetics, the mode demonstrates paradoxical twists of light/dark, evil/good and madness/reason. What is terrifying is also often pleasurable, giving rise to Gothic's characteristic ambivalence and common critical linkage to the sublime, Burke's and Kant's notion of elevating terror. Gothic orientations are confused and confusing; critics rarely agree if Gothic's impulse is conservative or subversive, confining or liberatory, perhaps because 'it is often both, simultaneously'.[57] If 'Gothic repeatedly stages moments of transgression because it is obsessed with establishing and policing borders, with delineating strict categories of being',[58] then it also, simultaneously and emphatically, questions and undermines these very borders and categories.

From its inception, Gothic has been a liminal, hybrid mode; much like Frankenstein's creature and Shelley's 'monstrous progeny' which tells his tale, it is 'assembled out of bits and pieces'[59] and drawn 'from an uneasy conflation of genres, styles, and conflicted cultural concerns',[60] which blend 'the ancient and the modern', the high and the low, the comic and the tragic. Maggie Kilgour explains the Gothic as a 'hybrid of the novel and the romance', noting that Gothic 'feeds upon and mixes the wide range of literary sources out of which it emerges and from which it never fully disentangles itself', including graveyard poetry, folklore, British theatre and German literature.[61] Gothic texts are often scattered, layered and fragmented, constructed as they are by frame, nested and epistolary narratives, multiple narrators, partial and damaged manuscripts, layered palimpsestic commentary, and 'irrelevant digressions, set-pieces of landscape description that never refer back to the central point'.[62] Gothic texts are described as polyphonic, polysemic, dialectical, comprised of a 'contending discourses',[63] dialogical and highly intertextual for the ways they blend, blur and engage previous texts 'not all of them literary'.[64] Such paradox, excess and interdiscursivity make Gothic difficult to define and contain. Like many of its iconic monsters, the Gothic mode shapeshifts, infects the other genres it encounters and rematerialises into new forms. Gothic has been theorised as a mode of returns and revivals, refusing to stay in its location in time, space, culture or form. Because of its characteristic 'mobility and continued capacity for reinvention',[65] 'internal heterogeneity' and endless mutations, Gothic is 'not containable to one period',[66] genre, culture or medium. If *Gothic* seems an 'ambiguous, shifting term', it is because it represents 'shifting and ambiguous' textual occurrences.[67] More than simply a genre, Gothic 'goes beyond the merely literary',[68] perhaps more aptly described as a mode, discourse and/or a rhetoric, a point to which I return in the last section of the introduction.[69]

Given such complexity, it has become difficult (and often undesirable) for critics to offer a comprehensive definition. It is not my intention here to offer such a definition, nor is it to offer an overview of Gothic history. In working with *mētis*, the rhetorical art of cunning and polymorphy, I wish to emphasise Gothic's flexibility as a genre, a style, a mode, an aesthetic, a rhetoric and a discourse through which monstrosity, uncanniness and liminality are expressed. While the boundaries, horrors and Otherness explored in Gothic narratives reveal nationally, culturally, socially and historically specific questions and/or anxieties, the Gothic mode most frequently probes the limits of *logos* (language and reason) and rebels 'against a constraining neoclassical aesthetic ideal of order and unity'.[70] In speaking of Gothic as rhetoric and discourse, I aim to emphasise the persuasive power of Gothic to not only portray but ultimately generate a posthuman worldview in which matter is alive and selves are plural and porous.

Although Gothic has been theorised as a crisis mode, emerging at times of socio-cultural stress as a response to or perhaps beacon of fears, trauma or anxiety, I want to link it to *krisis*, a timely and powerful response to the Enlightenment and the model of Man it propagated. Pointing at once to nonlinear time and timely rhetoric, *kairos* means the right time and right measure. Chronos offers a concept of measurable time, quantitative and linear; *kairos* offers a qualitative version or vision of time, 'the special position an event or action occupies in a series' or 'a season when something appropriately happens that cannot happen just at "any time," but only at *that* time'.[71] In other words, *kairos* links events occurring in the present to events of the past and future, understanding them as part of a larger series, season or whole. As Robert Leston argues, 'Because it deals with temporality, . . . kairos is perpetually concerned with the flux and becoming of life', prompting much consideration of limits, relations and perceptions.[72] Thus, *kairos* invites considerations not only of purposeful rhetorical action, but also of the enmeshment of semiosis, time, situation and environment[73] and the ways in which particular styles, topoi, figures and frames emerge as timely, appropriate or opportune to captivate audiences. *Kairos* 'means a time of tension and conflict, a time of crisis', but this crisis carries opportunity to accomplish something that could not be accomplished some other time.[74] *Kairos* is therefore also *krisis*: 'not a problem to be solved, but a kairotic opening' through which the world is shaped.[75] *Kairos* envisions what should be breaking into the present moment, so that 'something new' emerges 'out of old and dying conditions'.[76]

Gothic – the coherent code for the fragmented subject and cryptic 'vessel' for an enchanted worldview[77] – had a timely emergence in the late eighteenth century, working against the grain of Enlightenment and humanism. Gothic might be fragmented, excessive, paradoxical and ambivalent, but such traits seem to be the 'right measure' for our posthuman, liminal times.

Gothic in the *Long* Long Nineteenth Century

Gothic is a *kairotic* mode, emerging again and again with timely new forms and narratives to suit new contexts. Not merely reactive or exploitative, Gothic is 'interrogative'[78] and agonistic: a site of encountering, questioning, struggling and grappling with our fears and anxieties along with our notions of subjectivity, reality and ethics. Agonistic is not the same as antagonistic; agonism denotes a transformative 'response-producing encounter' that occurs when bodies, cultures or genres actively engage across difference.[79] As 'we' increasingly interrogate the limits of our selves and grapple with our responsibilities in the posthuman liminal age, Gothic has perhaps never been more timely. Yet, in line with *kairos* nonlinear time and Gothic's characteristic temporal dissonance, I want to develop my analysis of Gothic's present posthuman, post-anthropocentric value by turning to *fin-de-siècle* Gothic, suggesting that its narrative topics and strategies have renewed force for contemporary readers. Although the tendency is to read *fin-de-siècle* Gothic in terms of post-Darwinian crisis, from a rhetorical perspective, we can read it in terms of *krisis*: a timely, wily response to the disenchantment of the world and the rise of the Anthropocene. From an examination of *fin-de-siècle* Gothic, I tease out the *kairotic* and *mētic* dimensions of the Gothic mode more generally, exploring Gothic's attendant timeliness and wiliness in depicting a world beyond and without Man.

I want to begin my study of Gothic in the Victorian age, taking a long view of the long nineteenth century, described by Canon Schmitt as the *long* long nineteenth century.[80] If the long nineteenth century spanned from the French Revolution to World War I, then the *long* long nineteenth century includes the present and perhaps also the future. This long view situates the Victorian era alongside the present with an eye to future as part of the Anthropocene, a concept popularised by Paul Crutzen as the 'human-dominated geological epoch' in which the human has become 'a major environmental force' accelerating climate change.[81] Many critics situate the start of the Anthropocene with the Industrial Revolution while others link it to colonial contacts, which altered local environments and lifeforms.[82] Along with industrialisation and colonisation, the nineteenth century witnessed significant scientific developments that reshaped ideas about planet, species and environment, particularly, geology, evolutionary theory and ecology. In brief, Charles Lyell's *Principles of Geology* (1830–33) altered perceptions of human and geological time; Charles Darwin's works, especially *The Origin of Species* (1859), transformed understandings of human origins and nonhuman relations; and Ernst Haeckel's *Generelle Morphologie der Organismen* (1866) presented his theory of ecology, which emphasised relationships between organisms in an environment. At the same time, psychology introduced a realm of unconscious mental life and initiated debates over the locations and limits of consciousness. Collectively, these sciences called into question assumptions about time, matter and species, especially the primacy of Man. The 'Victorian imagination' was deeply engaged with questions about human relationships with the more-than-human world and the long-term environmental effects of modernisation, foreshadowing our 'contemporary ecological concerns' while illuminating 'the historical origins of many of our present crises'.[83] As I will demonstrate, Victorian Gothic literature thoughtfully intervened in these debates through its depictions of plural, porous, chimerical subjects entangled with technological and environmental forces.

The Victorian era for many is '*the* Gothic period.'[84] Gothic was 'seemingly everywhere' in Victorian fiction and culture,[85] cropping up in the domestic terrors of Charlotte, Emily and Anne Brontë, the urban settings of Charles Dickens, the clairvoyant sympathy of George Eliot and the sensational tales of Wilkie Collins as well as the Victorian fascination with death, 'ghosts, spiritualism and the occult'.[86] As I hope to demonstrate, Gothic seemed everywhere in the Victorian era, not simply because of its dark, lacy fashion or obsession with séances, but rather because the Victorians were witnessing a slew of changes that yielded new modes of subjectivity and reality, ones that profoundly unsettled who and what they thought they were. Late-Victorian or *fin-de-siècle* Gothic especially expresses responses to these changes. Inflected by evolutionary, biological and psychological theory, *fin-de-siècle* Gothic is characterised as more fragmented, more visceral, more excessive and more ambivalent than its eighteenth-century predecessor, emphasising metamorphic bodies and various indeterminacies of species, gender, race, sexuality and states (e.g., living-dead, liquid-solid-gas, young-old, etc.). Some of the most interesting and enduring Gothic icons, as Roger Luckhurst calls them,[87] were published during the era, including Robert Louis Stevenson's *Strange Case of Dr Jekyll and Mr Hyde* (1886), H. G. Wells's scientific romances like *The Time Machine* (1895) and *The Island of Doctor Moreau* (1896), Arthur Machen's *The Great God Pan* (1894) and *The Three Impostors* (1895), Richard Marsh's *The Beetle* (1897) and Bram Stoker's *Dracula* (1897). *Fin-de-siècle* Gothic emphasised transgressions of the order of species and the hierarchies of mind and matter, showcasing the permeable and questionable boundaries between human and nonhuman, mind and body, self and Other. I want to position my discussion of late-Victorian Gothic in relation to *mētis* and posthuman, post-anthropocentric theory to tease out the affective and philosophical dimensions of these boundary crossings and category blurrings.

I also want to blur temporal and disciplinary boundaries as I bring twenty-first-century texts into my analysis alongside late

Victorian Gothic. In including twenty-first-century fiction, film and media under the rubric of the *long* long nineteenth century, I inevitably gloss over important historical and socio-cultural distinctions between times, places and expressions. My intention is not to obscure the importance of situated knowledge and place-based, local analyses, but rather to acknowledge the continuing relevance of *fin-de-siècle* Gothic, to model the principles of métissage and to embrace the nonlinearity of *kairos*, of Gothic temporality and of what Rosi Braidotti calls posthuman time.[88] The intent of this temporal blurring is to 'connect and reconnect with relations, both close and far, across geographical and disciplinary lines',[89] 'because there is no linear time, but a thousand plateaus of possible becomings, each following its own multidirectional course'.[90]

The Second Braid: Post-Anthropocentric Thought

Entanglements of Self and Other

Gothic Mētis emphasises what might be termed Gothic's posthuman, post-anthropocentric leanings and associated value for posthuman theory and rhetoric. Most simply, posthumanism critiques 'the humanist ideal of "Man"'[91] as 'the measure of all things',[92] while post-anthropocentrism challenges the speciesism and exceptionalism attached to this ideal.[93] In my analyses, I blend critical posthumanism and post-anthropocentrism with adjacent theories like new materialism, material or corporeal feminism, speculative realism[94] and Object-Oriented Ontology (OOO). These theories unite in their critique of European humanist ideologies and subjectivities, particularly the value for a 'coherent, rational self' believed to be autonomous, agentic and enlightened[95], separate and above other creatures, objects or 'things'. OOO embraces the value of 'things', working with Martin Heidegger's 'tool being' in *Being and Time*, which Graham Harman argues 'gives birth to an ontology of *things themselves*' in which objects have lives or existences of their own, independent of and often beyond the perception of humans (or other things with whom they come into contact).[96] New (sometimes vital) materialists share OOO's interest in what Jane Bennett calls 'thing power', or 'the strange ability' of manufactured objects 'to manifest traces of independence or aliveness, constituting the outside of our own experience.'[97] The theories illuminate the mind in matter and the embodied nature of mind while highlighting the power of more-than-human and nonhuman subjects in the dramas of the world.

Although posthumanism often evokes an engagement with technological discourses and techno-human hybridity (most famously in Donna Haraway's cyborg), it is a diverse theoretical mode for deconstructing and dismantling humanist ideologies and discourses of self/Other with a call to develop alternative subjectivities in response. I apply the critical posthumanism of scholars like Cary Wolfe and Rosi Braidotti, treating the theory as a 'generative tool' for rethinking 'the human'[98] outside of the confines of humanist *Man*. As Karen Barad outlines, posthumanism is no grand celebration of the death of Man, nor is it 'an uncritical embrace of the cyborg' as a saviour, but rather a critique of 'human exceptionalism' and a prompt to become 'accountable for the role we play in the differential constitution and differential positioning of the human among other creatures'.[99] Posthumanists align with new materialists and corporeal feminists in their challenge to humanist models of self which separate the human from nature, elevate it over the nonhuman and hierarchise the mind over body, instead emphasising the interconnections between body and mind as well as humans, nonhumans and environment. Critical posthuman scholars underscore that 'the boundaries of the human subject are constructed rather than given', that there are no 'essences' to things like humans, animals, or machines[100] and that 'the "human" is not a neutral term but rather a hierarchical one that indexes access to privileges and entitlements'.[101] The goal is to deconstruct the dualisms that give rise to exploitative hierarchies, such as human/animal, culture/nature and self/Other.

New materialists argue that it matters *how* we matter and make the body the 'very "stuff" of subjectivity.'[102] Karen Barad's complex theory of agential realism (derived from quantum physics) challenges the 'prior existence of independent entities or relata' along with the 'metaphysics of individualism'.[103] Her concept 'intra-action' or 'intra-activity' suggests 'the mutual constitution of entangled agencies',[104] assuming that specific materialities and agencies emerge *through* relationships (more formally, quantum entanglements).

Intra-activity demonstrates that all matter is 'in-the-process-of-becoming . . . iteratively enfolded into . . . ongoing differential materializations' and that '"human" bodies are not inherently different from "nonhuman" ones'.[105] New materialists like Barad and Stacy Alaimo posit that a view of the body-in-motion coupled with an understanding of our '[interconnections] with the wider environment marks a profound shift in subjectivity',[106] demonstrating that humans and nonhumans are mutually constituted, as integral parts '*of* the world . . . part of the world in its differential becomings'.[107] If 'relata do not preexist relations' but rather emerge from 'specific intra-actions', then our particular intra-actions through which 'we' are 'co-constituted and entangled' with 'others' draw us into particular relationships – certain ways of living and being that come with contextual responsibilities.[108] This is not an issue of human agency, though, but rather 'an ongoing responsiveness to the entanglements of self and other'.[109] Posthuman theories unsettle ontological and epistemological assumptions about human being, its distinctions from things, environment and other creatures, and therefore its exceptionality and primacy. In the best cases, these theories call the human to develop responsible and response-*able* relationships with the many human, nonhuman, more-than-human and inhuman entities we live with and depend on.

Posthumanist, new materialist and/or post-anthropocentric theories share Gothic's engagement with an enchanted world of 'sentient space and place' and multiplex, porous selves. In some ways, posthumanism might be inherently Gothic and Gothic might be inherently posthumanist, for, as Botting defines it, Gothic is the necessary 'negative aesthetics' working alongside, within and against Enlightenment and reason. Gothic forms, figures and formulae have long been associated with anti- and counter-humanist ideologies as well as ontological states that come 'before, beyond, and alongside the humanist subject'.[110] A posthuman, post-anthropocentric perspective aligns with Castricano's Gothic worldview and adds new nuance to Gothic criticism, with its focus on ontological and epistemological uncertainty, liminal states, hybrid and subaltern identities, unstable binaries, monstrous becomings and the 'sentience of space and place.' By 'urging' us to see beyond the physical and the anthropocentric, Gothic invites the recognition and experience of relationships between humans and the more-than-human world, sustaining a 'view of a sentient world in spite of mechanical philosophy' and continuously sending 'aftershocks along the fault lines of anthropocentrism' since its 'seismic' emergence in the eighteenth century.[111]

Posthumans, Monsters and Others[112]

Posthuman and Gothic scholars are united by their interest in liminal ontologies and epistemologies, especially those demarcating the human subject from 'its Others: the monster, the stranger, the alien and . . . the posthuman'.[113] Along with Haraway's cyborg, Frankenstein's Creature has become something of a posterchild for the posthuman. Like the cyborg, the unnamed 'monster' is a blend of organic and mechanic, natural and artificial, human and animal, alive and dead. As Elaine Graham writes, 'he confuses many of the boundaries by which normative humanity has been delineated'.[114] Significantly, the Creature expresses a subjectivity 'outside of the human(ist) paradigm'[115] yet from within, since he is capable of reason and self-expression and thus possesses *logos*. Indeed, as Anya Heise-von der Lippe's reading of Shelley's novel illuminates, the text illustrates 'the conceptual difficulties of adopting a posthumanist perspective'[116] since humanism is the necessary container for posthumanism. Posthumanism is not really an 'after' humanism, and the posthuman is not really an 'after' the human, but more properly a deconstruction of humanist Man, challenging his speciesist, universalising and patriarchal nature.

Differently conceptualised humans than Man, posthumans defy categorisation and confuse ontologies. The posthuman is conceived as a liminal creature 'inhabiting the boundary between the human and the almost-human'[117] whose 'boundaries undergo continuous construction and reconstruction',[118] calling into question the very nature of these boundaries and 'the fixity of "human nature"'.[119] Posthumans exist 'between between' dualities and binaries – a type of 'becoming'[120] in the Deleuze-Guattarian sense of a 'creative *involution*', which results from symbioses, contagions, 'transversal communications' and other miscellaneous or multispecies alliances that challenge kinships restricted to 'filiation.'[121] 'Posthuman bodies', as Halberstam and Livingstone describe them, are 'bodies-in-process':[122] heterogeneous and always *becoming* something else through their *involvements* with other creatures, things and environment. Becoming is a unique evolution, one that does not necessarily progress or regress in a series or rely on ancestry, but rather generates novel assemblages and alliances, which for Deleuze and Guattari are necessarily 'minoritarian' against 'majoritarian' Man.[123] That is, *becomings* shift subjectivities away from the restrictive self/Other dichotomies and the politics of dominance associated with humanism to open innovative opportunities for identity, kinship and community, often working along lateral lines as opposed to linear, hierarchical ones.

Posthumans are 'Queer, cyborg, metametazoan, hybrid', but they are not some 'obsolescence of the human' and do not 'represent an evolution or devolution of the human'.[124] The 'post' means neither 'superseding the human [nor] coming after it'.[125] As Wolfe explains posthumanism, it is much like Jean-François Lyotard's concept of post-modernism always already inhabiting modernism.[126] Posthumans are not so much a 'post', then, as an alternative, always already running alongside (possibly within) humanism. Posthumans resemble Haraway's cyborg: 'resolutely committed to partiality, irony, intimacy, and perversity' in their 'oppositional' nature[127] and resistance to hierarchical difference both amongst humans '(whether according to race, class, gender)' and between them and nonhumans.[128] Posthumans offer a porous, multiplex, malleable[129] and ultimately enlarged model of human being, one that is 'transversal', relational and rhizomatic in its allegiance to nonhumans, inhumans, abhumans and the more than human world.[130]

Although monsters and posthumans are not necessarily synonymous, they are both liminal creatures who dwell 'at the gates of difference',[131] thriving in, on and between the margins of humans and their Others. Monsters serve complex cultural and rhetorical functions: they reveal, portend, symbolise, demonstrate[132] and ultimately unsettle 'what has been constructed . . . as natural, as human'.[133] Monsters serve both to mark 'the fault-lines' of human identity 'but also, subversively, to signal the fragility of such boundaries'; it is 'their simultaneous demonstration and destabilization' of norms that makes them 'monstrous'.[134] While monstrosity has been used to pathologise and demonise racial, gender, sexual, political, physical or mental difference, it also offers a trope for porous, heterogeneous and fluid models of self/subjectivity. The 'promise of monsters' is their 'blurring of boundaries' and the ways they unsettle 'the "ontological hygiene" by which . . .Western culture has drawn the fault-lines that separate humans, nature and machines' since at least the Enlightenment.[135] The monstrous is an 'invitation to explore . . . new and interconnected methods of perceiving the world' and to break 'either/or' logic in favour of 'either/and'.[136] The monster's heterogeneity resists hierarchies and binaries, offering instead a model for 'polyphony' and polymorphism.[137]

Betwixt and Between-Between: Liminality in Thinking and Being

Monsters and posthumans are liminal beings who point to the opportunities for liminal thinking and subjectivity. Liminal thinking and liminal selves resist fixed epistemologies and ontologies, moving between domains while embracing hybridity, heterogeneity, fluidity and fuzziness. Anthropologist Victor Turner is credited with developing the theory of liminality as a 'change from one state to another' involved in various rites of passage. The 'liminal *persona*' is a 'transitional-being' who is 'at once no longer classified and not yet classified'.[138] Liminal beings are boundary-dwellers and threshold-beings, existing 'betwixt-and-between' states, identities or categories. Turner links liminality to malleability, 'ambiguity and paradox, a confusion of all the customary categories'.[139] Liminal or 'fuzzy thinking'[140] engages the world as is – a flux of transient, porous subjects and objects. Limits are 'thresholds of encounters with others',[141] which bring the self into productive contact with alterity. To be liminal is not to be limitless, though: bodies and selves might be transversal, relational, plural and porous, but they have boundaries, however permeable.

The Third Braid: Mētis *in Myth and Rhetoric*

Metis/*Mētis*

Critics interested in post-anthropocentrism, more-than-human sentience and liminal or marginalised states have turned to *mētis* as a mode of thinking, being and relating that operates in the domains where *logos* does not. *Mētis* is a slippery, wily, shifty intelligence that works as/by intuition, on the fly and in the shadow of reason. Appealing 'more through *pathos* than *logos* or *ethos*, . . . emerging relationally from shifting and ambiguous situations' and operating 'with quick maneuvers that elude logical apprehension' and '[outsmart] brute force',[142] *mētis* is an intelligence 'which is alien to truth and quite separate from *epistēmē*, knowledge'.[143] *Mētis* 'always appears more or less below the surface' and in 'practical operations' that do not attempt to explain or justify their 'procedures',[144] often illustrated by embodied arts like weaving, where a weaver calls as much upon unconscious knowledge as they do conscious skill. This cunning intelligence has been described as 'tactics' by Michel de Certeau: subversive, creative and '*artistic* tricks' and clever ways of 'making do' with the available materials, spaces, resources and situations.[145] Perhaps 'the paragon of *mētis*' most familiar to the literary and cultural studies crowds is the crafty Odysseus from Homer's *Iliad* and *Odyssey*, described as '*polumētis*, "of many wiles," [and] *poikilomētis*, "of manifold artifice"'.[146] *Mētis* also manifests in deities like Metis, her daughter Athena and the disabled blacksmith god, Hephaestus, whose outwards facing feet embody and enable his *mētis*;[147] animals such as foxes, octopuses, seabirds and snakes; equipment like hunting traps and fishing nets; the skills of weavers, carpenters, midwives, navigators and politicians; and the rhetorical skills of the Sophists, known for persuasive tricks and twists, such as turning a weaker argument against the stronger.

As Marcel Detienne and Jean-Pierre Vernant explain in their famous study of *mētis*, *Cunning Intelligence in Greek Culture and Society* (1978), *mētis* is 'a type of intelligence and thought, a way of knowing' that denotes 'pliability and polymorphism, duplicity and equivocality, inversion and reversal'.[148] Through its various semantic and mythic associations, *mētis* represents an assortment of mental, physical and rhetorical traits drawing on metamorphosis, multiplicity, border crossing and weaving as well as braids, nets and tricks. Despite its complexity, *mētis* encompasses what Detienne and Vernant[149] describe as a 'coherent body of mental attitudes and intellectual behaviour', combining 'flair, wisdom, forethought, subtly of mind, deception, resourcefulness, vigilance, opportunism' and lifelong 'skills and experience'. *Mētis* is an intelligence used in 'situations which are transient, disconcerting, and ambiguous' and 'do not lend themselves to precise measurement, exact calculation or rigorous logic'.[150] Because it allows one to be multiple, flexible and adaptive, *mētis* equips those who possess it with a set of skills necessary to navigating and surviving treacherous, shifting situations and spaces. Whether they be god, human or animal, one with *mētis* becomes 'more multiple, more mobile, more polyvalent than' the 'multiple, changing . . . polymorphic powers' they might face.[151]

In Greek myth, the cunning trickster Metis is a goddess deceived and devoured by a god in pursuit of absolute power. One of Tethys and Oceanus's three thousand daughters, Metis's eponymous cunning intelligence made her the 'wisest among gods and men'.[152] Through her cunning, she tricked Cronus into drinking the pharmakon 'which forced him to disgorge first the stone and then the children whom he had swallowed', with whose help 'Zeus waged the war against Cronus and the Titans'.[153] After Metis helped him defeat Cronus and ascend to supremacy as king of the gods and men, Zeus took her as his first wife; however, when he discovered that her cunning intellect would be passed onto a son destined to usurp his place as ultimate sovereign, he tricked the trickster into a game of shapeshifting, swallowing her whole (sometimes as a liquid and others as a small creature, like a fly). Although Zeus deceived and devoured her (and in some versions, raped her), Metis was too cunning to be destroyed; she remained 'hidden beneath the inward parts of Zeus' so that 'the goddess might devise for him both good and evil'.[154] From Zeus's belly, Metis gestated and clothed her daughter, Athena, who springs forth fully grown and armoured from her father's head. Through his integration of the metamorphic Metis and usurpation of her powers, Zeus becomes the *Mētieta* (Wise Counsellor, All-Wise or Cunning One) while Metis is largely erased and forgotten.

The Metis myths reveal the porosity of body and mind and plurality of self. Metis (pregnant with Athena) becomes part of Zeus who in turn becomes *Mētieta*, demonstrating both embodied intelligence and multiplicity of being. A shapeshifter, Metis's ability to '[turn] into many shapes'[155] reveals her 'bodily difference'[156] and the 'somatic cunning' or 'bodily intelligence' that is *mētis*.[157] This 'somatic cunning' is shared by figures like Hephaestus, the disabled blacksmith god of fire and metallurgy whose sideways facing feet allowed him to 'move from side to side more quickly'[158] and offer the 'visual symbol of his *mētis*, his wise thoughts and his craftsman's intelligence'.[159] *Mētis* is 'a type of intelligence and of thought, a way of knowing'[160] often framed as a corporeal one, an 'intelligence as immanent movement'[161] that 'demands a view of the body and its thinking as being double and divergent',[162] plural, porous and polymorphic. Ancient treatises on *mētis* promote the ability to turn many ways and show divergent selves for divergent contexts; that is, a new self for each occasion, a postmodern or perhaps posthuman plurality.

The Shifting, Shimmering World

Mētis was not the special purview of gods and kings in Greek classics. Many animals were also invested with *mētis* and admired for their cunning intelligence and artful *technē*. Two animals stand out as exemplars of *mētis*: the octopus, who can change both colour and shape, and the fox, known for tricks and twists. Detienne and Vernant devote a chapter to 'The Fox and The Octopus' in their study of *mētis*, inspiring Debra Hawhee's work on 'Animal Tricksters.'[163] As per Oppian in his *Treatise on Hunting and Fishing*, the fox was 'the most scheming of wild animals', admired for her subterranean lair, with myriad entrances and corridors, and artful ability to evade capture, 'by ambush' and 'by noose'.[164] The fox's mind is as 'misleading, enigmatic, [and] polymorphic [as the] earth', adaptable to any circumstance.[165] Foxes are known for their tricks, like playing dead, and their reversals, such as using their tail to mimic the prey they turn round to capture,[166] all skills which illustrate their *mētis*.

Mētis's alignment with more-than-human sentience is emphasised in the Orphic theogonies, where Metis is not a goddess but a genderless primordial power. The Orphic 'Phanes-Metis' is 'an androgynous god with a twofold nature, being both male and female' and a 'bisexual being'.[167] In Orphic myth, Phanes-Metis (also known as 'Erikepaios, . . . Eros, Zeus, Bromios and Protogonos' or 'the firstborn') emerges from the Cosmic Egg, the source of life formed in the Aither by Chronos.[168] Phanes translates to 'the Dazzling One',[169] and the Orphic tradition treats them as a primordial deity, investing them with the seeds of all life and a power that 'weaves, plaits, links, and knots together the threads whose interlacing composes the tissue of Becoming' and braids 'the sequence of generations and events in a single complex'.[170] In some versions of Orphic myth, Zeus swallows Phanes-Metis, not as his wife, but rather 'to reverse creation' and 'create the universe anew', becoming both king and creator.[171]

Through its various conceptual and semantic associations, *mētis* connotes the shifting, shimmering world[172] and the cunning ways of knowing and operating 'concealed by the form of rationality currently dominant in Western culture'.[173] *Mētis*, as per Detienne and Vernant's and Lisa Raphals's detailed studies, appears 'as multiple (*pantóiē*)'; shimmering, variegated or 'many-coloured (*poikílē*); [and] shifting (*aiólē*)', with 'its field of application . . . the world of movement, of multiplicity and of ambiguity'.[174] Michel de Certeau emphasises that the cunning 'ways of operating' captured by *mētis* 'go much further back' than antiquity, 'to the immemorial intelligence displayed in the tricks and imitations of plants and fishes', noting a 'continuity and permanence' in cunning tactics – 'from the depths of the ocean to the streets of modern megalopolises'.[175] Detienne and Vernant theorise that this continuity between animals and Man is precisely one reason why *mētis* has remained in modern philosophy's shadows and subsumed to *logos*. That prudence is an attribute possessed by humans and animals alike 'calls into question the radical separation between man and beasts, between reasonable beings and the rest'.[176] Since models for *mētis* emerge from a shared domain of human-nonhuman intelligence as well as a domain of human-nonhuman struggle (e.g., fishing, hunting, trapping), they emphasise ambiguity and the permeable boundaries between 'human' and 'animal'. Not restricted to human minds, then, *mētis* is an intelligence circulating throughout nature and perhaps even matter itself.

Return of the Repressed

Although central to Ancient Greek myth, philosophy and society, *mētis* has been mostly glossed over by Western historians and philosophers for several possible reasons, including its ties to pathos, embodiment (female, disabled or non-normative bodies particularly), powerful (monstrous) women, animals, the more-than-human world and nonhuman consciousness, duplicity and pliability. *Mētis* has been difficult to study in part because there are neither 'treaties . . . nor . . . any philosophical systems based on the principles of wily intelligence',[177] and as Lisa Raphals points out, there is no English equivalent for the term *mētis*.[178] Because of its shadowy nature, '*mētis* must be tracked down elsewhere, in areas which the philosopher usually passes over in silence or mentions only with irony or with hostility' to highlight his 'reasoning'; indeed, '*mētis* is conspicuous by its absence'.[179]

Much like Zeus ate Metis, dominant Western philosophy has consumed *mētis*, either absorbing it into new models or eliminating it entirely. Raphals posits that dominant Greek philosophers appropriated and redefined the qualities of *mētis* to suit their 'epistemological priorities',[180] such as ordering, straightening, stabilising and organising the fluid, polymorphic and unpredictable qualities of the world. Sarah Kofman makes a similar claim that 'Plato, in the name of Truth, would relegate this entire conceptual idea to darkness, and condemn' its modes of being, thinking and relating.[181] Critics like Raphals, Detienne and Vernant, Kofman and Nandita Biswas Mellamphy have suggested that 'the entire foundation of Western thought from Plato onward has been firmly anchored' by the exclusion of *mētis*.[182] Yet, as Mellamphy aptly points out, 'the stable, continuous and regulated world of the Olympian gods', defined by the hermeneutic, the dialectical and the hierarchical, 'cannot fully digest Metis because she cannot be fully domesticated by hierarchies (even reversed and transformed ones)'.[183] Metis – who defeated the Titans, known for their *biē* or brute force, and survived Zeus's ingestion –demonstrates the power of *mētis* to overthrow those seemingly more powerful and to threaten 'any established order': *mētis* 'operates in the realm of what is shifting and unexpected in order the better to reverse situations and overturn hierarchies which appear unassailable'.[184] Because of its shifting, subversive nature, *mētis* is not the foundation of a new order, but rather a continuous movement of constant becoming. As de Certeau highlights, 'Whatever [*mētis*] wins, it does not keep'.[185] What Raphals describes as 'metic intelligence'[186] is 'distributed and duplicitous',[187] that is, multiple, pliable, twisted, oblique and ambiguous as 'opposed to what is straight, direct, rigid and unequivocal'.[188] Perceived as 'dangerous', 'unmanageable', 'multiple, undulating, and tentacular', *mētis* is 'a mode . . . incompatible with the law, the fixed[,] . . . the determined'[189] and 'capital-*T Truth*'.[190]

Through both association and denigration, then, *mētis* has been aligned (perhaps *maligned*) with that which the enlightened subject rejects as dangerous, tricky, shadowy, oblique, twisted and counter to a dominant order that prizes mind over body, reason over sensation, unity over multiplicity and straightness over the double, divergent and twisted. The exclusion of *mētis* from much Western thought points to the perceived danger of *mētis* to *logos*, to reason, to order and indeed to Man himself, as 'the measure' and sovereign. Zeus's betrayal and consumption of Metis have become a metaphor for the ways that dominant Western philosophy has swallowed and subsumed feminine, disabled, nonhuman and otherwise alternative viewpoints. Exhuming Metis and her cunning[191] is a means of reviving an overlooked, difficult to define, yet powerful way of knowing, being, thinking and operating, one that embraces the liminal, the feminine, the nonbinary and the nonhuman and challenges (or perhaps allows us to circumvent) the dominant Western cultural paradigm that separates humanity from nature, mind from body and multiplicity from ontology.

I follow the line of critics like Michelle Ballif, Shannon Walters, Biswas Mellamphy and Kristin Pomykala, viewing *mētis* as a way of knowing, being, communing and moving most apt for the postmodern, post-patriarchal, posthuman, postcolonial, post-truth and networked sensuous terrain of agonistic indeterminacy known as the present. Feminists, philosophers, rhetoricians, disability scholars and post-anthropocentric theorists have variously engaged in the rediscovery and rejuvenation of Metis/*mētis*. To this mix, I hope to add Gothic studies. Gothic – the mode of reversals, revivals, revenants and returns – may help to revive Metis and her consumed cunning; in doing so, it may offer forms of liminality that act as renewals.

Gothic Mētis

Gothic *mētis* (Gothic + *mētis*) emerges at the intersection of Gothic criticism, *mētis* studies and posthuman, post-anthropocentric theory, offering a multi-pronged movement towards the plural, porous and polymorphic and away from the straight, unified and fixed. Rhetorical criticism with elements of Critical Discourse Studies (CDS)[192] offers the weft[193] that threads these domains together. Rhetorical criticism and CDS provide theory, language and tools for a nuanced, multilevel textual analysis that complements literary studies and cultural studies. Researchers in CDS study how discourses[194] intersect with ideology, identity and equity, and together, CDS and rhetorical criticism illuminate how signs, symbols, artefacts, bodies and structures circulate power. In the pages that follow, I work with a contemporary and expansive view of rhetoric, one that does not restrict it to human subjects and especially not to Man. The recent post-anthropocentric turn of rhetorical criticism frees rhetoric from its traditional confines as a skill reserved for agentic, cultured humans. Taking rhetoric beyond humans and human culture, rhetoricians have provocatively and productively expanded rhetoric to include nonhuman, ecological and material/object forms.

The scholarly revival of Metis/*mētis* is a project that seems aligned with Gothic's artistic and critical lineage. I am curious about these aesthetic and conceptual overlaps, and I believe that Gothic's 'negative aesthetics',[195] hybridity and mutability allow it to uniquely showcase *mētis* in its myriad forms. In my study, I explore some iterations and materialisations of *mētis* in Gothic media, *mētis*'s applications for Gothic criticism and the reciprocal value of the Gothic for both critical posthumanist and rhetorical theory. Ultimately, I propose a distinctly Gothic *mētis* – a cunning monstrosity that operates in multiples, metamorphosis and transgression. By cunning monstrosity, I do not mean simply devious or grotesque, but that which is ingeniously heterogenous, cleverly open to alterity and artfully malleable. This cunning monstrosity is grounded in the multiple, porous, communicative body and Deleuze-Guattarian *becomings*: crafty *involutions* of heterogenous kinships. While Metis might not initially seem like a Gothic figure, I hope to demonstrate her utility for Gothic studies as a patron goddess for the double, the divergent, the devoured and the deviant, offering a feminine and multiplex counterpart to the Roman two-faced Janus.[196] Just as Gothic represents a space for depictions and articulations of *mētis*,

mētis offers several conceptual tools to analyse the Gothic, adding nuance to ongoing conversations about Gothic's rhetorical life inside and outside of literature. My project treats Gothic as not only a style of literature but also a style of rhetoric that renders the liminal, the monstrous, the uncanny, the abject, the multiplex, the ineffable and the divergent – that is *mētic* – dimensions of being and life. Gothic has long provided an artistic, discursive space to engage liminal identities and multiplex, non-anthropocentric consciousnesses: consciousness outside the brain, outside the human and outside the 'norm'.

Mētis is both the theme and the vehicle of this study.[197] Along with bricolage and *métissage*, I draw on Dolmage's '*Mētis* methodology' as outlined in *Disability Rhetoric*, which resists 'the forward march of logic' by moving 'sideways and backward' and engaging with interdisciplinary research.[198] A text inspired by *mētis* resembles what Dolmage calls 'an extraordinary body': 'double, divergent, flawed, incomplete, surprising, in need of others'.[199] This is in line with Hans Kellner's suggestion to historians to 'get the story crooked!'. For Kellner, 'the straightness of any story is a rhetorical invention'[200] that attempts to render flat, straight, hermetic or neat that which is complex, complicated and contested. Put simply, a *mētistic* approach encourages the blending of the 'ancient and modern' and the use of hybridity, bricolage and occasional digressions to challenge linearity and one-dimensional thinking in research writing.

Throughout the chapters, I explore Gothic *mētis* in all its variety as representation, rhetoric and even as praxis – a responsive, crafty and embodied openness to alterity, multiplicity and metamorphosis. The texts studied here are meant to be representative rather than definitive, depicting the range of wily corporealisations, responsive monstrosities and rhetorical multiplicities that characterise Gothic *mētis*. Chapter 1 expands on *fin-de-siècle* Gothic, situating this multifaceted form in the shifting terrain of the late-nineteenth century. A time of shapeshifting species, genders and races, the *fin de siècle* set the stage for Gothic to rematerialise into new forms with greater attention on metamorphic, hybrid and polymorphic identities. In this chapter, I analyse an assortment of *fin-de-siècle* Gothic shapeshifters and tricksters through the overlapping lenses of *mētis* and posthumanism, including Richard Marsh's Beetle,

Arthur Machen's impostors from *The Three Impostors* and Vernon Lee's Oriana from 'Prince Alberic and the Snake Lady.' My analysis explores how from a posthuman perspective, these cunning monsters might unsettle the British in service of the Othered. This chapter also establishes several conclusions about *mētis* to structure the analyses in the chapters that follow.

Chapter 2 continues the discussion of *fin-de-siècle* Gothic with attention to the ecological framings of its 'abhuman' monsters.[201] Metamorphic, hybrid and polymorphic bodies showcased the breakdowns of human identity as it overlapped with other species. While obviously meant to be spectacular and horrific, these chimerical renderings of human-nonhuman entanglements reflect and perhaps generate contemporary post-anthropocentric, new materialist models of human being. My analysis connects H. G. Wells's fiction to Donna Haraway's concept tentacularity, *mētic* modes of matrixed and adaptative being and speculative Gothic. This chapter also begins a larger theme of the chapters ahead, using the *mētic* Greek adjectives *polyplokos* (*poluplokos*, twisted and complex) and *polytropos* (*polutropos*, manifold and versatile) as conceptual tropes for porous, plural and polymorophic modes of being common to *mētis*, Gothic, and posthumans – modes of multiplex, mutable selves.

Chapter 3 covers material on multiple personality and multiple consciousness with Stevenson's 'Gothic gnome' *Strange Case of Dr Jekyll and Mr Hyde* at its centre. The focus is on *polytropos* ethos as multiplex, shifting, shimmering character. Stevenson's *Strange Case of Dr Jekyll and Mr Hyde* engages with and shapes a larger discourse of mental disunity and plural selves circulating within dominant Western psychology since the late nineteenth century. It also offers a wealth of material for considering the multiplex, plural and fragmented nature of identity and consciousness and how this might be embraced as a postmodern, posthuman tactic. This chapter extends the conversation about Gothic's role in rendering plural, porous subjectivity begun in the previous chapters.

Chapter 4 is likely the most ambitious chapter, moving from ethos to embodiment and acting as both a tangent and a bridge. This chapter analyses microbiome discourse and its Gothic-inflected rhetoric of human estrangement, continuing the discussion of *polytropos* by moving from a focus on 'Hyde to the Holobiont':

the contemporary plural framing of human being emerging from discourses of microbiology, symbiosis and ecology. Although characteristically distinctive domains, the postmodern plural self emerging from contemporary psychology shares several traits with the holobiont, including a radical rewriting of human being that shifts notions of normalcy and health away from matters of purity, unity and dominance. Critical and popular microbiome discourse emphasises the uncanny, abject and monstrous nature of human being. This chapter extends the consideration of Gothic beyond the literary and into the discursive, applying elements of CDS to my analysis.

Chapter 5 broadens the focus of the previous chapter, shifting from the microbiome to mycorrhizae, the symbiotic networks of filamentous fungi and tree roots. Working with two contemporary films, *Gaia* and *In the Earth*, and Arthur Machen's late nineteenth-century novella, *The Hill of Dreams*, this chapter analyses Gothic tales of fungal forms and networks along with their abilities to contaminate and communicate with humankind. This chapter explores the ways the Gothic mode may help to render the cryptic yet vibrant lives of nonhumans, like fungi. In returning to previous considerations of networks, networking and *mētis* with contemporary rhetorical criticism in mind, this chapter paves the way for Chapter 6's discussion of the already and innately 'ecological' nature of Gothic.

Chapter 6 returns to the *fin de siècle* with a study of Vernon Lee's writing on the genius loci, or spirit of place. Lee's travel writing offers both a powerful depiction of more-than-human rhetoric and a thoughtful praxis for engaging in interspecies rapport. Specifically, I align Lee's interspecies rhetoric with *mētistic* tactics, linking her work to contemporary studies of more-than-human and ecological rhetoric. Lee's application of spectral tropes invites a consideration of eco-Gothic and with this, Gothic's larger ecological relevance. Gothic's role in rendering the more-than-human world and the plural, porous modes of subjectivity that bind us to it offers fertile material for rhetorical criticism and environmental communication studies, which are increasingly seeking posthuman, new materialist, more-than-human and inhuman rhetorics to unsettle the field's lingering anthropocentrism and androcentrism.

The book concludes with a return to where it began, with a discussion of the liminal, posthuman, post-anthropocentric present. I describe the Anthropocene as our *pontos*: a treacherous space through which we must open a path, a *poros*. At the heart of the postscript is this notion of *poros*, which relates to finding a path through shifting contexts by way of *mētis*. *Poros* is also the root of *porous*, an opening or a path through which we might navigate the posthuman subjectivity noted by Braidotti and modelled by Gothic. While many paths might be explored through the overlaps of Gothic *mētis*, I focus on *mētis*'s applications for Indigenous Gothic and posthuman rapport.

My ultimate hope for the pages ahead is to demonstrate how reading Gothic alongside and through *mētis* – and *mētis* alongside and through Gothic – enriches critical understanding of the rhetorical and ethical possibilities for the polymorphic, the plural, the monstrous and the multiplex, especially in the liminal, posthuman present.

1

Fin-de-Siècle *Shapeshifters and Gothic Tricksters*

After living in Victorian literary dispersions throughout most of the era, Gothic rematerialises as a popular mode in late nineteenth-century fiction. Until the century's end, Gothic was seemingly everywhere and nowhere in Victorian literature, infusing popular works by writers like Charles Dickens and Emily and Charlotte Brontë in sometimes explicit and sometimes subtle ways. From about 1880 onwards, however, Gothic reemerged into the Victorian literary scene as a popular mode, with some of the best-known Gothic tales published during the period, including Robert Louis Stevenson's *Strange Case of Dr Jekyll and Mr Hyde* (1886) and Bram Stoker's *Dracula* (1897). The Gothic of the 1880s and 1890s is both recognisable as and distinctive from its eighteenth-century predecessor: it is more visceral and more chaotic than first-wave Gothic, presenting extremely heterogeneous narratives and remarkable shapeshifting, chimerical monsters. This chapter examines some *fin-de-siècle* Gothic shapeshifters and the ways they embody the flux of the nineteenth century's end wrought by a confluence of scientific, technological, sociocultural and imperial changes. Equipped with *mētis*, the art of cunning and polymorphy, Gothic shapeshifters, like Richard Marsh's Beetle and Arthur Machen's Helen Vaughan, unsettle the various boundaries between human/nonhuman, male/female and dominant/subaltern while playing clever tricks on English men and women. In the chapter ahead, I relate such Gothic shapeshifters to the trickster, a mythological figure of liminality, 'change, ambiguity, paradox, defiance, laughter, buffoonery, and even cruelty'.[1] Tricksters are found in myths around the world, and Gothic myths are no exception.

Tricksters are thought to be some of the most ancient and most common mythic characters across human cultures.[2] Well-known tricksters include Hermes, the Greek messenger and mediator, Loki, the mischievous Norse god, Anansi, a cunning Akan spider, and Coyote, central to many North American Native myths as not only a trickster but also a creator. The trickster is an in-between, liminal figure associated with limits, boundaries, passages and other 'point[s] of contact' between cultures and categories.[3] Sometimes fools, sometimes godlike, sometimes malicious and sometimes humorous, tricksters are ambivalent, mutable and transgressive, defying categorisation as human or animal, good or evil, creator or destroyer, often being both. Frequently, they are 'chaos-inducing' figures 'intent on challenging the existing order of things'.[4] Whether that challenge be good or bad depends on one's perspective. While one cannot say with any confidence that what tricksters create benefits humankind, it is certain to at least unsettle the old and usher in the new. The *fin-de-siècle* Gothic shapeshifters under study question, subvert and challenge (sometimes even overturn) dominant orders, much like the mythic Metis helped to defeat the powerful Titans. In situating Gothic tricksters alongside Metis, *mētis* and critical posthumanism, I hope to demonstrate that what is poison for some is a remedy for others; more specifically, what is poison for the patriarchy and Empire is a remedy for the Othered.[5]

This chapter analyses an assortment of *fin-de-siècle* Gothic shapeshifters and tricksters, moving sideways, backwards and obliquely through the domains of late Victorian Gothic, contemporary critical posthuman theory and classical Greek myth. My intent is to outline one strand of Gothic *mētis* by exploring the trickster as shapeshifter, boundary-breaker and unsettler. Metis was a trickster, known for cunning words and wily embodiment. Capable of taking many forms and using clever tricks, she deceived Cronus and unsettled the order of the Titans. Her eponymous *mētis* is the cunning of tricksters, a mode of interlacing opposites that introduces an element of chaos or confusion into dominant systems. Too tricky, too ambivalent and too fluid, *mētis* is not the foundation for a new order but a way to introduce play into an existing one. As Michel de Certeau explains in his theory of tactics, such cunning defies the 'proper' and 'belongs to the other' and can thus never supplant the dominant: 'Whatever [*mētis*] wins, it does not keep'.[6] *Mētis* is about being more hybrid, more shifting and more cunning than the flux around us, seemingly emerging most forcefully in times that are shifting and uncertain. It is perhaps no surprise, then, that tricksters emerged with force in the shifting terrain of the late nineteenth century and again in our contemporary uncertain age, characterised as models for both political deceivers and posthuman aides to guide us through liminal post-truth, post-anthropocentric times.

Tricksters are also models for transgressive and transdisciplinary research. They are 'recursive, rather than linear' and unbound by category.[7] Working like a trickster, I intend to veer from *fin-de-siècle* Gothic to myths of monstrous women with *mētis*, focusing especially on Metis and her subversive tactics. *Mētis* is a mode of weaving, twisting and turning, which I align with Nicholas Royle's theory of veering as a shift of perspective and the action 'of changing course or direction' drawn from the French verb *virer*, 'to turn or turn around'.[8] Veering is both physical and psychological; one can veer towards or away from bodies, things or attitudes. Since 'veer' is the root of 'environment', for Royle, 'the theory of veering' seeks to turn away from anthropocentric perspectives (by extension patriarchal and colonial ones) and into uncanny ones that align nonhumans with humans, the masculine with the feminine, the local with the global and the strange with the familiar.[9] 'Veering can be deliberate or unintentional', and it is a not a movement that depends 'on any logic of origin or destination: it is an uncertainly perverse, unfinished movement *in the present*'.[10] To veer is to twist, to turn, to swerve, to diverge and/or to deviate (along with many things).[11] It is therefore aligned with shapeshifters, tricksters and generally those with *mētis*, whose cunning tactics are capable of perverting and subverting hegemonic identities and orders.

After introducing the *fin de siècle*, known as a time of flux wherein identities and powers were shifting, I turn to an analysis of some classic *fin-de-siècle* Gothic tricksters, including Richard Marsh's Beetle, Arthur Machen's impostors and Vernon Lee's Snake Lady from 'Prince Alberic and the Snake Lady' (1897). In the next chapter, I probe the porous lines between humans, animals and environment presented in *fin-de-siècle* Gothic, exploring the human-animal hybrids and human/animal reversals common to H. G. Wells's scientific romances, while Stevenson's Dr Jekyll, another *fin-de-siècle* Gothic shapeshifter, is discussed in Chapter 3.

Fin-de-siècle *Flux*

Fin de siècle captures both an era and a sentiment, one often wrapped up in notions of cultural and imperial decline as the nineteenth century and reign of Queen Victoria approached their end.[12] While the British Empire expanded from 1870 to 1900, the developing global market and the rising international status of Germany, the United States and Japan paradoxically situated the Empire at both its peak and its decline.[13] Challenges to the Empire from within its colonies, such as the second Boer War (1899–1902), and by critical British subjects, like Olive Schreiner, further enhanced the tenuousness of Empire and fuelled 'fantasies' of British racial and imperial degeneration,[14] fantasies that were exacerbated by quick expansion, increasing immigration and rising crime in London, the heart of the Empire. As Max Nordau famously describes the *fin-de-siècle* moment and its zeitgeist in his oft-quoted *Degeneration* (1892),

> One epoch of history is unmistakably in its decline, and another is announcing its approach. There is a sound of rending in every tradition, and it is as though the morrow would not link itself with to-day. Things as they are totter and plunge.[15]

Nordau laments how 'Over the earth the shadows creep with deepening gloom, wrapping all objects in a mysterious dimness, in which all certainty is destroyed and any guess seems plausible. Forms lose their outlines, and are dissolved in floating mist.'[16] While he amplifies the crisis of decay and decline common to degeneration discourse, Nordau's emphasis on transition and dethronement[17] aptly describes a period known for rapid change and generational clashes. In the 'transition from old to new,' there was no certainty in Britain's 'continued enlightenment and improvement',[18] yet for many late Victorians, this uncertainty was a source of excitement.

A time of paradox and ambivalence connecting the Victorian to the Modern, the *fin de siècle* is understood today as a culture of interlocking decay and renewal or 'cultural decline and spiritual rebirth'.[19] Sally Ledger and Roger Luckhurst describe the period as 'an epoch of endings and beginnings' and 'an excitingly volatile and transitional period' that was 'fraught with anxiety and with an exhilarating sense of possibility'.[20] Given the complexity of the era's political, cultural, artistic and technological dimensions, I shall offer some generalisations that are no doubt oversimplifications. My aim in this section is to highlight the ambivalence and amorphousness that characterised the *fin de siècle* and with this, set the stage for the analyses that follow in this chapter and the rest. The era is characterised by several 'new' developments of note: new modes of gender and sexuality (such as the New Woman and homosexual), new sciences (such as criminal anthropology, psychical research and sexology), new technologies (such as the telegraph, the telephone and the camera), new perceptions of time and space (elicited by new tele-technologies and the increasing speed of travel) and new modes of artistic expression (such as Decadence and newly emerging genres, like science fiction, detective fiction and the weird).[21] The 'Naughty Nineties' produced much experimental literature that defied previous forms of Victorian art, especially realism and its alleged moralising purpose.[22] For example, Decadent writers like Oscar Wilde and Arthur Symons sought to experience and express new sensations in literature, embracing the mysterious, the unorthodox, the occult and the exotic as they pursued 'the truth of spiritual things' and endeavoured to articulate the unsayable, 'exquisite' nature of feelings, as Symons explained it.[23]

The paradoxical sense of decay and renewal underpinning the *fin de siècle* showcases a much broader fixation on duality or doubleness in the period. Partially because of the larger spirit of juxtaposition, paradox and ambivalence, the late nineteenth century became the golden era of literary doubles, giving rise to classic Victorian doubles like Jekyll/Hyde, Dorian Gray and Trilby/La Svengali.

It was also an era defined by 'double consciousness', as Michael Saler notes and as discussed in Chapter 3. However, these dualities were not always black and white, but often many shades of fuzzy interlocking grey. Late-Victorian writers presented dualities like human/animal, civilised/primitive, light/dark, etc. as porous and complementary, 'juxtaposing oppositions without necessarily resolving their contradictions' and ultimately embracing 'hybrid, "both/ and" perspectives' while rejecting 'starker binary distinctions and . . . essentialist, "either/or" ontologies'.[24] The *fin de siècle* was a period of unsettling 'traditional, hierarchical oppositions – rational and irrational, masculine and feminine, fiction and non-fiction, disenchantment and enchantment', etc., oppositions that were 'often found to be coterminous' upon scrutiny.[25] A time when 'Forms [lost] their outlines, and [were] dissolved in floating mist',[26] the *fin de siècle* was a fluid, plural, in-between era: a time of 'Sexual Anarchy', where 'men became women [and] women became men',[27] evolutionary chaos, where Men became beasts and beast became kindred, and colonial reversals, where foreigners became local and imperialists became 'savages'.

In the following two chapters, I address the Darwinian and psychological inflections of these hybridities and reversals, focusing on porous webs of relations in Chapter 2 and plural forms of consciousness in Chapter 3. Here, I am interested in examining how *fin-de-siècle* Gothic writers represented these hybridities through shapeshifting, species-and-gender-bending monsters.

Shapeshifting Gothic and Gothic Shapeshifters

Characterised as a liminal era of transitions, transgression, clashes and confusion, the *fin de siècle* offered the perfect backdrop for a Gothic revival. Although, as Luckhurst notes, there is no simple reason for Gothic's renewed popularity,[28] the widespread sense of flux coupled with emergent sciences and technologies provided ample material to furnish contemporary tales of terror and horror. Glennis Byron posits that expanding late-Victorian 'concerns about national, social, and psychic decay' cultivated fertile ground for 'Gothic monstrosity [to reemerge] with a force' unmatched since first-wave Gothic at the end of the eighteenth century.[29] On the one hand, nineteenth-century Gothic narratives continued eighteenth-century Gothic traditions: crypts, ruins and tombs; vampires and doubles; ghosts and uncertain hauntings; madness and extreme emotions; concerns with a remote past, uncouth customs and all manner of transgression. Late-Victorian Gothic also retains its predecessor's characteristic scattered, layered and excessive narrative style, sometimes taking it to new extremes of multiplicity, fragmentation and excess. On the other hand, *fin-de-siècle* Gothic emerges as a 'genre'[30] in its own right, demonstrating new inflections drawn from Darwinism, degeneration, ecology and psychology. Ever the shapeshifter, Gothic takes on new forms and themes in the *fin de siècle*, apropos for the shapeshifting era. *Fin-de-siècle* Gothic is also potentially more hybrid than original Gothic, characterised by blends with horror, science fiction, romance, detective fiction and the weird, acting as the foundation from which these genres emerge.

The flux and ambiguity of the *fin-de-siècle* zeitgeist finds expression in the shapeshifting, chimerical monsters that populate its literature. *Fin-de-siècle* Gothic has been described as more 'somatic' and visceral than its eighteenth-century predecessor, showcasing heightened attention to bodily metamorphosis and multiplicity,[31] as illustrated by Stevenson's metamorphic Jekyll/Hyde or Stoker's iconic shapeshifting villain, Dracula, who can grow younger, 'transform himself to wolf,' bat, mist or 'elemental dust' and can even 'become so small' that he can 'come out from anything or into anything, no matter how close it be bound or even fused up with fire'.[32] Dracula's complex representation also evokes fluid gender and sexual identities, so that he is both masculine and feminine as well as queer (with his penetrative teeth, sensuous red lips and seduction of women and men alike).[33] This blending of elements, species, genders, sexuality, ages and states (living death) was a common formula for *fin-de-siècle* Gothic monsters, who were even more excessive and more liminal than Mary Shelley's chimerical Creature. Such multiplex, metamorphic monstrous bodies have been described as 'abhuman' – 'not-quite-human' and 'characterized by . . . morphic variability, continually becoming not-itself, becoming other'[34] – and 'overdetermined' – 'open to numerous interpretations' by condensing intersectional 'fragments of otherness into one body'.[35]

With *mētis* in mind, I want to relate these shapeshifting, chimerical Gothic monsters to tricksters who unsettle seemingly unassailable orders, beginning with Richard Marsh's *The Beetle* (1897).[36]

Marsh's novel focuses on an ambiguous, amorphous creature 'born of neither god nor man',[37] a 'liminal man-woman-goddess-beetle-thing'[38] endowed with supernatural and mesmeric powers known alternately as 'the Beetle,' 'The Woman of Songs' and 'The Oriental.' The vengeful Beetle is a priestess from the cult of Isis who comes to *fin-de-siècle* London hunting her/his/its former lover, the great statesman Paul Lessingham, who it had formerly enslaved in Egypt and wishes to recapture. As a Liberal Member of Parliament, Lessingham synecdochally stands for the English government and by extension, the English nation, with the attack against Lessingham's individual sovereignty paralleling an attack against Britain's national sovereignty.[39] Marsh's text shares many similarities with *Dracula*,[40] most obviously in the threat of a nefarious, shapeshifting foreign villain who 'penetrates the very heart of England, the city of London',[41] in search of English flesh and blood. Like most *fin-de-siècle* Gothic novels, the story of the Beetle unravels via multiple, shifting and sometimes embedded perspectives, in this case four main narrators: the vagrant clerk Robert Holt, the middle-class inventor Sydney Atherton, the New Woman (and love interest of Lessingham) Marjorie Lindon, and the private investigator Augustus Champnell. Readers discover at the novel's end that two of these tales (Holt's and Lindon's) are in fact packaged and presented by others. A tale of reverse colonisation whereby an ancient, Eastern threat invades contemporary England, *The Beetle* emphasises the unsettling of English on the levels of nation, identity and language. I will unpack this point further in the next few paragraphs.

Throughout the novel, the metamorphic Beetle plays nefarious 'tricks' on characters, ranging from 'conjuring trick[s]' and tricks 'of [the] imagination' to 'devil's trick[s]', including kidnapping and sexual assault.[42] Mesmerism[43] is one of the 'trickster' Beetle's artifices in her '*modus operandi*'[44] through which she not only dominates the wills and minds of others but 'tricks' them of their consciousness, voice and volition. Lessingham relates that when he was seduced, mesmerised and imprisoned by the Beetle as a youth in Cairo, she 'robbed' him of his willpower and 'trick[ed] [him] of [his] manhood': 'I lay there like a log. She did with me as she would, and in dumb agony I endured'.[45] Later in London, the Beetle, as both man and insect, violates the mesmerised Holt: as a man, he probes the helpless Holt's face with his fingers and kisses him with his 'blubber lips'; as a giant bug, it mounts Holt's body, embracing his face with its 'huge, slimy, evil-smelling body' and 'myriad legs'[46] in what has been described as a monstrous 'copulative engagement'.[47] The mesmerised Holt is 'driven' by the Beetle; unable to control his body or words, he is impelled to burglarise Lessingham's home and 'constrained to shout out, in [unrecognisable] tones . . . "THE BEETLE"'.[48] Mesmerised characters like Lessingham and Holt find themselves either rendered 'dumb' or forced to ventriloquise the Beetle's words. Most others who encounter the monstrous Beetle are left shocked, mad and aphasic, illustrated by Marjorie Lindon's hysterical narrative at the end of the novel,[49] where she commits to paper what she will not speak and destroys her text repeatedly in a ceaseless rewriting of her trauma.[50]

The Beetle's slippery, shifting identity is the highlight of the novel. Taking on various disguises and forms, they appear sometimes old, sometimes young, sometimes male, sometimes female and sometimes as a giant bug. As a 'child of Isis', the Beetle is associated with transmigration 'of the soul [and] of the body', specifically assuming the form of a beetle after her alleged death in Egypt.[51] Like many *fin-de-siècle* monsters, the Beetle demonstrates the layered Othering of species, gender, race, sexuality and state (both alive and dead). Its identity is presented as compounded, uncertain and unfixed.[52] When the first protagonist, Robert Holt, encounters the creature, he is unsure of not only its age, gender and nationality but also its species: 'I could not at once decide if it was a man or a woman. Indeed at first I doubted if it was anything human'.[53] Layering racialised and animalised traits, descriptions of the Beetle emphasise its 'saffron yellow' wrinkled skin, hairless small head, 'blubber lips,' 'absence of chin' and 'abnormally large' nose so extravagant that 'it resembled the beak of some bird of prey', which collectively give the '[disagreeable suggestion] of something animal' and 'something not human'.[54] Aside from being 'oriental to the fingertips', their racial identity is otherwise left uncertain. Drawing from assorted racial stereotypes, the characters can discern only that the figure is from the East, a possible 'Arab' with 'more than a streak of negro blood'.[55]

Foreign tricksters like the Beetle invade Victorian England, breaking all manner of boundaries, especially those long cherished by the English as demarcations of self/Other, male/female, civilised/savage and dominant/submissive. As a shapeshifter with fluid species, gender, age and sexuality, the Beetle unsettles typical identity categories and renders the identity of other characters uncertain because 'hers is too fluid to constitute a reference point' as the Other to the self.[56] The Beetle's powerful mesmeric skill is crucial to unsettling these boundaries. Mesmerised subjects were said to be connected to and dominated by the mesmerist's will, and there were complex class, gender and racial stereotypes attached to the roles of mesmerist and mesmerised. Women, colonial subjects and the mentally or physically infirm were perceived as passive, penetrable and submissive and therefore both apt and appropriate to be mesmerised by one assumed to be more masculine, more dominant and more civilised.[57] Marsh reverses the gender and racial roles assumed in the typical mesmeric relationship by making the mesmerising villain thoroughly foreign, sometimes female and sometimes homosexual. In doing so, he calls into question English security and authority.

In the next section, I relate Gothic tricksters to *mētis* by analysing Arthur Machen's twisted tales of cunning tricksters, like Helen Vaughan from *The Great God Pan* and the 'impostors' from *The Three Impostors*. Machen's work illuminates some ways that we can observe *mētis* at play in Gothic fiction at the level of both character and narrative, with his fragmented at times disorienting narratives filled with rhetorical twists, turns and reversals. His tales of liminal, amorphous creatures, cunning deceivers and nefarious tricksters demonstrate the dark side of *mētis* and the ambivalence of tricksters more generally as they are not in service to humanity although they might create or destroy something occasionally to our benefit.

Arthur Machen's Tricksters

Welsh writer Arthur Machen's late nineteenth-century fiction is both exceptional and exemplary of *fin-de-siècle* Gothic, featuring unspeakable acts of horror, insalubrious sexual desires, multifarious and hybrid forms of identity, the blending of the mystical with the scientific and the clash between Judeo-Christian and Pagan beliefs. His 'heterogenous' work 'does not easily fit any one form, genre, category, or style', labelled by critics as Decadent, Gothic, horror and/or weird.[58] Machen himself was something of a shapeshifter, sometimes identifying as Welsh and other times as English and remodelling his style over a very long literary career.[59]

Machen's tales of occult horrors display a profound fascination with the liminal: hybrid and shapeshifting villains, mystical-scientific experiments that breakdown boundaries between mind/matter/spirit and borderland spaces that exist on the margins between places and times. Perhaps best known is *The Great God Pan*, where Dr Raymond conducts a nefarious occult neurological experiment on his teenage ward, Mary. In his isolated laboratory buried in the Welsh countryside, Raymond aims to transgress the 'fathomless abyss that separates the world of consciousness from the sphere of matter' and access the 'spirit-world', the 'real world', which exists beyond the everyday world, an act that the ancients called 'seeing the god Pan'.[60] Raymond believes that this 'real' world lies hidden in the 'familiar lines and paths' of the human brain[61] and can be exposed by 'a trifling rearrangement of certain cells'.[62] His experiment is a 'success', leaving Mary catatonic and impregnated by Pan, the goat-god of the wild. In Greek myth, Pan is the son of trickster Hermes and is known for mischief, panic and lust, his wildness and lustfulness symbolised by his half-man half-goat body. Machen presents Pan as an amorphous 'presence, that was neither man nor beast, neither the living nor the dead, but all things mingled, the form of all things but devoid of all form'. An encounter with Pan is said to 'dissolve' the 'sacrament of body and soul'.[63]

The result of Mary's union with Pan is the monstrous progeny Helen Vaughan: a hybrid, soulless, inhuman creature, who is known to have many aliases but no true name as 'Only human beings have names'.[64] As the daughter of the nebulous Pan, Helen herself is duplicitous, mischievous and metamorphic. She hides her monstrous nature under a reassuring exterior of 'wonderful' and 'strange beauty'.[65] Helen becomes a cunning femme fatale who preys on London gentlemen, seducing them into unspeakable (no doubt sexual) acts and leaving a wake of 'suicidal mania' behind her in London. Helen's perversion drives the narrative so that by the end of the novel, several characters have been killed, shocked to death or left with a lingering horror. In a spectacular scene well known to Gothic scholars, Vaughan is said to transform from 'woman to man, from man to beast, from beast to worse than beast' and ultimately to 'a substance as jelly' in the throes of death,[66] losing 'sexual specificity, species specificity, and the specificity that distinguishes form from matter'.[67]

Content aligns with style in Machen's fiction. Liminal, unstable bodies are portrayed through vertiginous narratives and unspeakable scenes. Much like *fin-de-siècle* Gothic more generally, *The Great God Pan* is composed of shifting narrative perspectives (from third person to first person), multiple narrators, embedded letters and scattered newspaper clippings, culminating in the final chapter titled 'The Fragments', which includes an eyewitness account of Helen's spectacular reversion and several fragmented letters. The multiple perspectives and multiple embedded interpretations create what J. Halberstam describes as 'interpretative mayhem' and an 'excess of meaning', reminding us of the 'ornamental excess' of Gothic architecture, with its 'gargoyles and crazy loops and spirals'.[68] Gothic for Halberstam involves the breakdown of genres, of meanings, of categories and of language itself, as 'the inability to categorize' correlates to 'the inability to narrate'.[69] Dr Matheson's report on Helen's death demonstrates the latter of these typical Gothic rhetorical moves:

> I watched, at last I saw nothing but a substance as jelly. Then the ladder was ascended again . . . (*here the* MS. *is illegible*) . . . for one instance I saw a Form, shaped in dimness before me [. . .] a horrible and unspeakable shape, neither man nor beast.[70]

Helen's breakdown of identity manifests equally in a breakdown of language, with Matheson wavering between descriptive attempts and expressive failures. Vague nouns like 'substance', 'Form' and 'shape' are paired with adjectives like 'horrible and unspeakable', determiners like 'neither', ellipses and incoherent, illegible text, producing what Kelly Hurley defines as typical *fin-de-siècle* Gothic rhetorical strategies: 'occlusion', obfuscation, 'the multiplication and confusion of narrative layers, . . . constant interruptions of the story being told' and 'a simultaneous movement towards and convulsive retreat from' its monstrous spectacles.[71] Such 'unintelligible writings, and the unspeakable' are key 'Gothic Conventions'[72] as defined by Eve Kosofsky Sedgwick and will be discussed throughout the chapters ahead.

Machen's *The Three Impostors or The Transmutations* (1895) features a series of narrative twists, tricks and reversals, including transmutations of character, plot and setting, transmutations of body and mind and transmutations of narrative. The novel is a tangled episodic tale of incredible coincidences, chance meetings, overheard anecdotes and marvellous encounters on the everyday streets of *fin-de-siècle* London. The various tales are connected by Dyson and Phillipps, bachelor friends prone to traversing London, who upon their many walks encounter the titular three impostors: deceivers and tricksters who disguise themselves, telling lies to entice and entrap their audience. Beyond Dyson and Phillipps, the novel features a cast of bizarre and sometimes confusing characters, many of whom are revealed as impostors in pursuit of a young man with spectacles. The stories told by these individuals in their various guises and disguises make up the bulk of the narrative of *The Three Impostors*. The interwoven tales carry the reader throughout the south of England and Wales, from the city to the desolate countryside and even to the Rocky Mountains of North America (the changes in landscape are one of the novel's 'transmutations', as per Joshi).[73] The stories, often labelled adventures, encounters or novels,[74] describe all manner of transmutations, tricks, traps and transgression, including the random discovery of a famous Roman antiquity, the gold Tiberius, a murderous North American cult, torture devices that trap their owners and men turned into mummies or dissolved into slime.

Impostors tell tales in which they are cast as victimised protagonists, often innocent, hapless, destitute and haphazardly thrown into alliances with people revealed to be disguised, nefarious, predatory and somehow involved with occult knowledge or supernatural forces; yet, the narrative reversals reveal the opposite: these taletellers are the ones disguised, nefarious and predatory – cunning and subversive members of a secret Pagan cult hidden in the heart of London searching for the stolen gold Tiberius and the young man with spectacles who took it. Readers are left knowing that the tales are lies, yet perhaps wondering what, if anything, is true. Lies wrapped in lies and nestled in disguise, tricks, traps and ruses – these impostors are tricksters of the most nefarious sort. Inspired by *1001 Arabian Nights* and Robert Louis Stevenson's *The New Arabian Nights* (1882) and its sequel *The Dynamiter* (1885),[75] the book itself is a trap, as Stefania Forlini suggests, with a circular narrative, which, in the form of an ouroboros, begins where the tale ends and ends where it begins in a deserted house on the outskirts of London.[76] Forlini's insightful reading of Machen's novel highlights how it transgresses and unsettles the boundaries between 'past and present', 'the local and the global', self and Other, 'fiction and non-fiction' and even the discursive and the material, as its narrative effects compel certain *affects*, such as 'disgust and horror' along with 'questioning' and contemplation.[77]

Machen's fiction reveals the ways *mētis* can be used to disguise, deceive and entrap as well as to reverse perceptions. Moving to an analysis of Vernon Lee's fiction in the section ahead, I probe another line of Gothic tricksters through a reading of Lee's *fin-de-siècle* Gothic fairy tale, 'Prince Alberic and the Snake Lady' (1896), which tells the story of a fairy cursed with a snake body and her magical tapestry. Lady Oriana's long, twisting snake body fascinates the young Prince Alberic and offers a particularly striking version of Lee's subversive femme fatal as well as an apt illustration of *mētis*. There are several *mētic* elements that I plan to tease out of this tale, including the associations between *mētis* with shapeshifting and the coiled movements of the snake as well as the denigration of female powers associated with the myth of Metis. In line with the Metis myths, Oriana demonstrates the repression of the feminine, the hybrid and the nonhuman in patriarchal culture along with their power to unsettle it. Associated with the flexible, the crooked and the curved,[78] *mētis* is upheld by rhetoricians as an embodied cunning ideal for navigating agonistic engagements and subverting authoritarianism. In my analysis of Lee, I unite the curved, flexible elements of *mētis* with the temporal dissonance and transgressive elements of Gothic. Lee's twisted Gothic fairy tale about a benevolent snake godmother demonstrates the possibilities for Gothic *mētis* to be read as cunning monstrosity in service to the Othered.

Snake Ladies and Shedding Skin

The final *fin-de-siècle* Gothic shapeshifter I want to relate to *mētis* is Vernon Lee's Oriana, the snake lady. A cunning gender-bending, species-blurring ancient fairy, Oriana exemplifies Lee's characteristic interest in femme fatales, gender fluidity, feminine and queer desire, category confusion and patriarchal subversion. Lee's short stories are celebrated examples of Victorian feminist and queer thought. Her work will be discussed again in Chapter 6. My focus here is on her subversive, twisted *fin-de-siècle* Gothic fairy tale, 'Prince Alberic and the Snake Lady' (1896), which illustrates her fascination with transgression, gender indeterminacy, queer forms of engagement and transhistorical, transspecies rapport.

Lee's 'Prince Alberic and the Snake Lady' weaves together genres, times, genders and species to craft a Gothic fairy tale of familial doubles haunted by unfulfilled ancestral promises. Set in seventeenth-century Italy, the tale tells the story of the cursed fairy Oriana, 'condemned for no fault, but by envious powers to [the] dreadful fate'[79] of being a snake unless freed by a worthy cavalier. Oriana's fate becomes entwined with the House of Luna after Alberic the Blond swears but then breaks an oath to remain faithful to her for the ten years necessary to release her from her curse. Generations later, the Marquis Alberic takes Oriana as his illicit wife only to abandon her in the ninth year to join a monastery. In the textual present, Oriana forms a connection with the heir to the Duchy of Luna, young Prince Alberic, who is both the namesake and likeness of his ancient relatives. In something of a gender-reversed fairy tale, Prince Alberic is locked away in a tower by his grandfather, left uneducated, unsocialised and unloved. The sensitive, effeminate young prince embodies many of the traits of the classic fairytale princess: delicate, beautiful features, a caring and sensitive nature and a deep connection with the nonhumans and objects who form his isolated community. Able to transform into her human shape for one hour every evening, Oriana becomes Alberic's benevolent godmother who provides him with the courtly training denied by his grandfather. After two previous Alberics break their oath to remain faithful, the young prince seems destined to undo the snake lady's curse. But there is no happily ever after in

Lee's fairy tale: Oriana is killed, Alberic starves himself to death and the Duke, haunted by his misdeeds, gives into a life of debauchery that is ultimately his and his house's demise.

Oriana first appears as an image in a faded Gothic tapestry depicting her and Alberic the Blond, which hung in the young prince's room partially obscured by a large crucifix atop a dresser.[80] When it is revealed that 'she ended off in a big snake's tale, with scales of the most vivid . . . green and gold', the Duke Balthasar Maria orders the tapestry removed lest it '[feed] the thoughts of youth on improbable events' or contribute further to Alberic's 'violent excite[ment]' at the sight of the snake lady's tale.[81] The Snake Lady tapestry is not only a record of Alberic's lineage but a means for transhistorical and transspatial rapport. As Mary Patricia Kane highlights, the tapestry acts as 'both a decorative inscription of the past and the site of supernatural or transhistorical communication with the past'.[82] The tapestry also transports Alberic from the lifeless Red Palace, where 'there were no live creatures but snails and toads, which the gardeners killed',[83] to a vibrant world populated by colourful, textured 'leaves and fruits and flowers' and 'curious live creatures', including 'various birds, big and little, butterflies on the lilies, snails, squirrels, mice, and rabbits, and even a hare'.[84] The tapestry seems to materialise in the lands at the Castle of Sparkling Waters, where Alberic is sent as punishment after destroying a tapestry of Susanna and the Elders[85] hung in replacement of the Snake Lady. At Sparkling Waters, Alberic is mesmerised by the grapevines, lush fields and lively creatures, 'with the growing sense that he was in the tapestry, but that the tapestry had become the whole world'.[86] For Duke Balthasar Maria, the Castle of Sparkling Waters is 'a terrible place', bereft of furniture and 'little better than a ruin' inhabited by peasants.[87] 'Ignominiously discarded' as the home of House of Luna, Sparkling Waters becomes an exploitable resource, mined to ruin for its 'ready-cut stone'.[88] Yet, for Alberic, the place is enchanted and formative, a reversal or subversion of the enfant sauvage Romantic myth in which an escape from civilisation liberates and expands the soul.[89] In something of a Gothic reversal, ruination is a source of renewal and encroaching nature is liberating rather than oppressive.

The Castle of Sparkling Waters also represents a reversed, perverse Garden of Eden, inhabited by an amicable, edifying grass snake.

Oriana acts as a benevolent, nurturing godmother to Prince Alberic, teaching him manners, fashion, swordcraft, literature and politics. Her complex representation evokes Eastern mythologies of 'benevolent dragons'[90] and various snaky women from legend, notably the Lamia, a vampiric creature from classical myth with the head and breasts of a woman and the body of a serpent, made famous by John Keats's 1820 poem.[91] As Catherine Maxwell and Patricia Pulham note, 'snake women, especially those that can temporarily change their shape, have long been portrayed as dangerously alluring or sexually provocative', influencing 'the iconography of the classic *femme fatale*',[92] a figure Lee was well known to play with in her work. In Greek and Christian mythologies, snakes were used to refer to the sinuous beauty and dangerous influence of women upon men.[93] Oriana's challenge to patriarchal and religious authority is clear by Duke Balthasar's '[acts] of hostility' against her and the priest's descriptions of her as a 'demon . . . witch, malefica or stryx'.[94] She is framed as dangerous to Alberic not only because she might excite his youthful mind on 'improbable events', but because she might excite his youthful lust so that 'another member of the house of Luna . . . may succumb to her arts and be faithful to her for the ten years needful to her disenchantments'.[95] Oriana's snake tail has been described as phallic, contributing to her complex 'cross-cultural and cross-gender' representations.[96] A fairy, shapeshifter, snake-lady and trickster, Oriana's hybrid nature challenges binary divisions of gender, species, morality and time; she is masculine and feminine, human and animal, good and bad and the past in the present.

As Oriana's depiction suggests, although snakes are often associated with evil and sin in Western traditions, they are also models for shapeshifting and renewal, with their twisting, coiled bodies symbols for flexibility and adaptiveness. In its various representations in culture and myth, the serpent moves between 'the entangled knots of religious, cultural, and political identity',[97] acting as 'multivalent' signs of 'sexuality, fertility, guardianship, vengefulness, magic, healing, and boundary-crossing' as well as 'deception, hubris, and terror'.[98] Oriana's hybrid body 'attests to a potential for transgression and diversity'[99] and aligns her with *mētis* as 'a *poluplokos* being'.[100] Marcel Detienne and Jean-Pierre Vernant explain that the Greek adjective *polyplokos/poluplokos* referred to 'a living, interlacing, network,' which described the octopus with its 'thousand arms', the snake with its coils, the labyrinth with its tangle of halls and passages and the monster Typhon's snake-like appendages.[101] Kristin Pomykala elaborates that to be *polyplokos* is to be '"complex" or "tangled," a form of *mêtis* reaching out with tentacular and serpentine feelers' into tangles, rhizomes, 'dark and winding subterranean passageways and watery depths' within which we experience our entanglements with earth and other creatures.[102] It is in such dark and dangerous liminal territory that identities are challenged, and we may 'slough off old skin' to become better adapted to the agonistic terrain of our interdependency.[103] Lee's *mētistic* engagement with nonhuman subjects is discussed further in Chapter 6.

Assembling Mētis

The Beetle, Helen Vaughan, daughter of Pan, and Oriana the snake lady demonstrate the threat of bodily difference – especially hybrid, feminine and fluid bodies – associated with Metis and her *mētis*. In Hesiod's and Apollodorus's myths, Metis was an Oceanid[104] who embodied the fluidity and metamorphosis of water and could turn 'herself into any shape she pleased'.[105] In the Orphic theogonies, Phanes-Metis is 'an androgynous god with a twofold nature, being both male and female', a 'bisexual being' who carrying 'the germ of all things' in the universe was '[endowed] with all its diversity of forms'.[106] Rhetoricians like Jay Dolmage speculate that one reason for *mētis*'s exclusion from dominant Western philosophy is because it is primarily associated with female, nonbinary and animal bodies.[107] Much like Metis and Phanes-Metis, these *fin-de-siècle* Gothic shapeshifters represent the ways certain bodies and identities have been used to uphold andro- and anthropocentric models of self in the Western humanist tradition. Queer, androgenous, chimerical, animal and ambivalent, the *fin-de-siècle* Gothic shapeshifters discussed above are tricksters who unsettle British identity and language through their hybrid identities, shapeshifting bodies and uncertain intentions. From this analysis, I wish to extrapolate a few points crucial for understanding *mētis* and my application of it in a discussion of posthuman, post-anthropocentric Gothic.

Firstly, I want to emphasise *mētis* as a mode aligned with the feminine, nonhuman, nonbinary and queer. Most obviously, *mētis* is anthropomorphised as the shapeshifting goddess Metis and the trans-gender, bi-sexual and nonhuman Orphic Phanes-Metis.[108] I use *queer* to denote both non-heterosexual 'forms of intimacy' and 'a practice of resistance' geared towards disrupting hegemonic power structures and identities,[109] meanings that are illustrated by the deities Metis and Phanes-Metis, the 'bi-sexual' being. Although not exclusive to women, *mētis* is affiliated with the feminine throughout Greek literature, where 'women are depicted as creatures of [*mētis*]' because they must use 'trickery and deception in the face of the forces of the patriarchy' given their lack of political voice or brute strength.[110] Metis and her eponymous cunning are etymologically, conceptually and mythically tied to an assortment of monstrous women who resist, challenge, subvert and unsettle patriarchy. For example, Jay Dolmage traces the layered associations between Metis, Medusa and Coatlalopeuh, a Mexican Indigenous Earth and fertility goddess discussed by Gloria Anzaldúa in *Borderlands*.[111] Dolmage unpacks the complex links between these cunning women, including their powerful intelligence and resistance to rhetorical traditions that vilify female, embodied and mixed voices. Evelien Bracke connects Metis to Euripides's Medea and the mythical enchantress Circe,[112] while Biswas Mellamphy similarly associates Metis and Medea, connecting the 'Pelasgian Titan' and 'foreign priestess of the chthonic Hecate' with the 'fringe Hindu goddess first worshipped by criminals and outcastes', Mahakali.[113] Collectively, these mythic women represent multiplex and malleable ways of being and relating that counter binaries, 'purity' and 'coherence', also seen by Anzaldúa's mestiza consciousness[114] and the similarly hybrid métissage discussed in the introduction.

Secondly, I wish to underline *mētis*'s relation to the twisted, the curved and the divergent and the new perspectives this might yield. According to Marcel Detienne and Jean-Pierre Vernant, 'pliability and polymorphism, duplicity and equivocality, inversion and reversal' are the 'essential features of *mētis*', qualities that they link 'to the curve, to what is pliable and twisted, to what is oblique and ambiguous' against that which 'is straight, direct, rigid and unequivocal'.[115] Those with *mētis* (*polymētis*, 'of many wiles') are *polytropos* ('full of twists and turns'), *poikilomētis* ('of manifold artifice'), *polymēchanos* (of many contrivances)[116] and *polyplokos* ('complex' or 'tangled').[117] *Mētis* is a mode of being, thinking and reading that resembles Royle's concept of veering, associated with turning, subverting, perverting, twisting, detouring, etc. For Royle, veering 'impels us to think afresh and otherwise about . . . borders or opposition' and 'disturbs presuppositions' regarding such oppositions, unsettling distinctions between 'the literal and figurative, the physical and psychological, the external and internal, the literary and the real' or just about any binary.[118] Veering 'is not straight'; it 'entails a movement between' and a 'peculiar neither-nor but also both-at-the-same-time' orientation[119] that resonates with *mētis* as a power that 'weaves, plaits, links, and knots together the threads whose interlacing composes the tissue of Becoming' and bind 'generations and events in a single complex'.[120] As Detienne and Vernant explain, Metis is simultaneously 'Day and night, light and darkness' as well as 'male and female', their 'polymorphic power' working to '[transcend] these oppositions'.[121]

Thirdly, *mētis* is a mode of the 'between', as Christopher Long describes it, 'a transformative political intelligence' that paradoxically blends 'cunning, deception and craftiness' with 'wise counsel and political acumen'.[122] As a shapeshifter, trickster and witch,[123] Metis possessed a fluid body and rhetoric, which allowed her to transgress, twist, defy and overturn dominant orders, using her wiliness to unseat the power of Cronus and the Titans. Long highlights that *mētis* can lead to 'transformative effects' and holds the possibility 'for a different politics', 'one rooted in the transformative capacity of words' rather than brute force (the *biē* of the Titans and the force of patriarchal or colonial domination).[124] For Long, this 'other politics' via *mētis* embraces the feminine and the androgenous – to which I would add the nonhuman – operating on a shifting terrain of contact with alterity and 'competing claims for justice . . . in the face of irreconcilable differences'; a *mētic* politics of the 'between' or liminal 'entails the capacity to weave such differences together into the fabric of a community' equally 'strong' and 'flexible' and ultimately capable of responding 'with openness and creativity to the tensions endemic to the play of difference'.[125] Similarly, through her analysis of Metis, Medea and Mahakali, Biswas Mellamphy emphasises *mētis* as a netlike intelligence that binds opposites and 'disjunctively conjoins a fabric or network of relations', yet for her, 'it [is] impossible to build an alternate politics from and upon' *mētis*; it is a cunning that gains power 'through the paradoxical contiguity of oppositions', operating by way of the 'undomesticated and barbaric' and proceeding by 'contagion rather than by way of logic, law, and legitimacy'.[126]

Finally, the liminality, paradox and heterogeneity of *mētis* situate it within the 'fuzzy logic' of decolonial, posthuman and post-anthropocentric thought. *Mētis* embraces a hybridity and temporal dissonance that resists the hard and concrete differences imposed upon selves and the world by a dominant Western colonial logical, which '[suffocates] the many non-binary, non-discrete, and non-exclusive epistemologies that existed before the conquest'.[127] Operating by contagion and subversion, *mētis* 'constitutes a threat to any established order'; by remaining 'shifting and unexpected', this intelligence works 'to reverse situations and overturn hierarchies which appear unassailable'.[128] Because *mētis* 'does not keep' what it gains[129] through reversals and subversions, it does not replace a dominant paradigm with another; rather, it unsettles in an endless process of becoming. The interlacing opposites, non-human connections and fluidity of *mētis* reflect the posthuman, post-anthropocentric theory discussed in the introduction. Thus, rhetorical critics have viewed *mētis* as a tool for interspecies, posthuman rapport, discussed at length in Chapters 4 through 6.

Gothic Tricksters

The various *fin-de-siècle* shapeshifting monsters discussed above are ambivalent, paradoxical, tricky and subversive. Whereas the blends of genders, species, sexualities and states they demonstrate is an ultimate horror in Stoker, Marsh and at times Machen, for Lee, it offers possibilities for transgressive hybridity. Like all tricksters, Gothic tricksters twist, pervert and subvert various categories and systems, introducing incongruity, 'havoc and change' into just about any order, no matter how 'tightly controlled and well-preserved'.[130] While I cannot say that Gothic tricksters are on the side of humanity, it does seem that there is something possibly fruitful to glean from the ways they unsettle the British Empire and patriarchy. Read through the lenses offered by *mētis*, trickster theory and posthuman, post-anthropocentric philosophy, tales of shapeshifting Beetles and hybrid snake ladies highlight flexible, fluid ways of navigating if not unsettling inadequate epistemological paradigms, like those of European humanism, for the ways they denigrate feminine, non-binary, non-European, nonhuman and disabled perspectives. Gothic tricksters might not be good for Mankind, but they might work in service of the Othered.

Even as narratives end with monsters ostensibly contained or killed, monsters and tricksters alike are rarely destroyed, and the ruined houses, questionable mental states, lingering traumas and uncertainties they leave behind in these tales generate long-lasting effects. Although these *fin-de-siècle* Gothic tales do not show us the triumph of the marginalised against speciesist, imperialist, patriarchal, queer-phobic European powers, we can see the ways these monstrous tricksters have unsettled British identity, nation and language. It is important to note the ambivalence of *mētis*, however, lest it seem like some special trait of ethics or mode of justice. Associated with cunning, duplicity, trickery, deception and subversion, *mētis* is a trait of both kings and jesters, despots and rebels. In its ambivalence, *mētis* aligns with both Gothic narrative and a trickster disposition. A mode of 'the between', the fluid, the paradoxical and the discordant, *mētis*, like *fin-de-siècle* Gothic, demonstrates Patricia MacCormack's claim that what might be 'horror for some' is 'the very opening of the world to others'.[131] It is only a 'very particular kind of subject' who finds porous, plural and fluid identities horrifying; the horror experienced by Stoker's, Machen's, Marsh's and Lee's characters 'need not close off the possibility that . . . readers would negotiate their own subjectivity and elements of alterity' with an openness to diversity.[132] Put a little differently, what is poison for the patriarchal or the colonial is a remedy for the Othered. The negative connotations attached to shapeshifting beetles and snake ladies need not preclude contemporary readers making our own meanings as posthuman, post-anthropocentric subjects. The discussions about liminal, hybrid bodies, minds and methods outlined here are continued in the next two chapters on tentacularity and flexible plurality.

2

Gothic Tentacularity

'Yet the sight I had to witness was horrible, almost beyond the power of human conception and the most fearful fantasy. Something pushed out from the body there on the floor, and stretched forth, a slimy, wavering tentacle.'

Arthur Machen, *The Three Impostors*[1]

'There is never just one tentacle, but many.'

Eugene Thacker, 'An Exegesis on Tentacles'[2]

'Tentacularity is about life lived along lines – and such a wealth of lines.'

Donna Haraway, *Staying with the Trouble*[3]

From the tales of amorphous goat-gods, shapeshifting beetles and fairy snake-ladies, we can discern the particular fascination with human-animal hybridity laced throughout *fin-de-siècle* Gothic. Across the fragmented narratives of human ruination and liminal, shapeshifting identities, these Gothic tales question the definitions and limits of human identity, and in their query, emphasise the porous lines demarcating humanity from the mass, mess and maze of the more-than-human world. Picking up on the previous chapter's discussion of *polyplokos* being as 'a living, interlacing, network',[4] this chapter examines late-Victorian Gothic depictions of human-animal-ecological entanglements through the overlapping lenses of *mētis* and Donna Haraway's concept of tentacularity.

Haraway explains tentacularity as 'life lived along lines', in networks, and 'in the generative recursions that make up living and dying' in the Chthulucene, her play on the Anthropocene denoting the collaborative worldbuilding, or sympoiesis, of human and more-than-human communities.[5] For Haraway, tentacular creatures, tentacular tales and tentacular thinking work to counter 'human exceptionalism and bounded individualism'.[6] Essentially, tentacularity and *polyplokos* both define and emphasise twisted, coiled, liminal, hybrid and networked modes of being and relating. To be tentacular or *polyplokos* is to embrace the shifting, shimmering domains of life expressed in the interdependencies of creatures and environment, no matter how painful or horrifying they might be. Gothic generally, and *fin-de-siècle* Gothic specifically, model the kinds of fluid, boundary-breaking and tentacular modes of being and engaging promoted by Haraway's tentacularity.

Working with Haraway, I argue that *mētic* myths and *fin-de-siècle* Gothic tales are two of the 'myriad tentacles [that] will be needed to tell the story of the Chthulucene'.[7] Metis, her Orphic counterpart, Phanes, and the *polyplokos* octopus model rhizomatic and fluid identities that operate in 'contact zones', which are liminal spaces of collaborative worldbuilding in which myriad entities 'meet, clash, and grapple with' and ultimately transform each other, often in 'highly asymmetrical' power relations.[8] *Mētis* itself is tentacular and multiple: a cunning ability to extend, to withdraw, to undulate, to coil and also to entangle dualities and asymmetries. In the next section, I elaborate on how *fin-de-siècle* Gothic rewrites human identity and kinship, which reveals its posthuman, post-anthropocentric leanings. Inflected by Darwinian science, ecology, degeneration theory and myriad human, natural and mental sciences, these terrifying tales interrogate previous conceptions of Man and his position in the Great Chain of Being. They also illustrate the ways that posthumanism has been circulating alongside and within humanism since the Enlightenment, acting as a counter rather than a beyond or 'after' humanism. I then turn to H. G. Wells's Gothic-inflected scientific romances to exemplify some specific examples of *fin-de-siècle* Gothic's posthuman, post-anthropocentric perspectives. Turning back to tentacularity and *polyplokos* being, I conclude with a discussion of Gothic speculation.

Fin de siècle, Fin de *Man*

As the previous chapter established, the *fin de siècle* witnessed the cumulative and amplified effects of a century's worth of scientific and cultural rewritings of British identity, including new conceptions of gender, sexuality, embodiment and consciousness. My focus in this chapter is on the new understandings of species and human being developed by emergent nineteenth-century sciences, like evolutionary theory and ecology, and as depicted in *fin-de-siècle* Gothic. Although the European humanist model of a rational and exceptional human remained idealised,[9] its certainty was undermined by new sciences that deconstructed human being and 'remodel[ed]' it into sometimes radically new forms.[10] Martin Danahay highlights that even though evolution became an established biological principle in the late nineteenth century, it remained a controversial subject in wider Victorian society due to the challenge it posed to human exceptionalism, 'unsettling . . . the boundary between the human and the animal' while revealing human ancestry to be the result of random events rather than a divinely ordered design.[11] After publishing *On The Origin of Species* (1859), Darwin continued to develop his ideas on human ancestry in works like *The Descent of Man* (1871) and *The Expression of the Emotions in Man and Animals* (1872), the latter of which might draw the most 'direct connections between humans and animals',[12] correlating human and nonhuman facial, vocal and bodily expressions.[13] In *Descent*, Darwin argues, 'man bears in his bodily structure clear traces of his descent from some lower form' and these traces are also observable in mind, leading him to conclude that 'there is no fundamental difference between man and the higher mammals in their mental faculties'.[14] Darwin's general message was that humans are also nonhumans: our bodies and minds are of the same substance.

Evolutionary theory was the foundation for German naturalist and biologist Ernst Haeckel's theory of ecology.[15] His *Generelle Morphologie der Organismen* (1866) presented ecology as the study of 'the relationship of the organism to the surrounding exterior world' considered 'in the broader sense all the conditions of existence'.[16] *Ecology* derives from the Greek *oikos*, meaning home or place of being, and framed nature as a 'household' of 'relationality, continuity, and, ultimately, unity';[17] however, Devin Griffiths and Deanna Kreisel highlight that nascent 'ecological theory did not assume that these interactions were coherent, harmonious, or tightly integrated'.[18] Rather, the understanding of ecology held by nineteenth-century scientists 'emphasized a dynamic sense of transformation', treating ecologies as 'open', 'complex and evolving'.[19] Griffiths and Kreisel claim that following Darwin's work, many Victorian thinkers developed creative, 'extremely wide-ranging and flexible' views of ecologies, which included not only 'interactions between living bodies' but also their connection with 'the various organic and inorganic materials that constitute their environment.'[20] Alongside ecology, symbiosis emerged as a way to understand complex interrelations between organisms. Studies of symbiosis examined organisms who seemed to live together as one organism and were difficult to distinguish from one another, such as lichen or coral polyps. Ecology together with evolutionary theory and symbiosis presented a view of dynamic bodies entangled with other bodies, some of those bodies human, many nonhuman, some even inorganic. In this view, humans are intimately connected with other species and the environment around them. This model of dynamic porous bodies and more-than-human interactions is the foundation for both *fin-de-siècle* Gothic and contemporary posthuman and new materialist theories (discussed later in this chapter).

Divergences aside, *fin-de-siècle* Gothic tales almost universally explore the knotted question of 'who is Man?' and foreground his kinship with other creatures and environment. In their creative engagements with evolutionary theory and ecology, late Victorian Gothic writers stretch Darwin's web of relations and Haeckel's 'household of nature'[21] to radical extremes, depicting human-animal and other human-hybrid monstrosities. Kelly Hurley describes such monstrosities as the 'abhuman': a metamorphic, 'admixed, fluctuating, abominable' human/nonhuman hybrid that might be 'wolfish', 'simian', 'tentacled', 'fungoid' or 'simply "unspeakable" in its gross, changeful corporeality'.[22] The abhuman emphasises that humans are indistinct from nonhumans and malleable in both body and identity. Discussed further in Chapters 5 and 6, the rhetoric of ineffability so common to *fin-de-siècle* Gothic may not simply obscure to horrify or perform clever rhetorical tricks of obfuscation, but may showcase more-than-human agencies and humankind's imbrication in the material world. As Dr Chambers from Machen's 'Novel of the White Powder' articulates,

> the universe is verily more splendid and more awful than we used to dream . . . a mystic, ineffable force and energy . . . and man, and the sun and the other stars, and the flower of the grass, and the crystal in the test-tube, are each and every one as spiritual, as material, and subject to an inner working.[23]

Machen is one of several *fin-de-siècle* Gothic writers who explores the tensions between vitalism and materialism, ultimately arriving at a view of vital matter wherein mind or spirit and matter are one in the same and with this, Man is enmeshed in Nature.

Filtering *fin-de-siècle* Gothic through post-anthropocentric, posthuman and new materialist theory adds new domains to ongoing conversations about Gothic's explorations of kinship. Discussing changing eighteenth-century dynamics of family and marriage, Robert Miles posits that Gothic '[expresses] a concern with kinship patterns in a changing society',[24] and his point rings true for the *fin-de-siècle* context albeit for slightly different reasons. In its portrayals of the porosity and plasticity of human being, *fin-de-siècle* Gothic renders the shifting 'kinship patterns' of humans and nonhumans in the late-nineteenth century. Despite – or perhaps because of – what Elaine Showalter identifies as an intense longing for 'strict border controls' policing the lines of identity,[25] *fin-de-siècle* Gothic showcases again and again the breakdown of identity categories; the porosity of subjects, objects and environments; and with this, the fundamental ambiguity of how to demarcate (or elevate) Man from his Others. While such multispecies models of self were horrific to writers like Richard Marsh, for writers like Vernon Lee, these porous models of self-other-environment were sources of enchantment and interspecies rapport, reminding us that 'What might be monstrous' to some 'may represent a figure of emancipation for' others[26] – horror for Man is the very opening of the world for his Others.[27]

If Gothic emerges alongside and underside the Enlightenment in the eighteenth century, offering narratives and discourse to challenge, question or counter humanism, then by the end of the nineteenth century, it has established itself as fundamentally posthuman. This is to say that by the time of the late nineteenth-century British Gothic revival, Gothic had cemented its 'negative aesthetics' and its status as counter-humanist mode, trading in the monstrous, the uncanny and the liminal. With its increased attention to polymorphy, hybridity and the rhizomatic connections of life – past, present and future, human and more-than-human – *fin-de-siècle* Gothic demonstrates the heightened sensitivity to the networked nature of body, mind, time, space and species that characterises posthuman, post-anthropocentric thought. Not an exclusively twenty-first-century development, posthumanism, rather, as Cary Wolfe perhaps best articulates, is much like Jean-François Lyotard's 'paradoxical rendering of postmodernism' in that 'it comes both before and after humanism',[28] always already existing within and alongside it, perhaps much like how Metis and her *mētis* remained undigested by the consuming patriarch. In its fixation on vital matter, porous and hybrid bodies and the limits of human being, *fin-de-siècle* Gothic secures and extends Gothic's original 'protest against the disenchantment produced by industrialisation and Enlightenment'.[29] To narrow the focus beyond the broad range of *fin-de-siècle* Gothic, in the next section I focus specifically on the late nineteenth-century romances of H. G. Wells.

'Precarious Man':[30] *Evolution and Ecology in H. G. Wells*

H. G. Wells's Gothic-inflected scientific romances offer popular examples of how late nineteenth-century fiction explored the tenuous dominance and false exceptionality of Man. An essayist and a novelist, Wells wrote extensively on topics related to biology, evolution and ecology, or the interrelations of species within environments. His nonfiction and fiction alike have garnered critical attention for their thoughtful reflections on developing sciences and their implications for contemporaneous and future humans.[31] In some of his most provocative essays on biology and evolution, Wells lampoons and unsettles anthropocentric perspectives by emphasising humanity's fragile dominance and uncertain future. For example,

'Man of the Year Million' (1893) satirically predicts that man 'will undergo further modification in the future, and at last cease to be man, giving rise' to a new kind of being, comprised of a large brain and a small body that is nourished 'by immersion a tub of nutritive fluid'.[32] Other late nineteenth-century essays by Wells offer a less satirical and perhaps less hopeful framing of human evolution. 'Zoological Retrogression' (1891) troubles Victorian faith in evolutionary progress, reminding his readers that 'there is almost always associated with the suggestion of advance in biological phenomena an opposite idea'.[33] Wells questions the assumption that 'organic evolution' ends with Man as the apex creature as well as the certainty in 'man's permanence or permanent ascendency'. At the end of the essay, he suggests that 'Nature' might be 'equipping some now humble creature' with the necessary traits to 'sweep *homo* away into darkness from which his universe arose'.[34]

Wells's later essays, like 'On Extinction' (1893) and 'The Extinction of Man: Some Speculative Suggestions' (1894), explore the possible end of humankind and rise of another dominant species. 'On Extinction' ends in what Martin Danahay describes as a 'prophetic mode', moving from 'dinosaurs, to the dodo and the bison, to the human species' in its narrative of dead or dying species.[35] Finally, and perhaps significantly for a chapter called Gothic Tentacularity, Wells's 'The Extinction of Man' speculates about an advanced cephalopod species '[emerging] to challenge human hegemony'.[36] Here, Wells chastises 'the excessive egotism of the human animal' to imagine itself exempt from extinction. Although 'man is undisputed master at the present time', it 'has been so with other animals' and will no doubt be so again. He highlights 'even now man is by no means such a master of the kingdoms of life as he is apt to imagine'; the sea, for example, is 'mysterious' and 'beyond his control' and may someday, simply for 'mere idle sport', progenerate a new species that will unseat Man from his terrestrial dominance. Wells offers crustacea and cephalopods as strong contenders to adapt to terrestrial life and develop a taste for human flesh. He speculates that even the smallest of creatures, like ants and bacteria, may ultimately facilitate 'the fall of humanity'.[37] Collectively, his works have been interesting to scholars in Critical Animal Studies (CAS) and eco-criticism, for the ways they render Darwinian webs of relations and human-animal interdependencies, and more recently, posthumanism, for their depictions of human-technological interfaces, alien and nonhuman intelligence and future possibilities for humankind.

At the heart of much of Wells's *fin-de-siècle* fiction is what CAS scholars describe as the human/animal divide and an engagement with Jacques Derrida's 'question of the animal'. As Derrida contends, this is not a singular question, but a call to interrogate traditional reductive, essentialist notions of 'the animal' and with this, to notice the ways that nonhumans have been denied subjectivity in dominant Western philosophy, leading to their exploitation.[38] Derrida and CAS scholars after him have underlined the human/animal divide as the most fundamental distinction in Western philosophy,[39] emphasising, as Sherryl Vint puts it, that subjectivity itself has been 'premised upon the separation of human from animal'.[40] Wells's fiction inevitably and emphatically questions if not denies this separation, offering instead a model of self premised on the inclusion of the nonhuman in the human. His 'evolutionary speculations' emphasise 'human impermanence, imperfection, insignificance, and, most especially "degradation"'.[41] For Wells, the lines demarcating Man from Beast were both arbitrary and permeable. Fictional depictions of humanoid animals, animalised humans, sentient aliens and edible humans are just some of the ways he challenges this divide.

Wells's early fiction is famous for probing the implications of evolutionary theory, perhaps especially the porosity and ambiguity of the human/animal divide and the speculative futures of humankind suggested by evolution. Influenced by the work of his one-time teacher T. H. Huxley, Wells often presents pessimistic or uncertain futures for humankind, challenging the assumption of increased progress from simple to complex and primitive to civilised. Wells and Huxley alike viewed natural selection as inherently brutal, with no guarantee that humankind would improve over time. Much of his early work demonstrates the potential devolution of humanity, especially *The Time Machine* (1895), Wells's first novel, which tells of a bleak far-future where animal life has been significantly depleted, human-made structures have deteriorated and the bourgeoisie and proletariat have so radically split that they have evolved (or devolved) into separate species, both animal like. The Morlocks are described as inhuman, strange 'white animal[s]'[42] and are associated with deer, apes, spiders, lemurs, ants, sea-anemones, worms, vermin and rats as well as generalised animalistic traits, including luminous eyes, hairy bodies and a stooping quadruped posture. It is eventually confirmed that the Eloi are 'mere fatted cattle . . . preserved and preyed upon' by the Morlocks.[43] Depicting not only 'The Sunset of Mankind',[44] *The Time Machine* depicts the intermingled sociological and ecological deterioration that follows from Man's domination of nature.

In two of his later *fin-de-siècle* novels, *The Island of Doctor Moreau* (1896) and *The War of the Worlds* (1898), Wells explores the evolutionary past and future limits of humankind along the human/animal line. In *The War of the Worlds*, the highly evolved Martians easily dominate and invade the British. Wells's narrative of reverse colonisation involves a reversal not only in the sense that England is the colonised instead of the colonising nation, but further in suggesting that the Martians do not recognise the native British as sentient beings, treating them as the English treat nonhumans. Easily bested by the technologically advanced Martians, the English in the novel are recast as 'lesser' beings through comparisons to the nearly-exterminated Tasmanians, the vanished bison and dodo and a variety of other nonhuman animals, including rabbits, insects, infusoria and rats, undermining the Victorians' sense of dominance twofold. Wells's scientific romance depicts the English as exiled not only from their homes but also from their position as 'master[s]' of nature, which the narrator describes as their 'dethronement' as the 'empire of man' declines.[45] Peter Kemp claims the comparisons of humans to nonhumans are intended 'to disturb man by reminders of his kinship with the natural world',[46] but they also reinforce these connections, demonstrating Wells's characteristic ambivalence. The narrator realises 'the immensity of . . . space and nature' along with his own 'feebleness' in the face of the Martians.[47] The novel thus illustrates the Victorian recognition of humankind's enmeshment in the more-than-human world, subject to the same competition and consumption that other creatures face.

Many of Wells's short stories also emphasise the permeable lines between humans and nonhumans along with the possibilities for nonhuman sentience. For example, 'In the Abyss' (1896), 'The Sea Raiders' (1896) and 'The Empire of the Ants' (1905) depict intelligent nonhumans capable of advancing beyond and beside humans. Like *The War of the Worlds*, 'The Sea Raiders' (1896) showcases Wells's fascination with tentacled creatures, in this case a newly discovered species of giant squid named Haploteuthis ferox, who prey upon humans in search of food. This story reflects Wells's 'The Extinction of Man', where he muses that some highly advanced cephalopod may develop a taste for human flesh, unseating our position as a dominant species as they hunt us for food. 'In the Abyss' (1896) describes a previously unknown undersea civilisation of 'phosphorescent quasi-human forms' existing alongside terrestrial humans.[48] In what seems an early commentary on human pollution, the narrator says that these 'strange denizens of the deep sea' must deal with 'our ships, our metals, our appliances . . . raining down' upon them and sometimes smiting and crushing them.[49] Lastly, 'The Empire of the Ants' (1905) narrates the rise of a highly evolved species of ants in the Amazon who are quickly learning to use tools and organise against humans. The story's narrator Holroyd realises that man has 'but a precarious hold upon' the more-than-human world, asking 'Who were the real masters?'.[50]

The Island of Doctor Moreau is perhaps Wells's most provocative exploration of the arbitrary line separating humans from animals and the tenuous nature of human exceptionalism. Taking place on a small, unknown and unnamed volcanic island somewhere in the Pacific, the story is told by Edward Prendick, the sole survivor of a shipwreck, who is rescued by a schooner only to be abandoned again on Moreau's island, the site of his laboratory and home to the 'monstrosities' known as 'Beast Folk'[51] – hybridised creatures made up of different animals (like Hyena-Swine and Ox-Bear) and humanised in appearance and mannerisms through Moreau's experiments with vivisection, grafting and hypnosis. Many critics have discussed the ways in which the novel's depictions of the 'Beast Folk' undo the distinctions between human and animal by calling into question those qualities thought to be uniquely human. Laura Otis, for example, explores the Beast People's traits that undermine Prendick's assumptions about nonhuman animals and their capabilities: they can talk, build houses, walk erect and 'even try to think'.[52] The novel's depiction of vivisection underscores the paradox underpinning scientific studies of human physiology: the key to better understanding the human is to understand the nonhuman. Indeed, British neurologist David Ferrier made this paradox explicit when he famously claimed, 'It will be my endeavour to show you that what is true of the monkey is strictly true also of man.'[53] The portrayal of vivisection in the novel has received much critical attention, and critics like Mason Harris note the novel's conflicting and conflicted response to the practice as we view Prendick act as both horrified, sympathetic witness to the pain of vivisected animals and disdainful critic of the anti-vivisection movement, which he refers to as 'the silly season' in England.[54] Wells himself was a well-known supporter of scientific experimentation, including vivisection, yet the text challenges the efficacy and value of such practices by revealing the human subject as part of a continuum, or as Darwin phrased it in *Origin*, an 'inextricable web of affinities',[55] one that linked *Homo sapiens* with nonhuman subjects and the broader ecologies that house them.

The novel depicts Prendick's shifting, inconsistent responses to Moreau's Beast People and eventual questioning of his own humanity. At first, the island inhabitants appear to Prendick as 'strange brutish-looking fellows' who although 'human in shape', possess the 'unmistakable mark of the beast', leaving him to question whether the creatures are 'man or animal'.[56] With his erroneous conclusion that these are humans who have been animalised through vivisection, Prendick fears he shall be next. He eventually learns, however, that the Beast Folk 'were not men, had never been men. They were animals, humanised animals, – triumphs of vivisection.'[57] His differing interpretations of the Beast Folk underline two Victorian responses to Darwinian theory highlighted by Michael Parrish Lee: anxiety over the uncanny '"humanness" of animals' and the threat that the human might easily transform into the animal.[58] As Lee suggests, Prendick's encounters with the Beast Folk throughout the novel throw his own humanity into question. Beginning with his certainty that Moreau can turn him into a 'beast', Prendick later believes that he has 'caught something of the natural wildness' of the Beast Folk after he has been left alone with them on the island, recalling 'how soon [he] fell in with these monsters' ways'.[59]

Prendick is constantly mistaken for one of Moreau's creatures by the Beast People, and despite his various attempts to distinguish himself from and elevate himself above them to the status of full human (thus master), he is never entirely successful. The Ape-Man remains fixated on the fact that Prendick is 'a man, a man, a five-man, like [he],' highlighting their shared trait of hands with five fingers (a contrast to the misshapen hands of the other Beast Folk).[60] Furthermore, Prendick's reciting of The Law – the ritualistic formula for humanity based in the uncertain refrain, 'Are we not Men?' – unites him with the Beast People in a 'kind of rhythmic fervour'.[61] Rohman asserts that the Law 'insists upon the *instability* of human subjectivity and the concomitant need to establish and reestablish the boundaries of the human'.[62] Thus, Prendick's humanity is rendered uncertain by his need to secure it alongside the Beast Folk. When he is eventually rescued and returns to England, he cannot convince himself that the men and women he meets are not also Beast People or that he himself is a reasonable creature; rather he feels like 'an animal tormented with some strange disorder in its brain which sent it to wander alone, like a sheep stricken with gid'.[63]

On the surface, the text seems to confirm the human/animal divide, most obviously in the way that the novel depicts the regression of the Beast People as inescapable. In the chapter 'The Reversion of the Beast Folk', Prendick claims that 'day by day, the human semblance left them' and that 'the change was . . . inevitable', recalling Moreau's previous claim that despite his best efforts (with vivisection, grafting and hypnosis), 'somehow the things drift back again: the stubborn beast-flesh grows day by day back again'.[64] However, upon closer scrutiny it becomes clear that the human/animal divide is never secure in the novel. Reading the novel through theoretical lenses like CAS or posthumanism reveals that comparisons used to mark difference also – paradoxically and perhaps unintentionally – express a relation between human and animal, resulting in what Matthew Calarco describes as 'indistinction': the eradication of supposed distinctions between humans and animals, and by association between subject and object, self and other, mind and matter.[65] Rhetorically, the novel draws parallels between animals, Beast People and humans through the use of terms like 'beast' and 'brute,' which are applied equally to Moreau's beastly servant M'Ling, the animals who make up the 'ocean menagerie' and the captain of the *Ipecacuanha*. Prendick himself is counted among the 'beasts and cannibals and worse than beasts' aboard the *Ipecacuanha*.[66] Furthermore, the novel is populated by what Hurley calls 'beastly men' – the drunken captain of *Ipecacaunha* and his crew, who are all too happy to kick Prendick off the boat and go adrift again on the ocean; Montgomery, who degenerates into alcoholism; and Moreau, who is 'remorseless' in his scientific pursuits and lacks what Hurley labels the 'civilizing human emotions of compassion and pity'.[67]

Wells's novel also disturbs the clear divide between human/animal when Prendick is paradoxically led to realise his affinities with the Beast People by his focus on their difference; in recognising the 'grossness' and 'grotesqueness' of their hybrid animal bodies, Prendick realises 'the fact of [their] humanity'.[68] When Prendick comes face-to-face with the fugitive Leopard Man, who, after breaking The Law and consuming animal flesh, risks being sent to Moreau's House of Pain, he tells the reader,

> It may seem a strange contradiction in me, – I cannot explain the fact, – but now, seeing the creature there in a perfectly animal attitude, with the light gleaming in its eyes and its imperfectly human face distorted with terror, I realised again the fact of its humanity.[69]

This encounter with the Leopard Man seemingly challenges Prendick's assumptions about the Beast Folk and by extension his own relationship to nonhuman animals, evoking Derrida's 'The Animal That Therefore I Am (More to Follow)', in which Derrida claims that when we accept that the animal 'has its point of view regarding me', we come to face 'the abyssal limit of the human'. The subjectivity of nonhumans prompts us to see ourselves as also subject to 'the gaze'[70] of others.

In his characteristic ambivalence, however, Wells goes only so far in taking Prendick or his readers to 'the abyssal limit of the human' and not seemingly beyond. His presentations of the Beast Folk are clearly coded with racist and imperialist theories that marked the non-European as animal-like, as an intermediary between animal and human, as a 'missing-link' or an evolutionary antecedent to the fully human European, theories used to justify and endorse the colonial project based upon a de-humanisation of non-Europeans. Moreover, Moreau acts as a spokesperson for scientific materialism in his incessant 'repudiation of the flesh'.[71] Moreau is modelled after the figure of the Baconian scientist, whereby the scientist must '[assert] his humanity by forcing nature to submit' to his dominance.[72] In this model, the assertion of the human/animal boundary is essential – the exploitation of animals in the pursuit of scientific knowledge is necessary 'to fulfil human potential'.[73] *The Island of Doctor Moreau* highlights that scientists like Moreau must thus deny and denigrate embodiment, a disembodied perception of selfhood common to Western science, which feminists and posthumanists have criticised.[74] In his 'easy dismissal of the suffering of others', Moreau bolsters the European humanist 'metaphysics of subjectivity derived from the human-animal boundary', including a distanced relationship to the material world.[75] When the Beast Folk cannot hide their animal bodies, Moreau's response is to 'turn them out when [he] begin[s] to feel the beast in them'.[76] CAS critics align with post-anthropocentric and new materialist critics by emphasising the embodied nature of human being as a way to challenge the logocentric Cartesian focus on the mind as the essence of human identity and to recognise that 'Homo sapiens' shares the 'same biological origin as the plethora of [nonhuman] species' with whom we hold 'greater or lesser degrees of kinship and common experience'.[77]

For Prendick, his ties to animality and to materiality remain a source of horror and contempt. Upon his return to England, he seeks to rediscover a humanist model of subjectivity, one that is based on the logocentrism of the Enlightenment and a disavowal of embodiment and the 'animal' life it recalls. In his quest to discover and nurture 'whatever is more than animal within [him]', Prendick turns to the study of chemistry and astronomy, ironically claiming to find solace and hope in 'the vast and eternal laws of matter' while in actuality looking for 'bright windows in this life of ours, lit by the shining souls of men',[78] suggesting what is in fact a hope to recuperate a exceptionalist definition of the human that denies our shared embodiment with other animals. Regardless of this ambivalence and paradox (or perhaps because of it), as I explain in the final section of this chapter, Wells's fiction and the larger *fin-de-siècle* context from which it is drawn offer provocative materials for contemporary posthuman, post-anthropocentric readers.

The Tentacular and Tentacularity

While *fin-de-siècle* Gothic writers may have provocatively unseated Man from his apex position in the Great Chain of Being for sensational effect, Wells and many of his fellow popular writers offered a model of ecological awareness that resonates not only with contemporaneous studies of evolution and ecology but also contemporary science and philosophy. The human-nonhuman entanglements imagined by Wells and other *fin-de-siècle* Gothic writers gesture towards corporeal feminist and new materialist theories of porous embodiment and human/nonhuman interdependence. Borrowing heavily from microbiology (discussed in Chapter 4), new materialists embrace the 'filthy lesson' of symbiosis: because humans are multilayered microbial colonies and sites 'of contamination and abduction by alien forces',[79] they 'have never been individuals'.[80] Corporeal feminists and new materialists collectively aim to counter humanist 'fantasies' of individuality and sovereignty, of 'human uniqueness in the eyes of God, of escape from materiality, or of mastery of nature'.[81] Concepts like Stacy Alaimo's trans-corporeality or Karen Barad's intra-action emphasise that the boundaries between us and the environment are porous, that 'the substance of the human is ultimately inseparable from "the environment"'[82] and that humans and nonhumans are 'mutually constituted' as integral parts '*of* the world . . . part of the world in its differential becomings'.[83] In this Mobius-strip model of embodiment,[84] distinctions between self/other or inside/outside are arbitrary or constructed, and the nonhuman is an intimate part of the human. For theorists like Barad, it matters *how* we matter, and our mutuality with and dependence on nonhumans mean that 'we' are 'co-constituted and entangled' with our 'others',[85] which might oblige us to become responsive to their needs. Although horrific for Man, *fin-de-siècle* Gothic demonstrates various ecological networks and the intimacy between individual humans and the various entities populating the more-than-human world with whom we are entangled. In these ways, writers like Wells productively challenge the self/other dynamic of humanist subjectivity as they trouble the boundaries between human/animal, mind/matter and subject/object.

Along with ecology, symbiosis emerged in the nineteenth century as a concept for theorising the interdependencies between species, but with attention to embodiment over environment. Developed through the work of 'Swiss botanist Simon Schwendener' and 'Belgian zoologist Pierre-Joseph Van Beneden', symbiosis redefined what most Victorians referred to as parasitism, an all-encompassing term for relationships between organisms, both helpful and harmful.[86] Symbiosis addressed 'complex biological relationships in which it was often difficult to distinguish where one organism ended and another began'.[87] While a discussion of nineteenth-century understandings of symbiosis is beyond the scope of this study, we might turn to Wells's work for a brief window into this developing idea as it emerged for Victorians. Symbiosis became a way to understand relationships between different organisms who seemed to live together and move together as one organism 'but could also be divided into different organisms separately able to perform life functions'.[88] In 'Ancient Experiments in Co-Operation', Wells uses symbiosis to challenge the Victorian view of nature as pure competition and to promote a 'Socialist . . . synthesis' as an ideal evolution of society.[89] Colonial organisms, like coral polyps, hydrozoan and Polyzoa, are treated as models for all creatures, including 'higher animal(s)' like ourselves, who 'are, in fact, *colonies* of imperfectly-separated amoeboid cells', a 'co-operative union of individuals' so complete that we perceive ourselves as individuals.[90] Wells opines, 'It is as startling and grotesque as it is scientifically true, that man is an aggregate of amoeboid individuals in a higher unity'.[91] From here, he uses his imagination, discussed more below, to pursue 'a fascinating line of speculation' that ventures if humans are already 'aggregate[s] of amoeboid individuals in a higher unity', in the future we might 'coalesce' into ever greater '"colonial" grouping[s]' reflective of 'Siamese twins and double-headed monstrosities' or perhaps even 'strange forms' like 'human trees with individuals as their branches and so forth'.[92] Along with his provocative visions of human evolution, Wells predicts that future society will 'be an organism' capable of a 'perfect sympathy of feeling' if not developing a feeling of its own; 'Men will be limbs', and 'Not only will there be "forty feeding like one," but forty writhing like one'.[93]

In emphasising such evolutionary and ecological webs, *fin-de-siècle* Gothic offers a vivid model of what Haraway terms tentacularity. Tentacularity for Haraway, 'is about life lived along lines', in networks, and 'in the generative recursions that make up living and dying' in the Chthulucene.[94] The 'multispecies muddles' of the Chthulucene illustrate the tentacular figures, tentacular tales and tentacular thinking Haraway promotes in *Staying with the Trouble*. Here, she identifies tentacular figures as 'fingery', 'fibrous', 'flagellated', braided, matted, tangled, networked and tendrilled, including humans, spiders, squid, 'neural extravaganzas', 'myofibril braids, matted and felted microbial and fungal tangles, probing creepers, swelling roots . . . nets and networks'.[95] Tentacularity writ large illustrates the dual-pronged objection to individuality offered by biology and philosophy, which makes 'human exceptionalism and bounded individualism' impossible to think.[96]

Although her Chthulucene might evoke H. P. Lovecraft and his famous (or perhaps infamous) cosmic horror, Haraway rejects these associations, explaining her term as a compound of the Greek roots *khthôn* and *kainos*, roughly meaning *earth* and *time*.[97] The Chthulucene is '[a] timeplace for learning to stay with the trouble of living and dying' with our multispecies kindred 'on a damaged earth'.[98] While her dismissal of Lovecraft for his misogyny, racism and nihilism is understandable, her descriptions of the Chthulucene nonetheless evoke the uncanny and at times dreadful human and more-than-human assemblages of *fin-de-siècle* Gothic and Lovecraft's later cosmic horror inspired by it. In his well-known letter to *Weird Tales* editor Farnsworth Wright, Lovecraft described 'mankind' as a 'negligible and temporary race' and explained that his stories 'are based on the fundamental premise that common human laws and interests and emotions have no validity or significance in the vast cosmos-at-large'.[99] Based in this philosophy, Lovecraft's horrors depict humankind mentally and physically transformed by encounters with ancient nonhuman forces. As I have argued elsewhere,[100] while Lovecraft framed human insignificance and impurity as horrific, his emphasis on human vulnerabilities and nonhuman influence evokes contemporary trends in biology, ecology and post-anthropocentric theory. His provocative depictions of human-nonhuman intimacies mirror contemporary post-anthropocentric theorists like Haraway's call to develop multispecies kinships, even if they are risky, contaminating, unsettling or disadvantaging to humankind. As I discuss further in Chapters 4 and 5 on microbiomes and mycorrhizae, Gothic is ripe with images of multispecies becomings, rhizomatic collectives and what Patricia MacCormack describes as relations 'that should not be': relations that are experienced through 'the vast connective tissue' entwining all 'materiality, animality, life, and reality'.[101]

Haraway explains that her name Chthulucene comes from the 'denizens of the depths, from the abyssal and elemental entities, called chthonic' and charts her theory of tentacular thinking via 'demon familiars', such as the 'Pimoa cthulhu' spider,[102] 'snaky Medusa' and other 'mobile, many-armed predators' like the octopus.[103] For Haraway, tentacularity connotes 'abyssal and dreadful graspings, frayings, and weavings'.[104] A contrast to the 'sky-gazing Anthropos', tentacular creatures are dreadful and chthonic; that is, 'of, in, or under the earth and the seas'.[105] Spiders, octopuses, gorgons and other 'leggy', 'loopy' tentacular creatures are better 'than any inadequately leggy vertebrate of whatever pantheon' to navigate the 'multispecies muddles' of the Chthulucene.[106] Predatory and playful, tentacular creatures entangle, knot and weave relations, stories 'and consequences but not determinisms', staying 'both open and knotted'.[107] Tentacles are one of Wells's favourite 'predatory extremities'[108] found frequently in his fiction, including the Haploteuthis ferox of 'The Sea Raiders', the unknown orchid of 'The Flower of the Strange Orchid' and the tentacled Martians of *The War of the Worlds*. As seen in his comments on hydrozoa and polyzoa in 'Ancient Experiments in Co-Operation', tentacled creatures are also models for symbiotic relations and perhaps even future sociality. Across Wells's works and other tentacular tales of *fin-de-siècle* Gothic, tentacles emerge as signs of otherworldly contact and more-than-human (or perhaps inhuman, nonhuman and/or unhuman) intelligence. For late Victorian and early modern writers like Wells, Machen, William Hope Hodgson and Lovecraft, tentacles were not only markers of alien, nonhuman, monstrous beings, but also signs of nonhuman intelligence reaching out from other realms of time, space and being to connote, perhaps probe, the limits of humanity, materiality and identity.

Dreadful Figures and Tentacular Tales: Cunning Models for the Chthulucene

As Haraway argues, the post-anthropocentric present calls for a shift in perspective, from the 'sky-gazing Anthropos' to the dark chthonic depths wherein we 'entangle with the ongoing, snaky, unheroic, tentacular, dreadful ones'.[109] To this end, I want to suggest two avenues for such dreadful figures and tentacular tales, both of which turn to the past to engage the present. The first of these pathways returns us to Ancient Greece and the tales of Metis and *polyplokos* beings like the octopus while the second winds us back to the *fin de siècle*.

Mētis, the Twisted and the Dreadful

A protagonist in 'the webbed tales of the Chthulucene',[110] octopuses are also commonly evoked in classical narratives of cunning as exemplars of *mētis*. In his second-century A.D. *Treatise on Fishing*, Oppian outlines his admiration for the octopus's elusive, tricky nature, which allows it to catch its prey by surprise while under the cover of darkness.[111] A 'being of the night', the octopus's '*mēchanē*[112] enables it to merge with the stone to which it clings', to change both its colour and shape as it blends into its environment and mimics its prey.[113] Such trickery and polymorphy have made octopuses models of *mētis*, exemplifying the 'essential features' identified by Marcel Detienne and Jean-Pierre Vernant's detailed analyses: 'pliability and polymorphism, duplicity and equivocality, inversion and reversal' as well as that which is curved, 'pliable and twisted' in contrast to the 'straight, direct, rigid and unequivocal'.[114] A figure of polymorphy and flexibility, the octopus was described by the Ancient Greeks as a 'living knot of mobile, animated bonds' or 'a knot made up of a thousand arms, a living, interlacing network, a *polúplokos* being'.[115] The adjective *polyplokos*, readers may recall, also describes 'the snake with its coils and folds', 'the labyrinth, with its mazes and tangle of halls and passages' and other twisted, complex entities.[116] In this same vein, we can place Medusa's snakelike head as 'a direct symbol of her cunning, calling up the curving and polymorphism of mêtis'[117] and the netlike, networked intelligence of Metis herself, as highlighted by Nandita Biswas Mellamphy's analysis. Metis and her dreadful monstrous peers like Medusa, Medea and Mahakali model a 'chthonic matrix' – 'a prehuman and overhuman assemblage' emblematic 'of an emergent planetary-wide "network-centric condition"', which is 'nonhuman/inhuman, heterogeneous, and multiple, consequently less and less anthropocentric'.[118] Biswas Mellamphy highlights that despite the tendency to anthropomorphise figures like Metis and Mahakali, they are more properly 'inhuman and/or overhuman'.[119] Metis illustrates this through her metamorphic trickster body, which can in quick 'succession, become a lion, a bull, a fly, a fish, a bird, a flame or flowing water'.[120] As I discuss in Chapter 4's analysis of microbiome discourse, we can also describe ourselves as *polyplokos*, that is, a living interlacing network: 'a chimera . . . containing . . . [nonhuman] others'.[121] Tentacularity reminds us that we ourselves are rhizomatic webs of other creatures.

Through its various conceptual and semantic associations, *mētis* brings attention to the shifting, shimmering world and the cunning ways of knowing and operating not proper to Man. Along with nonhuman intelligence, octopuses demonstrate '*polytropiē*', a constant movement that counters 'immobility and rigidity'[122] and thus the kinds of 'bounded individualism' criticised by Haraway. Odysseus, the *polymētis*, shares the epithet *polytropos* with the octopus, as the classic example of the '*polútropos* one, the man of a thousand tricks, . . . who can turn a different face to each person'.[123] Eustathius calls Odysseus an octopus in his commentary on *The Odyssey*.[124] The octopus models a type of ethos, or character, promoting a flexible volte-face nature, which may be deceptive in some contexts yet receptive in others. Ampharaos, for example, advised his son to 'make your mind most like/the skin of the rocky sea creature/in all the cities you visit'.[125] Similarly, the sixth-century poet Theognis advises to develop 'a many-colored *ēthos*' and to adopt 'the temper of the convoluted octopus, which takes on/the look of the rock it is in converse with'. Theognis's ultimate point is that 'Skillfulness is better than inflexibility'.[126] Debra Hawhee explains in her discussion of the *mētic* octopus that 'For the ancients, the octopus . . . was a figure of flexibility';[127] its ability to '[reach] out in all directions through its countless, flexible and undulating limbs'[128] evokes 'a modality of response constantly bound up in its flexible, adaptive movement between things',[129] while its 'polymorphic powers' make it 'as supple and fluid as the water in which it moves'.[130] In line with Haraway's tentacularity, then, *mētis* allows those who possess it – whether octopus, goddess or human – to flow with an everchanging world, to move between categories, to undo binaries and to stay flexible, multiple and adaptive in moving 'along lines', in networks and 'in the generative recursions that make up living and dying' in the Chthulucene.[131]

Gothic Speculation

Although Haraway dismisses Lovecraft and excludes his brand of horror from her model of the Chthulucene, I propose that in doing so, she overlooks the possibilities that Gothic has to offer in speculations of the tentacular relations she promotes. Her claim that 'Lovecraft could not have imaged or embraced' the 'myriad intra-active entities-in-assemblages – including the more-than-human, other-than-human, inhuman, and human-as-humus'[132] modalities she outlines seems false since as MacCormack highlights, Lovecraft is a writer of 'becomings,' rhizomatic collectives and relations 'that should not be', which are grounded in 'the vast connective tissue' entwining all 'materiality, animality, life, and reality'.[133] While Lovecraft is not my focus here, I use him and his work as an example of the posthuman, post-anthropocentric tendencies we can observe more collectively across the Gothic mode. Returning to Wells and the late nineteenth-century context, I aim to tease out some of Gothic's speculative possibilities.

In 'The Future in America: A Search After Realities' (1906), Wells describes his 'habit of mind' as one that

> confronts and perplexes my sense of things that simply are, with my brooding preoccupation with how they will shape presently, what they will lead to, what seed they will sow and how they will

> wear. At times, I can assure the reader, this quality approaches otherworldliness.[134]

Wells's habits of otherworldly speculation have led some to view him as prophetic and are no doubt the foundation of his engaging fiction. Wells seems even to predict Haraway's theory of tentacularity in 'Ancient Experiments in Co-Operation', where he links human beings to colonial creatures, like coral polyps and hydrozoan, and likens us to lichens. Indeed, it seems that Wells would agree with Haraway that 'we are all lichens'.[135] He pursues 'a fascinating line of speculation' in 'Ancient Experiments' that leads him to assume the sentience of not only various pack and flock animals, but even cities, ships and phagocytes: 'strange unities[136] [who] wander through the body, here engorging bacteria, and there crowding at an inflamed spot or absorbing an obsolete structure'.[137] This same line of speculative thinking leads him to imagine the 'extensive modification' of humankind into 'strange forms' like 'human trees'.[138] In his final work, *Mind at the End of its Tether* (1945), he speculates that 'the human story has come to an end' and some other species, perhaps 'an entirely alien strain' or some 'new modification of the *hominidae*', will inherit the Earth. While Wells restricted himself to an 'up or down' model of evolution and degradation for species, in considering 'the death of Man',[139] the human trees, highly-advanced Martian octopuses, phosphorescent aquatic quasi-humans, tool-using ants and chimerical beast people springing from his imagination and common across *fin-de-siècle* Gothic are the kinds of posthuman imaginaries that help us to think tentacularly.

Along with the imaginative possibilities stemming from its monstrous figures, *fin-de-siècle* Gothic seems one of the 'myriad tentacles [that] will be needed to tell the story of the Chthulucene'[140] because of its characteristic excessive, fragmented style and ambivalence. Gothic's narratives are notoriously fragmented and multivocal, unravelled via letters, diaries, journals and newspaper clippings (as seen in Gothic classics such as *Frankenstein*, *Strange Case of Dr Jekyll and Mr Hyde* and *The Three Impostors*). These multiplex, intertextual, sometimes contradictory, sometimes incomplete and sometimes unreliable narratives seem to resonate with symbiotic (that is, tentacular) connections, which as Jeanette Samyn highlights, can be 'messy, rife with relationships that are painful and asymmetrical, but also full of possibility'.[141] If life and human being are a mess, mass and maze of 'multispecies muddles', then it seems we need messy and labyrinthine styles to narrate these entanglements and relationships. As I unpack further in the chapters ahead, late nineteenth-century Gothic rhetoric is 'a vertiginous excess of meaning', reminding us of the 'ornamental excess' of Gothic architecture and its 'gargoyles and crazy loops and spirals'. Gothic demonstrates 'a rhetorical extravagance that produces, quite simply, too much',[142] but this excess seems apt for rendering multiplex ecological subjects and engagements. The heterogenous entanglements and metamorphic, chimerical bodies displayed across late Victorian Gothic '[manifest] evolutionary forces in all their teeming presence while also harkening the new forms of subjectivity emerging' for the posthuman present.[143] Gothic's characteristic ambivalence also seems useful in telling tentacular tales, which are neither optimistic nor cynical about the possibilities for a future co-existence between humans and nonhumans.[144] Gothic might offer a palate cleanser for overly utopic renderings or catastrophic narratives of symbiosis, neither of which capture the ambivalent reality of ecological power asymmetries. While perhaps unpalatable to Man, Gothic ambivalence seems to be the right flavour for multispecies muddles.

Referring to Gothic speculation, I aim to link Gothic to the speculative fiction and the speculative thinking outlined by Haraway as fundamental to tentacularity and in doing so, gesture towards both Horace Walpole's original meaning and the possibilities for Gothic in the present. Haraway uses the abbreviation SF to refer to the blend of 'science fiction, speculative fabulation, string figures, speculative feminism, [and] science fact' she views as fundamental to unsettling anthropocentric, individualistic perspectives in favour of symbiotic ones. SF renders tentacular figures in tentacular tales, which are meant to challenge perceived boundaries between fact and fiction, matter and discourse, human and nonhuman, self and other, and many others. Such speculative thinking embraces the chthonic, the dreadful and the uncanny in a quest to produce novel forms of thinking, feeling, doing and narrating that mesh humans together with their 'oddkin'.[145] Such descriptions of SF resemble Walpole's original meaning of 'Gothic' (outlined by Frank) as a 'speculative' mode, granting access to an uncanny 'alternative universe' that allows for the '*sentience of space and place*'[146] and includes myriad inhuman, unhuman and more-than-human subjects. As a mode of what Tzvetan Todorov calls the fantastic, the Gothic 'belongs to the modality of the "as if"',[147] granting access to the uncanny fabulations Haraway imagines as productive avenues for unsettling anthropocentric thinking. Yet, in conversations about SF's ability to render the uncanniness of the more-than-human world, Gothic is strangely absent. Given the mode's temporal dissonance and with *fin-de-siècle* Gothic's multispecies muddles in mind, I would suggest that Gothic offers the kind of tentacular speculations apt for the posthuman present. In rendering a world without and beyond Man, Gothic speculations might unsettle some of the lingering anthropocentrism still haunting us in the Chthulucene.

The next three chapters trace tentacularity through Gothic fiction, rhetoric and film, moving from late nineteenth-century to early twenty-first century contexts. These chapters explore some ways that Gothic participates in the post-anthropocentric turn along with the theoretical and rhetorical possibilities its fragmented, excessive and speculative style offers. With this, I also explore how Gothic style articulates the cunning character, rapport and rhetoric *mētis* inspires.

3

Jekyll's Polytropos *Ethos*

'With every day, and from both sides of my intelligence, the moral and the intellectual, I thus drew steadily nearer to that truth, by whose partial discovery I have been doomed to such a dreadful shipwreck: that man is not truly one, but truly two.'

Robert Louis Stevenson, *Strange Case of Dr Jekyll and Mr Hyde*[1]

Few Gothic texts have achieved the cultural status of Robert Louis Stevenson's 'Gothic gnome',[2] *Strange Case of Dr Jekyll and Mr Hyde* (1886). The quintessential modern tale of humankind's pluralism, the story follows lawyer John Gabriel Utterson's attempt to unravel the mystery surrounding his old friend, Dr Henry Jekyll. The plot centres on Jekyll's increasingly odd behaviour and seemingly inexplicable relationship with the dark stranger, Mr Edward Hyde, who Utterson fears is blackmailing Jekyll. It is eventually revealed, however, that the nature of Jekyll's relationship with Hyde is far more disturbing and complex, for Hyde and Jekyll are in fact *one*. Although markedly different in appearance and personality, Jekyll and Hyde share the same body, the same consciousness and even the same crimes. In his 'Full Statement of the Case', Jekyll reflects on the seemingly divided nature of psyche, concluding that 'man is not truly one, but truly two', and someday 'will be ultimately known for a mere polity of multifarious, incongruous, and independent denizens'.[3]

An enduring tale of psychic pluralism and grappling with divergent parts of the self, Stevenson's text has spawned countless adaptations in both theatre and film, has informed a wealth of critical discussions and has inspired the phrase 'Jekyll and Hyde' as a synonym for split or bi-polar personalities in contemporary vernacular, most often depicting the contrast between a 'good' and 'bad' persona. In fact, Stevenson's Gothic 'case' has influenced scientific discourse on multiple personality disorder (MPD now dissociative identity disorder or DID)[4] on an international scale as demonstrated by the contemporaneous writings of F. W. H. Myers in England, Morton Prince in the United States and Lewis Bruce in Scotland and contemporary work by Mick Cooper in the United Kingdom.[5] Stevenson's provocative tale represents a longstanding Gothic engagement with the double, the doppelganger, duplicity, duality, fragmentation, possession, dreams, the unreliability of memory and the instability of identity. Critics have framed Gothic as an ideal mode to probe and render the 'personal sense of the war within', feelings of 'psychic disintegration . . . the breakdown of identity[,] . . . the decentering of the Self' and, as noted in the introduction, the subject 'in a state of deracination, . . . finding itself dispossessed in its own house, in a condition of rupture, disjunction, fragmentation'.[6]

In this chapter, I want to return to Robert Miles's claim that 'Gothic has found itself embroiled within a larger, theoretically complex project: the history of the "subject"'; yet, I want to challenge the association between the fragmented subject noted by Miles and a 'wound' or 'rift in the psyche',[7] suggesting instead that Stevenson's famous novella can be read as an example of the cunning multiplicity and polymorphic personalities associated with both dissociative identity disorder and *mētis*. *Polytropos*, Greek for turning many ways, manifold, versatile and wily, signals the shapeshifting of *mētis* and a crafty self-stylisation to fit divergent audiences linked to Sophist rhetoric and Michel de Certeau's cunning tactics.[8] As the previous chapters have outlined, *mētis* represents a domain of multiplicity, from the shimmering, shifting movement of the more-than-human world to the chimerical character of embodiment to the manifold nature of human consciousness. *Mētis* does not manifest in that which is one or unified; it is 'multiple and diverse'.[9] The image of Metis living on within Zeus as his counsel is one reason why *mētis* is associated with hybrid bodies and multiplex minds. When Metis is consumed and integrated by Zeus, she is 'no longer a singular entity',[10] and perhaps never was; as a shapeshifter and water goddess, Metis was already fluid and already multiple, a point further emphasised in the Orphic tradition of androgynous, amorphous Phanes-Metis.

Read from the perspective that multiplicity can be tactical rather than pathological, the *Strange Case of Dr Jekyll and Mr Hyde* urges a flexible, manifold ethos[11] that works with (rather than against) the disjointed, plural and malleable nature of the human psyche. Plural models of psyche and self have been linked to the 'post-modern' world of increased connection and flexibility as well as the posthuman, post-anthropocentric world of human-nonhuman assemblages and 'multispecies muddles' that make up Haraway's Chthulucene.[12] Jekyll's deadly attempt to remodel himself as a unitary, upright subject stands as a testament to the value of plural, flexible and hybrid models of self. Reading Stevenson alongside discourse on dissociation (i.e., psychic splitting) from the nineteenth century to the present via critical posthumanism and *mētis*, I argue for the rhetorical and intellectual value of multiplicity and fragmentation along with the Gothic mode's role in articulating it. I end by discussing recent psychology that promotes psychic plurality and challenges cohesion (in both identity and narrative) as a sign of mental wellness.

The Invention of Multiple Personality

Historians have identified at least three main waves of interest in double or multiplex consciousness in modern Western culture, beginning with the late eighteenth-century emergence of animal magnetism.[13] As sporadic reports of double consciousness in European and American medical literature emerged throughout the nineteenth century, interest in dual and multiple personality reached an all-time high in the final decades. Most recently, North America saw an influx of reported cases of multiple personality disorder (MPD) in the 1970s and 1980s, which resulted in what M. Boor labels an 'epidemic'.[14] Ian Hacking argues that each wave of MPD's popularity in diagnosis was facilitated by its linkage with important social issues, such as spiritualism in the nineteenth century and child abuse in the twentieth. Speaking of the nineteenth century, Hacking claims that the assorted reports on dual, alternating or double consciousness prior to 1875 made no sense until they were filtered through psychology's studies of memory and personal identity.[15]

Marquis de Puységur's experiments with animal magnetism laid the foundation for much modern work on dual or multiplex personality. In his 1784 experiments with animal magnetism, Puységur (Armand Marie Jacques de Chastenet), a student of Franz Anton Mesmer, discovered 'magnetic somnambulism' or 'magnetic sleep', characterised as a somnambulistic state in which entranced subjects displayed noticeable alterations in personality. Puységur describes his experiments with a farmhand patient, Victor Race, who became 'profound, prudent, [and] clear-sighted' rather than 'a naive peasant who can barely speak a sentence' when he was magnetised. Puységur claims that magnetised, Victor became 'someone whom I do not know how to name'.[16] He also observed that subjects typically forgot what had transpired during the magnetic state while they were in their normal or waking state, concluding that 'the demarcation is so great that one must regard these two states as two different existences'.[17] Magnetic sleep revealed that the mind was divided and that people possess a second consciousness quite distinct from their normal, everyday consciousness, which might display unique personalities, tastes, value judgments and mental acuity. Radical changes in personality in somnambulists are found throughout the history of animal magnetism and early hypnotism. Puységur's characterisation of 'two different existences' in human beings and his discovery of magnetic sleep 'introduced a radically new view of the human psyche and opened up a fresh vista of psychological inquiry'.[18] Observation of the mind was no longer confined to 'the rational, conscious layers of the psyche,'[19] and in these depths multiple and incongruous selves might be discovered.

From 1875 to the end of the century, cases of dual or multiple personality were reported with increasing frequency. Both naturally occurring and artificially produced modifications in personality (by suggestion under hypnosis) were popular items in psychological research, with well-known psychologists like Pierre Janet, Alfred Binet and Charles Féré researching somnambulism and suggestion in France; F. W. H. Myers and William Crookes of the London Society for Psychical Research and psychologist Henry Maudsley researching divided and multiplex consciousness in England; and Morton Prince and Boris Sidis exploring the cases of multiple personality in The United States. In England, psychologist, Henry Maudsley, for example, argued that the mind was divided into antagonistic halves in the brain itself, putting forth a view of the human as physiologically and psychically divided. Similarly, Darwin's *The Expression of the Emotions in Man and Animals* (1872) presented his hypothesis that humans retained emotions found in their animal ancestors, which suggested a subject divided between brute and civilised nature. Collectively, nineteenth-century mental sciences like neurology, psychology, mental physiology and psychoanalysis developed a model of consciousness and identity predicated upon inner division and conflicting states of being.

My past work on multiple consciousness has focused particularly on dissociation[20] – a splitting of certain mental processes (thoughts, emotions, memories and sense of identity) from conscious awareness – and it is in this context that I would like to situate Stevenson's work although I acknowledge that in many ways, the *Strange Case of Dr Jekyll and Mr Hyde* is not really a text about dissociation: Jekyll remains conscious of Hyde just as Hyde is clearly conscious of Jekyll. Dissociation indicated that there might be many 'minds' operating simultaneously within each human being, and studies of dissociation became the cornerstone for Victorian theories of consciousness, the structure of mind and the nature of individual personality. It is in the milieu of interest in dissociated consciousness and multiplex identity that Stevenson wrote and published his *Strange Case*, which coincided with other important treatises on these topics. Indeed, Hacking marks the advent of multiple personality discourse just prior to Stevenson's publication, identifying the July 1885 publication of the case of Louis Vivet, a man said to manifest up to eight separate personalities, as the catalyst. Vivet's case, originally published in France, was made known to the broader English audience in the 'Psychological Retrospect' section of the *Journal of Mental Science* in January 1886, written by A. Myers, and then again in the November *Proceedings of the Society for Psychical Research* by his brother, F. W. H. Myers, in a piece entitled 'Multiplex Personality'. In the following year, French psychologist Pierre Janet published an article outlining his theory of dissociation, and Eugène Azam published *Hypnotisme, double conscience et altérations de la personnalité: le cas Félida X*, in which he discusses the well-known case of Félida X, a woman whose secondary personality came to supersede her primary one.[21] In 1889 Janet published *L'automatisme psychologique* in which he attempted to outline a new scientific theory of psychological pathology with dissociation at its core. Dissociation quickly became a topic widely discussed in medical, scientific, social, legal and literary circles.

To what extent Stevenson was aware of and influenced by contemporaneous reports of double, alternating, split, multiple and dissociated personalities has been debated by scholars. However, if Stevenson's sources of inspiration for *Jekyll and Hyde* are difficult to discern, the same cannot be said for the influence the text has had on theories and language of dissociation and self-plurality more generally. Stevenson's novella has been understood by critics as a pivotal piece in the discursive formation of 'multiple personality' as an object of knowledge, inspiring significant works like Myers's work on 'Multiplex Personality' in England and Prince's work on multiple personality in America.[22] Prince is most obviously indebted to Stevenson. His *Dissociation of a Personality* (1905) tells the story of Miss Christine Beauchamp, a pseudonym for Clara Norton Fowler, who, according to Prince, is 'an example in actual life of the imaginative creation of Stevenson'.[23] Miss Beauchamp possessed 'several personalities', one of whom she described as 'a devil' and another as 'her Mr. Hyde'.[24]

Because of the nature of both evidence (divergent life-stories for divergent personalities) and treatment (automatic writing and/or constructing a coherent autobiography), dissociation has a particularly literary or discursive quality. The fact that 'the whole language of many selves had been hammered out by generations of romantic poets' and Gothic novelists[25] has led many psychologists to dismiss the veracity of MPD/DID. For example, Ray Aldridge-Morris (1989) and H. Merskey (1992) claim that MPD is the product of the public fascination with sensational stories like Prince's *Dissociation of a Personality*, Thigpen and Cleckley's *The Three Faces of Eve* (1957) or Flora Rheta Schreiber's *Sybil* (1973), with Merskey claiming that there was a notable increase of reported cases after the publication of these texts.[26] Aldridge-Morris calls MPD an 'exercise in deception'[27] and sees it as a cultural phenomenon rather than an independently occurring mental disorder; Mayer-Gross et al. (1954, 1977) claim that multiple personalities were always artificial productions, due to medical attention and literary interest; and Merskey argues that widespread publicity for the concept makes it uncertain whether any case can now arise without being promoted by the suggestion of popular culture. In the same vein, Robert Rieber maintains that nineteenth-century 'popular literature . . . flooded the minds of the public with fascinating macabre psychological novels', citing the work of Stevenson and Edgar Allan Poe as examples.[28] Rieber claims that tales like Stevenson's 'had a formidable impact on the reading public', forming a circuitous path of interest that moved 'from the scientific literature to pop culture and back again'.[29] Ian Hacking admits that MPD 'has dined all too well on cheap novellas, tabloid newspapers, movies and above all else, television';[30] however, this is not to undermine or challenge veracity so much as to acknowledge that common understandings of non-unitary mental states like hysteria, possession, somnambulism and multiple personality have been predominantly formed by 'the literary imagination',[31] perhaps more specifically, the Gothic imagination.

In what follows, I examine Stevenson's novella, especially Henry Jekyll's 'Statement', which serves as an autobiographical account of his experiments with Hyde and painful attempts to unify his divergent, plural personalities into the coherent, upright gentleman demanded by Victorian middle-class culture. Jekyll's 'Statement' reveals the literary or rhetorical quality of DID along with its treatments, which have been limited in their demand for subjects to craft a coherent self-narrative. Working with *mētis* and critical posthuman theory, I identify the possibility for a flexible ethos to be extracted from Jekyll's narrative of failure. This reading somewhat challenges critical interpretations focusing on repression and regression, which most commonly inform discussions of Stevenson's novella. While I do not deny the consonance between the Jekyll/Hyde dyad and contemporaneous discourses of degeneration, criminality and atavism or the obvious theme of repression in the novel, I find the emphasis on these overlaps limits the multivocal interpretations embedded within the text – written as it is as a 'drama of letters' from multiple authors.[32] By linking Jekyll's multiplex personality to *polytropos* ethos drawn from *mētis*, posthumanism and non-western attitudes about dissociation, we can see plurality as *generative* rather than degenerative. After examining Jekyll's 'Full Statement of the Case', I return to late nineteenth-century discussions of dissociation and multiplex personality promoting flexible multiplicity as ontology (way of being) rather than pathology (disorder of being), which I link to the contemporary neo-dissociation movement and its embrace of a healthy self-plurality. Ultimately, I argue that the Gothic mode reveals the rhetorical and intellectual value of the multiplex, duplicitous and fragmented.

The Tenuous 'I' of Dissociative Narrative

Henry Jekyll's 'Statement' expresses one of the most quintessential testaments to the innate multiplex nature of human being. Jekyll writes,

> With every day, and from both sides of my intelligence, the moral and the intellectual, I thus drew steadily nearer to that truth, by whose partial discovery I have been doomed to such a dreadful shipwreck: *that man is not truly one, but truly two*. I say two, because the state of my own knowledge does not pass beyond that point. Others will follow, others will outstrip me on the same lines; and I hazard the guess that *man will be ultimately known for a mere polity of multifarious, incongruous, and independent denizens*.[33]

Jekyll identifies the 'thorough and primitive duality of man', yet considers it 'the curse of mankind that these incongruous fagots were thus bound together – that in the agonised womb of consciousness, these polar twins should be continuously struggling'.[34] Jekyll's statement oscillates between distance and proximity to Hyde and, by extension, between a view of self-plurality as both pathological and ontological, by which I mean plurality is framed as both abnormal and innate to human being. While Hyde might be characterised as 'lower', 'worse' and 'pure evil' in contrast to Jekyll, Jekyll cannot deny that he is 'radically both', with 'a second form and countenance substituted, none the less natural' than the first.[35] Jekyll indicates that he knows Hyde, if not fully, 'from very early' so that from a young age he becomes 'committed to a profound duplicity of life' with a desire to 'house' these disparate elements in separate identities.[36]

Much like the larger text, Henry Jekyll's autobiographical 'Full Statement of the Case' is 'a complex weave of voices'.[37] Jekyll's account begins as a typical autobiography might, with the date of his birth and a linear presentation of the events that mark the appearance of his second self and his decline into misery. But unlike a typical autobiography, which seeks to 'construct a unitary and autonomous subjectivity',[38] Jekyll's autobiographical (or confessional) statement stresses the divisions within his self and fails to produce a coherent self-narrative. Jekyll's statement contains many of the typical narrative elements common to dissociative patient accounts: an inability to view the self holistically, a refusal to accept alter personalities as part of the 'I' and an unpredictable and unstable use of pronouns. Jekyll begins his 'Statement' grounded in the seeming stability of the first-person pronoun, viewing Hyde as an element of himself: 'There was something strange in my sensations, something indescribably new . . . I felt younger, lighter, happier in body'. Jekyll's claims that 'I knew myself' and 'This, too, was myself' shortly give way to the use of 'it' rather than 'he' or 'I,' the use of third-person distance in references to 'Henry Jekyll' and 'Edward Hyde' and claims such as 'He, I say – I cannot say, I' in the descriptions of Hyde's actions.[39] Yet, when one might expect Jekyll to distance himself the most from Hyde – that is, in his description of the murder of Carew – Jekyll narrates the event from the first-person perspective: 'Instantly the spirit of hell awoke in me and raged. With a transport of glee, I mauled the unresisting body, tasting delight from every blow.'[40] These permutations of 'I,' 'he,' 'it,' 'Henry Jekyll' and 'Edward Hyde' are unpredictable, even for a subject who might be prone to dissociations of personality. For example, when Morton Prince asks Miss Beauchamp's alter Sally to write an autobiography as a secondary self, she restricts her pronouns to 'she' and 'I'.

It is perhaps telling that Lanyon's command to the hysterical Hyde is 'compose yourself'.[41] His command indicates the importance of coherence in self-representation and points to the treatment used by psychologists like Janet and Prince for patients with hysteria and MPD. Linking it to dissociation, Janet maintained that hysteria is 'a malady of the *personal synthesis*', an inability of the subject to 'compose' herself and tell a coherent story of her identity.[42] Thus, the cure for this malady is to integrate the multiple sensations, perceptions and memories which comprise one's own experience and personality into a unified 'I'. Similarly, Prince asks Sally to compose an 'autobiography', the value of which for Prince 'lies in the description of a dissociated mind, and of the alleged cleavage of consciousness dating back to early childhood'.[43] By locating the origin of this 'cleavage' in consciousness, Prince could learn of the events which led to Christine's creation of Sally as a separate personality. Prince positions himself in much the same way as Utterson, acting as 'Mr. Seek' in his 'Hunt for the Real Miss Beauchamp', the story of whom is revealed through a series of letters written between personalities that Prince must record and decode. Like Stevenson's, much of Prince's text is comprised of letters: letters within letters, letters left from one personality to another, letters from Sally or Miss Beauchamp to Dr Prince and letters which demonstrate the switch from one personality to another in the act of the writing. Janet's work, likely the earliest to use narrative to bridge gaps between selves in service of a unified, harmonised personality,[44] ushered in this longstanding psychotherapeutic use of 'a logically sequenced self-narrative as a mechanism through which one gains wellness' and '[recovers] from DID', a treatment that remains popular today despite increased pharmacological treatments for mental illness.[45]

Part of the lingering appeal of Janet's treatment is no doubt the common associations drawn between memory, identity and narrative, especially in Western psychology discourse. As psychologist Laurence Kirmayer suggests, our ordinary memory is full of gaps and holes, so 'we must work . . . to close the gaps and mend the ruptures in experience', which we do partially through narrative reconstruction.[46] Elizabeth Howell writes that 'The "self" is plural, variegated, polyphonic, and multivoiced', so the experience of unity is 'an illusion' created by 'the mind's capacity to fill in the blanks and to forge links', often through 'narration'.[47] As Kirmayer outlines, from a philosophical and psychological perspective, 'the self [is] a narrative construction', that is, 'a coherent story we construct about our actions, and the *I* is the narrative center of gravity in our story'; however, there might be 'multiple stories . . . with different narrative centers' and thus 'multiple selves' in one *person*. Dissociation represents a 'disturbance of self-organization' and self-unity, which may or may not require correction, depending on one's cultural context.[48] Kirmayer argues that 'cultures differ in their tolerance for [narrative] gaps' and for 'the radical shifts in perspective that accompany shifts in states of mind', noting that cultures that demand a coherent self-presentation have limited avenues to express healthy multiplicity.[49]

Although Jekyll does not dissociate Hyde, his 'Statement' is interesting to consider in the context of DID patient narratives and psychotherapeutic treatments for the ways it reflects the innate multiplicity of the psyche, the Western socio-cultural pressure to cohere these divergent dimensions and the broader implications of multiplex being for dominant western culture, especially the models of subjectivity it allows. In the Western world, to achieve a 'socially credible personhood', dissociative gaps and contradictions in disposition or behaviour must be joined together by a narrative of self-continuity: 'Simply put, it is not socially adaptive to show one's fragmented personality'.[50] Kirmayer points out that many non-Western cultures recognise and accept the shifting and multiplex nature of the self (in terms of personality, identity and/or subjectivity). However, the Western self is expected to be 'univocal' and therefore 'must constantly strive to reconcile or rationalize inconsistencies and lacunae' in their self-presentation. This univocal model of self also demands continuity and rationality, expressed in a linear narrative that rationalises our motives and behaviours.[51] Kirmayer suggests that the Western subject 'is engaged in a constant process of minimizing or subduing alternate voices' even 'if multivocality is intrinsic to the human condition'.[52] Amy Louise Miller highlights that in Western cultures, 'The reality of self is constructed as being local and unified' to such an extent that 'unity is the sole allowably "normal state"'. Miller calls this the 'local view' of self:

self is 'attached' to and 'bounded' by the body in time and space. In this system, 'I' am a separate individual 'who exists locally within the boundary of my skin', with my thoughts taking place within the boundary of my mind, which is bound to my brain and located 'inside my head' with an 'assumed one-to-one relationship between my mind and my body'.[53]

Case studies of dissociative phenomena involving psychic-splitting, multiple personality and somnambulism challenged traditional Western assumptions about the nature of identity as being unified and integrated as well as the assumption that a healthy person has only one mind. Stephen Braude suggests that dissociative states 'challenge various familiar assumptions about the nature of personhood', especially the tendency to assume a one-to-one 'correlation between persons and bodies'.[54] Because it revealed the capacity for many minds, multiple consciousnesses and implanted thoughts, dissociation challenged the belief that individuals possess only one 'mind' and destabilised the Enlightenment belief in a rational, agentic subject (i.e., Man). Although some psychologists (e.g., Janet and Myers) conceded that the secondary self could be creative if not superior to the dominant self in terms of intelligence and disposition, for most, dissociation (and similar fluctuations and multiplications of personality) was a sign of pathology, and the therapeutic goal was to integrate various personalities into a coherent and socially sanctioned whole.

Thus, Jekyll must not only cohere his divergent selves into a robust integrated whole, but this self must also conform to those traits most prized for middle-class British Victorian masculinity: independence, stability, rationality and unity. That Hyde is associated with femininity, animality, pathos, excess and mutability makes him all the more dangerous to Jekyll's ideal, perhaps idealised, model of self. Associated with apes, monkeys, troglodytes, multiplicity, embodiment and hysteria, Hyde is clearly aligned with traits rejected by conventional models of not only masculinity but more broadly humanity as it exists in the European humanist tradition. Jekyll, through his fluid and multiple identity, can no longer identify himself as a comprehensive subject. His inability to say 'I' when speaking of himself suggests that more is at stake than his pronominal confidence; this inability points to a radical collapse of his masculine identity, one that is exacerbated by Hyde's association with hysteria.

Jekyll's 'Statement' offers something of a window into the experience of lived self-plurality and the consequences of too rigid a view of self. Dr Jekyll, 'the prototypical Victorian gentleman', is required by his society to demonstrate 'gravity-repression-goodness-humanity-morality' as opposed to the 'recklessness-freedom-evil-bestiality-villainy' of Hyde.[55] His splintering into two selves is a 'consequence of a society which constellates order with goodness and disorder with badness'[56] as well as unity with health and multiplicity with pathology. Psychologists since Stevenson's time have confirmed Jekyll's claim that 'man will be ultimately known for a mere polity of multifarious, incongruous, and independent denizens'; however, as Mick Cooper argues, whether this multiplicity will lead us 'to the same "dreadful shipwreck"' depends entirely on how 'this plurality is lived out: in a spirit of either/or-ness, repression, and divisiveness, or in a spirit of both-ness, liberation, and dialogue'.[57] As myriad psychologists have argued (and rhetorician Cathryn Molloy articulates), 'no compelling reason exists to privilege' cohesion in self-narration.[58] In a culture or society that 'celebrates heterogeneity and diversity, self-plurality may emerge as a potential means of maximizing one's possibility for actualization'[59] – generative rather than degenerative. Kirmayer argues that too much pressure for rationality, consistency, univocality and continuity may lead to pathology, and he encourages a flexible, polyphonic self as a healthier model to strive for.[60] Jekyll's story demonstrates that the horror attached to multiple selves is not the multiplicity but rather the demand for unity. This is not to discount the distressing nature of DID or dissociative gaps in memory, but rather to argue for the value of fragmentation and plurality in identity and its representation: embrace your inner Hyde!

Flexible Multiplicity

In the following section, I explore some divergent models of the multiplex self articulated in mental science discourse from the late nineteenth century to the present, working with *mētis* and posthumanism in mind. I am especially interested in F. W. H. Myers's 'Gothic' psychology, which countered many mainstream interpretations of subconscious states and divergent selves as pathological, treating them instead as cunning means to self-expansion and elevation. Following my reading of Myers, I turn to contemporary (largely American) psychology discourse promoting self-plurality as a post-modern – perhaps also posthuman – tactic to generate selves just as fluid and hybrid as the contemporary post-modern, posthuman world.

'Gothic Psychology' and the Multiplex Self

The work of English philosopher and psychical researcher F. W. H. Myers offers a starting point to an alternative story of multiplex identity circulating alongside the pathology frame in Western psychology discourse. Thematically, the works of Stevenson and Myers share many concerns: the mutability of personality, the capacity for spontaneous fluctuations of self and a view of humans as composed of many selves. There are also some striking similarities in the language used by Stevenson and Myers in their explorations of our multiple natures, including parallel descriptions of the 'inco-ordinate elements of the polity of our being'.[61] Critics have debated the extent to which Myers and Stevenson might have influenced one another. Myers famously took a noted interest in the *Strange Case*, predicting that Stevenson's reputation would be made by the text and writing to Stevenson twice with suggestions for revision that he believed would make the tale adhere more closely to 'observed psychological fact'.[62] Although Stevenson never followed through with Myers's recommendations, Myers nonetheless lauded Stevenson's work in his obituary for him in the *Journal of the Society for Psychical Research*, writing that *Jekyll and Hyde* was 'of such special value to the psychologist' for the ways it 'offered one of the most striking examples on record of the habitual uprush and incursion into ordinary consciousness' of subconscious ideas 'without sense of effort or choice or will'.[63]

Throughout his career, Myers was intrigued by this 'uprush' of ideas from the subconscious 'into ordinary consciousness', and he was particularly interested in the study of liminality, more precisely 'conscious life beneath the threshold or beyond the margin' and what he called the 'multiplex and mutable character' of 'the personality of man'.[64] His 'thesis of multiplex personality' was 'namely, that no known current of man's consciousness exhausts his whole consciousness, and no known self-manifestation expresses man's whole potential being'.[65] In his posthumously published *Human Personality and its Survival after Bodily Death* (1903), he writes, 'I regard each man as at once profoundly unitary and almost infinitely composite, as inheriting from earthly ancestors a multiplex and "colonial" organism – polyzoic and perhaps polypsychic in an extreme degree'.[66] Myers presents a tentacular model of psyche: heterogenous and rhizomatically connected to other lifeforms. It also resembles a pre-Jungian model of the collective unconscious and Jung's view of the unconscious 'extend[ing] outwards – like a field – beyond the self.'[67] I'll return to the posthuman, post-anthropocentric implications of this view of psyche at the end of this chapter.

Myers conceived of consciousness in terms of spectra and thresholds. As William James explains it, Myers segmented the mind into the supraliminal and Subliminal, believing that our everyday supraliminal self/consciousness was only a small fraction of the 'psychic spectrum' while the Subliminal 'represents more fully our central and abiding being', a region 'with possibly the most heterogeneous contents'.[68] Our conscious self is thus just 'one small part of an extended psychical entity'; Myers thought that we could catch a glimpse of our subliminal self under the right circumstances and that our subliminal self could be superior to our everyday conscious self. He believed that humans possessed psychical capabilities of which they were only dimly aware and saw mediumship and automatism as evidence of 'subliminal Selves, or more briefly of a subliminal Self', arguing that 'no Self of which we can here have cognisance is in reality more than a fragment of a larger Self, – revealed in a fashion at once shifting and limited'.[69] Against the grain of mainstream psychology, Myers argued that the subconscious or subliminal secondary personalities revealed in trance, dreaming and automatic writing 'potentially possessed a higher intelligence than one's waking or supraliminal personality and often served to convey messages of guidance'.[70] As he explains in a piece for the May 1889 *Journal of the Society for Psychical Research*,

> each of us, we may say, contains within himself the potentiality of an unknown number of personalities, some at least of which may be educated to become so readily recurrent as his primary personality, although no one of them can – anymore than his primary personality – be made to manifest itself in a really continuous manner.[71]

Thus, for Myers, divergence and incongruity were innate rather than pathological traits of human personality.

Drawing on a typical Victorian rhetoric of self-help and evolution, Myers promotes psychic plurality as a mechanism through which humankind might improve. He asks, 'who assures us that even here and now we have developed into the full height and scope of our being?'[72] In an industrial analogy, Myers equates our brains to a 'vast manufactory, in which thousands of looms, of complex and differing patterns, are habitually at work'.[73] Since we inherited this 'factory' from our ancestors, it is only sensible that we would need to rearrange and update the floor plan, moving and removing any obsolete machines and replacing them with newer models. He suggests that modern humans require modern minds to suit their modern context – a similar claim made by the postmodern psychologists discussed in the section below. Myers credits Mesmer and his students with discovering a 'new branch of moral as well as physical therapeutics' that acts as 'a nascent art of self-modification; a system of pulleys (to return to our previous metaphor), by which we can disjoin and reconnect portions of our machinery which admit of no directer access'. Through careful self-fashioning – or perhaps self-weaving – we can cast off 'the cloak which our rude forefathers have woven themselves against the cosmic storm' and find ways 'to shift and refashion it as our gentler weather needs'.[74] Just as our waking and sleep states have 'come to co-exist for us in advantageous alternation, so also other states may come to coexist with these, in response to new needs of the still evolving organism'.[75]

For Myers, 'If we are multiplex beings, let us get the advantage of our multiplicity. If we are modifiable by circumstance, let us learn to modify ourselves'.[76] Much like a posthumanist or like Theognis in his conception of 'octopus ethos' discussed in Chapter 2, Myers views the human personality as 'a much more modifiable complex of forces than is commonly assumed'.[77] Moreover, the proximity between the degenerate and the superior or the normal and the abnormal 'shows us how often the word "normal" means nothing more than "what happens to exist"'.[78] Myers thus proposed a view of human multiplicity contradicting many of his peers and geared towards 'bringing out that composite or "colonial" character which on a close examination every personality of men or animals is seen to wear'. Human consciousness for Myers is rhizomatic and 'cannot be truly expressed in any linear form. Even a three-dimensional scheme, – a radiation of faculties from a centre of life, – would ill render its complexity'.[79]

In his eulogy for Myers, American psychologist William James claims that 'the human mind' has 'largely [been] an abstraction,' figured as a 'sort of sunlit terrace' by the classic academic and psychologist. However, more recently,

> the terrace has been overrun by romantic improvers, and to pass to their work is like going from classic to Gothic architecture, where few outlines are pure and where uncouth forms lurk in the shadows. A mass of mental phenomena are now seen in the shrubbery beyond the parapet. Fantastic, ignoble, hardly human, or frankly non-human are some of these new candidates for psychological description . . . The world of mind is shown as something infinitely more complex than was suspected; and whatever beauties it may still possess, it has lost at any rate the beauty of academic neatness.[80]

Although James is discussing the 'romantic' psychology of Myers, which has since been reappropriated as 'Gothic' by writers like Andre Breton and Sonu Shamdasani,[81] his comments could be readily applied to other 'romantic improve[rs]' of psychology, which may include Gothic writers like Stevenson, Arthur Machen and Bram Stoker, 'who explored the human mind in all its troubling complication, without the artificially imposed linearity of mainstream scientific discourses'.[82] Gothic fiction explores the 'Fantastic, ignoble, hardly human, or frankly non-human' aspects of human psychology noted by James, exposing 'the dark, tangled corners of the human mind',[83] which cannot be neatly rendered. And if, as James suggests, 'Nature is everywhere gothic, not classic. She forms a real jungle, where all things are provisional, half-fitted to each other, and untidy', then the convoluted storylines, embedded fragments, multiple and sometimes contradictory narrators, impostors, doubles and shapeshifters of Gothic's narrative landscape represent a contrast to the 'far too neat'[84] storylines of scientific discourse. After my discussion of the postmodern plural *polytropic* self that has emerged from late-twentieth-century psychology discourse, I will return to the value of fragmented, nonlinear narratives in self-expression, turning again to Stevenson's work and Gothic more generally.

The Postmodern, Posthuman *Polymētis*

While myriad modern theories of fragmented human psychology have circulated since the late nineteenth century,[85] the late twentieth century saw the rise of a positive plural-self discourse, largely following from the renewed interest and emphasis on dissociation in psychology. Dissociation came to be seen as existing along a continuum, with most dissociative experiences considered part of normal psychological functioning and multiplicity considered an innate – if not ideal – trait of human consciousness, personality or ethos. Psychologist Mick Cooper notes that plurality is becoming more commonly accepted as a normal state of human being, with an increasing number of people viewing themselves as multiple. Shifting from unified tales of singular, reasonable and consistent protagonists, contemporary subjects are more likely to craft plural self-narratives, in which they present themselves as two or more characters and frequently 'shift among multiple, often contradictory self-representations'.[86] In what John Rowan and Cooper describe as 'a self-pluralistic approach', an individual may not always be unified or consistent, yet they are still viewed as whole. This perspective 'sees the self as . . . woven into the fabric of a multi-dimensional universe'.[87] Increasingly, the unitary, consistent and continuous self is viewed as 'an illusion our minds attempt to create' when in reality we need 'multiple and varied "selves" . . . to carry out the many and diverse activities of our lives'.[88] While there is no doubt that experiences of mental disunity and self-fragmentation continue to prompt serious psychological treatment, there is also greater attention to a 'path of "authentic pluralism"', which Rowan and Cooper characterise as 'an openness towards multiple irreducible principles, multiple worlds, and dialogue'.[89]

Late twentieth-century plural-self discourse extends and amplifies Myers's framing of self-plurality as a creative tactic for a flexible subject in a continuous state of becoming. Multiplicity or self-plurality can be 'creative' or 'adaptive', allowing 'the individual to maximize their potentialities' and 'make the most of the multiple opportunities that a postmodern world presents'.[90] Flexible multiplicity might even be a postmodern necessity according to psychologists like Rowan and Cooper, who view 'the notion of a unified, monolithic self' as 'increasingly untenable' if not 'a relic from a bygone era' in 'an ever-fragmenting social world'. As Rowan and Cooper explain it, in a socio-cultural milieu where celebrities 'reinvent their identities as swiftly as . . . [politicians] reinvent their politics, transformation, flux and plurality' are traits for contemporary subjects to embrace.[91] Leon Rappoport, Steve Baumgardner and George Boone similarly note that the 'development of a pluralistic sense of self' is not only encouraged, but 'all but require[ed]' for healthy 'social-emotional adjustment . . . in postmodern societies', which value 'flux, multiplicity, and transformation', thus yielding subjects who constantly reinvent themselves, taking on new and divergent personas or identities and ultimately acting as shapeshifters. Neither good nor bad, this polymorphy is characteristic of a postmodern, perhaps posthuman and post-truth, society and the flexible ethos it demands.

This flexible, fluid, plural subjectivity has become a tactical means of navigating an increasingly plural, multiplex, shifting world. A 'one-with-the-potential-to-be-many' is 'a unified Being-towards-the-world which has the possibility of Being-towards-its-world from a variety of self-positions'.[92] In other words, a multiplex, shifting world requires a multiplex, shifting subjectivity. Cooper describes 'the postmodern man [*sic*]' as 'playful' and adaptive in their plurality, a contrast to 'the deadly seriousness and mutual antagonisms of the more repressive forms of lived-plurality', such as those illustrated by Henry Jekyll.[93] While Jekyll becomes Hyde to 'resolve his conflict between gravity and gaiety' in a 'highly repressive society', a plural, polymorphic ethos is well-suited to a contemporary sociocultural environment that 'celebrates heterogeneity and diversity'.[94] Contemporary self-plurality discourse therefore promotes the post-modern *polymētis*

– a cunning polymorphic self who uses divergence to fit shifting contexts. Embracing a spectrum of selves to suit a range of contexts or identifying with a new sense of self at a new phase of one's life are some ways to avoid the kind of painful, morbid splitting represented by Jekyll.[95] In Homer's *Odyssey*, Odysseus is known as *polymētis* as well as *polytropos*, meaning that he is an expert in tricks and possesses a polymorphic identity.[96] *Polytropos* denotes the flexible multiplicity of both 'the octopus and the man of *mêtis*': 'the *polútropos* one' is an active subject of change; his 'supple and shifting' nature allows him to present 'volte-faces' and remain flexible in character, capable of responding to any situation that may arise.[97] It may be deceptive to disguise one's identity or to adopt the volte-face, yet the ruse is a necessity shared by many beings and a viable tactic of survival and flexibility.[98] As the sixth-century poet Theognis advises us, 'have the temper of the convoluted octopus' and 'turn towards all friends a many-colored *ēthos* / joining with whatever temper each one has'.[99] Translated slightly differently, Theognis's point is to 'Follow the example of the octopus with its many coils (*polúplokos*)'.[100] In other words, be polymorphic, flexible and adaptative in both personality and rapport.

Mētis offers 'an alternate vantage' through which dissociation (including DID), multiplicity, plurality and fragmentation 'could be framed as inventional play' rather than purely 'reactionary maladaptation'.[101] From this vantage point, we might view multiplicity, fragmentation and dissociation as cunning ways to develop an ethos suited to shifting, postmodern times. Cathryn Molloy's rhetorical study of DID suggests that alters (e.g., alternate personalities) might be read more positively as 'tactics'. Quoting de Certeau, Molloy posits that as a tactic, alters may help one to '"use, manipulate, and divert" the material world' and resist the pressure to '"impose" on it orderly, cohesive narratives'. She suggests that 'fragmentation . . . might be . . . a way for a person to live many lifetimes in one', offering a creative form of ethos that allows the fragmented subject to present a different self to suit a different context.[102] *Mētis* seems to be what Molloy is looking for when she seeks 'a positive, transgressive and entirely healthy, if socially unacceptable' way for fluctuating identities to 're/de/construct ethos' depending on context.[103] It is the type of tactical cunning that transgresses the limits of self/other.

The self-plurality promoted as a post-modern tactic for post-modern subjects might also be described as a posthuman or post-anthropocentric one. As the introduction outlines, the posthuman is a multiplex, fluid being, one who exists 'between-betweens', as per J. Halberstam and Ira Livingstone, constantly expanding its boundaries to enlarge and diversify its constitution. If humanist Mankind sought to purify himself from feminine, animal, emotional, hybrid and fluid elements, then posthumanist, post-anthropocentric humankind seeks to infect and mutate itself through all manner of nonhuman and queer contagion – the various 'becomings' and involutions noted by Deleuze and Guattari. The posthuman ethos is *polytropos*, that is, manifold, versatile, and wily, and what Rosi Braidotti might describe as 'transversal',[104] connected to multiple nonhumans, trans-corporeal or porous, if not trans-species or multi-species. A posthuman, post-anthropocentric subjectivity embraces the multiple, the fragmented, the divergent and the shifting – in brief, the *mētic.*

Jekyll's 'Statement' demonstrates the volte-face quality of the *polymētis* and the tactical, creative potential of multiplicity, yet it is not a model of its success. Rather, in attempting to unify, straighten and rectify his divergent, plural selves, Jekyll limits himself to a Cartesian model of self, ill-suited to accommodate the flux and paradox of the *fin de siècle* and even less suited for the posthuman, post-anthropocentric liminal world of the present. The horror of *Jekyll and Hyde* seems less the tension between good and evil or the rise of Hyde as 'pure evil', but rather the Victorian (and by extension dominant modern Western) pressure to present a coherent, unified self in place of a divergent, plural one. As this chapter has outlined, plurality might not only be natural, but also desirable – a creative tactic to defy, subvert or mitigate various social oppressions, larger social traumas or hegemony more generally. Multiplicity exceeds and explodes the dualities and binaries of Western humanist logic informing dominant models of self and expression. Binaristic models offer easy dualisms through which to structure realities, categorise entities and ascribe values; oppositions, like good and evil, higher and lower, spirit and matter, soul and body and masculine and feminine form the basis of Christianity, patriarchy, colonialism and European humanism. Victorians were more comfortable admitting the possibility of duplex or double personality because it was at least consonant with religious ideology and accepted understandings of human duality. Multiplicity destabilised these easy dualisms and opened several uncharted, and possibly uncontrollable, areas of psychic and social life to speculation.

'Fantastic, ignoble, hardly human, or frankly non-human' Gothic Rhetoric

It is perhaps significant that Jekyll frames his plurality as dehumanising and 'unmanning'.[105] The dissociative subject, the multiplex subject, the 'not-I' is the Other to the stable humanist subject, symbolically rendered feminine and non-human. Multiplex being is what Deleuze and Guattari would describe as 'minoritarian' against majoritarian Man. Multiplicities work through symbiosis and 'involution', the types of becomings that yield new subjectivities through mutation, contagion and alliance in movements away from filiation, progress and evolution. Multiplicities draw humans into packs and assemblages with nonhumans: 'Each multiplicity is symbiotic; its becoming ties together animals, plants, microorganisms, mad particles, a whole galaxy'.[106] Multiplex being is thus a movement away from humanist Man and the modes of being, relating and expressing associated with him. The dominant Western subject's univocality reflects its fantasy of being master – to itself and to others, indeed of 'all it surveys' – 'a cultural fiction that is wearing thin'.[107] The possibilities that the human psyche is fragmented and the self is unknowable undermine humanist conceptions of the subject as the basis for knowing, understanding and constructing knowledge, and thus the Master (or perhaps 'measure') of all things. In this final section, I want return to Gothic and its role in dismantling the myth of a unified, purified Man and its ability to articulate a fragmented, multiplex alternative. Although a large topic, I hope to offer a few useful generalisations drawing on the previous chapters and to carry forward to the next.

Gothic's hybrid, at times nonlinear and often multiplex or fragmented narrative style does not simply layer inconsistency to confuse and terrify (although these are certainly effects); rather,

Gothic style – hybrid, fragmented, multivocal and excessive – seems designed to represent fluid, shifting selves and counter discursive attempts to flatten their complexity. Molloy frames the fragmented subject's resistance to cohesive self-narrative as 'rhetorical savvy' and promotes 'nonlinear, fragmented, opaque narratives' as ways to 'honor gaps and fissures in memory' and plural, shifting identities.[108] She argues that 'Narrative coherence [is a] mechanism through which a frightening past is finally rendered definitively knowable, and thus conquerable' in psychotherapy.[109] I would add that narrative coherence is also a mechanism through which the complexity, multiplicity and polymorphic possibilities of nature are flattened in the quest to render them understandable and controllable.

Thus, James's comments on Myers's Gothic psychology point to the larger value of Gothic's excessive, ornate, fragmented style in narrating porous, plural models of self. The 'sensational,' 'baroque' style and 'convoluted narratives, subterranean passages' associated with Gothic fiction[110] are not only apt models for the human mind, but for the rhizomatic (tentacular) webs of consciousness that extend beyond it. As James suggests and Anne Stiles highlights, scientific writing that attempts to 'force nature into uncomfortable linear narratives' is 'at best, an imperfect fit'; late-Victorian Gothic's 'snarled plotlines' of 'multiple narrators, embedded texts, instances of doubling and mistaken identity, and numerous indications of narrative instability and unreliability' posed a contrast, a criticism and 'a corrective' to the rigid, linear narratives of scientific writing and the linear 'inflexible' worldviews behind them.[111] Stevenson himself turned to Gothic as he struggled to articulate models of consciousness, life and evolution, bemoaning the limits of scientific discourse to express them.[112]

Gothic's themes, characters, plots and narratives collectively challenge 'the bounded, individualistic, model of the self that has dominated Western cultures for at least the last two hundred years,'[113] a model associated with patriarchal and imperial domination. Gothic reveals a world of many minds – multiple minds within the same body, multiple minds within the same text and perhaps also multiple minds extending beyond the human. In fact, Gothic seems to act as a 'password'[114] to what Jungian philosopher Barbara Eckman describes a 'subjective universe' in which the 'multiple consciousnesses in the world' are 'released from their Enlightenment imprisonment within human brains', leading instead to a view of 'multiple consciousness, some human, others inhuman' and 'some located within human psyches, others located outside, in nature and even elsewhere'.[115] The next chapter examines how Gothic creeps up in discourse on the multiple consciousness and multispecies collective of the human microbiome.

4

From Hyde to the Holobiont: The Monstrous Microbial Self

'Zeus put her into his own belly first, that the goddess might devise for him both good and evil'; there 'she remained hidden beneath [his] inward parts.'

Hesiod, *The Theogony*[1]

As the previous chapters have established, Gothic unsettles notions of unity and purity both philosophically and rhetorically. An impure form filled with impure content, Gothic forms, styles and contents disturb orders of thinking, being and expressing. Although its disordered narratives and monstrous characters cultivate horror, Gothic mechanisms also perform important ideological work. The confusion wrought by Gothic narratives and their monsters productively unsettles the limits of oppositional structures like mind/body, self/Other, subject/object and human/nonhuman, creating a 'fuzzy logic' that is promoted by posthuman and decolonial theory. Reading Gothic alongside and through *mētis* emphasises the ways that the mode has challenged and countered units of measurement that attempt to flatten complexity, restrain deviance and straighten the twisted, whether they be genres, personalities, species or individuals. These theoretical and expressive traits are some of the reasons why I have aligned Gothic with critical posthumanism and *mētic* intelligence. In all these domains, the multiplex, the hybrid and the twisted are prised models for thinking, being and relating. This chapter picks up on these discussions and interweaves them in an analysis of contemporary microbiome discourse.

Microbiomes are highly intriguing and slightly mystifying, especially for the ways they rewrite human identity. They are the habitats, collective genomes and surrounding environment of our microbiota: the 'community of tiny living things'[2] dwelling on and in our bodies, predominantly in the gut. Studies have correlated the microbiome to human health, consciousness and even personality. Most disturbing and exciting, though, is the new, uncanny if not posthuman model of human being emerging from microbiome studies, described by some as the 'holobiont.'[3] Connecting conversations about microbiomes and symbiosis, the holobiont offers a new conceptualisation of humans as hosts to assemblages of symbionts rather than bounded, discrete 'individuals'.[4] Conceptually, the holobiont encapsulates the porous and plural model of human being dominating discussions of the microbiome under study in this chapter although not all writers discussed here refer to it directly. Biologist Scott Gilbert sums up the holobiont as a 'plurality of ecosystems', framing humans as 'symbiotic webs' that connect to other symbiotic webs, both larger and smaller.[5] Like Gilbert, Margaret McFall-Ngai is one of many well-known scientists who pointedly remind us that we are 'more microbial than human', more properly 'nested ecosystems' than individuals.[6] McFall-Ngai concludes that much like the Hawaiian bobtailed squid central to her research, 'each one of us is a chimera of sorts', tentacular creatures with internal crypts haunted by and inhabited by Others.[7] Within our bodies we find what Marcel Detienne and Jean-Pierre Vernant might describe as an 'interlaced network', a 'living knot of mobile, animated bonds'[8] comprised of myriad bacteria, archaea, lower and higher eukaryotes and viruses, which reaches outward to connect to the other networks that comprise the Earth's ecosystems. As science populariser Ed Yong remarks, 'we are legion . . . Always a "we" and never a "me" . . . heed Walt Whitman: "I am large, I contain multitudes"'.[9]

In probing our 'Otherhood' with microbes[10] and challenging the scientific and philosophical belief in the bounded individual self, microbiome research has led popular scientists to expound a new model of human being, one that is plural, porous and polluted (and perhaps more than a little *Gothic*). Discussions of the human microbiome surprisingly parallel the Gothic novel's presentation of the self 'in a state of deracination' after 'finding itself dispossessed in its own house, in a condition of rupture, disjunction, fragmentation' and multiplicity.[11] Echoing nineteenth-century anxieties over mind control and radical materialism, microbiome discourse is especially reminiscent of *fin-de-siècle* Gothic writing, depicting human bodies and minds polluted by alien, foreign or nonhuman forces and broken down to their primordial origins. Microbiome discourse thus seems to bring the Gothic subject out of the realm of fiction and into scientific, critical and public discourse on topics like embodiment. The point that I would like to make in this chapter is that the *polyplokos* (tangled, complex) and *polytropos* (manifold, flexible) subject of nineteenth-century Gothic tales finds new expression in public discourse on the human microbiome, most obviously in depictions of humans as porous, multiplex, malleable and contaminated by heterogeneous nonhuman entities. In these at times radical rewritings of human being as abject and uncanny, it is not difficult to discover what I call a Gothic tint to the discourse. That is not to say that microbiome discourse *is* Gothic, but rather that their narrative styles sometimes overlap in excessive emphasis on – if not delight in – human-nonhuman hybrids, porous and amorphous being and human ruination.

While bacteria, germs, infections and miasma populate Gothic texts in interesting ways, this chapter is not about microbials in Gothic but rather about the Gothic shades in microbiome discourse, which is rife with hauntings, ghosts, the living-dead, monsters and vestigial sins. Microbial entities transport the past into the present and the Other into the self, gesturing towards possible futures – both promising and horrifying. This chapter explores these Gothic inflections of contemporary popular microbiome discourse and with this, the *polyplokos*, *polytropos* microbiome. More specifically, I analyse examples of popularised science and popular science writers discussing the radically chimerical holobiont self that is revealed by microbiology.

To develop my analysis, I apply elements of Martin Reisigl and Ruth Wodak's (2009) Discourse Historical Approach (DHA) to

Critical Discourse Studies (CDS), critiquing the nomination (naming), predication (qualification) and argumentation (justification/questioning) strategies used by various journalists, scientists and critics in their discursive constructions of the microbiome, human embodiment and identity. More broadly, the DHA emphasises five types of discursive strategies,[12] which construct self/Other positions and thus establish 'us' vs 'them' discursive dynamics.[13] DHA is necessarily interdisciplinary, drawing on various methods and methodologies to analyse data from numerous genres. Sensitivity to socio-cultural and historical context is crucial, and the analysis is often said to be 'problem-oriented', intended to 'deconstruct' hegemonies by 'deciphering the ideologies that serve to establish, perpetuate or resist dominance' coded into discursive data.[14] DHA analysis emphasises the constructedness of identity, especially collective identities, which are primarily built along lines of inclusion and exclusion and are inherently unstable. Taking a slightly divergent (perhaps Gothic) approach to DHA, I am less interested in how microbiome discourse constructs an us/them dynamic but rather in how it breaks down such a dynamic.

With these breakdowns in mind, my analysis reveals Gothic-inflected framings of human identity: uncanniness, through which the familiar human body, mind and identity are made strange; abjection, which draws attention to the ways liminal beings disturb 'identity, system, order';[15] and monstrosity, which emphasises the liminal, chimerical, porous and heterogeneous nature of human being. Ultimately, human being is rendered strange, polluted and nonhuman in a rhetoric of thrilled if not sublime disgust. Before moving to this analysis, I outline the ontological and epistemological confusion wrought by microbiology since its inception in the late seventeenth century. This chapter concludes with a discussion of contaminated ethics, most simply cooperative contamination.

Tricky Microbes

Microbes are tricksters, difficult to classify, categorise, qualify, quantify and control. Much like mythic tricksters, microbes are known for their incongruity, ambivalence and transgression. Sometimes helpful, sometimes essential, sometimes pathogenic and sometimes deadly, they exist between states, transgress boundaries and defy categories, crossing between bodies and species. Viruses, for instance, hover 'between living and nonliving', combining animate and inanimate traits,[16] while archaea are said to be wily, 'unruly' single-celled organisms for the ways they 'resemble bacteria under a microscope' but are technically a distinctive species. There is even a class of archaea called the Lokiarchaeota, named after the 'elusive, anarchic and ambiguous' Norse trickster Loki.[17] Microbes unsettle ontological paradigms not only because they are so complicated, so duplicitous and so ambiguous, but also because they lead to new models of bodies, environments and species, acting as key players in evolution and symbiosis. Since the mid-seventeenth century, microbiologists have sought to understand these mysterious yet ubiquitous creatures. In *Micrographia* (1665), Robert Hooke praised the advancements of lenses that rendered the '*Earth . . . quite a new thing to us, and in every* little particle *of its matter; we now behold almost as great a variety of Creatures, as we were able before to reckon up in the whole* Universe *it self*'.[18] Antonie van Leeuwenhoek's specially crafted lens revealed a world swarming with what he described as animalcules, tiny 'animals' found in places like rainwater and the human mouth. Later described as protozoans, these animalcules were observed by van Leeuwenhoek to be 'above a thousand times smaller than the smallest ones [he had] ever yet seen'.[19] Studies like Hooke's and van Leeuwenhoek's revealed that what once seemed like solid, stagnant matter was pulsating with myriad microscopic entities.

In recent decades, microbiology has emerged as one of the most popular and public of sciences – spreading into all realms of society, scholarship and culture while cultivating a newfound appreciation for our microscopic peers. Contemporary microbiology yet again challenges extant paradigms of species, matter and life. For approximately 100 years, microbes were treated as agents of disease and decay, following from the influential work of nineteenth-century microbiologists, like Louis Pasteur and Robert Koch, who framed microbes as foes and contaminants and ushered in the 'war on germs.' As Heather Paxon highlights, 'Pasteurian' attitudes figure microbes as antagonists to human health and propagate 'germophobic subjects' in the process.[20] As scientists today discover the crucial role that microbes play in human and environmental health as well as evolution, previous conceptions of microbes as contaminants and 'germs' are being refined by more nuanced understandings of symbiosis. Many bacteria and viruses are essential to human health while others demonstrate an ambiguous, dual nature, acting in some cases as boons, others as banes. Contemporary microbiology extends the study of disease and pathogens into other realms of health and environment, correlating human and environmental microbiomes and generating excitement for the possibilities that microbes hold in areas of medicine, philosophy, politics and environmental protections.

Reframed as the basis of all life, microbes offer a window into both the past and the future of human being as well as a bridge between human, nonhuman and environment. Contemporary microbiologists view microbes as crucial to our wellbeing and fundamental to our health, presenting the microbiome as an extension of our *selves*. There is even a push within the scientific community for medical professionals to reframe host-microbial relationships to encourage appreciation for microbial flora and fauna as the foundation for human health if not life itself, with a 2006 United States Institute of Medicine forum calling for 'a truce in the war on germs'.[21] The turn away from a view of 'the human body as a battleground on which physicians attack pathogens'[22] has led to a turn towards ecological framings of human health and embodiment. Elizabeth K. Costello et al. argue that 'the human body can be viewed as an ecosystem', reframing health as a matter of 'park management' requiring 'a multipronged approach of habitat restoration, promotion of native species, and targeted removal of invasives'.[23]

Studies of the gut microbiome have also unsettled long-held ideas about human consciousness and personality. Research on the gut-brain axis reveals that gut microbes not only aid in digestion, hormone production and nutrient absorption, but also 'communicate with the brain along neuronal lines', which acts like a '"bacterial broadband"'.[24] This communication is theorised as multidirectional, with microbes not simply receiving but sending signals to influence mood, behaviour (especially eating behaviour) and perhaps also personality.[25] Gut microbes help with the production of dopamine and serotonin, neurotransmitters associated with feelings of pleasure and happiness.[26] Several recent studies 'have shown that gut bacteria can use these signals to alter the biochemistry of the brain',[27] and the microbiome, especially dysbiosis (an imbalance in gut microbiota), has been correlated with autoimmune disease (particularly 'gut' related autoimmune diseases, like Crohn's disease), anxiety, mood disorders (e.g., depression and bipolar disorder), autism, eating disorders and obesity. Joe Alcock et al.'s study of eating behaviour reveals that our microbiome manipulates us in myriad ways, including behaviour and mood, feelings of anxiety, pain perception and food preferences, ultimately concluding that 'microbes can influence hosts through hormones' while calling into question the notion of self-control.[28]

Shifting away from Cartesian conceptualisations of the pineal gland as the epicentre of consciousness, the 'dark murky depths' of our intestines are now thought of as crucial to cognition and self, representing 'our main point of contact with our fellow microbes' while mediating 'our relationship to the world outside our bodies'.[29] The gut-brain axis gives new meaning to notions of gut feelings, butterflies in the stomach and perhaps also *mētis*. Continuing to counsel Zeus after her ingestion, 'Metis operates at gut level, in the very belly of the patriarch – the site of darkness and gestation and hunger'.[30] *Mētis* is said to be an embodied, tentacular intelligence, associated with the primordial powers that weave together all life, powers which scientists like Lynn Margulis and Scott Gilbert have linked to microbes like bacteria. Microbiomes, Metis and *mētis* thus illuminate Elizabeth Wilson's claim in *Gut Feminism* that the 'gut is an organ of mind: it ruminates, deliberates, comprehends'.[31] An embodied model of mind resituates consciousness as it unsettles mind/body dualism and associated mind/matter hierarchies.

Had the Ancient Greeks possessed microscopes, they would have associated microbes with *mētis*: cunning *polyplokos* (rhizomatic) and *polytropos* (manifold) tricksters, turning and twisting 'so swift, and so various, upwards, downwards, and round about'.[32] The next section unpacks the posthuman, post-anthropocentric and new materialist implications of the holobiont.

'Homo Microbis':[33] The Holobiont

Given the exciting ways microbiology is rewriting narratives of health, identity and consciousness, it is no surprise that microbes have captivated the minds of scientists, philosophers and media alike, leading to what Heather Paxson and Stefan Helmreich describe as 'microbiomania.' Although scientists have cautioned against the hype of microbiome research, it is easy to find hyperbolic claims about the power of microbes to shape us and control us (or for us to manipulate and control them). Microbiome science has inspired a slew of research regarding the potential implications and ethical quandaries attached to the study, collection and manipulation of microbial populations, including the epistemological and ontological questions that follow from new understandings of human being. Microbiome research asks anew age-old questions about the nature and boundaries of human bodies, the composition and limits of mind and consciousness and the relationship(s) between body and mind, mind and matter and human and nonhuman. Indeed, microbiome science has led to a profound paradigm shift in understandings of human being – from the classical Cartesian model of a reasoning, agentic, unified subject who is separate from and above nature to a contemporary posthuman, new materialist ideal of a chimerical, open, ecological self who is symbiotically entangled with nonhumans and environment, described by Helmrich as '*Homo microbis*' and illustrated by the holobiont. As Gilbert, Jan Sapp and Alfred Tauber famously emphasise, 'there have never been individuals'; the 'thousands of bacterial "species" (themselves genetic composites)' living inside us 'belie any simple anatomical understanding of individual identity' and evade 'the self/nonself, subject/object dichotomies that have characterized Western thought', including health and medicine.[34] The holobiont offers a new way to frame the human as a multispecies collective or community. Gilbert explains that the concept of the holobiont 'disrupts the tenets of individualism that have structured dominant lines of thought' from biology to philosophy along with politics and economics, making it a powerful challenge to 'what it means to be a person'.[35]

Excitement for the posthuman and post-anthropocentric potential of microbes and microbiomes is obvious in contemporary scholarship. Multiple, porous, burrowing and thoroughly ambiguous entities, microbials have been cast as 'allies',[36] 'buddies',[37] 'actors', 'a generative multitude or crowd',[38] 'companion species'[39] and protagonists[40] in posthuman narratives of becoming, agentic matter, porous embodiment and 'queer kinship networks'.[41] The posthuman, post-anthropocentric and new materialist connotations of microbiology are clear: Man is not who he thinks he is and is no longer at home within or master of his own mind or body, and certainly not of the Earth. Microbiology reveals a world pulsating with evermoving and everchanging matter, which circulates through interlocking systems that fundamentally align the human with the more-than-human world. In the popular and critical embrace of symbiosis and hype for the potential of what Gilbert describes as 'literally "becoming with the other"',[42] rhetors have evoked Gothic tropes of the uncanny, the abject and the monstrous, pronouncing the nonhuman, impure nature of humans.

In tracing these Gothic-inflective discursive elements, I wish to do more than, to paraphrase Alexandra Warwick, showcase that where we find the uncanny, we find Gothic;[43] rather, working with Jodey Castricano's definition of Gothic as a mode that renders the ineffable more-than-human world and drawing on the associations between Gothic, *mētis* and critical posthumanism mapped thus far, I hope to demonstrate the rhetorical and philosophical life of the fragmented, discontinuous Gothic subject as they exist outside the pages of fiction.[44] *Mētis*, appropriately for its modalities and mechanisms, is ever present yet perhaps often subtle and rarely explicit in this analysis, manifesting in the polytropic, cunning nature of microbes and the tentacular entanglements they suggest.

Unsettling Man in Popular Microbiome Discourse

My analysis borrows elements of CDS generally and the DHA method outlined by Reisigl and Wodak more specifically. CDS involves multi-tiered analysis that situates specific textual analyses in larger socio-cultural contexts and in relation to matters of power, ideology, identity and/or social inequities. It connects detailed textual analysis with wider discursive and political concerns,[45] such as the pervasive ideologies that support the dominant powerful groups in society, whose values appear to be commonsense. Discourse is a complex, complicated term in CDS. To clarify my use, I define discourse as denoting both topic-specific language (e.g., microbiome discourse, environmental discourse, etc.,) and semiotic ways of construing worldviews. Most simply, discourse is a way to categorise speech, text or conversation, which often carries the more theoretical meaning as the production and circulation of systems of power. Typically, what binds a group of statements or texts into something called a discourse is not only a shared topic but also shared social contexts or shared institutional ties and the ideologies that inform them. Largely influenced by Michel Foucault's corpus of work on the intersections between power, identity and discourse, CDS aims to critique social ills and inequity by engaging closely with texts, however defined. Following from Norman Fairclough, I use 'construe' to indicate the power of discourses to shape, rather than simply depict or represent, reality.[46] As critics since Foucault have stressed, discourses are entwined with and produce material effects, shaping the identities, perspectives and expressions of their users and receivers.

I borrow from Reisigl and Wodak's DHA method, applying nomination (naming), predication (qualification) and argumentation (claims about identity and embodiment) to my analysis. Most simply, nomination is about how people and things are named or referred to. As Reisigl and Wodak explain it, nomination strategies produce the 'discursive construction of social actors, objects, phenomena, events, processes and actions'.[47] Predication strategies qualify positively or negatively what is constructed by nomination, attributing the 'characteristics, qualities and features . . . [of] social actors, objects, phenomena, events, processes and actions'.[48] Claims about truth and rightness offer some forms of argumentation, my study of which most simply asks, 'what arguments are employed in discourses'[49] about microbiomes? More specifically, I focus on popular microbiome discourse, especially the naming of microbes, microbiomes and the human (nomination) and claims about implications for identity and multispecies relations (argumentation) following from new understandings of microbiomes. My materials for this analysis include editorials and scientific accommodations (popularisations of science by journalists) found on popular publications (e.g., *Newsweek*, *Nature* and *The Times*).[50] After an analysis of these collective materials, I turn more specifically to a discussion of popular science writer Dorion Sagan's work on symbiosis, symbiogenesis and the radical rewriting of human identity elicited by studies of the microbiome.

Seething Zoos of Microbes: Popular Microbiome Discourse

Examining popular microbiome discourse reveals the successful end to the war on germs and subsequent shift to 'park management' promoted by scientists. Microbes are no longer simply foes or antagonists to be fought, protected against or eliminated in human dramas of disease and decay. In today's popular microbiome discourse, microbes are often figured as 'friends', 'frenemies', 'buddies',[51] 'compadres',[52] 'critters',[53] 'bugs'[54] and 'members',[55] with terms connoting various degrees of proximity (friends, compadres, buddies, members) and distance (frenemies, critters, bugs). Several writers use metaphors and analogies to liken human bodies to houses or vehicles, framing microbes as 'inhabitants',[56] 'residents',[57] 'a huge community of permanent tiny neighbors',[58] 'stowaways',[59] 'colonists',[60] 'lodgers',[61] 'hitchhikers',[62] and (my personal favourite as a Gothic scholar) 'denizens' 'dwelling'[63] in our bodies. Microbiome discourse most often circulates ecological framings of the human body. Based on the scientific understanding of the microbiome as a series of ecosystems, popularisers, bloggers and journalists describe our microbiome as an 'interior wilderness', 'rain forest', 'prairie',[64] 'landscape',[65] 'garden',[66] 'rainforests or coral reefs', or use terms like 'an ecology on legs',[67] 'menagerie',[68] 'zoo',[69] 'colony' and even 'an entire world'[70] to describe us. While the suggestion that humans contain 'an entire world' within us retains suggestions of human exceptionality, most terms used to denote microbes and microbiomes in popular discourse seem to take us down a rung on the Great Ladder of Being, reminding us of the nonhumanity we house within.

Predication strategies typically ascribe positive or negative qualities to the actors or objects named in discourse. In the case of microbes, the qualities popularisers attributed to them were not necessarily good or bad but most often ambivalent. Many popularisers layered paradoxical depictions of our microbial 'frenemies' with whom we have a 'complicated' relationship.[71] Our bodies may be 'haunted by millions of microbes', but the 'ghosts in [our] machine' are mainly 'friendly'. Modifiers (e.g., adjectives and adverbs) often emphasise the difference or strangeness, multitude, prevalence and volume of microbes. For example, terms like 'alien',[72] 'mysterious' and 'ghostly'[73] are coupled with claims that our microbiomes are the 'invisible', 'hidden half of ourselves'[74] that offer 'uncharted territory'[75] and an 'unexplored landscape'.[76] Modifiers like 'seething'[77] and 'Teeming'[78] work alongside repeated intensifiers ('very,' 'every') and numbers like hundreds, several hundred, millions and trillions to emphasise not only the volume of microbes but also the ways they vastly outnumber us, dominating the cells in our body.

Many popularisers emphasise our impurity in claims about the ubiquity and volume of microbes. '100 trillion bacteria of several hundred species bearing 3m non-human genes' are said to dwell 'in the nooks and crannies of every human being'.[79] Moheb Costandi writes, 'from the minute you are born, microbes begin to colonize every exposed surface and organ of your body' with 'about 500 different bacterial species call[ing] your intestines home'. Popularisers amplify the pollution and impurity of the microbiome by emphasising the volume and ubiquity of microbes, stressing that 'Teeming masses of bacteria are in your mouth, on your skin, up your nose and on the surface of your eye' so that 'No matter how well you wash, nearly every nook and cranny of your body is covered in microscopic creatures'.[80] Comparisons emphasise that even if 'it might sound perverse', most of our DNA 'is not "ours," but belongs to cohabiting bacteria', leading to common claims that 'More than half your body is not human', that 'we are only 10 percent human' or that microbial cells 'exceed the count of your own body's cells by 10-to-1'.[81] A rhetor's choice of pronouns (perspectivation) reveals different degrees of proximity and distance from these 'teeming masses' inhabiting our bodies, with most popularisers or journalists opting to use second person rather than first person to describe our microbiomes.

The revelation that humans are hosts to myriad microscopic critters has prompted many writers to reject the notion of individuality. For example, an article in *The Economist* claims that 'People are not just people' while others write, 'you are not what you think you are', 'your body isn't just you', or our bodies are filled with 'inner aliens'.[82] The microbiome forces us to think of the self 'in the first-person plural' and 'to alter conceptions of what and who we are',[83] especially the notion that we are unified, seamless selves. As Alexander Kriss puts it, microbiome studies 'demonstrate a complex mutuality between us and living matter that is, strictly speaking, not us,' which 'fundamentally threatens dominant Western conceptions of the self'.[84] The microbiome is 'challenging our notion of what it means to be human',[85] turning the world 'inside out' and 'upside down' as it leads us to question 'the idea of what, biologically speaking, a human being is'.[86] These new framings of human being have been described as 'humbling',[87] unsettling human hubris and narcissism with the revelation that we might not be 'any different from a coral reef' or that 'little, ignorant bacteria could be in charge' of the world.[88] As microbiomes reveal that there are no individuals, the loss of self- and species-boundaries causes many to redraw the lines of humanity. 'Microbes maketh man',[89] but, clearly, they also unmake him.

Popularisers have been quick to hype up the panic attached to the loss of a stable, unitary self and its boundaries, presenting claims of microbial control, especially of human minds, personality, consciousness and will. Yong notes that learning microbes can 'sway the brain – the organ that, more than any other, makes us who we are' – is 'a disquieting thought' since we attach such importance to free will; the fact that the 'unseen forces' of microbes can manipulate our cravings, personalities and behaviours evokes 'many of our deepest societal fears' and 'darkest fiction', which 'is full of Orwellian dystopias, shadowy cabals, and mind-controlling supervillains'.[90] Such narratives of microbial control also evoke nineteenth-century tales of menacing foreign mesmerists, hypnotising villains, hapless automatons and dissociations of personality, which came to dominate *fin-de-siècle* Gothic fiction, like Richard Marsh's *The Beetle*. In some ways, contemporary microbiome discourse and late nineteenth-century Gothic showcase similar fears that our porous, malleable being may be subject to foreign or alien influence. Although scientists are *fairly* certain consciousness and autonomy are not under assault by microbes, popular writers like to emphasise that microbes are 'pulling the strings',[91] acting as 'our puppet master'[92] and 'doing something to us',[93] with many pointed second-person claims like 'microbes manipulate your Mind', influence 'your thoughts and moods'[94] and may 'even control your brain' as they 'outright manipulate their hosts, including humans'.[95]

Collectively, the message is that humans are not who we think we are. We are not the sovereign masters of our own minds and bodies (or health or evolution) and are fundamentally imbricated in the drama of the more-than-human-world. Before turning to the implications for Gothic *mētis*, I briefly explore Dorion Sagan's Gothic-posthuman inflected rhetoric.

Dorion Sagan's 'Beautiful Monsters'[96]

Popular science writer and eco-philosopher Dorion Sagan has written extensively on symbiosis, evolution and ecology. Along with his mother, Lynn Margulis, Sagan has popularised concepts like symbiogenesis, a theory of bacterial-driven evolution for eukaryotic cells, and endosymbiosis, a term for a symbiotic relationship in which one organism inhabits another, or as Margulis and Sagan explain it, 'the co-opting of strangers, the involvement and infolding of others'.[97] According to Margulis and Sagan, human evolution is a story of 'cell gorgings and aborted invasions' from which 'merged beings that infected one another were reinvigorated by the incorporation of their permanent "disease"'.[98] Although he does not widely discuss the microbiome *per se*, Sagan's writing on human-microbial entanglements and the chimerical nature of Man has been influential in theorising what Stefan Helmreich refers to as '*Homo microbis*': an alternative to Homo sapiens that accounts for 'the never pure, the ever-swarming, the ever-connected, [and] ever-multiple body'[99] as well as the unstable, nonlinear, nonhuman nature of human being. Across many of his works, Sagan presents a multiplex, multispecies model of human being, working towards his self-proclaimed 'lifelong efforts to decenter the human.'[100] While his work has an obvious posthuman and post-anthropocentric tint, I want to suggest that it also has a Gothic flair, trading as it does in tropes of haunting and monstrosity as he takes his readers on a journey into life's 'ghostly archive and living tombs',[101] including those within our own bodies.

Sagan parallels psychology's challenge to a monolithic concept of mind by unsettling 'a monolithic conception of "the" body' in his writings on 'New Biology', symbiosis and 'gene-trading bacteria'.[102] New Biology teaches that humans are not individuals, but 'multiple beings' with a 'chimerical nature'.[103] Sagan argues that 'there is no racial, let alone genetic purity in life'; we are all 'part virus' and the 'offspring' of 'promiscuous . . . genetic indiscretions and transgressions'.[104] Through emphasis on contamination and multiplicity, he rhetorically estranges dominant Western paradigms of health and identity that rest on purity and unity. For example, he posits that 'What we call "human" is . . . impure, laced with germs', the product of 'morphed diseases' resulting from 'organisms that ate and did not digest one another' and other forms of infection and merger.[105] Sagan describes the symbiotic self as 'a monstrous breach of Platonic etiquette in favor of polymorphous perversity'[106] through which the 'boundaries of selfhood'[107] have expanded by incorporations of 'strangers, others',[108] nonhumans and 'what once would have been called inanimate matter'.[109] With Gothic style, he claims that 'our very existence' stems from 'the ancient "failure" of Lilliputian[110] vampires' and that our bodies are palimpsests of 'phantomlike' traces of ancestral cells and 'spirochete remnants . . . haunt[ing] the phenome' in 'the deepest, most ancestral levels of our being'.[111]

For Sagan, our monstrous, contaminated nature is the foundation for an expanded view of self and consciousness. That life stems from 'impure origins' and various 'infections'[112] leads him to view the self as ecological and multispecies oriented, its 'boundaries . . . expanding' to make 'the "I" . . . a figure of large numbers'.[113] Within our bodies are myriad other 'selves', including cells, which Sagan frames as the 'minimum self' with 'lives and sentience of their own'.[114] In line with posthuman, post-anthropocentric and *mētic* thought, he postulates, 'The human body is not Platonic and separate; it is ecological, microecological, and connected'.[115] Importantly, Sagan rejects the framing of 'recognizing mind-like behaviors in nature' as anthropomorphism, 'pathetic fallacy, personification, [or] superstitious pre-scientific thinking',[116] highlighting the limitations for expressing the intentionality and intelligence of nonhuman subjects. In what he describes as 'the return of the scientific repressed', 'the non-anthropic, the non-human, the post-human, the transhuman, the more-than-human, [and] the animal' have come to the fore of biological inquiry.[117]

More Microbe than Man: Posthuman Gothic Framings of the Microbial Self

In a discourse pairing epideictic wonder with disgust, popular writers repeatedly emphasise that we are nonhuman, more than human and less human than we think, our bodies teeming with swarming microbial Others. Claims about how our bodies are 'haunted by millions of microbes' or filled with 'inner aliens'[118] both excite and estrange in their challenge to a unified, purified human. As Helmreich sums up the symbiogenetic self, 'humans are tangled mixtures, Frankensteins, of a welter of teeny microbial friends and enemies', with traces of relic viruses and 'microorganismic inheritances'.[119] While the discovery that 'man is not truly one'[120] famously agonised Jekyll and other Gothic protagonists, it has become normal to think of the self 'in the first-person plural',[121] challenging traditional notions of human unity, purity, sovereignty and exceptionality. Jekyll was correct that 'man will be ultimately known for a mere polity of multifarious, incongruous, and independent denizens',[122] only he might not have guessed those 'denizens' would be dwelling in 'our intestines'.[123] In depicting the human as fragmented, multiplex, possessed, dispossessed, 'alienated, divided from themselves, no longer in control of . . . passions, desires'[124] or bodies, popular discussions of the human microbiome bring the Gothic subject – a self 'finding itself dispossessed in its own house, in a condition of rupture, disjunction, fragmentation'[125] – out of the pages of eighteenth- and nineteenth-century Gothic literature and into the centre of contemporary inquiry.

Although some claim that microbiome research sounds like dystopian or science fiction,[126] I want to suggest that its discourse also rings of Gothic sentiments and styles. In fact, Margulis explicitly describes symbiosis's rewriting of biology, life and evolution as 'some Gothic . . . novel' replete with 'Faustian thrill'.[127] While I would not go so far as to describe holobiont discourse as 'Gothic', I do want to suggest that this discourse presents a model of the

Gothic self, trades in Gothic tropes and demonstrates the 'Gothicity' Hurley identifies in late-nineteenth century biomedical discourses like evolution, ultimately producing a modern 'abhuman': ambiguous, morphological and otherwise 'discontinuous' in identity. For Hurley, degeneration, pre-Freudian models of the unconscious, Darwinism and sexology revealed a human subject 'fractured by discontinuity and profoundly alienated from itself', the implications of which were perceived as disastrous and traumatic – 'one might say "gothic"' – by a majority of the population.[128] Something similar can be said of contemporary microbiology, which produces an abject, monstrous version of the human: porous, teeming with nonhumans, and 'haunted' by matter that is 'not us' – a view Margulis admits is 'unsettling' if not 'frightening'.[129]

Just as critics have highlighted the Gothic inflections of discourses like degeneration, psychoanalysis, Darwinism and sexology, I want to highlight the thematic and rhetorical overlaps between microbiology and the Gothic, given their shared domains of contaminations, transgressions, mutations, revenants and revivals. Microbiology discourse is populated by motifs of haunting and resurrection, from bacterial ghosts[130] to living-dead viruses to revived ancient microbes, or 'waking the dead' as it is colloquialised.[131] Monstrous vampires, zombies, werewolves and mummies are popular figures used throughout microbiology discourse[132] and not merely vehicles through which microbials materialise into fiction, film, games and art. There is even a recent special issue of the *Journal of Molecular Biology* devoted to 'Jekyll and Hyde: Bugs with Double Personalities',[133] its front cover depicting a bacterium with a top hat divided in two, one half blue with a monocle and smile, and the other half red, dishevelled and scowling with vampiric teeth in an obvious homage to the Victorian gentleman and his degenerate half.[134]

Thus, just as images of infection, decay and humans invaded or besieged by invisible forces offer common fodder for Gothic fiction and film, microbiology, as both a science and a discourse, takes on Gothic inflections. As a science devoted to making the unseen seen and lifting the veil between macroscopic and microscopic worlds, microbiology exposes invisible, ambiguous, transgressive and ubiquitous entities living alongside and inside us – contaminating, colonising, consuming and mutating us – unsettling the boundaries between self/Other, human/nonhuman, living/dead and past/present while emphasising that what we humans have repressed, shunned and harmed will return with a vengeance to curse us and our future generations.[135]

Holobiont discourse recontextualises monstrosity as an ethical trope for situating the human in the wider web of more-than-species relations. While monstrosity has often served as a dehumanising frame used 'to rationalize xenophobia and prejudice' against 'women, racial and sexual minorities, political radicals or those with physical or mental impairments',[136] it has more lately been resituated or reappropriated (i.e., recontextualised) as a reminder that 'in all our heedless entanglements with more-than-human life, we humans too are monsters'.[137] For Sagan, microbes, the Earth and life itself are 'beautiful monsters', as are we, enmeshed as we are in its multispecies, chimerical webs.[138] Sagan and Margulis's work on symbiogenesis – the 'Gothic' story of life – reveals that 'Life has been monstrous almost from its beginnings'; ancient 'prokaryotes (bacteria and archaea) gave birth to monsters' who still inhabit us and all other eukaryotes.[139]

In this sense, the holobiont evokes Julia Kristeva's notion of the abject (along with Hurley's abhuman). For Kristeva, the abject is that which 'disturbs identity, system, order' or that which 'does not respect borders, positions, rules', summed up as 'the in-between, the ambiguous, the composite'.[140] More complexly, abjection details with tension between I/not-I and the various taboos and rituals designed by cultures to separate the self from the non-self, the human from the nonhuman and the pure from the impure. Abjection has to do with borders and with excluding that which threatens the integrity of those borders, especially the borders of the self: 'abjection is above all ambiguity', one that brings the hermetic and unified subject into contact with what threatens it.[141] It is not simply about purity or cleanliness, though; abjection both constitutes and unsettles the self, 'simultaneously beseeches and pulverizes the subject', as the 'I' discovers the Other is within rather than without its borders, that the Other constitutes the 'very *being*' of the Self, 'that [the self] *is* none other than abject'.[142] As Kristeva asks, 'How can *I* be without border?'.[143] Different from and 'more violent' than uncanniness (discussed below), abjection 'notifies us of the limits of the human universe', 'confronts us . . . with those fragile states where man strays on the territories of *animal*' or with the borders between the civilised and primitive.[144] Kristeva discusses the pre-separation of self and Other through a maternal lens, but there might also be a symbiotic lens through which to consider 'the archaism'[145] of the self and its relationship with the chaos of the pre-symbolic (or the mess and mass of the nonhuman world that humans are part of). Microbiomes reveal that 'uncanniness, foreignness is within us', that the 'other is my ("own and proper")' body.[146]

Microbiology's rewriting of human identity as a chimerical blend of self, Other and environment produces a Gothic-inflected discourse that emphasises not only the abject (porous, polluted and liminal) and monstrous (chimerical, nonhuman) nature of human being, but also its uncanniness. Although Freud identifies several types of feelings of the uncanny in his famous 'The Uncanny' (1919), the crux of his argument is perhaps that 'the uncanny is that class of the frightening which leads back to what is known of old and long familiar', or, more precisely (borrowing from Friedrich Schelling), 'everything is *unheimlich* that ought to have remained secret and hidden but has come to light'.[147] As Freud would have it, the uncanny is the anxiety associated with the breakdown of borders, which results in the loss of the self as subject. Critics like Kristeva and Nicholas Royle have shown that the uncanny above all has to do with the experience of indistinct borders, particularly the border between self and Other. The experience of the uncanny is in many ways related to a border-crossing, a blurring of boundaries (between the familiar and strange, the self and Other, reality and fantasy). According to Royle, 'the uncanny . . . has to do with a sense of ourselves as double, split, at odds with ourselves'.[148] Royle claims that the uncanny involves feelings of uncertainty or estrangement, especially 'regarding the reality of who one is' and 'one's sense of oneself (of one's so-called "personality" or "sexuality", for example)'.[149] The uncanny has to do with 'a sense of strangeness, mystery or eeriness,' and more particularly, 'a sense of unfamiliarity which appears at the very heart of the familiar' and the reverse 'sense of familiarity which appears at the very heart of the unfamiliar'; to that end, the uncanny is not simply 'the weird or spooky', but rather the 'disturbance of the familiar',[150] perhaps especially the familiarity of the self.

In suggesting the Gothic inflections of holobiont discourse, I hope to avoid what Alexandra Warwick describes as the mundane and 'rather mechanical conclusion: here is an example of the uncanny [or the monstrous or the abject], therefore an example of the Gothic'.[151] Returning to CDS, *mētis* and previous claims regarding the Gothic's skill in rendering porous, plural selves, I want to say something of the deeper ideological impact of the Gothic tropes haunting holobiont discourse and the uncanny model of self this discourse offers. In Critical Discourse Studies, the goal of analysis is often to uncover dynamics of ideology, power and identity at play in the discursive construction of subjectivity. CDS often boasts an ethical orientation, a desire for social justice or social change and an attention to silenced, marginalised and oppressed voices or perspectives. CDS (reflecting its frequent homebase of social sciences) has traditionally addressed social ills, like poverty, oppression and discrimination; however, more recently, there has been an ecological turn, extending considerations beyond human society and towards the environment along with the myriad more-than-human subjects who populate it. Arran Stibbe's critical discourse analysis work with ecolinguistics and ecology, for example, critiques ecologically harmful discourses and promotes those encouraging respectful relationships between humans and environment.[152] While Stibbe's work thoughtfully highlights that 'the problems faced by oppressed groups are not just social but ecological',[153] he remains largely focused on how ecological problems, like climate change, impact marginalised humans. Given how the microbiome illustrates the nonhumanity within the human, it seems that greater attention to nonhuman subjects is also necessary. My supposition is that Gothic discursive frames like the abject, the monstrous and the uncanny might be useful to this end.

Nicholas Royle and Timothy Morton have linked the uncanny to contact with nonhumanity and the more-than-human world. In *The Ecological Thought* (2010), Morton writes, 'The more ecological awareness we have, the more we experience the uncanny'.[154] For Morton, this is because the environment itself is uncanny, and so are we. He discusses how 'strange strangers' inhabit places like cities and forests, crowding them so that places that appear empty 'seem to become entities in themselves'. The 'creepiness' of 'discovering the mesh', Morton's term for the entanglements of humans, more-than-humans and other lifeforms, of discovering that 'there is something else – someone else, even' leads to 'ecological awareness'. For Morton, the uncanny is the foundation of ecological awareness because it arises from our experience of the 'total interconnectedness' of all things.[155] Uncanniness emerges from our contact with strangely familiar and familiarly strange entities, which include ourselves. Humans are holobionts and are therefore 'strange strangers': homes to nonhuman entities who make the lines of self and Other both porous and ambiguous.

Our imbrication in the mesh, mess, maze and mass of the more than human world begins with our microbiomes, and our awareness of this might lead us to expel limiting notions of subjectivity and ethics. As Kristeva's theory of the subject as always in-process[156] reveals, abjection is productive in its unsettling of the boundaries of the self.[157] In the liminal space of abjection, the human 'I' can be dethroned[158] and a humanist model of self can be ejected. Abjection is a process of the self constantly establishing and re-establishing its nature, and what is rejected, refused, accepted or included is significant (and socio-culturally determined, as Kristeva's theory of the foreigner suggests[159]). As Marek Tesar and Sonja Arndt posit, abjection helps 'us to explore the liminal spaces in-between conceptions of the human "I" and a posthuman "I"', spaces of transition, transformation and entanglement; this liminal space offers 'an opportunity to engage with the Otherness' or foreignness that Kristeva argues is 'already always present' within us, making us all 'strangers, even to ourselves'.[160] Abjection estranges, but it is productive and can expel anthropocentric notions of the subject or the self and with this, expand the limits, meanings and responsibilities of the human 'I'.

Holobiont discourse defamiliarises the self in productive ways as it reveals the porousness and interdependencies of entities within the world, a reality that is both horrifying and promising. In this vein, posthuman, post-anthropocentric and new materialist critics have issued a collective call to embrace impurity, contamination and infection as models for and modes of ethical engagement between humans, nonhumans and environment – a call that I describe as contaminated ethics.

Contaminated Ethics

Through its insistence on the monstrous, abject and uncanny nature of human being, holobiont discourse brings the Gothic subject out of the realm of fiction and into scientific, critical and public discourse on topics like embodiment, environment and ethics. In microbiome narratives, we find new iterations of abhuman, *poly-plokos* being as humans are revealed to be complex, tangled 'living, interlacing networks'. Humans are 'bodies tumbled into bodies',[161] and posthuman, post-anthropocentric and new materialist critics have argued this has profound implications for identity, kinship, community and ethics. Shifting our perspective from individuals to holobionts emphasises that transformational encounters with difference are necessary for our continued existence. Considering our innate impurity and intimate connections with nonhumans and environment, post-anthropocentric theorists argue that we must develop a praxis for human-nonhuman-environmental care, especially if we are to survive our contemporary era of environmental precarity (Tsing) and trouble (Haraway). The twenty-first-century horrors of 'pollution, mass extinction, and climate change' illuminating our collective vulnerability to ruin reveal that we require 'livable collaborations' to stay alive.[162] To this end, theorists like Donna Haraway, Anna Tsing and many others argue for us to embrace 'contamination as collaboration'.[163] According to Tsing, who explores the paradoxes and intricacies of multispecies relationships and ecological devastation in her study of mushrooms, contamination can be a means of transformative cooperation. Contamination is 'transformation through encounter' that 'makes diversity' and facilitates 'work across difference', including work 'across species'.[164]

Tsing gives us an important reminder that despite the hyperbolic praise for symbiosis laced throughout critical theory, scientifically, symbiosis is not utopic: there is no guarantee that hosts will remain intact, healthy or alive, making it at times 'ugly or otherwise'.[165]

The point of contaminated ethics is that we need to accept if not embrace these infectious, uneven exchanges, which, as Jeanette Samyn argues, can help us to navigate 'ecologies [that] are open and messy, rife with relationships that are painful and asymmetrical, but also full of possibility' for modelling 'a way out of bounded individualism and anthropocentric hubris'.[166] There are no stable 'self-contained units'[167] in symbiotic assemblages like the holobiont. Such 'encounter-based collaborations' are relational and 'ever-changing'.[168] To work with and through extreme contemporary asymmetries,[169] we need to cultivate an openness to these transformative encounters our Others offer. Posthuman, post-anthropocentric – I dare say 'Gothic' – subjectivities reflect this openness. Breaking from humanist notions of progress or telos, posthumanism embraces 'the complex and random processes of mutation', which can never be mastered by humans[170] and leaves us open to 'continuous construction and reconstruction'[171] in a process of endless becoming. Contagion is a mode of Deleuze-Guattarian becoming, involving a 'creative *involution*' of heterogeneous Others to create subjectivities based in multiplicities and assemblages.[172] Through modalities of infection and mutation, post-anthropocentric subjects become-*with* others in 'unexpected collaborations and combinations' – a process Haraway describes as 'making oddkin'. That 'nothing is truly sterile' is simultaneously a 'terrific danger, basic fact of life, and critter-making opportunity'.[173]

Holobiont discourse adds new evidence supporting the Gothic mode's value for narrating chimerical identities and perspectives. With uncanny vision, we discover that what appears to be stagnant or stable matter is really a symbiotic multispecies mesh and that what we thought was self is an 'otherhood' of nonhuman beings. There is no purity in existence, and thus what might be abjected in processes of self-construction is the limiting assumption that there is. Holobiont humans are monsters, 'bodies tumbled into bodies', so 'the art of telling monstrosity requires stories tumbled into stories'.[174] Curiously, though, as Chapter 2 established, outside of Gothic studies, Gothic is rarely mentioned as mode for telling these stories. Writers like Margaret Atwood and Haraway have turned to sci-fi and speculative fiction, as have Tsing, Swanson, Gan and Bubandt, who link monsters and ghosts to 'sensibilities from folklore and science fiction' that might guide us through 'the indeterminate conditions of environmental damage' and nature's uncanniness.[175] However, Gothic, the fragmented mode of uncanniness, abjection and monstrosity, seems even more apt for telling stories of symbiotic entanglements that unsettle anthropocentric and exceptionalist thinking. Gothic is one explicit response to Enlightenment Europe's attempt 'to banish monsters' and the heterogeneity found so 'abhorrent to Enlightenment ways of ordering the world', which divided life into separable beings and clear categories. These 'ecological simplifications of the modern world [are] products of the abhorrence of monsters'.[176] Despite their horror, Gothic's depictions of 'visceral connections with the unlike' reflect and inspire a 'voracious drive for proximity with alterity' that reminds us how humans, 'the earth and life are nothing more than a mesh of unlike entities coexisting',[177] sometimes within the same body.

Gothic seems to offer a palate cleanser for the hyperbolic praise and posthuman promise of 'microbiomania', which can obscure the sometimes asymmetric, painful (but nonetheless necessary) engagements of symbiosis. Microbes reveal the 'terrible beauty' of living matter, which has 'no special allegiance' to humanity.[178] Symbiosis is not a love story but a Gothic story of ambivalence and a horror story for the Anthropos, who can be overturned by the smallest of nonhuman heroes. As I discuss in the next chapter, examples of contaminated ethics can be found throughout Gothic media, especially eco-Gothic, wherein microbial encounters are common sites of horror, but also increasingly an ethical awareness stemming from challenges to humanism and humankind's destructive, greedy nature.

5

Gothic Fungus: Mycorrhizae, Mētis *and Monstrosity*

'Make rhizomes, not roots, never plant! Don't sow, grow offshoots! Don't be one or multiple, be multiplicities!'[1]

Microbiomes, 'our Being made of beings',[2] remind us of our imbrication in the ecologies that house us, haunt us and could potentially harm us. Microorganisms are far more ancient and far more resilient than Man, and scientists predict that just as microbial life began long before human life, so too will it continue long after our end. Although microbes are no longer foes in scientific or medical dramas, they still frequently populate Gothic and horror, often signalling the demise of the Anthropos and the rise of monstrous alternatives. In this chapter, I move from the invisible denizens of the microbiome to the pulpy 'denizens of ruins'[3], exploring a fungal strand of microbial horror and its post-anthropocentric appeal.

Fungi constitute a mysterious and 'peculiar tribe'[4] of beings; long classified as plants yet more closely resembling animals, the fungal kingdom contains a unique and wide diversity of organisms capable of designing rich landscapes and engaging in enriching multispecies relationships. Along with bacteria, fungus has played a crucial role in Earth's history, forming terrestrial landscapes while 'shaping environments for themselves and others'.[5] Although fungi have been abhorred as pathogens and 'vilified' for their associations with death, decay, pestilence, disintegration and ruin,[6] they have also been praised as models for symbiotic relationships, bringing about connection rather than infection.[7] Since the 1990s, the sequencing of fungal genomes has provided a wealth of data on fungal evolution, processes of adaptation and diversification, leading to research on fungi's potential for agriculture, forestry, medicine, industry and even alternative fuels. For mycologists like Paul Stamets, the applications of fungi are practically limitless. Indeed, according to Stamets, mushrooms have the power 'to save the world'.[8]

It is perhaps no wonder, then, that fungi have become popular symbols denoting the rise and fall of aeons in the overlapping contexts of popular science, popular culture and post-anthropocentric theory, taking on layered symbolism as productive parasites and prolific worldbuilders. Capable of 'burst[ing] categories and upend[ing] identities',[9] filamentous fungi (my focus here) spread out gossamer-fine fungal tubes called hyphae, which penetrate substrates to absorb nutrients and branch into mycelia. When mycelium joins with tree roots, it creates an underground labyrinth of mycorrhizal networks that connect life in a forest or other ecosystem. These mycorrhizal networks, which transmit and receive messages along with nutrients, have been colloquially described as being like the Internet or more playfully, the Wood Wide Web. Models for networked communications and multispecies collaborations, mycorrhizal networks have become sources for both hopeful narratives of symbiosis and horrific depictions of pollution, infection and decay.

Linking these transgressive and responsive traits to the cunning intelligence and multiplex *polyplokos* being of *mētis*, this chapter explores recent depictions of wily fungal networking in eco-Gothic, showcasing a tradition of Gothic media in which fungi connote queer ecologies, 'queer' in the double sense of non-heterosexual intimacy and resistance or disruption to normative identities, structures and systems.[10] These queer fungal networks pulse and pulsate beneath the Anthropos in rich subterranean worlds, which Anna Tsing argues often goes unnoticed by humans, who 'can't venture underground to see the amazing architecture of [these] underground [cities]'.[11] Peering into fungi's 'underground city' of mycorrhizal networks, Tsing posits, leads one to discover 'the strange and varied pleasures of interspecies life' and attunes us to their 'underground stories'.[12] Following 'mushroom tracks,' which are 'elusive and enigmatic', can take us 'on a wild ride – trespassing every boundary'.[13] Following mushroom tracks seems inevitably to take us into Gothic *mētic* terrain: subterranean labyrinthine networks, boundary-crossing, transgression and liminality, such as states of living-death and processes of decay.

In this chapter, I want to follow the mushroom tracks laid out in recent eco-Gothic tales, focusing specifically on the post-anthropocentric fungal horrors of Jaco Bouwer's *Gaia* (2021) and Ben Wheatley's *In the Earth* (2021), two films depicting mycorrhizae as ancient god-like foils to Man and the Anthropocene. Through their ambivalent speculations on a '*world-without-us*',[14] Bouwer's and Wheatley's films portray the interlocking transgressive and responsive potential of cunning mycorrhizal networks. My analysis frames mycorrhizae as 'living, interlacing network[s]'[15] that model the rhizomatic being, relating and thinking discussed by Deleuze and Guattari and promoted in extension by posthuman critics. As per Deleuze and Guattari, the rhizome 'connects any point to any other point'[16] and thus denotes a manner of being and becoming that does not emerge from a single, central point of origin. Characterised by multiplicity and a creeping proliferation, the rhizome transgresses boundaries and defies notions of hierarchy, centrality, limits and individuality. Moving rhizomatically, I align eco-Gothic with post-anthropocentric theory and rhetorical criticism. *Mētis* has proven a fruitful concept through which rhetoricians have filtered discussions of transspecies and ecological rhetoric. Working with an assortment of research on fungus, new materialism, post-anthropocentrism, weird and Gothic media, I analyse these films and locate them within a tradition of queer Gothic ecologies and *mētistic* rhetoric[17] – that is, transgressive and adaptive interspecies communication involving the blending and blurring of human, environmental, non-human and technological elements.

Crypts and Creeps

Fungi can be construed as cunning, responsive and perhaps a little monstrous – creeping and creepy, transgressive and hybrid, chimerical and awesome. Because they are liminal entities existing between taxonomies (such as plant and animal, life and death), fungi have been 'hardly allowed a place among Nature's lawful children'.[18] In *The Romance of the Fungus World* (1925), R. T. Rolfe and F. W. Rolfe describe mushrooms as 'queer fellows' who are 'Nurtured in death and decay', using terms like 'bizarre', 'lurid', 'bloated and leering', 'dainty and graceful' and 'uncanny' to characterise these ambivalent 'pariahs of the plant world', who elicit both 'wonder and loathing'.[19] These associations have carried into myth and fiction,[20] where fungi are depicted sprouting 'from the black earth alongside the bleakness of gravestones, catacombs, and within cracked arcane tunnels'.[21] Mushrooms and mould crop up repeatedly in Gothic landscapes, from the rot and decay of mouldering abbeys and family estates, like Edgar Allan Poe's House of Usher, to the fungal monstrosities of weird writers like William Hope Hodgson, H. P. Lovecraft, Thomas Ligotti and Jeff VanderMeer.[22]

Despite the obvious appeal of black, unctuous, creeping, living-dead and graveyard-decorating fungus for Gothic writers, there has also been a persistent engagement with fungus-as-gateway to interspecies worlds and nonhuman engagement, showcasing the cunning intelligence of the more-than-human world. The effects of the 'Minute fungi' spread across the House of Usher, 'hanging in a fine tangled web-work from the eaves', extend beyond atmospheric creepiness, leading Roderick to believe in 'the sentience of all vegetable things' along with the symbiotic entanglements of things like fungi, houses, people and trees.[23] While Poe construes this as madness, Roderick Usher's worldview seems consonant with both science and posthuman, post-anthropocentric and new materialist theories.

Lovecraft's fiction similarly resonates with contemporary understandings of symbiosis and its posthuman inflections.[24] 'The Shunned House' (1924) tells of a fetid old house in Providence, notorious for a nebulous 'white fungous' said to contour tree roots, patches of mould and chimney smoke into 'ghoulish, wolfish', 'queer', 'quasi-human or diabolic outlines'.[25] The 'fungous loathsomeness'[26] is revealed to be a monstrous mycelium spreading out from the body of a long-buried vampire. Consuming and colonising, the anthropomorphic fungus bites, chews, drains and decays its victims into an assemblage of fungus, vapour, earth and root in which time, space, matter and lineage become 'queerly distorted' in a 'kaleidoscopic vortex of . . . unaccountable heterogeneity'.[27] Lovecraft's narrator claims that such 'secrets of inner earth' are 'not good for mankind', revealing elements of matter, substance and energy that humans, 'for lack of a proper vantage-point, may never hope to understand'.[28] Although horrific for Man, these fungal networks emphasise the contaminated ethics discussed at the end of Chapter 4 and illustrate what new materialist Stacy Alaimo describes as trans-corporeality: a reminder that 'the human is always the very stuff of the messy, contingent, emergent mix of the material world'.[29] For Alaimo, our porosity and permeability invite greater attention to the more-than-human networks connecting all life and encourage us to develop multispecies kinships, no matter how painful (or horrific) they might be. I return to Lovecraft towards the end of the chapter.

Recent eco-Gothic media, defined by Andrew Smith and William Hughes as 'an ecologically aware Gothic',[30] have amplified the transgressive nature and posthuman appeal of fungus in provocative narratives of fungal infections mutating humankind and unsettling our dominion over nature. *The Last of Us*, an action-adventure videogame (2013) turned popular HBO series (2023), depicts a post-apocalyptic United States ravaged by cannibalistic humans ('the Infected' or 'clickers') infected by *Cordyceps*,[31] a genus of ascomycete fungi[32] (sac fungi) known for parasitizing arthropods and other fungi. Similarly, M. R. Carey's *The Girl with All the Gifts* (2014; adapted for film in 2016) is set in a post-apocalyptic United Kingdom where humankind has been overtaken by a *Cordyceps* infection. Both narratives depict a quest for a cure that ultimately does not materialise, with humankind teetering on the brink of total collapse while a new dominant species rises. Eco-Gothic fungi are thus often harbingers of humanity's end, suggesting the fragility of the Anthropocene and perhaps our dominance as a species. Fungi are known to be ancient and resilient worldbuilders, capable of outlasting us and perhaps even superseding us as the dominant species.[33] Yet, these narratives are not simply nihilistic renderings of our inevitable demise as a species, but rather reminders of our opportunities to open ourselves to ecological entanglements (perhaps contaminations) and experience the worlds of fellow creatures.

Fungal Gothics are thus often *mētistic* Gothics, grounded in dynamic hybrid becomings and responsiveness to alterity.

In what follows, I situate fungi within the space of an eco-Gothic animate environment and relate it to Gothic *mētis* as a rhizomatic, responsive monstrosity. I am especially interested in fungal communication as an embodied, ecological rhetoric that encourages a *mētistic* engagement with an ancient more-than-human world. I pursue this analysis along two main lines: a brief discussion of Arthur Machen's eco-oriented occultism, best exemplified in *The Hill of Dreams* (1907), and a more robust analysis of Bouwer's and Wheatley's films.

A 'study of corruption'[34]: *Arthur Machen's* The Hill of Dreams

Arthur Machen's work on occult, ancient knowledge and liminal selves and spaces presents a post-anthropocentric vision of an animate, affective more-than-human world. As previous chapters outlined, his early works like *The Great God Pan* and *The Three Impostors* explore the 'mystic, ineffable force and energy' of the universe[35] and the vitality or consciousness of the material world, depicting what Karen Barad describes as the 'radical aliveness' of matter.[36] Although his stories of human transmutation and hidden, buried occult forces are no doubt drawn for sensational effect, elements of his work reveal his Romantic vision of a world imbued with mind and ripe for human engagement. In fact, Machen claims his whole literary vision (and particularly *The Great God Pan*[37]) stems from his desire 'to pass on the vague, indefinable sense of awe and mystery and terror that [he] had received' from 'the form and shape of the land of [his] boyhood and youth.'[38] In *Far Off Things* (1922), Machen describes his formative engagement with the 'strange worlds of river and forest and bracken-covered slope' of Caerleon-on-Usk, for which he 'never lost [his] sense of its marvels'.[39] He was 'an enchanted student' of 'an enchanted land' that 'never was illuminated by common daylight, but rather by suns that rose from the holy seas of faery and sank down behind magic hills'.[40] For him, this was 'no earthly land'[41] but home to fauns, nymphs and the Little People, an ancient fairy race long hidden in the Welsh hills and forests.

Machen was born in Caerleon-on-Usk but spent much of his adult life in London, and in both these settings, we can observe his deep fascination with the United Kingdom's Roman and Celtic history. His home village was the site of the Roman town of *Isca Silurum*, and many of his early stories are set in the Welsh countryside, depicted as an enchanted fairyland filled with wonder, mystery and the lingering affective remnants of an ancient past, which, whether Roman or fae, laid hidden in the earth in 'the places beneath the hills',[42] reminiscent of the Land of Summer in Celtic mythology: an ancient realm hidden deep within the earth and connected by 'secret mounds and tunnels to our world'.[43] His autobiographical writings and fiction alike portray Caerleon-on-Usk as an animate, occult space, a literal and figurative borderland to what Mark Valentine describes as 'also a borderland between this world and another world of wonder and strangeness'.[44] Works like *The Great God Pan* accentuate the permeability of these borderlands as figures like Pan transgress the bounds of time, space and matter. London, too, was merely the veneer for Pagan, occult forces; its labyrinthine streets the sights of both wonder and horror and filled with reminders of humankind's imbrication in nature, such as Helen Vaughn's reversion from woman to ape to bacteria 'even to the abyss of all being' in *The Great God Pan* and Francis Leicester, who becomes a 'dark and putrid mass, seething with corruption and hideous rottenness, neither liquid nor solid, but melting and changing . . . and bubbling with unctuous oily bubbles' in *The Three Impostors*.[45] In Machen's works, both 'the mesh of the streets' and the 'mesh of the hills'[46] unsettle distinctions between human/nonhuman, mind/matter, past/present and visible/invisible as they reveal hidden occult forces pulsating beneath the earth, streets and skin, ready for engagement.

Machen's semi-autobiographical novella *The Hill of Dreams*[47] depicts his interest in enchanted, animate landscapes, affective more-than-human subjects and porous embodiments that act as access points between humans and an ancient earth. *The Hill of Dreams* tells the story of Lucian Taylor, whose 'separation from mankind' and life as a lonely, struggling writer in London parallels Machen's own story.[48] In his introduction to the novella, Machen tells of his struggle to write the book, the painstaking plotting and planning of which removed the sense of wonder or mystery in writing.[49] He claims that 'the thought of the old land had come to [his] help' when he was otherwise stymied by and disenchanted with his work.[50] Lucian is similarly inspired by the Welsh countryside, specifically a decaying Roman fort atop a hill.[51] The crumbled fort sits within a forest of anthropomorphic trees and atop a 'black and unctuous' earth that nourishes 'an abominable fungus'.[52] The novella demonstrates Lucian's obsession with the hill and the lingering effects of his sensuous encounters with it, which shape both his character and art.

Lucian's wanderings throughout the Welsh 'outland and occult territory' take him into a haunted fairyland populated by 'ghostly' trees with branches like 'bones' and a blood-red pond (the sun on a pond).[53] It is a 'fairy' place, where,

> Not a branch was straight, not one was free, but all were interlaced and grew one about another; and just above ground, where the cankered stems joined the protuberant roots, there were forms that imitated the human shape, and faces and twining limbs that amazed him. Green mosses were hair, and tresses were stark in grey lichen; a twisted root swelled into a limb; in the hollows of the rotted bark he saw the masks of men.[54]

Lucian realises that '*the wood was alive*'.[55] Amongst the tangled 'faun-like' brambles,[56] he spends an afternoon napping naked on the 'black and unctuous' ground, with his porous body offering a conduit for rapport with the ancient animate earth. In what has been described as a copulative engagement or sexual coupling with the earth,[57] Lucian 'shuddered as he felt the horrible thing pulped beneath his feet'; 'The turf beneath him heaved and sank as with the deep swell of the sea', and 'Quick flames . . . quivered in the substance of his nerves, hints of mysteries, secrets of life passed trembling through his brain.'[58] When he awakes, he blushes as he recalls some 'visitant' with dark eyes and scarlet lips, which he says kissed him.

Machen's novella emphasises the ways that fungus contaminates to communicate with adjacent lifeforms. Infected by his engagement with the 'abominable fungus', Lucian suffers from 'occasional fits of recollection, both cold and hot' while a 'flame' that 'never faded' burns within him. For the rest of his life, he is plagued by outbursts of a 'sudden sense of awful hidden things, and . . . that quivering flame through his nerves that brought back the recollection of the matted thicket'.[59] Lucian's intimate contact with earth transforms him as it 'enmeshes him in transspecies associations that threaten to dissolve the boundaries of his body and mind'.[60] Playing with fungi's taxonomical and ontological confusion, the novella follows what Ella Mershon describes as a decompositional logic that counters the typical movement of the bildungsroman, charting Lucian's decline and dehumanisation rather than his healthy development. Contaminated by the fungal earth, Lucian struggles to feel at home in a world of humans, who he views as 'animals,' 'putrid filth, moulded into human shape' that 'defiled the earth, and made existence unpleasant, as the pulpy growth of a noxious and obscene fungus spoils an agreeable walk'.[61] Lucian 'felt that when he lay dead beneath the earth, eaten by swarming worms, he would be in a purer company than . . . when he lived amongst human creatures'.[62] Fungus's decompositional properties also seem to dissolve boundaries between human and more-than-human language, and much of the novella charts Lucian's attempt to 'translate' not simply the beauty of nature but its voice and affect into English.[63]

Lucian commits to discovering a perfect language for both literature and landscape, these two concepts overlapping as the landscape animates his writing and his writing depicts the landscape. His first manuscript was 'a pious attempt to translate into English prose the form and mystery of the domed hills, the magic of occult valleys, the sound of the red swollen brook swirling through leafless woods'.[64] The trees murmur, mutter, speak, take counsel and argue, but Lucian finds their language 'strange, unutterable' and 'inarticulate', so his 'Wooden sentences . . . clogged the pen'.[65] Lucian's literary experiments involve incorporating 'nature' into his work, using pigment made from 'red earth' and 'the unctuous juice of a certain fern which he thought made his black ink still more glossy'.[66] Perhaps a sign of madness, a nod to experimental Decadent style or an ode to ineffable more-than-human semiosis, Lucian's book,

> was written all in symbols, and in the same spirit of symbolism he decorated it, causing wonderful foliage to creep about the text, and showing the blossom of certain mystical flowers, with emblems of strange creatures, caught and bound in rose thickets.[67]

His writing is ritualised, sensuous and nonlinear; the phrases 'stung and tingled as he wrote them'[68] and rewrote them in endless obsessive revisions, his text becoming a collection of scattered fragments and layered, palimpsestic comments. Mershon views Machen's novella as a perverted 'fin-de-siècle bildungsroman that contests and subverts the logic of self-formation', turning the typical plot of maturation and socialisation into one of fungal 'transspecies' contamination.[69] As he composes his text, Lucian himself seems to decompose, losing his sense of reality while becoming 'inhuman' and monstrous.[70] In an ambiguous yet fitting denouement, Lucian seems to end his life merged 'into the mildew and mold of a moldering home' that may or may not be his own.[71]

Critics have read Lucian's contact with the 'abominable fungus' as an example of queer fungal intimacies and queer ecologies that breakdown taxonomical and ontological boundaries. For Mershon, Machen's novella displays 'queer forms of belonging' that unsettle notions of self-contained bodies and systems in favour of openness and collectiveness in 'language-making, self-making, and world-making'.[72] As Dennis Denisoff describes it, queer ecology emphasises 'desires and attractions that operate beyond human models of engagement', species or identity, offering 'emotional forms of co-constitution' that help to undermine 'human exceptionalism'.[73] Queer ecology emerges at the intersection of queer theory and ecological thought in an attempt to resist binary and fixed categories, like human and nonhuman, domestic and wild and urban and wilderness, and in doing so, reshape how humans interact with the more-than-human world.[74] Catriona Sandilands explains that queer ecology aims to 'disrupt prevailing heterosexist' notions of 'sexuality and nature' while also seeking 'to reimagine evolutionary processes, ecological interactions, and environmental politics in light of queer theory'.[75] Queer ecology thus both critiques how heteronormative ideas about gender can influence ideas about the more-than-human world and undermines binary framings of nature, accentuating, much like posthuman and new materialist criticism, that nature does not fit into binaries, is not separate from Man and most certainly does not exist simply to be penetrated or dominated by him.

Thus, as Machen's work demonstrates, Gothic fungi are not merely 'agents of dissolution', pollution, decay and demise; they are models for dynamic multispecies collaborations and communications through which both humans and nonhumans are transformed, or transmuted, as per Machen. Fungi dissolve the boundaries and undermine the perceived binaries between self/Other, human/nonhuman, nature/culture, matter/discourse and mind/matter. Eco-Gothic tales of fungal entanglements are not merely the stuff of nightmares, but also tales that encourage ecological sensitivity and ecological entanglements. Underpinning the horror of infection, mutation and decay is a helpful reminder of ecological entanglements and possibilities for multispecies flourishing and a push towards the contaminated ethics discussed in Chapter 4. To engage the more-than-human world may 'sting' and it may contaminate, but these at times painful, asymmetrical exchanges are the foundation for transformation. As Patricia MacCormack prompts, what might be 'horror for some' is 'the very opening of the world to others'.[76] Moving into a reading of *Gaia* and *In the Earth*, I want to link Gothic fungus to *mētis* and argue for the value of monstrous *mētistic* rhetoric in the context of post-anthropocentric ethics and interspecies rapport. I argue that *mētis* facilitates the transformational encounters with difference promoted by post-anthropocentric theorists like Tsing and modelled by eco-Gothic narratives.

Mētic *Monsters in* Gaia *and* In the Earth

To postulate the *mētic* nature of Gothic fungal entanglements, I turn to two recent eco-horror films showcasing the cunning, adaptive nature of fungi, more specifically mycelium and mycorrhizae: Jaco Bouwer's *Gaia* (2021) and Ben Wheatley's *In the Earth* (2021). Both films depict remote forests inhabited by ancient entities known variously as spirits, gods, goddesses or simply Earth, which manifest as massive fungal networks. Through *mētic* tactics of trickery, disguise, infection and subversion, these cunning fungal networks seek to unsettle the Anthropocene and stop the seemingly unstoppable human geological force destroying the planet.

Mētic Mycorrhizae: *In the Earth*

Wheatley's *In the Earth* is set in the UK during a pandemic that resembles but is not specified as COVID-19. Emerging from social isolation, Dr Martin Lowery travels to Gantalow Lodge to research mycorrhizae's agricultural applications. Martin is also searching for his former colleague (and likely lover), Dr Olivia Wendle, who has gone non-contact researching mycorrhizae in the local woods. At the lodge, he discovers the legend of Parnag Fegg, an earth spirit said to haunt the area. The main plot depicts Martin and park ranger Alma journeying into the forest to look for Olivia. They discover that Olivia worships Parnag Fegg as does her estranged husband, Zack, who builds idols and offers human sacrifices to Fegg. Parnag Fegg defies explanation. Alma describes her as a mythic forest spirit used to explain missing persons and thus warn locals about the dangers of the deep woods. For Zack, Fegg is a god, the spirit of an ancient necromancer and alchemist who transmogrified himself into a monolith when under attack by locals.[77] However, Olivia defines Parnag Fegg as a process rather than a person – a method for opening communication with the very Earth itself via light, sound and ritual. She claims that Parnag Fegg translates to sound and light in local dialect: parnagus = sound and fegg = light. Whatever or whoever Fegg might be, it manifests as a massive mycorrhizal network that extends through the forest, likely the entire United Kingdom and possibly throughout the planet, at the centre of which is a monolith not appearing on any maps of the area.

Mycorrhizae figure large in Wheatley's folk-infused eco-horror. Described by Martin as the earth's brain, mycorrhiza is an intricate subterranean mesh of fungus and tree root (*Mycorrhiza* is a compound of *mukès* and *rhiza*, Greek for fungus and root, respectively). Mycorrhizal networks form by mycelium, filamentous fungi's underground networked colony of hyphae, spreading out and connecting with surrounding plants at the intra-and extracellular level[78]. Highly adaptive, integrative, flexible and communicative, mycorrhizae form symbiotic associations between fungi and plants, but as Tsing notes, 'mutual benefits do not lead to perfect harmony', with fungi sometimes parasitising roots and trees sometimes rejecting the fungus.[79] Scientists explain the mycorrhizal network as 'a complex adaptive social network' able to integrate heterogenous species who 'interact, provide feedbacks and adapt'.[80] Colloquially described by American mycologist Paul Stamets as 'the earth's internet' and popularised as the Wood Wide Web, mycorrhizal networks '[carry] information across the forest' and transport microbes.[81] Far more than a network of resource transactions and exchanges, mycorrhizal networks demonstrate multispecies communication; these networks allow plant-to-plant dialogue between the same and different species, leading to changes in growth, photosynthetic rate, nutrition, defence against plagues and pathogens and drought resistance, among others.[82] While plant communication was once 'dismissed as fantasy',[83] mycorrhizae research is quickly uncovering its reality, with studies like G. Kim et al.'s suggesting that plants may use a form of language in which different molecules act as *words*.[84] In fact, mycelium is thought be sentient.

In the Earth depicts mycorrhizal networks as ancient, sentient and communicative, drawing on mythological associations between fungi, the supernatural and 'mythical beings' like 'fairies, witches and so forth'.[85] Parnag Fegg might be an alchemist, possibly a witch or perhaps something far more ancient and ineffable. Who or whatever Fegg is, it has called Olivia and others to its forest, which Olivia believes is its attempt to tell humans how to live with other creatures in the precarious present. I return to mycorrhizae in my sections on mushroom rhetoric and *mētistic* communication below.

Subverting Anthropos: *Gaia*

While Wheatley's film depicts a possibly fruitful collaboration between humans and the more-than-human Earth, Bouwer's *Gaia* warns that we have already lost the chance to reconcile with Mother Earth, or as Bouwer calls her, Gaia. *Gaia* also takes place in a remote forest where humans are said to disappear. Set in South Africa, Bouer's film portrays two forestry workers, Gabi and Winston, on a mission to collect trail cam footage. On the way, their drone is knocked down by a mysterious man, sending Gabi on a recovery mission that leaves her injured and separated from Winston. In the forest, she meets a father and son named Barend and Stefan, who live illegally and off the grid, with no technology or ties to modern civilisation. Through sacrifice and prayer, the duo worships an entity they call Mother, God and Goddess. For Barend, perhaps like Spinoza, 'nature is scripture',[86] and it is in nature that one finds God.

Bouwer's depiction of Gaia draws upon ancient myth and contemporary eco-theory. In Greek myth, Gaia is the Goddess of Earth and mother to the Titans[87] (and Metis's grandmother). To Hesiod, Gaia represents the beginning of the world and a stable foundation for all creatures to emerge from.[88] More recently, Gaia names a theory of living, interlocking planetary ecosystems that most simply posits 'the Earth is alive'.[89] English chemist James E. Lovelock is credited with the 'Gaia hypothesis', which proposes that 'the growth, death, metabolism and other activities of living organisms' regulate elements of Earth's 'atmospheric gases . . .[,] surface rocks and water'.[90] Gaia is said to resemble 'a superorganism' or more properly 'an enormous set of nested communities that together form a single global ecosystem'.[91] As Dorion Sagan explains, 'Gaia refers to the biosphere understood not as environmental home but as body, as physiological process' because of the ways Earth's biosphere seems to '[behave] *as* a body'.[92] Sagan explains that 'Sociologically, Gaia ties into animism, native Americanism, and ecologism' while also providing 'a sort of immanent goddess that for many at last suggests a welcome departure from a transcendent God'.[93] Donna Haraway situates Gaia in her Chthulucene, in contrast to the Anthropocene and 'sky-gazing' Anthropos.[94] Working with Bruno Latour's 'Gaïa stories' for 'the "Earthbound"'[95] and Isabelle Stengers's conception of Gaia as a 'fearful and devastating power that intrudes on our categories of thought' if not 'on thinking itself', Haraway presents 'Earth/Gaia [as] maker and destroyer, not a resource to be exploited or ward to be protected or nursing mother promising nourishment'.[96] Haraway takes Gaia as Lovelock intended – less a goddess than a system who cannot and does not care about the desires or intentions of humans or any other specific creature: 'Arising from Chaos, Gaia was and is a powerful intrusive force' and not our 'hope for salvation'.[97] Despite her connotations as Mother Earth, Gaia is not here to nurture us, as Bouwer's film warns.

Bouwer's film presents Gaia as an ancient intelligent networked being inhabiting a remote South African forest, whose tendrils possibly stretch around the globe. As Barend explains to Gabi, 'the largest organism on the planet lives right here, beneath us. Older than human history, it's been growing, waiting, ripening' and now 'it's ready to spread' – an entity who was 'here long before apes started dreaming of god'.[98] The film begins with an overhead shot of the massive forest and Gabi stating, 'Imagine there was a time when the whole world looked like this' and 'long after we're gone, this *thing* will still be here'.[99] Gabi's comments preface the message of the film, which is that humankind is a blight that Gaia, the 'Mother of Creation and Destruction',[100] is about to eradicate. The film frames humankind's relationship with nature in terms of conflict, with Barend claiming that the industrial revolution was our declaration of war. Gaia is losing, but not for much longer. Humankind cannot be saved, and as Barend tells Gabi, 'Rather than mercy, wish for a swift end to the Anthropocene'.[101]

At once open and hostile, these ancient fungal entities reach out to humans, telling us that we have overstepped our bounds but will soon be brought back into the mesh (or pulp) of the more-than-human world. I read these entities as *mētic* monsters and argue that their rhetorical power can be seen as an example of *mētis*, emphasising the embodied, twisting and affective power of cunning and adaptive intelligence to undo hierarchies, adapt to agonistic entanglements and navigate treacherous spaces.

The Polyplokos *Monster and* Mētistic *Rapport*

The fungal networks of *In the Earth* and *Gaia* are a *polyplokos* monster: a twisted, coiled, rhizomatic creature endowed with *mētis* who acts as a cunning 'living trap'.[102] In these films, *polyplokoi* beings send out their many tendrils and use their *mētis* to entrap and subvert humanity in cunning ways. Rather than fight through brute force, Parnag Fegg and Gaia use *mētic* tactics of disguise and infection, much like Metis who overthrew the more powerful Titans through her wiles and magic potion. *In the Earth*'s Parnag Fegg sends out a fungal infection – the common ringworm – to call people to the monolith in the forest. The ringworm is a bond with Parnag Fegg, who plants a thought in their minds that grows like a seed, as Olivia puts it. Olivia, Zach and Martin, who are all infected with ringworm, have the same experience of being called – an undeniable and irresistible urge to come to the forest. As mycorrhizal networks send out signals to draw resources to itself, Olivia posits that the ringworm is this signal and that they are the resources.

The circular ringworm mimics the eye-like hole in Parnag Fegg's monolith as well as the mycorrhizal network Olivia has mapped and the spore cloud that encircles and entraps their camp. The circle of the monolith looks much like an eye opened to the forest, with camera shots zooming outward from the hole into the trees, illustrating Marcel Detienne and Jean-Pierre Vernant's claim that 'Every animal with *mêtis* is a living eye which never closes or even blinks'.[103] Circles also evoke fairy rings and their associations with fairies and elves[104] as well as views of the earth 'as a self-repairing, closed system', as in Gaia theory or Louis Pasteur's *cercle de vie* theory, which argued all matter returns to the soil and the atmosphere in putrefaction.[105] Given Fegg's association with alchemy, the circle also resembles the Ouroboros, which expresses the circularity of life and unity of being, commonly depicted as a snake swallowing its tale. Circles; rhizomatic tangles in roots, tree branches and mushroom patches; and tendrilled, tentacular, hyphae-like fibres extending everywhere are common images throughout both films, eliciting the sense that Fegg and Gaia are omnipresent and omniscient as well as what Haraway would call tentacular. As Detienne and Vernant's study reveals, circles, bonds, 'knots, ropes, meshes and nets' are fundamental expressions of *mētis*, with 'the most prized cunning of all' being '"duplicity" . . . which conceals its true lethal nature beneath a reassuring exterior'.[106]

In both films, spores demonstrate the duplicity and subversion of *mētis*. Spores are traps, but they are also bonds that facilitate interspecies rapport. Parnag Fegg releases a spore cloud that encircles Olivia's camp and entraps her, Alma and Martin. When Alma attempts to escape and inhales the spores, she is suddenly connected to the light and sound of the forest and overwhelmed by the rich sensory data that leaves her struggling for breath and for words. Spores play an even larger role in *Gaia*. The forest is ripe with spore clouds circulating an infectious fungus that prefers homo sapiens as its host. Gabi inhales spores soon after getting injured in the forest, and the film traces her mutation into one of Gaia's 'apostles': mindless mushroom monsters[107] in line with the *Cordyceps*-infected humans of *The Last of Us* and *The Girl with All the Gifts*. Gabi's infection begins with dreams of coughing up hyphae-laced phlegm and of sprouting lichens and toadstools on her body, which soon becomes reality. Once infected, Gabi and her partner Winston transform into colourful, textured fungal landscapes. By the end of the film, Gabi is a colourful patch of toadstools, lichens and Laetiporus bound to the floor of Barend and Stefan's cabin. Ultimately, Gaia makes Stefan her vessel and sends him to spread her infectious fungi throughout the Anthropocene. As Barend tells him, 'She has chosen you, my son. Your body . . . our message'.[108] Her message is that humankind is about to witness its greatest reckoning. But we will not be undone by *biē* or brute force; Gaia's cunning tactics of contamination will lead us to our demise. The film ends with Stefan in a city cultivating a rapidly spreading fungus, making the film's tagline, 'She will transform us', seem both a promise and a threat.

Through ingestions of spores and other fungal forms like sacraments made from mushrooms, characters in these films are transformed and bound to the earth in ways that change their perceptions and perspectives, such as enhancing visual and auditory perception to commune with the 'light and sound' of Parnag Fegg or opening bodies to Gaia's mutational becomings. These *polyplokoi* monsters are cunning and subversive, using disguise and tactical infections rather than brute force to unsettle the destructive, powerful Anthropocene. In doing so, they illustrate how *mētis* allows the seemingly weak or small to cunningly overturn those who appear stronger and larger, as in Metis's attack against the Titans or Sophist tricks of rhetorical reversals. *Mētis* reveals that the survival of the fittest does not always entail that the larger dominate.[109]

Mētis is also present in these films as a tool for posthuman, post-anthropocentric communication. Connoting metamorphosis and 'the indeterminacy of both subjects and objects', *mētis* is a cunning that 'transgresses the boundaries separating the gods, humankind, and animals'.[110] As discussed further in Chapter 6, rhetoricians have linked *mētis* to posthuman and ecological rhetoric,[111] with critics like Kristin Pomykala and Shannon Walters theorising *mētis* as an embodied intelligence for 'becoming with' other creatures and a rhetorical strategy for cooperative movement between human, animal and technical bodies.[112] We can associate *mētis* with *technē* as Janet Atwill explains it: 'a domain of . . . intervention and invention' that is 'often associated with the transgression of an existing boundary'.[113] *Technē* is associated with technology, but it is 'never reducible to an instrument or a means to an end'; rather, because *technē* is as much an art as an instrument, it 'intervenes' with boundaries and 'creates a path that both transgresses and redefines that boundary'.[114] *Technē* is thus bound up with both *mētis*, the art of cunning and polymorphy, and *kairos*, the right time and the right measure, known also as the 'power to discover and invent new paths'[115] of engagement.

If the *polyplokoi* monsters in these films use their *mētis* and develop *technē* to communicate with humans, then the humans develop their own to talk back. Fungi is one tool used to this end, with characters ingesting mushrooms in rituals to open channels of rapport. While sacrament and sacrifice are predictable vehicles for communing with alleged gods, these films depict characters using far more cunning tactics for rapport, which I want to link to *mētis* (cunning) and *technē* (artful technology). *In the Earth*'s Dr Olivia Wendal – both a witch and mad scientist – weaves light, sound, mushrooms, science and ancient rituals associated with the *Malleus Maleficarum* to commune with Parnag Fegg. She has discovered a unique version of *Malleus Maleficarum* with sections in a local dialect describing Fegg as 'light' and 'sound'. Zack uses sacrifice and idolatry to commune with Parnag Fegg in what he describes as a purer form of communication; however, Olivia has devised an elaborate language of light and sound, using a system of speakers, microphones, strobe lights, an electric organ and a mixing board, which collectively allow her to hear what the roots and trees are saying and respond back in the language she has devised from their patterned replies.[116] Olivia is convinced that whatever is here wants to communicate, claiming that 'If it wants to talk, then we have to listen'; she needs to know 'how we can live together without destroying one another.'[117] Importantly, though, as Zach claims, the forest knows what it wants and does not need humans to manage it.

These films along with Machen's novella thus demonstrate the communicative abilities of fungus and by extension the more-than-human world. Significantly, the attempts to render fungal communication necessarily turn to Gothic. In the final section, I explore how these films illustrate more-than-human rhetoric and the struggle to find human terms to define and engage it.

Gothic Mētis *and the Ineffable More-than-Human World*

Fungus has formed an infectious and engaging 'thread that runs, mycelium-like' throughout Gothic and its adjacent modes of horror and the weird, depicting simultaneous 'wonders' and 'terrors'.[118] Not only cryptic and creepy, fungus is also communicative, adaptive and responsive, as Gothic tales from Machen to Wheatley have expressed. Fungal rhetoric like other forms of more-than-human expression can be difficult for humans to discern and even more difficult to articulate in many languages, perhaps especially English, which Tla-o-qui-aht activist Gisele Maria Martin describes as 'an ecologically illiterate language'.[119] Timothy Morton expresses a similar point in *Humankind*, where he asks, 'Can I give voice to [an ecological being] in this book?', determining that 'there is no pronoun entirely suitable to describe ecological beings'; first, second and third person perspectives all seem to obscure the particular symbiotic entanglements of ecological subjects, as Morton theorises them.[120] The struggle to find a term to express the ecological subject leads Jodey Castricano to the 'fourth person', 'which not only combines the first, second and third person points of view but exceeds them' as a person not equivalent to 'one'.[121] Castricano highlights the tendency of English grammar to separate subjects and objects, and therefore to suggest a separation between them in reality, a worldview associated with European Enlightenment and associated humanist models of self/Other. These comments on the limits of English to express ecological subjectivity are reminiscent of William James's remarks about Myers's 'Gothic psychology' in Chapter 3 and Sagan's points in Chapter 4 regarding the limits of scientific language to describe nonhuman selves so that one must force multiplex realities into flat representations or resort to what gets dismissed as anthropomorphism, 'pathetic fallacy, [or] personification'.[122] Before turning to some ways that Gothic writers attempt to transgress and extend these rhetorical limits, I want to first outline how and why we can view fungus as rhetorical, by which I mean artful and responsive.

Given the intermingled critical, scientific and public discourse on the Wood Wide Web, it seems clear that fungal networks are communicative and rhetorical, that is, responsive to the marks of others and creatively leaving tracks for others to follow. George Kennedy's conceptualisation of nonhuman rhetoric is particularly helpful in explaining fungal rhetoric. For Kennedy, rhetorical energy exists in all organisms, including plants, who use 'coloration and scent' as a type of rhetoric essential for their survival.[123] Kennedy's comments on rattlesnake rhetoric are also helpful for envisioning a fungal rhetoric, particularly a mycorrhizal one. Much like 'a rattlesnake's rhetoric consists of coiling or uncoiling itself',[124] hyphae coil as they penetrate plant cells to form symbiotic entanglements. Kennedy proposes that like humans, nonhumans model a rhetorical process consisting of invention, arrangement, memory, style and delivery. Arguing for a type of 'proto-rhetoric', Kennedy notes the ways that other creatures *deliver* their messages through facial and physical expression, movement, gesture, vocal/tonal inflection, colour, shape and movement. Kennedy argues that 'Writing or marking' can be observed not only in human languages, but also in the ways animals 'mark' their territories with scent, express themselves through movements and sounds and generally leave traces of themselves on their environment for other organisms to read.[125] Kennedy's claim that even 'the most primitive form of marking is a vehicle for rhetoric' is echoed by Nathaniel Rivers, who defines rhetoric as '*all* the ways we mark and are ourselves marked, bitten, or stung',[126] expanding our thinking about rhetoric to encompass semiotic engagements available to all creatures, including animals, plants and fungi, who may, as Machen's novella reveals, reach out to sting us.

We can view mycorrhizal networked interactions as rhetorical, specifically deliberative[127] in that they are geared towards judgements based on advice about future actions: a signal that suggests an attack invites the receiver to consider a future course of action, much like a signal that suggests responses to environmental stimuli, root and stem growth, etc. We might also note the inherent ethos, pathos and logos of mycorrhizal or any nonhuman communication. The sender of a message, 'whether consciously or not', also sends 'a sign of . . . credibility and good will (ethos)', stimulates an emotional response in their audience (pathos) and provides evidence (logos), such as 'giving the call that denotes a predator', if their message is to be successfully received.[128] Studies of nonhuman or more-than-human rhetoric identify energy, marking and sensation as the foundations of nonhuman communication as well as materials or tactics available for transspecies communication. Bouwer and Wheatley both capitalise on film's ability to communicate beyond words, using colour, movement, strobing lights and cryptic sounds to render fungal rhetorics as legible for human audiences. Fegg and Gaia are most likely to express themselves in the dancing of spores, the blooming of mushrooms and the creeping, extending coiling and penetrating movements of hyphae. I discuss the eco-critical, posthuman, vital materialist turn in rhetorical criticism and critical attempts to locate rhetoric beyond the human further in the next chapter.

Gothic writers and scholars alike have often mused upon the limits of human language to express the animacy of nonhumans, the 'sentience of space and place' and the liveliness of the more-than-human world. In *Far Off Things*, Machen outlines this struggle, which we see equally conveyed in his fiction:

> It is only music, I think, that could image the wonder of the red sky over the faery dome, and the gathering dusk of the night as it fell on the rocks of that high land, on the streams rushing vehemently down into the darkness of the valley, on the lower woods, on the white farms, gleaming and then vanishing away . . . if at all, can such things be expressed, since they are ineffable; not to be uttered in any literal or logical speech of men. And if one looks a little more closely into the nature of things it will become pretty plain, I think, that all that really matters and really exists is ineffable; that both the world without us – the tree and the brook and the hill – and the world within us do perpetually and necessarily transcend all our powers of utterance, whether to ourselves or to others.[129]

Machen's tendency towards the unspeakable and rhetorically abstract in his fiction seems to illustrate his point that the world within and without us is beyond our comprehension and cannot be described by our language. We see similar strategies in Lovecraft's fiction as he attempts to render the invisible movements of microscopic creatures who exist beyond human understanding and description. In 'The Colour Out of Space', Mrs Gardner is said to '[scream] about things in the air which she could not describe' without using 'a single specific noun, . . . only verbs and pronouns. Things moved and changed and fluttered, and ears tingled to impulses which were not wholly sounds'.[130] Breakdowns in matter, boundaries and identity almost inevitably lead to breakdowns of language in Gothic. Perhaps this is why Gothic's most prevalent and repeated rhetorical strategies involve fragmentation, excess, digression, obfuscation and disorientation: the 'sentience of space and place' defies linear and realist representation. The rhizomatic structures of ecologies seem to find apt expression in the 'narrative chaos'[131] of Gothic.

Gothic's rhetorical strategies highlight the limitations of realist expression to capture the 'ineffable' liveliness of the more-than-human world. As Adrian Tait points out, even if writers like Machen adopt a new materialist or post-anthropocentric sense of a vibrant more-than-human world in which mind and matter overlap, they still encounter the difficulty of 'conceptualizing' and 'hence representing' these categorical breakdowns.[132] The ineffable is not simply that which one struggles to express but an encounter with that which is beyond human understanding and categorisation. Michael T. Wilson reveals that the ineffable is 'first a religious concept, the thing that cannot be described entangled with the word that cannot be uttered', not only an 'encounter with the divine' but also the 'numinous' and the overwhelming awe it inspires;[133] it is thus an experience that is 'category-resistant'.[134] Castricano posits that the encounter with the ineffable is an encounter with the sentience of space and place, with the uncanny breakdowns of subjects and objects and the 'site of an inexplicable interaction between psyche and matter'.[135] Not always definable as people, places or things, ecological subjects are not reducible to 'one' and may be best expressed by fluttering and pulsing movements and tingling, stinging sensations. Machen and Lucian overlap in their movement away from realism, with Lucian ultimately disbelieving 'that language could present the melody and the awe and the loveliness of the earth'. Despite his best efforts, he could not 'win the secret of words, to make a phrase that would murmur of summer and the bee, to summon the wind into a sentence, to conjure the odour of the night into the surge and fall and harmony of a line'.[136] Such things might be better felt than defined.

Significantly, the backdrop to these films is the Anthropocene, with emphasis on the deleterious effects of humankind's consumptions, colonisations and extractions. Appropriately, colonisers are colonised by fungus, and through this contact, identities, bodies and perspectives are transformed. The monstrous connections with alterity and transformations that fungi offer can be salutary, as the comments on contaminated ethics at the end of the previous chapter suggest. While the monstrous fungal networks of Fegg and Gaia decentre Man and subvert anthropocentric autonomy, they also highlight the value and necessity of what Tsing calls transformational encounters with difference or collaborations through contamination. Fungi's communicative potential is certainly monstrous: it infects, transgresses, hybridises and transforms, yet it also responsive, cunning and adaptive – that is *mētic.* Despite the horror, these films remind us of the importance of our communion with the Earth, of our need to be cunning and adaptive in ecological rapport and the need to honour our obligations to nature, even when it stings or disadvantages us, as without the more-than-human-world, we cannot live (let alone live together without destroying one another). Fungi are ancient and resilient, likely to survive long after other forms of life have ceased to find Earth liveable. That fungi emerge from ruin is perhaps why they so frequently crop up in tales of a collapsing Anthropocene and populate our imagination of what Machen (and Thacker after him) refers to as the world 'without us'. Fungi represent resilient, adaptive and interconnective more-than-human forms of life as much as they represent disease, death and decay. In the end, just as there is no mercy for Gabi, there may be no mercy for us; we who have colonised and mined Earth might need to offer our bodies for the inhabitation and resource extraction of other creatures. Gabi's opening comments are appropriately prescient. Long after we are gone, 'this *thing* will still be here'. As the monstrous Melanie in *The Girl with All the Gifts* remarks as the last of humanity falls to the *Cordyceps*: 'It's not over. It's just not yours anymore'.[137]

6

Gothic Mētis *and More-than-Human Rhetoric*

'To feel solidarity is to feel haunted.'

Timothy Morton, *Humankind*[1]

Previous chapters have aligned Gothic and *mētis* as conceptual and rhetorical modes for engaging the liminal, construed as an in-between space wherein categories, states and identities are blended and blurred. Filtered through posthuman and new materialist theory, liminality connotes plural, porous selves and their entwinements or co-constitutions[2] with Others. Late nineteenth-century writer Vernon Lee conceptualised such liminal spaces as a type of 'limbo' wherein mysterious 'diverse vital forces'[3] haunt and engage each other, a space of 'unnamed mystery into which various things enter' in an 'atomic affinity' that can be sensed but rarely named.[4] In limbo, 'the order of time and space is sometimes utterly subverted' as 'the power of outdoor things, their mysterious affinities, can change the values even of what has been and what has not been'.[5] Limbo is the 'Kingdom of Might-have-been',[6] including unfulfilled desires, the 'mysterious affinities' between humans and the more-than-human world and the forgotten 'power of outdoor things' to engage us. This chapter explores how Vernon Lee depicted the haunting presence of such forgotten engagements and her attempts to commune with myriad ineffable more-than-human entities.

An avid traveller and prolific writer, Vernon Lee sought to experience and portray the agentic nonhumans she discusses in *Limbo and Other Essays* (1897). While she at times lamented the paucity of language to capture the magic and vitality of nonhumans, her writings nonetheless demonstrate a sincere attempt to render and engage the uncanny more-than-human world, which for Lee was not a setting for human art and activities but a protagonist in worldly dramas beyond our understanding. Along with her provocative stories of hauntings and alluring femme fatales, Lee wrote extensively on her travels across Western and central Europe and the spirits she encountered in the places she visited. Collectively, Lee's work demonstrates her attunement to the past, to nonhuman and ecological selves and to the haunting exchanges between them. I am particularly interested in her essays on the genius loci, or spirit of place, and her associated depictions of and engagements with sentient landscapes and locales. Lee develops the genius loci as a rhetorically powerful concept for engaging environmental affinities, one that unsettles humanist conceptions of subjectivity, language and rapport and prompts us to engage with them on nonhuman – or perhaps *supernatural* – terms. This final chapter expands on previous discussions of Gothic's rhetorical tropes and tactics by returning to Lee's work and relating it to the contemporary posthuman turn in rhetorical criticism. A larger goal of this chapter's analysis is to highlight the utility of Gothic tropes like spirits, ghosts and haunting in ecological or environmentalist discourse, especially in stories of the excluded, marginalised, silenced and forgotten more-than-human relations that haunt Man in the Anthropocene.

Lee's work is part of a broader *fin-de-siècle* Gothic-Decadent movement that engaged an enchanted, animate landscape, in which trees, rivers, streams, mountains, soil and rocks are invested with vitality and with rhetorical *technē* (that is, artful invention, intervention and articulation).[7] Her contemporaries like Arthur Machen similarly sought to acknowledge, describe and perhaps ultimately commune with nonhuman entities populating and animating the allegedly inanimate more-than-human world around them. Dennis Denisoff's recent work on *Decadent Ecology* describes the ways that writers like Lee were sensitive 'to transspecies co-reliance' and communication in ways that 'decenter . . . our self-image as environmental guardians' and emphasise 'the naïveté of our claims to [environmental] management'.[8] Decadent framings, as per Denisoff, offer an alternative to discourses of environmental rights, protections and management, depicting an environment beyond human understanding, regulation and control. Instead of trying to 'translate ecological communications into a human discourse', Lee encourages us to listen to ecosystems and become receptive to 'intercourse on nonhuman terms'.[9] With Denisoff's claim in mind, I want to interpret the nonhuman ecological signals of engagement in Lee's work via recent work on non-anthropocentric rhetoric, eco-Gothic and the sensuous, embodied and entangled art of rhetorical cunning: *mētis*. After outlining Lee's enduring fascination with hauntings, I then discuss how she construes the genius loci as an ecological subject in her essays on travel and landscape. Lee's work expresses not only a post-Darwinian sensitivity to nonhuman subjectivity but also a vital materialist sense of human-more-than-human-interdependencies. In the final sections of the chapter, I examine the rhetorical applications of hauntings and spirits for engaging environmental affinities and fostering a transspecies rapport.

Spectres and Hauntings in Lee

Vernon Lee had a self-proclaimed 'foolish passion for the Past' that gave her a profound respect for ghosts, for spirits and for hauntings.[10] For Lee, hauntings need not involve the spirits of the dearly departed, but rather, as she explains in her preface to *Hauntings and Other Fantastic Tales* (1890), the impressions of the Past as it invades the Present: 'My ghosts are what you call spurious ghosts . . . of whom I can affirm only one thing, that they haunted certain brains, and have haunted . . . my own'.[11] In 'Faustus and Helena: Notes on the Supernatural in Art' (1880), Lee explains that when she speaks of ghosts, she does not mean 'the vulgar apparition which is seen or heard in told or written tales', but a 'vague feeling we can scarcely describe, a something pleasing and terrible which invades our whole consciousness'.[12] What she calls 'the real supernatural' is 'born of the imagination and its surroundings, the vital, the fluctuating, the potent', and to experience it takes us 'beyond and outside the limits of the possible, the rational, the explicable'.[13] She found comfort in the past and the ways it infuses the present with life, with a 'soul' and ultimately with possibility.[14] Lee said she 'crav[ed] . . . the supernatural, the ghostly' as a relief from the 'prosaic' modern demand for reason and 'logic'.[15] While her friend hated old houses because '*There seemed to be other* people in [them] besides the living. . .', Lee found 'rapture' in the atmosphere of nonhuman sentience and presence, seeking out the 'crowd[s] of ghosts'[16] haunting old houses, crumbling churches, dense forests, babbling brooks, old towns or high mountains.

Lee's late-Victorian ghost stories often depicted suppressed desires or marginalised subjectivities, highlighting excluded female and queer perspectives. 'A Wicked Voice' (1887), for example, is a tale of queer spectral seduction. The story subverts gender stereotypes and heteronormative desire in its portrayal of the attraction between contemporary composer Magnus and the long-dead homme fatale, Zaffirino, whose exotic melodies had the power to kill as well as seduce. By the end of the story, Magnus begs to be haunted by Zaffirino's deadly voice, 'delicate, voluptuous . . . strange, exquisite, [and] sweet beyond words'.[17] Lee's tales of hauntings have resonated with feminist critics for the ways they showcase excluded or marginalised subjects[18] like women and their 'unfulfilled' and/or 'unspeakable' desires.[19] Emma Liggins identifies queer desire, '"other" sexualities outside the realms of heteronormativity' and 'gender indeterminacy' as predominant themes of Lee's *fin-de-siècle* ghost stories.[20] She argues that the spectral encounter at the heart of the 'fashionable' ghost story was used by women writers 'to address what remained "unseen"' or 'unacknowledged' in women's everyday lives,[21] such as the limitations of binaries to structure their sexualities, identities or desires. Hauntings in Lee are thus invitations 'to explore alternative subjectivities' and fluid identities,[22] including the androgynous[23] and, as I want to highlight, the more-than-human.

Along with marginalised feminine and queer perspectives, Lee employed the spectral and supernatural to highlight the excluded nonhuman, ecological affinities haunting modern civilised selves. In her essays on travel, landscapes and locales, she filters her deep engagement with place through tropes like hauntings, spirits and magic. In *The Enchanted Woods: And Other Essays on the Genius of Places* (1905), she explains that even commonplace city parks and backyards can be seen as enchanted places, 'full of spells and of adventure without end, drawing one, up that dark, gliding river, into their hidden heart'.[24] Enchanted woods transport us outside of time and place; following 'one path, now another, . . . up and down, endlessly, aimlessly', we give into 'roving, galloping' fancy and become 'the willing victims of great wizards and fairies'.[25] Lost in 'the magic gloom' of dark thickets and creaking branches of such enchanted forests, the heart '[stops] with delightful fright' as uncanny 'oaks and beeches loom in the dusk, colossal, the pale branches take threatening appearances, as of elephants or writhing snakes'.[26] It seems that wherever she went, Lee felt the 'haunting' presence of more-than-human sentience inhabiting uncanny trees, dark thickets, 'babbling and singing' brooks and 'the whispering brake of reeds', a 'presence' which revealed that places were not 'merely . . . stone, water, grass or trees', but the home of spirits.[27]

Lee's sensitivity to a spiritual reality and lively commerce underpinning seemingly mundane spaces and places aligns with critical work on the spectral as a liminal space to engage across time, bodies and species. Julian Wolfreys's work on spectrality highlights the unsettling nature of hauntings, which can disturb and disrupt the limits of identity. The spectral 'appears in a gap between the limits of two ontological categories' but is part of neither category; this liminality (as seen in the case of being both/neither alive/dead or present/absent, visible/invisible) marks the spectral as 'the limits of determination', one that resists oppositional categorisation.[28] Spectres are often 'frightening' and 'uncanny' because they 'disturb' the lines separating 'the living from the dead', the past from the present and the self from the Other. Andrew Bennett and Nicholas Royle relate the indeterminacy of the spectral to 'a denial or disturbance of the human' since ghosts mark the transition from the 'fundamentally human' to the 'inhuman' as well as the fuzziness of the lines between these categories.[29] The spectral blurs category distinctions, the most salient of which might be the subject/object divide. Philosophically and rhetorically, spectres thus represent those entities who exist outside the bounds of 'subjectivity' (and with this, the bounds of time, space, place, psyche and body).

In Lee's writing, hauntings and spirits often represent 'subjects' who exist beyond the limitations of Man and of his perceptions, including dynamic nonhuman vital forces. Examining several of her depictions of the genius loci in the pages ahead, I link Lee's work to eco-Gothic and the new materialist turn in rhetorical studies. Her spectral renderings of sentient landscapes and agentic nonhuman entities illustrate more-than-human rhetorical invention while modelling *mētistic* tactics to engage across species, bodies and times. Through writing like Lee's, we can learn to recognise what Anna Tsing calls 'the tracks and traces of nonhumans'[30] and devise cunning tactics for transspecies, trans-environmental and transhistorical rapport. Ultimately, Lee's work illuminates the utility of supernatural tropes to describe and engage an animate earth otherwise ineffable and eerie.

Genius Loci: *The Spirit of Place*

From 1897 to 1925, Lee wrote extensively on her travels through Western Europe, describing her interactions with the spirit and dispositions of places: the genius loci. Originally a Roman concept, the genius loci denoted 'the spirit or deity that inhabited a place', which was later taken more 'figuratively to [refer to] the associations or inspirations derived from a place'.[31] Leonie Wanitzek claims that Lee's constructions of places like Italy signify 'a particular mental as well as actual landscape'.[32] Denisoff's more recent study of Lee suggests that in addressing her emotional connections to place, Lee does more than simply recall her personal experiences or feelings; rather, Lee's 'fusion of the physical landscape with the subconscious, magic, and the mystic' acknowledges that landscapes are invested with lives, feelings and experiences[33] at once spiritual and material. I want to suggest that Lee's renderings of the genius loci do not simply depict her perceptions of or feelings about the places she visits but more properly construe an ecological subject with whom one can converse and form friendships.

Lee defined herself as a 'votary of the *Genius Loci*',[34] with the concept appearing in most of her essay collections.[35] In her introduction to 1899's *Genius Loci*, she describes the genius as something of a nonhuman or ecological person:

> A divinity, certainly, great or small as the case may be, and deserving of some silent worship. But, for mercy's sake, not a personification . . . No, no. The Genius Loci, like all worthy divinities, is of the substance of our heart and mind, a spiritual reality. And as for visible embodiment, why that is the place itself, or the country; and the features and speech are the lie of the land, pitch of the streets, sound of bells or of weirs.[36]

Significantly for Lee, the genius loci is not a personification but more properly 'an embodiment' of place with 'features and speech' and feelings 'Quite irrespective of their inhabitants, their written history'[37] or human feelings or perceptions. Lee understood that 'places have moods and emotions on their account, [and] seem to feel something which they transmit to us'.[38] She writes,

> the whole place (how shall I explain it?) becomes a sort of living something . . . a whole living, breathing thing, full of habits of life, of suppressed words; a sort of odd, mysterious, mythical, but very real creature; . . . something absolutely indefinable in shape and kind, but warm, alive.[39]

Lee's descriptions of the genius loci render places as subjects rather than settings. Places are 'warm', living 'creature[s]' who communicate, who breathe, who feel, who change and who transmit as much as they receive. At times, Lee's sense of the genius loci's 'immanent presence' is so palpable, 'so great' that she must look over her shoulder 'to make sure that no one [is] behind [her]'.[40] The genius does not simply inhabit 'a given turn of a road; or a path cut in terraces in a hillside, . . . in the meeting-place of streams, or the mouth of a river'; Lee believed that 'more strictly, *he is it*'.[41]

Lee's vision of nonhuman persons extends beyond swaying trees and babbling brooks to include environmental entities less likely to evoke movement, action and sound: mountains and their marble. While mountains seem hard and immobile, Lee felt that the 'spectral white crags' of the marble mountains '[have] a will' and 'act as if alive'.[42] Mountains 'rear, they turn on their side and roll over; they take hands, and begin, at least, to march and to dance, if not . . . to skip like young rams rejoicing'.[43] These mountains make 'us draw deep breaths of strenuous pleasure as we watch them'.[44] From her time in the Apennines, she is convinced that

> mountains are always doing something, and very often doing something to us. They are never, in the first place, without movement. Even when we are not causing them to furl and unfurl by changing our place . . .; even when they are not giving us their splendid topographical drama, they never become motionless when we become stationary. Their ravines, whenever we look down, seem actively to burrow and twist, sucking our thoughts like whirlpools'.[45]

Because mountains are so active, energetic, and affective, 'One can be, not exceptionally, but always, in sympathising commerce with [them]'.[46] Lee's writing illuminates that even the most seemingly inert matter is constantly 'doing something' and 'doing something to us' even if we do not immediately perceive it.

Thus, for Lee, places need not be personified because they are already persons, with personalities and proclivities independent of human perspectives. She maintained that the spirits of places 'can touch us like living creatures; and one can have with them friendship of the deepest and most satisfying sort'.[47] In finding 'intercourse with fields and trees and skies, with the windings of road and water and hedge', we find a rapport that fills our lives with uniquely nonhuman 'commerce . . . pleasure, curiosity, and gratitude'.[48] Far more than a personification, then, the genius loci suggests the sentience of space and place, the agency of nonhumans and the capacity for meaningful interspecies communication. Lee viewed 'ecology' as 'a verb – an action', a means of 'trans-historical, trans-spatial', trans-species and trans-corporeal engagements with 'vital spiritual forces' that transgress 'self, body . . . place . . . [and] time'.[49] Not simply an assemblage of 'co-reliant material entities', ecology for Lee was an active 'engagement with both the material and immaterial', framed in terms of 'haunting, mystery, loss, even nonexistence'.[50] I want to suggest that Lee develops what might be called a supernatural ecological rapport – that is, engagements with 'vital . . . fluctuating, [and] potent' nonhuman and more-than-human forces 'beyond and outside the limits of the possible, the rational, the explicable', as Lee would explain it.[51] For Lee, there is a 'divinity immanent in bricks and mortar and rock and stream',[52] and in her writing, haunted cities and sentient landscapes become agentic and artful, exerting dispositional changes on those who engage them. Such dispositional changes are the heart of rhetoric.[53]

As the next section unpacks, Lee's vision of entangled webs of rhetorical actors reflects contemporary post-human, new materialist notions of networked assemblages and more-than-human rhetorical energy. I am especially interested in Lee's attempts to communicate across time and species via kinetic and affective rapport. Lee's supernatural eco-rhetoric is not simply a rhetoric about ecology or an ecologically-sensitive rhetoric featuring spirits and hauntings, but an artful, embodied way to engage across temporal, material and taxonomic lines. Such *mētistic* practices demonstrate the power of *mētis* to confuse subjects and objects, to find a path beyond limits and ultimately to circumvent barriers to rapport. The ineffable more-than-human world might evade human language, but this does not mean we cannot engage it. Rather, as Lee prompts, this ineffability means we need to devise cunning tactics to expand our channels of rapport.

Mētis *and More-than-Human Rhetoric in Lee*

In this section, I argue that Lee's eco-rhetoric not only evokes contemporary debates about the nature of and possibilities for nonhuman rhetoric, but also, and perhaps more importantly, offers a rhetorically powerful model for engaging environmental affinities, one that unsettles humanist conceptions of subjectivity, language, and indeed, rhetoric. In using the term rhetoric, I mean to evoke not simply language use, but *artful* language use – a practice traditionally denied to nonhumans, often in tandem with *logos*, a term that conflates speech and reason. While it is accepted that nonhumans communicate (with both members of the same species and outsiders), ascribing language – and especially *artful* language – to them has remained tricky, largely due to denials of nonhuman consciousness, agency, inventiveness and intentionality. Yet, as rhetorician George Kennedy argues, within the world of animals and plants, we can observe 'various degrees of rhetoric among communications',[54] with some communications more inventive (or artful) than others. For Kennedy, communication's rhetorical quality is determined by energy both expended and received: from 'the emotional energy' prompting a message to the 'physical energy expended' in its delivery to 'the energy . . . coded in the message' to the energy necessary for 'decoding the message'. Most simply, 'Rhetorical assertion conveys energy and reaction in another energy source'.[55] Kennedy's theory of rhetorical energy highlights the extra-lingual and sensuous dimensions of rhetoric and opens rhetorical power to other entities, including mountains, trees, fungi and landscapes.

Lee's approach to eco-rhetoric can be described as sensuous. Sensation, that is 'the faculty of perceiving through the senses' and associated feelings or emotions,[56] has been theorised as a shared means of engagement experienced by humans and nonhumans, perhaps one that helps ecological communication. For example, Debra Hawhee's study of rhetoric alongside critical animal studies (a title Victorianists may appreciate: *Rhetoric in Tooth and Claw*) highlights the centrality of sensation for both rhetorical education and 'cross-species encounters', emphasising that the most 'sense-able' are also the most energetic properties of rhetoric: 'rhythm, sound, expression, style, movement'.[57] Sensation, energy, and embodiment are as central as *logos* to effective rhetoric and often the more profound catalysts for eliciting the 'dispositional changes' foundational to rhetoric.[58] As Hawhee emphasises, sensation is not unique to humans; thus, it might be a way to describe 'the overlapping and interactive worlds of humans and nonhumans' as well as a means for 'cross-species encounters [that] result in mutual movement and exchange'.[59] Sensation, and the energy exchanged between the sender and receiver of a message, is a 'process of *vivification*' that brings words to life and crosses the perceived boundaries between the discursive and the material.[60]

David Abram's well-known *Spell of the Sensuous* similarly frames sensation as a means of cross-species and more-than-human engagement. Abram promotes Maurice Merleau-Ponty's view of language as 'thoroughly incarnate', with words existing as 'active sensuous presences' in a 'material landscape', rather than purely symbolic representations of it.[61] As Abram explains it, Merleau-Ponty viewed human language as 'rooted in our sensorial experience of the world', which we begin to express by gestures and guttural sounds. Language is first learned by the body and not the mind.[62] Language for Merleau-Ponty as per Abram is 'rooted in our sensorial experience of each other and of the world' and is contingent on 'the reciprocal presence of the sentient in the sensible and of the sensible in the sentient'.[63] We can perceive the world as a 'perceiving self' because there is something to perceive, which in turn perceives us back: 'each of us . . . is both subject and object, sensible and sentient'.[64] An embodied, sensuous view of language expands its purview to include animals, who also express themselves gutturally and kinetically. Abram suggests that we can take this expansion much further by considering the participatory nature of sensation. In the sensory world, '*no* phenomenon presents itself as entirely passive or inert', so 'to the sensing body *all* phenomena are animate, actively soliciting the participation of our senses'. 'Each thing' and 'every phenomenon . . . is potentially expressive', with the 'power to reach us and influence us'.[65] Significantly, Merleau-Ponty expressed the 'consanguinity' between the human and the more-than-human world as 'flesh', uniting 'our flesh' with 'the flesh of the world'.[66] In this model, language too is 'flesh' grounded in the material, kinetic exchanges 'always already going on between our own flesh and the flesh of the world',[67] created and sustained by what Karen Barad would call 'the mutual constitution of entangled agencies'.[68]

Alive to the sensation of the more-than-human-world and believing that the spirits of places were tangible and could be viscerally experienced, Lee developed an affective, embodied and sensuous *technē* for engaging the genius loci. For Lee, the only way to gain a 'closer acquaintance' with nature is to move with it, to touch it, taste it and breathe it.[69] As she explains in 'A Walk in Maremma' from *The Enchanted Woods*, scrambling (a particularly active way to traverse a hill or mountain side) is 'the most intimate form of walking, the one bringing the most affectionate knowledge' of a place.[70] Because one is so actively engaged in navigating the terrain, 'one thinks about *it* – it only' and in doing so, can start to hear it express itself.[71] In her openness to the sensations of the land, Lee allows her 'soul . . . to cling to . . . undulations, bends of rivers, straightenings and snakings of road', realising 'how much of one's past life, sensations, hopes, wishes, words, has got entangled in the little familiar sprigs, grasses and moss' through the exchange.[72] Through walking, climbing, riding, driving, wandering and scrambling, Lee reads the various twists, turns, bends and intricacies of landscape and opens herself up to their energetic engagements and the dispositional changes that might follow. She sensed that 'there must be more' to the reality of the land, an underlying presence that gives it its '*timbre*' and calls out to those willing to listen.[73] Although this 'timbre' is difficult to express in human terms ('how shall I say it?'), it is tangible, perceptible and responsive nonetheless. This sensuous engagement with landscape is crucial to Lee's eco-rhetoric and a cunning way that she transgresses boundaries between human and nonhuman rapport.

In her attempts to describe the lives of nonhuman and environmental subjects in human terms, Lee frequently addresses the limits of language, noting that 'there is not even a single word or phrase to label' what she must, out of 'sheer despair,' call '*the lie of the land*: it is an unnamed mystery into which various things enter'.[74] This exercise, in describing the indescribable ecological subject, offers a lesson on the 'one-sidedness of language'[75] and the difficulty of finding 'reverent and tender enough expression for [places] in our practical personal language'.[76] Lee's writings demonstrate that although we cannot really speak another species' or entity's language, through observation and openness, we may learn something of it and devise cunning ways to circumvent barriers to rapport. Her eco-rhetoric thus hinges in part on her willingness to be affected by non-human energies, to give into 'the power of outdoor things, [and] their mysterious affinities, [which] can change the values even of what has been and what has not been' with 'the order of time and space . . . sometimes utterly subverted'.[77] Lee's sensuous eco-rhetoric is effective because it emphasises our imbrication within the messy, open ecologies of the world. Her physical engagements with the land seem to be a cunning way to experience nonhuman language and *vivify* her words, despite their limitations.

Lee's *technē* (an artful practice) for engaging across temporal, physical and categorical lines demonstrates her *mētis* and aligns her work with contemporary rhetorical criticism. Recently, rhetoricians have embraced *mētis* as an embodied intelligence and a rhetorical art capable of circumventing barriers between bodies and species. Metis was a shapeshifter with the ability to transform her body into animals, insects and elements, consumed by Zeus after she helped him trick Cronus and defeat the more powerful Titans. Other exemplars of *mētis* include animals like the sly fox and the polymorphic octopus, whose pliable body evokes 'a modality of response' and 'flexible, adaptive movement between things'.[78] Thus, *mētis*'s roots lie in human-animal exchanges, more-than-human subjectivities, the power of transformation, the ambiguity of identity and the transgressions of bodies, as in Zeus's consumption of Metis, who then lives on from inside his guts, advising him with her shrewd cunning. Recent rhetorical critics highlight the flexibility of *mētis* as a generative rhetorical concept that forms 'posthuman transrhetorical practices',[79] 'transgresses the boundaries separating the gods, humankind, and animals',[80] and ultimately helps 'human, animal and even technical bodies' move and work together.[81] Janet Atwill, for example, associates *mētis* with the 'indeterminacy of both subjects and objects' and the power to transgress the perceived boundaries between them.[82] Shannon Walters conceptualises *mētis* as 'an interspecies rhetoric' that both 'disturbs the traditional boundaries between humans and animals' and helps to redefine their 'kin relations'.[83] Because *mētis* is not unique to humans but an intelligence found in nonhumans and objects, engaging it (through sensation, for example) facilitates 'cooperation' and 'mediation' among diverse bodies and cognitive styles.[84] New materialist rhetoricians have extended *mētis*'s applications to include ecological entanglements between subjects and environments. These 'metistic rhetorics,' as William C. Trapani and Chandra A. Maldonado describe them, '[occur] in the middle space between actor and environment' and emphasise their entanglements, highlighting the porosity or fuzziness of the 'constitutions of human, animal, machine, the ecological, and their myriad combinations'.[85] *Mētistic* rhetorics showcase the inventional nature of nonhumans along with our susceptibility to their various energies, movements and dispositions.

Rather than suggest that we can save, fix or revitalise the environment as its special protectors or stewards, *mētistic* rhetorics like

Lee's highlight our entanglements with other creatures and environment, shifting from a view of humans separate from or above nature to one in which we recognise ourselves as participants in the 'agonistic composition of the world', those vulnerable interactions with 'other, wild objects', or 'outdoor things', 'capable of acting back in strange, sometimes threatening ways'.[86] To be clear, this is agonism rather than antagonism, a grappling with unpredictable and asymmetrical relations and not an animosity or hostility towards them. As intelligence, skill and rhetoric, *mētis* encourages us to be cunning, responsive and adaptive as we navigate 'the sensuous and agonistic terrain of our interdependency' with places and other creatures.[87] *Mētistic* rhetorics suggest that we need *more* and not *less* involvement with the more-than-human world, that we need to situate ourself as part of the material world in all its 'differential becomings' since we are all of the same substance, the same matter and the same vitality.[88] Thus, *mētistic* rhetorics are grounded in new materialist notions of interconnected human and nonhuman bodies, described by Jane Bennett as 'assemblages'. Drawing on Deleuze and Guattari's work, Bennett explains assemblages as 'living, throbbing confederations' of humans, nonhumans and things in which 'things' and nonhumans can 'act as quasi agents or forces with trajectories, propensities, or tendencies of their own' separate from human perceptions and beyond our control.[89] Lee's notions of 'vital . . . fluctuating . . . [and] potent' forces pulling humans, nonhumans and things into 'atomic affinity' gesture towards Bennett's view of assemblages, illustrating Bennett's suggestion that we 'shift from environmentalism to vital materialism' and thus 'a heterogeneous monism of vibrant bodies'.[90]

Through her *mētistic* blending and blurring of self and environment, Lee creates what Nathaniel Rivers describes as a strange environmental rhetoric, one that is uncanny, ambivalent, nonanthropocentric, contaminating and affective. Informed by new materialism and Object-Oriented Ontology, strange environmental rhetoric highlights the rhetorical power of nonhumans and environmental entities and encourages a position of 'deep ambivalence' in our relations to and representations of them. Ambivalence in this sense 'means equivalence or equivalency', a condition of 'contrary feeling-tones' simultaneously invested 'with both a positive and negative character'. In this 'oscillation of ambivalence', we might arrive at 'an attitude of equivalence' that acknowledges 'the rhetoricity of all being', not simply human being.[91] Deep ambivalence is 'neither the detachment of alienation nor the fantasy of decoding' the uncanny blends of the more-than-human world, but rather a type of 'coexistence' that is 'not reducible to one kind of relation or one source of causation'.[92] In Lee's terms, deep ambivalence highlights our affinities with the more-than-human world.

In acknowledging the consubstantial, co-constitutional and affective entanglements of humans, nonhumans, spirits, and environments, Lee offers a rhetorically powerful call to not simply appreciate or even protect nature, but to immerse ourselves in it and to give back to it as an active participant in our psychic, moral, and material lives, 'to pour a libation or hang up a garland in honour of the Genius Loci'.[93] Although she refers to this as a 'silly sentiment',[94] Lee's rapport with nature is one that is situated, adaptive, responsive and reciprocal and is thus something to be admired if not adopted. In construing the genius loci as an ecological subject, Lee presents a way to talk *to* rather than *about* Nature. Through writing like hers, we can learn to recognise what Tsing calls 'the tracks and traces of nonhumans'[95] and expand our view of rhetoric to include, as Rivers prompts, '*all* the ways we mark and are ourselves marked, bitten, or stung', including the 'discursive or non-discursive, human or nonhuman.'[96] Moreover, we can embrace an openness to non-normative, non-anthropocentric, and at times agonistic models of engagement, which may be classed under terms like Devin Griffiths and Deanna K. Kreisel's open ecology or Catriona Mortimer-Sandilands and Bruce Erickson's queer ecology.[97]

As such, Lee acknowledges that landscapes are agentic if not artful, using the means of persuasion and engagement available to them, and thus capable of exerting dispositional changes associated with rhetoric. She thus not only speaks elegantly about more-than-human or ecological subjects, but she also depicts their persuasive, communicative actions and how to engage them. Her concept of the genius loci reveals how rhetorical energy crosses temporalities and ontologies and thus gestures toward both post-anthropocentric and Gothic narrative styles.

Haunting More-than-Human Rhetoric

If rhetoric is indeed 'an energy existing in life' coded into 'subatomic particles,' as Kennedy claims and Lee illustrates, then it is an energy that extends beyond humans to include nonhumans, objects and matter along with its movements and entanglements more expansively. Perhaps rhetorical energy may also linger, leaving haunting traces to be read across time. Lee certainly thought so, as do myriad contemporary post-anthropocentric theorists, new materialists and eco-philosophers. In the overlapping domains of rhetorical criticism, anthropology and post-anthropocentric theory, spectral tropes have become popular means to represent excluded, marginalised and silenced nonhuman subjects and illuminate the forgotten ecological relations that haunt Man in the Anthropocene. The ghostly 'traces of more-than-human histories through which ecologies are made and unmade' form the 'haunted landscapes' of the Anthropocene.[98] Ghosts, revenants and hauntings remind us of our ancestral relations, like extinct creatures or 'the ghostly presence of ancestors inside us'[99] – our microbiomes and our cells inhabited by the ghostly traces of other cells. Species are interconnected and 'haunted' by other species:[100] we are all haunted.

Ghosts, spirits and spectres are not simply apt metaphors for the ghostly remains left in ancient forests, ruined spaces or our bodies; spectres remind us of our connections with other creatures. Tsing and peers argue that it is through attention to ghosts that we can learn to pay better attention to nonhuman lives and their living spaces, while Timothy Morton borrows from and amplifies Derrida's notion of 'spectrality' in his discussion of ecological thinking. For Morton, 'spectrality is the flavor of the symbiotic real',[101] the space that connects humans and nonhumans in the ecosphere. Morton says the 'symbiotic real' can be thought of as a 'spectral realm' in which all things are interconnected, making 'personhood . . . uncanny' as the self becomes not simply itself but also its 'spectral halo'.[102] Morton argues that 'To encounter an ecological entity is to be *haunted*' since 'we find ourselves obliged to think them not as alive or dead, but as spectral', which is to say ontologically 'ambiguous'.[103] Indeed, '*Spectrality is nonhumans*, including the "nonhuman" aspects of ourselves', and it is through spectres and the spectral that we might arrive at a more equitable exchange with more-than-humans, leading to what Morton describes as 'an ecocommunism, a communism of humans and nonhumans alike'.[104] Morton's characterisation of an ecocommunist spectral symbiotic real evokes Lee's sense of limbo and the 'fuzzy logic' of decolonialism and posthumanism. As biology and philosophy alike challenge the lines between 'life and nonlife', self and Other, mind and matter, human and nonhuman, 'we discover . . . that we coexist *with* and *as* ghosts, specters, zombies, undead beings and other ambiguous entities', a 'fuzzy' spectral realm that has been 'excluded from traditional Western logic'.[105] Thus, as Morton argues and Lee's writing suggests, 'To feel solidarity is to feel haunted'.[106]

Ghosts also attune us to nonlinear, non-western temporalities (Gothic temporalities, perhaps), reminding us that our present is a time 'haunted with the threat of extinction'.[107] Much like Lee, the editors of *Arts of Living on a Damaged Planet* prompt attention to the past to 'see the present more clearly', noting that 'Every landscape is haunted by past ways of life', by 'human and not human . . . "ghosts"', but also by '*imagined futures*'[108] – what possibilities we see for a space, such as a capitalist vision of development or a posthumanist dream of cohabitation. Tsing et al. emphasise that 'ladders are not the only kind of time';[109] ghosts and hauntings are another, one that offers a nonlinear temporality, what Lee might describe as an ongoing 'sense of the near presence . . . of the past . . . which looms all round'.[110] To counter Western humanist, capitalist and colonial narratives of the more-than-human world as separate, as inanimate and as inarticulate, we might, like Lee, allow our 'mind[s] to be swept along the dark and gleaming whirlpools of the past . . .',[111] 'extend our senses beyond their comfort zones'[112] and become open to eeriness and uncanniness of more-than-human rapport. Lee's writing demonstrates that *mētistic* tactics can be used to circumvent barriers to rapport, whether temporal, species or other.

While I would not suggest that Lee was writing Gothic tales when she was writing of the genius loci, I do find her depictions of the eery sentience of space and place interesting in the context of Gothic studies and the contemporary posthuman, new materialist and rhetorical quest to identify and develop the types of engagements that can cross temporal and taxonomic lines. Lee's rhetoric demonstrates the utility (or perhaps necessity) of Gothic tropes for engaging environmental affinities. In the final sections of this chapter, I discuss the ways that Gothic might facilitate greater ecological awareness.

Gothic Environmentalism

Despite its lengthy history as a study of human communication, rhetorical criticism has recently taken a post-anthropocentric and ecological turn, searching for insights into nonhuman and more-than-human forms of semiosis, engagement and rapport, which may include objects, animals, trees, plants and fungi, as well as more expansive forms, like landscapes, ecologies and environment. George Kennedy's work on general rhetoric and rhetorical energy has laid a foundation for this work as has the rhetorical recovery of *mētis*. Similar calls to unsettle anthropocentric and androcentric understandings of language, communication and rhetoric have emerged in adjacent fields like environmental communication studies, environmental criticism, eco-linguistics and eco-critical CDS. Within the interdisciplinary field of environmental communication studies, for example, questions are emerging over how to challenge the persistent nature/culture binary underlying Western thought and develop a 'more-than-human rhetoric' that extends rhetorical criticism beyond humanist dualisms and perspectives. Environmental criticism's turn towards 'more-than-human rhetoric' includes the rhetoric of coyote scat, Tilikim the captive orca, cookery, prairie wildflowers and earthquakes.[113] Along with the quest to develop more-than-human rhetoric, environmental communication studies has also turned to promoting darkness, uncanniness, toxicity, contamination, melodrama and ambivalence[114] to exhibit and engage an animistic world filled with selves existing beyond the human. In what follows, I situate the Gothic in this context.

As a mode preoccupied with the uncanny sentience of space and place, the ineffable more-than-human-world and 'the fringes, the unspoken, the peripheral, and the cast aside',[115] Gothic is well suited to articulate more-than-human encounters as well as facilitate the desired development of environmental criticism noted above. As Jeffrey Andrew Weinstock argues, the Gothic stages 'a peculiar sort of enchanted world . . . in which the line between subject and object becomes muddled and obscure' in a way that chastises 'human hubris' and upbraids its 'egotism'.[116] Weinstock gestures towards Gothic's potential to offer a lexis not only of fear, anxiety, terror and horror, but also a lexis of enchantment, estrangement and wonder that can be used to develop the 'more-than-human rhetoric' currently sought after from environmental criticism. The Gothic mode can generate 'curiosity' along with 'disgust',[117] which seems not only beneficial for narrating the lives of nonhumans, but also for unsettling some of the well-ingrained anthropocentrism plaguing humankind. Although its transgressive potential remains contextual and debated, Gothic is known to explore the margins and to question (perhaps even rupture) binaries, making it a good fit for the 'interrogation of the nature/culture dualism'[118] and to 'unearth' the 'marvelous' ways in which the environment delights, confounds and horrifies.[119]

The Gothic provides language, thematics and strategies that may aid in these critical and communicative endeavours. Considering the Gothic's engagement with enchanted and ruinous landscapes, temporal dissonance and revisitation, 'ontological confusion'[120] and its capacity for unsettlement[121] and revival,[122] the Gothic mode seems apt for environmental criticism, offering possibilities to transgress and unsettle boundaries, articulate a nonhuman perspective and stimulate an influential affect for environmental advocacy. Firstly, as a 'multimodal . . . transmedial'[123] and interdiscursive form, Gothic aptly accommodates science and theory to new contexts. A rich history of Gothic scholarship reveals the mode's capacity to infect other texts, genres, mediums and discourses, creating all manner of Gothic and Gothic-inflected hybrid forms. Gothic – through its mutable, infectious elements along with its popularity and ubiquity – accommodates,[124] that is translates, symbols, motifs, ideas and/or theories from texts to other texts, mediums and discourses. This is observable with psychology discourse, as discussed in Chapter 3, or as discussed in Chapter 4, in microbiology discourse – where one may find myriad Gothic-inflected accommodations amplifying the nonhumanity of the human, the uncanniness of the human body, the haunting nature of microbial traces and/or the vampiric, ghostly and monstrous nature of microbes. Discourses on ecology and the Anthropocene have also followed suit. The editors of *Arts of Living on a Damaged Planet* offer ghosts and monsters as 'two points of departure for characters, agencies, and stories that challenge the double conceit of modern Man', countering myths of 'Progress' and 'the conceit of the Individual'. Ghosts and monsters 'unsettle' Man 'by highlighting the webs of histories and bodies from which all life, including human life, emerges'.[125] These accommodations reveal Gothic's utility to stimulate readerly engagement outside of fiction.

One avenue for a Gothic environmentalism is to amplify the use of tropes like haunting, monstrosity and the uncanny in popularisations and criticism. Dorion Sagan's popular science writing is one example as is Timothy Morton's eco-philosophy, which has a notable Gothic flair in its use of tropes related to darkness, the uncanny, the spectral and the sublime.[126] Moreover, Gothic's interdiscursivity may facilitate a productive translation of temporal dissonance into other discursive contexts. Most simply, interdiscursivity (a concept from Critical Discourse Studies) signifies that discourses are open and often hybrid, linked in various ways so that one discourse subsumes or absorbs elements of others; further to this, interdiscursivity allows for recontextualisation, a process whereby elements of one discourse are incorporated into or appropriated by other discourses to generate new strategies for audience engagement.[127] Recontextualisation may create a discursive space for 'imaginaries,' or possible futures, to emerge.[128] Tsing et al. suggest that along with their legacies, '*Anthropogenic landscapes are also haunted by imagined futures*'.[129] A case can be made that despite Gothic's fundamental association with 'legacies of the past',[130] there is also a future-thinking tendency in many works, perhaps especially contemporary eco-Gothic texts, with their commentary on sustainability and application of various Indigenous worldviews,[131] which are themselves often future-thinking through the 'legacies of the past'. For example, Tewa scientist Gregory Cajete's work on native science and native ecologies encourages a view of past, present and future as interconnected, suggesting that turning back to Indigenous ways of being in the world, we can look forward to craft sustainable futures. In this model, not only is past, present and future interconnected, but humans and environment are interconnected in 'a tapestry of relationships that [has] feeling and soul'.[132] Situating ourselves in the more-than-human world as part of it, rather than above it, immerses us in cosmic rhythms and attunes us to dispositional changes.

Gothic affects may also aid in environmental criticism and environmental advocacy. Environmental communication studies has long engaged the question of how to communicate environmental damage and risk to the public in ways that will not only lead to understanding and acceptance, but will modify attitudes and actions (i.e., how to promote saliency). While studies of apocalyptic rhetoric and catastrophe narratives have often challenged the utility of doom, gloom and apocalypse in motiving the public to adapt more sustainable attitudes and habits, more recent research suggests that 'negative emotion' can more greatly impel the public 'to get involved in climate change discussion'.[133] To that end, contemporary theories of the 'toxic sublime' and 'environmental melodrama',[134] for example, suggest that a degree of paradox, discomfort, terror and perhaps even outright horror at environmental degradation and our role within it are exactly what the public need to question their attitudes and alter their behaviours. Morton claims that 'Not all of us are ready to feel sufficiently creeped out' by the Anthropocene and the ecological destruction industrial humans have wrought.[135] If Gothic affect 'hinges on the human self-preservation instinct' to 'scare, disturb, or disgust' us, as Xavier Aldana Reyes suggests,[136] then it seems that the Gothic mode may be useful to simultaneously (and paradoxically) tap into our anthropocentrism while making it horrific.

I believe that just as the Gothic provides a fictional space to dramatise philosophy and science poignantly and to articulate an ecological subjectivity, it also offers a powerful lexis and affect that has, can and should be embraced by environmental critics looking to enliven their field with nonhuman, magical and at times horrific narratives. This is not to endorse narratives of apocalypse or catastrophe, which can immobilise critics and publics, but to suggest that a degree of discomfort, unease, perhaps even terror and horror can productively recalibrate reader perspectives and audience engagements. Perhaps a Gothic-*mētistic* rhetoric is what environmental criticism is seeking. Reading Gothic may also be a tactic for developing ecological or post-anthropocentric sensitivity. Morton argues that 'one's "inner space" is a test tube for imagining' ecological subjects and for thus developing an 'ecological awareness' grounded in 'coexisting'. Much 'like a quaking peasant with a string of garlic, warding off the vampires',[137] we can perhaps ward off anthropocentric attitudes. The horror attached to some Gothic depictions of human and more-than-human entanglements 'need not close off the possibility that . . . readers would negotiate their own subjectivity and elements of alterity' with an openness to diversity.[138] Put a little differently, what is horror to some 'is the very opening of the world to others'.[139]

Encountering narratives of the cunning monstrosities revealed by Gothic *mētis* seems especially useful. The *polyplokos*, *polytropos*, porous and polymorphic beings and narratives covered through the lenses of Gothic *mētis* offer the bridge between self/Other, human/nonhuman, inside/outside, nature/culture, etc. needed to generate respect for nonhumans and environment and to challenge our persistent humanist assumptions about self, species and space. There is a lingering, affective, perhaps *contaminating*, quality to reading Gothic. Gothic readers may experience 'material effects in the post-structural sense of re-negotiating signifying systems and relations of difference and otherness in the world'.[140] Contemporary Gothic readers, like classic Gothic subjects, find themselves fragmented, discontinuous in identity, porous and subject to a reality in which matter is alive, purposive and responsive. Thus, they seem well poised to glean posthuman, post-anthropocentric insights from tales of cunning monstrosity.

Gothic is Always Already Eco[141]

As a genre that 'seeks to express the inexpressibly more-than-human' world,[142] Gothic clearly has something to say about nonhuman and more-than-human rhetoric that may be valuable to critics and readers alike. Conversely, in its turn to the posthuman, post-anthropocentric and ecological, rhetorical theory offers fresh perspectives on eco-Gothic and Gothic more generally. In this final section, I want to comment briefly on how Gothic scholars might apply rhetorical theory to Gothic studies and with this, to explore Jodey Castricano's claim that Gothic is always already eco.

Eco-Gothic has emerged as a popular topic in recent years in Gothic studies. Eco-Gothic (along with eco-horror) primarily explores Gothic's representations of the more-than-human world, often coded as 'Nature'. Andrew Smith and William Hughes define eco-Gothic as 'an ecologically aware Gothic' and link it to other modes of ecocriticism, claiming that 'Gothic seems' well-suited to express 'anxieties' about climate change, environmental degradation and species loss.[143] David Del Principe suggests that eco-Gothic offers 'a nonanthropocentric position' that highlights the agency of 'the environment, species, and nonhumans' while '[giving] voice to ingrained biases and a mounting ecophobia' related to 'humans' precarious relationship with all that is nonhuman'.[144] Del Principe posits that eco-Gothic may offer a 'more inclusive lens' through which to view the 'Gothic body' and its 'unhuman, nonhuman, transhuman, posthuman, or hybrid' nature and thus, human-nonhuman-environmental interconnections. Dawn Keetley and Matthew Sivils explain that 'the ecogothic is a literary mode at the intersection of environmental writing and the gothic' that often blends an 'ecocritical lens' with 'ecophobia', defined as the 'contempt and fear we feel for the agency of the natural environment'.[145] In most cases, Gothic's linkage to ecology is based in fear, unease, anxiety, contempt, terror or horror.

Working with rhetorical criticism, it is possible to add new nuance to ongoing conversations about Gothic's relationship to ecocriticism. For example, Smith and Hughes claim that the eco-Gothic presents the environment as 'a semiotic problem' and 'a space of crisis which conceptually creates a point of contact with the ecological'.[146] Rhetorical criticism reveals that although we may associate semiotics with human representation, 'Nonhuman life-forms also represent the world'.[147] Anthropologist Eduardo Kohn, working with nineteenth-century philosopher Charles Peirce's theory of semiotics, claims that 'Life is constitutively semiotic. That is, life is, through and through, the product of sign processes' or 'the creation and interpretation of signs'; even more than materiality, semiotics binds all forms of life.[148] Thus, 'All life is semiotic and all semiosis is alive',[149] and it is 'through our partially shared semiotic propensities that multispecies relations are possible, and also analytically comprehensible'.[150] From this perspective, a semiotic problem becomes a communicative opportunity, an opportunity for more-than-human rapport. Moreover, rhetorical theory confirms crisis as a 'point of contact with the ecological', as Smith and Hughes suggest. In rhetoric, a crisis can become a *krisis*, pointing to the concept of *kairos* as nonlinear time and timely rhetoric, with *kairos* often meaning the right time and the right measure. *Kairos* is also 'krisis': 'a deciding, a judgment', which calls 'into question' both 'our future survival' and 'our comportment toward nature in general'.[151] *Krisis* is thus not simply 'a problem to be solved, but a kairotic opening through which we shape the world to come'.[152] Rhetorical criticism can therefore reframe the semiotic problems of nature addressed in eco-Gothic so that the semiotic is an interspecies communicative space and crisis becomes *krisis*, or a kairotic opportunity transforming attitudes and practices. Gothic reveals that nature is not indifferent, but ambivalent – a space of contradictory impulses, asymmetry and limbo if not equivalence: 'to feel ambivalent is to be equivalent'.[153] Or perhaps, to return to Morton and Lee, to feel ambivalent is to feel solidarity, which is to 'feel haunted'.

Although not Gothic per se, Lee's essays on haunted houses, animate environments and ecological spirits illuminate Gothic's utility in the Anthropocene – our time of multispecies living, dying and haunting. While critics tend to frame Gothic's ecological and atmospheric sensitivity as 'eco-Gothic', following Castricano I take Gothic more generally to be already and always ecological, that is sensitive to the sentience of space and place and the affective exchanges between porous, plural selves and their symbiotic Others. For Castricano, Gothic might be 'unsettling because it posits the sentience of space and place, of non-human agency' and thus counters humanist framings of *nature* as passive, inert, inanimate and somehow 'separate' from the human.[154] Because of Gothic's ties to animism, Castricano suggests that it should be considered a genre which 'seeks to express the inexpressibly more-than-human',[155] a point with which I firmly agree. Gothic tropes like the uncanny, the abject, the spectral or the eery seem to provide means to describe and engage an inexpressibly animate Earth, with a self and agency beyond human understanding, management or control. Lee was painfully aware of what she described as the 'one-sidedness of language'[156] and the difficulty of finding 'reverent and tender enough expression for [the sentience of place] in our practical personal language',[157] which led her to concepts like the genius loci and a fascination with the supernatural, ghosts and haunting. Just as Lee turned to spirits, so should we.

Postscript: Gothic Poros

'We live in Gothic times.'

Angela Carter[1]

The early twenty-first century mood is one of uncertainty. Many of us are aware that we are living in the Anthropocene, and this awareness prompts serious consideration about who we are and who we should become. Much like the end of the nineteenth century, we find ourselves betwixt and between eras as 'One epoch of history is unmistakably in its decline, and another is announcing its approach'.[2] As we rend outdated traditions and dethrone 'views that have hitherto governed minds', it seems that 'all certainty is destroyed' and that 'forms [have lost] their outlines . . . dissolved in floating mist'.[3] Perhaps the greatest form we have lost is that of an exceptional, unified human and with this, the certainty that the world can be categorised into units of mind and matter, human and nonhuman or self and Other. At times, 'we seem to be drifting to some terrible doom'[4] as the 'shadows creep with deepening gloom, wrapping all objects in a mysterious dimness'.[5] But what is 'horror for some' is 'the very opening of the world for others'.[6] The loss of human exceptionality is an invitation to embrace posthuman interdependencies. As we unseat Man from his apex, new opportunities for self, for kinship and for rapport emerge. Drawing on the ideas mapped out in this study, I offer some final thoughts on how Gothic

+ *mētis* can help steer us through the shifting, uncertain times of the Anthropocene. To probe these pathways, I reflect on *mētis* as a skill of navigators and a tactic of transcultural, posthuman rapport.

Mētis is a cunning embodied intelligence well situated for the present. A networked intelligence of interlacing opposites and mode of continuous becoming, *mētis* equips those who possess it with a flexibility that allows them to be more fluid, more shifting than the fluid, shifting situations around them. *Mētis* is a posthuman alternative politics to Platonic Truth or Aristotelian binary logic, one that rests on matrices and divergence and does not keep what it wins. It is aligned with trickster logic and in affinity with Indigenous and ecological thought. *Mētis*'s matrixed, networked tentacular nature makes it of value in the decolonial quest to craft 'fuzzy logics' and posthuman ethics grounded in knowledge of symbiosis and symbiogenesis. The polyplokos (rhizomatic and complex) nature of our very bodies and minds (extending as they do along our gut-brain axis) entangles us into more-than-human webs, prompting us to expand our parameters of self and redefine subjectivity. Such views of a body enmeshed in nature is the foundation for many posthuman, post-anthropocentric and new materialists calls to ethics, prompting us to extend kinship beyond human communities to include the myriad more-than-human and nonhuman communities we depend on. That nothing is truly stagnant, stable or pure is an invitation to be artfully malleable, constructing subjectivity and relations along lateral rather than linear lines, through rhizomes rather than hierarchies. Significantly, *mētis* has been hidden in the belly of dominant Western patriarchal and colonial thinking. In turning back to the Metis myths and the tales of cunning that run adjacent to them, I hope to have uncovered one path to decolonial, post-anthropocentric praxis (a path that turns our attention back into ourselves). Metis and her *mētis* are associated with foresight or forward thinking, but not necessarily along lines of progress or teleology; rather, *mētis* moves laterally, connecting past with present and future, just as it combines self with other, inside with outside, masculine with feminine, human with nonhuman.

Mētis is a skill of navigators and helmspersons that helps them to plot routes and take 'cunning account of the unpredictability and instability of the waves', winds and weather.[7] Treacherous, shifting and uncertain contexts and spaces can be described as 'the póntos'. In Greek traditions, *pontos* 'means the great, unknown open sea, . . . where the shores are lost to view', especially when 'the sky and the water . . . become indistinguishable' as 'a single, dark, indistinct mass' with 'no point of reference to help one find one's way out'.[8] *Pontos* is 'a disturbing and mysterious space' in which paths are 'constantly obliterated', becoming 'closed as soon as [they] open'. *Pontos*'s counterpart is 'poros', meaning a 'route or path that the navigator has to open up through the pontós'.[9] Marcel Detienne and Jean-Pierre Vernant illustrate 'the interplay between Pontos and Poros'[10] through accounts of Odysseus or the Argonauts 'steering their way through the Clashing Rocks or the Black Rocks' and navigating areas in the sea where 'moving rocks rear up, constantly shifting both sideways and up and down'. When she wants to save Odysseus from the treacherous sea, Athena intervenes with her *mētis* to calm the winds and '[open] a route for him, indicating a poros which is both a solution and a way out'.[11] The Anthropocene is our current *pontos*, 'a disturbing and mysterious space' we must navigate with few clear directions or pathways to chart our course. As Detienne and Vernant explain it, 'in the most concrete sense *póros* means a path, passage or ford'; in an intellectual sense, *poros* 'means a stratagem, the expedient which the cunning . . . can devise in order to escape from an *aporía*'.[12] In certain traditions, *poros* 'is closely connected with *technē*' or artfulness.[13] *Poros* is also the root for porous, reminding us of the pathways or openings between our bodies, other bodies and the world around us. Playing with *poros*, I suggest new directions for studies of Gothic *mētis*. In doing so, I wish to remind readers that *mētis* is not the foundation for a new order of scholarship, but rather, a cunning way to divert from the norms and embrace the plural and polymorphic. True to its history and perhaps its power (to be incorporated within yet remain undigested by dominant orders), *mētis* is at times explicit and at times subtle in the suggestions that follow.

Gothic Métissage

Associated with the circular, the twisted and the curved, *mētis* inspires nonlinear and transgressive practices that blend and blur times, species, genres, cultures and traditions; *mētis* helps us to veer, twist, braid, pervert and subvert, as does the practice of *métissage* it informs. In *métissage*, a writer may mix and blend various languages, genres, myths, styles and traditions, sometimes to honour them, sometimes to challenge them and sometimes to extend them. Gothic itself might be a *métissage*; in its original form, it was a blend of the ancient and the modern, the romance and the novel, the conservative and the liberal, the English and the German. Since its original eighteenth-century emergence in England, Gothic has continued to blend, blur, twist, pervert and transform through its contact with various times and places. If Gothic emerged as a hodgepodge of disparate forms, discourses and sentiments, it has only continued to mutate into more hybrid, discordant forms. Today, one may find Gothic in all manner of places, in all manner of forms, and in all manner of cultural traditions. As Michelle Burnham sums up, 'a variety of nations, ethnicities, regions, and communities . . . have . . . adopted . . . [and] also transformed the genre and its conventions', leading to the creation of myriad *Gothics*, which includes Irish, Canadian, French, Southern, feminist and Indigenous, to name a few.[14] In each context, Gothic might be said to emerge as a unique form, reminiscent of or directly responding to earlier Gothic texts and traditions yet imprinted with the languages, histories, myths and cultures of the writers who have adapted it. Through a process of '*transculturation*', non-English writers, including (or perhaps especially) the formally colonised, can 'select and invent from materials transmitted by a dominant culture' and repurpose them, sometimes to subversive ends. Gothic has always offered such a 'contact zone' in which writers can 'grapple with', blend, blur and subvert genres, discourses and modes.[15] Such 'contact zones', as Mary Louise Pratt calls them, can be transformational spaces, geared especially towards crafting the kind of 'fuzzy thinking' or 'fuzzy logic' associated with decolonial efforts.[16]

While a study of intercultural or Indigenous Gothic is beyond the scope of this postscript, I would like to briefly outline an example of Indigenous Gothic *métissage* working with Canadian writer, Eden Robinson's fiction. Robinson is a coastal First Nations author from Kitamaat, British Columbia and a member of the Haisla and Heiltsuk First Nations. Her works like *Monkey Beach* (2009) and her more current trickster series[17] braid Gothic tropes into Indigenous mythology. Ghosts, monsters, ancestral spirits, sasquatch and tricksters like Weegit are just some of the common characters across Robinson's works, which probe serious issues like intergenerational trauma, lost languages and cultures from colonialism, the harmful legacies of the Canadian residential school system (and its genocide of Canadian First Nation and Métis cultures), sexual abuse and assault, addiction, racism, violence and death alongside more playful topics like Elvis and weed cookies. Temporal dissonance is common across Robinson's works, which tend to jump from past and present and from the everyday world to various spirit realms in which time and reality are stretched to their limits. For example, *Monkey Beach* illustrates the tensions between dominant colonial and Indigenous ways of knowing, the tensions between past and present (and the differing versions of each we might encounter depending on who is telling the story), as well as generational tensions, more specifically, the loss of languages and traditions in newer generations. The protagonist, Lisa Marie, experiences visions and dreams that land her in therapy, but her Grandma, Ma-ma-oo, treats them as a powerful gift given to Lisa by her ancestors. These tensions between various cultural interpretations of ghosts and spirits have both excited and challenged Gothic scholars, who have questioned the utility, efficacy and ethics of reading First Nations' literature using methods derived from Euro-Canadian cultural and literary frameworks.[18] However, as Michelle Burnham suggests, by limiting our understanding of Gothic to a European phenomenon, we limit our perceptions of what Gothic might mean.[19] *Métissage* emphasises the porosity of cultures and traditions, yet shows how they can remain distinctive, a hybridising practice that takes readers into the liminal, into the contact zone and the space of fuzzy logic.

A mode of revivals and recursions, Gothic might also be a mode of reconciliation. Reconciliation engages my thinking as a Canadian scholar who has conducted the work for this book on Blackfoot Confederacy Territory, who grew up in the land of the Six Nations of the Grand River and who spent many formative years as a graduate student on the unceded land of the Okanagan Nation. These lands have nourished my body as they have nourished my spirit, bringing me into rapport with past, present and future, dominant

Canadian and First Nations' cultures and literatures and the myriad more-than-human subjects who connect these domains. If Gothic can attune us to a fuzzy logic of past/present, subject/object, self/Other and mind/matter breakdowns, then perhaps it can also attune us to Indigenous perspectives, like those of Canadian First Nations, Métis and Inuit peoples, who encourage respect for relations, which might be past, present or future and encompass both human and nonhuman kindred. As Betty Bastien shares in *Blackfoot Ways of Knowing: The Worldview of the Siksikaitsitapi*, 'the fundamental premise of *Niitsitapi* ways of knowing is that all forms of creation possess consciousness'; the separation of 'nature and humans' is a Eurocentric worldview that obscures our alliances with, responsibilities towards and abilities to communicate with the 'cosmic forces' we depend on.[20] As Jodey Castricano argues in relation to *Monkey Beach* and in broader relation to Canadian Indigenous theories, stories like Robinson's demonstrate a generative 'collision between Indigenous thought and Western psychology', one that unsettles Eurocentric thinking about consciousness as restricted to human brains and encourages a greater appreciation of *all* our relations, whether they be past or present, human or non.[21] From its beginnings and especially in the Anthropocene, Gothic has 'ensured that we do not forget that we live in a sentient world',[22] a reminder that seems to resonate with increased efforts to decolonise and Indigenise thinking and education in Canada.

Writers like Robinson, who blend, blur and braid genres and traditions to generate new modes of thinking and relating, act like tricksters, those mythic beings of *mētis*. Liminal beings, tricksters can navigate liminal spaces, such as the contact zones between cultures and the rending of old traditions. The trickster creates one pathway outside of the colonial logic and anthropocentric attitudes that steered us into the Anthropocene. Neither good nor bad, human nor nonhuman, tricksters are not defined by categories or bound by limits. Tricksters are creative destroyers. As they unsettle the old, the often generate the new. They emerge from chaos and can navigate the *pontos*, shifting with its shifting tides as they shapeshift into fluid forms. As Gregory Cajete prompts, tricksters remind us 'to take responsibility' for attitudes and behaviours, not taking the 'easy route' out of the chaos they create.[23] The trickster 'personifies the process of change' as well as creativity and spontaneity and 'ties together the worlds of nature, gods and humans'.[24] Donna Haraway popularised the trickster Coyote as a model for feminist theory,[25] an icon for human relationships with the more-than-human world and ultimately a useful figure for rendering the Earth as a 'trickster with whom we must learn to converse'.[26] Neither for us nor against us, the Earth is perhaps ambivalent. Yet, if we cannot find our 'equivalency'[27] with Earth, it is sure to spell our demise.

Talking with Ravens and Crows

Monkey Beach opens to Lisa waking from a dream with crows talking to her possibly in Haisla: '*La' es* – Go down to the bottom of the ocean'.[28] She wonders if this is a cryptic message from the spirit world or merely her tired brain waking from dreams. Her mother suggests that maybe it is a sign Lisa 'needs Prozac', but Lisa senses that the crows 'were talking' to her even if she did not know 'what the crows are trying to say'.[29] Lisa and her family are searching for her brother, Jimmy, who has been lost at sea. She begins experiencing dreams and visions that prompt her to go to Monkey Beach, a home to b'gwus (Sasquatch) and the possible location of her brother. The crows appear to presage Lisa's visions and perhaps guide her through liminal spaces, such as those between the land of the living and 'the land of the dead'.[30] Their calls often preface contact with nonhuman forces, culminating at the end of the novel, where Lisa crosses into a spiritual realm where she communes with past relations, like her Ma-ma-oo. As she crosses between these realms, Monkey Beach is lined with 'crows, as far as the eye can see', flying 'in circles' as they 'swoop and dive and turn'; ultimately, Lisa '[realizes] they were dancing'.[31] Not only guides between realms, the crows are also guides to an animate more-than-world. After Ma-ma-oo advises him, Jimmy begins feeding crows for good luck in his swimming competitions, which they seem to bring.[32] He marvels at their intelligence throughout the novel, '[rambling] on about the virtues of the biggest brained member of the Corvidae family',[33] which also includes ravens, magpies and jays.

Crows and their corvid cousins, ravens, are one of the most popular trickster figures in Native American Indigenous mythology. Weegit, 'the cheeky, shape-changing raven'[34] trickster of Northwest Coast mythology, appears in several of Robinson's works. Weegit is said to have created 'the world and humans', but only 'out of boredom', claiming to steal 'the sun and the moon . . . to bring light to humankind' although it is apparent 'he did it so it would be easier for him to find food'.[35] Although the story of Weegit illustrates the duality of the trickster, who sometimes creates new worlds by accident or out of boredom, it also illustrates how humans have been communing with corvids for generations, with food-sharing one of our primary mechanisms. Raymond Pierotti recounts an Apache story about ravens, who led the People to food and then advised them 'It is our way to share what we have with others'. One large raven tells them, 'There will come a time . . . when our peoples will not speak directly to one another', but even if '*We will have different languages, different homes*', we will remain united by hunger for 'that is the way of beings on this Earth'. The raven prompts the Apache, to 'not ignore' their children, for 'they have come to invite you to a feast'.[36] This story demonstrates how Indigenous peoples '[learned] how to communicate with nonhumans by understanding nonhuman forms of communication'.[37] Ravens are known to work with both humans and wolves to help them acquire food and in turn, acquire food for themselves. As Betty Coon Wheelwright explains, these clever omnivores have learned to partner with mammals, like humans and wolves, whose 'teeth, claws, or tools' can 'open large mammals' for ravens to eat, and to reciprocate, the raven uses its aerial advantage to see prey and signal their locations.[38] Pierotti posits that 'this cooperative relationship with both humans and wolves' together with ravens' 'high intelligence' is the foundation for 'the respect shown to Ravens by Indigenous peoples'.[39]

Tricksters, companions, creators and guides, corvids have become a pervasive mythic figure in many human cultures.[40] Myths about them 'convey important information' regarding humans' relationships with nonhumans.[41] Studies of crows have revealed them to be some of the most intelligent, social birds (if not creatures), capable of interspecies friendship, tool use, problem-solving, facial recognition and even recursion, a crucial element of language enabling sentence building.[42] Wheelwright highlights that 'Ravens are individuals' with a striking, perhaps 'uncanny', 'capacity to form a relationship with humans'. Because they are so intelligent and so capable, corvids 'challenge many common assumptions about the superiority and uniqueness of the human species'.[43] It might seem like 'anthropomorphizing', but anyone who has spent enough time with corvids knows that 'humans have more in common with [them] than most of us ever imagine', and our friendships with them can '[remind] us where we began', in resonance with the more-than-human world.[44]

There is, of course, a Gothic history of talking with corvids, even if it has been framed as madness. Edgar Allan Poe's 'The Raven' (1845) equates the 'ungainly [fowl's] . . . discourse' with mimicry, evil and the devil.[45] Yet, the raven remains interlocutor and 'prophet', delivering some important message to the narrator and readers. Said to be of the 'days of yore',[46] the raven might represent an animate world reaching out to modern humans, who have been convinced that talking with birds is insane. For me, corvids are an important guide through the *pontos* of the Anthropocene, countering the denial of more-than-human sentience that led to it. To aid the Argonauts through the Black Rocks, Metis's daughter Athena 'sends them a bird' as a guide, described as a 'sea crow'. Athena herself is described as a sea crow and may occasionally take the form of a bird.[47] Exactly what kind of bird a sea crow is remains unclear. Although 'ancient naturalists, ornithologists and lexicographers' left records of the 'essential characteristics' of the sea crow, 'positive identification' is not possible,[48] with best guesses naming cormorants, gulls, grebes, puffins or jackdaws. Much like the bird-man-god, Weegit, 'The sea-crow' functions 'as an intermediary at the centre of a triangle of elements – the earth, the water and the air'.[49] Corvids are thus apt navigators for liminal spaces.

Although crows are not included in the list of birds mentioned in Detienne and Vernant's study of *mētis*, I believe that these crafty creatures embody this cunning, adaptive intelligence. I personally have befriended a family of crows, and through this friendship, I have learned arts of noticing and skills for transspecies rapport. For approximately seven years, two American crows (*Corvus brachyrhynchos*), named Brandon and Brenda, have come to visit my home every day, and each summer, they have brought their newly fledged babies to meet me and my husband (even our cat). At crucial times of this writing process, my crows have brought me gifts and with these, important messages. My personal favourite gift has been a small silver earring (a circle for *mētis*) complete with a heart and feather (the only thing better might have been a small bust of Poe).

Brandon came to us last fall to spend his final day. We could tell he was unwell: he was lethargic and barely eating. He sat in his favourite tree in front of the house all day. The next morning, I saw his lifeless body on the ground. I held him and wept. There was something magical about holding him, putting his little claws around our fingers and seeing just how old he must have been. His legs were thick and gruff with years of use, years of life – clutching food and bringing us gifts we will always cherish. We buried him beneath his favourite tree, the tree he had sat in for approximately seven years, often with Brenda, and every summer and fall with his annual brood. Next to his shrouded body, we placed peanuts and shiny trinkets he would have loved, including an enamel butterfly reminiscent of the one he brought me a few months prior. It was a few days before I could accept it was really him. Day after day, I watched the sky, hoping he would arrive. But soon it was clear it was Brandon, and we had to say goodbye. Brenda sat each morning in their favourite tree for several days, but she did not come to eat. She was mourning her partner, and we felt it alongside her. She seems to have a new partner (I've named him Beau) whom she now brings for her daily visits. On several occasions, she has accompanied me on walks, flying above me or following me home. About a week after we buried Brandon, I believe she brought us a gift: a small silver magnet in the shape of a T (which I have taken for Tasha and Thank You). It is difficult to express my love for these birds and my appreciation for the unique friendship they bring. Being in their company, the company of crows, I am more certain than ever that more-than-human interspecies friendships are not simply possible but necessary.

I believe that growing up reading Gothic works like Poe's, Lovecraft's and Machen's helped convince me to see a lively world of nonhuman subjects and agentic matter even from a young age. Reading Gothic has been a catalyst for expanding my sense of self, reality and ethics. The enchanted world of Gothic was a prompt to see the enchantment in my own world. I believe that reading Gothic can facilitate these changes in other contemporary readers, for whom more-than-human sentience and interspecies connections are joyous, not madness. While personal gnosis and unsupported testament rarely hold weight in academia, in a move – a veer, twist, swerve or perversion – away from the scholarly norm, I offer my experience as a Gothic birder to suggest an overlap between reading Gothic and communing with nature. What might be 'horror to some' is 'the very opening of the world for others'.[50]

Closing Lines on Liminal Times

Liminal times might be Gothic times, as Angela Carter famously called our present transformational moment. Gothic times require Gothic time: haunting reminders of the Past in the Present, including the Other in the self, and a hauntological sensitivity to futures not yet manifested. Posthuman critics remind us that 'ladders are not the only kind of time':[51] ghosts may be another. Turning to the past with an eye to the future might be one way to generate a posthuman, post-anthropocentric ethics. Moving backwards while looking forwards reminds us that the past is ever present, that the future is entwined with present and past and that our relations extend beyond our own moment or culture to include those before and after. A nonlinear model of time resists the humanist telos of human perfectibility and undermines associated dreams of unending advancing *Progress*. This temporal blurring is meant to reflect the intricacies of posthuman timescales, Gothic vision and North American Indigenous models of time, which are often cyclical rather than linear.[52] Circular or cyclical worldviews see all events as connected, regardless of when the event occurs, and with this, encourage a view that sees the interconnections between all beings. With such a view, we can extend the parameters of our relations and refine the nature of our relationships. Nonlinear or circular timescales may challenge European conceptions of past and present as distinctive categories, and with this, hierarchical views of life as one of progress from simple to complex. For posthumanists, largely following from Deleuze and Guattari, 'there is no linear time, but a thousand plateaus of possible becomings, each following its own multidirectional course'.[53] As Anna Tsing and peers argue in *Arts of Living on a Damaged Planet*, each present is haunted by both its pasts and its futures, its many possible lines of becoming.

Working with Gothic, known for temporal dissonance and a blend of the ancient and the modern, and the practice of *métissage*, known to blend and blur genres and traditions, I have suggested that looking to classics and the nineteenth century holds promise for understanding the present and orienting us towards a posthuman future. I have turned back to classics and the nineteenth century because I believe that these time-places hold important knowledge for us to consider in the present as we navigate liminality and embark on a pursuit to decolonise our thinking, writing and teaching. As David Punter has recently suggested, Gothic 'is about history', but it might also 'be about the future, about the various trajectories along which we might see ourselves evolving'.[54] In linking *mētis* with Gothic – the 'password' to inhuman, nonhuman and more-than-human worlds – my hope has been to illuminate their shared domain of posthuman, post-anthropocentric subjectivities and sentiments, which seem to be the right tenor for the present. Late nineteenth-century Gothic especially showcases a heightened sensitivity to the networked nature of body, mind, time, space and species, portraying the entanglements of mind, matter and environment sensationally yet sincerely. From a rhetorical perspective, we can read it in terms of *krisis*: a timely, wily response to emergent ecological subjects. Ecological subjects are multiplex, polymorphic and porous (in fact, monstrous); with the cunning of an octopus, they develop plural, flexible body-minds. Rather than repress or suppress their innate multiplicity or nonhumanity, ecological subjects embrace it to align themselves with the shifting, shimmering and ultimately porous more-than-human world around them. Gothic's emergence against the grain of Enlightenment and its restriction of fancy, coded as the belief in the animacy or sentience of nonhumans and matter, uniquely positions it to comment on the Anthropocene. With *mētis* and its rhetorical sister concepts like *kairos* in mind, we can glean new insights about Gothic's attendant timeliness and wiliness in depicting a world beyond and without

Man. My analysis has demonstrated that the Gothic mode depicts the ineffable more-than-human domain along with the means to engage it. In the current posthuman, post-anthropocentric world, such depictions and tactics seem especially timely.

Mētis has been hidden in the belly of dominant Western patriarchal and colonial thinking, perhaps gestating so it can progenerate new cunning for the present. Swallowed by Zeus to extend and secure his power, Metis was suppressed, and her special cunning – one associated with the feminine, queer and nonhuman – was absorbed and coopted. The Metis myths demonstrate how imperial and 'patriarchal dominion has always established its authority and won legitimacy by [subverting] the feminine',[55] the nonbinary, the queer and the nonhuman. Hesiod's *Theogony* is structured and propelled by such narratives of domination. Zeus's consumption of Metis facilitates the ultimate shift from the world of Chaos, which is 'radically unstable, ambiguous, and open', to the 'stable order of [his] regime'. Christopher P. Long emphasises that 'What begins in darkness and with a surplus of feminine fecundity' concludes 'in a surplus of masculine fecundity, with Zeus' birthing Athena.[56] Yet, as translations of the *Theogony* suggest, this chaotic, more-than-human and feminine energy (associated with Gaia and inherited by her granddaughter, Metis), is too cunning, too shifting and too tricky to be fully contained. Zeus does not digest Metis, who might be said 'to take counsel with, to debate, consider, or contrive together with' Zeus and thus 'suggests a kind of communal habit of thinking enacted between Zeus and Metis'. Long questions whether Metis was willing to be ingested, to be absorbed into the belly of the patriarch, highlighting that Hesiod's narrative is 'rife with nuance' stemming from the ambivalence of the middle voice he uses, which hints at Metis's possible collusion and agency. The 'reflexive power of the middle voice . . . turns its object back in upon the subject'.[57] Therefore, even if Metis was consumed by Zeus, she continued to contaminate him.

Just as it is difficult to know where to begin, it is difficult to know how to conclude. The Metis myths that tell of her unique cunning reveal the world as cyclical and highlight the porosity, the fuzziness, of things like a beginning, middle and end. Rather than move forward, perhaps we should move laterally, forging transversal alliances and crafting polymorphic identities. There is no easy way through the *pontos* of the Anthropocene, but one *poros* is to become *porous* – to open ourselves to the world and allow it to shape us as much as we shape it.

Notes

Introduction

1 *Mētis* is related to *mētiaō* ['to consider, meditate, plan'] and *mētióomai* ['to contrive']. From Lisa Raphals, *Knowing Words: Wisdom and Cunning in the Classical Traditions of China and Greece* (Ithaca and London: Cornell University Press, 1992), pp. xii–xiii. The Latin equivalent is *Sollertia*. The cunning, trickery, ruses and deceit associated with *mētis* find expression in *Raqa'iq al-hilal fi Daqaiq al-hiyal* ['Cloaks of Fine Fabric in Subtle Ruses'] (*c.* 1300), translated by René R. Khawam as *The Subtle Ruse, the Book of Arabic Wisdom and Guile*, and in Chinese works like the *I Ching* (*c.* 1000–750 BCE) and Sun Tzu's *Art of War* (*c.* 475–221 BCE). See Michel de Certeau, *The Practice of Everyday Life*, trans. Steven F. Rendall (Berkeley, Los Angeles and London: University of California Press, 1984), p. 21.

2 A reference to Sun Tzu's *The Art of War*, which also promotes the cunning ruses of *mētis* for turning victories against stronger opponents. De Certeau, *The Practice of Everyday Life*, p. xix.

3 De Certeau, *The Practice of Everyday Life*, p. xi.

4 Jay Dolmage, *Disability Rhetoric* (Syracuse: Syracuse University Press, 2014), p. 157, p. 5.

5 Raphals, *Knowing Words*, p. xii.

6 Janet Atwill, *Rhetoric Reclaimed: Aristotle and the Liberal Arts Tradition* (Ithaca: Cornell University Press, 1998), p. 9.

7 Rosi Braidotti, *The Posthuman* (Cambridge: Polity Press, 2013), p. 15.

[8] Nick Groom, 'Introduction' to Horace Walpole, *The Castle of Otranto*, ed. N. Groom (Oxford and New York: Oxford University Press, 2014), pp. ix–xxxviii, at p. xix.

[9] Frederick S. Frank, 'Introduction', Horace Walpole *The Castle of Otranto and The Mysterious Mother*, ed. F. S. Frank (Peterborough: Broadview Press, 2011), pp. 11–34, at p. 17.

[10] Marcel Detienne and Jean-Pierre Vernant, *Cunning Intelligence in Greek Culture and Society*, trans. Janet Lloyd (New Jersey: Humanities Press, 1978), p. 32.

[11] Mary Shelley, *Frankenstein; or, The Modern Prometheus* (Peterborough: Broadview Press, 1994), p. 83.

[12] See for example William Veeder, *Mary Shelley &* Frankenstein: *The Fate of Androgyny* (Chicago: Chicago University Press, 1986), p. 17.

[13] Jolene Zigarovich, 'The Trans Legacy of *Frankenstein*', *Science Fiction Studies* 45/2 (2018), pp. 260–72.

[14] Tony Davies, *Humanism* (London: Routledge, 2008).

[15] Mary Shelley, 'Introduction to Shelley's 1831 Edition', in *Frankenstein*, eds. D. L. Macdonald and Kathleen Scherf (Peterborough: Broadview Press, 1994), pp. 347–52, at p. 351.

[16] 'The Modern Prometheus' (1755) is an essay by Immanuel Kant cautioning against modern science's attempt to defy the natural order, which names Benjamin Franklin as an example.

[17] In Aeschylus's *Prometheus Vinctus* (*c.* 479–24 BCE), Prometheus essentially replaces Metis as the cunning deceptive Titan who aids Zeus in securing his sovereign power. See Detienne and Vernant, *Cunning Intelligence in Greek Culture and Society*, pp. 58–62.

[18] Hesiod, *Theogony*, 929a (*c.* 730–700 BCE) *https://www.theoi.com/Text/HesiodTheogony.html*, accessed 1 June 2022.

[19] Lydia McDermott offers an insightful analysis of Shelley's *mētis* and the ways her novel fits into the Metis myths in 'Birthing Rhetorical Monsters: How Mary Shelley Infuses *Mêtis* with the Maternal in Her 1831 Introduction to *Frankenstein*', *Rhetoric Review* 34/1 (2015), pp. 1–18.

[20] Shelley, 'Introduction to Shelley's 1831 Edition', p. 350, p. 351.

[21] *Mētis* applies to that which is 'woven, plaited or fitted together', like 'knots, ropes, meshes and nets' or anything that is produced by fitting many pieces together into a whole (Detienne and Vernant pp. 45–6). See also Emma Cocker, 'Weaving Codes/Coding Weaves: Penelopean Mêtis and the Weaver-Coder's Kairos', *Textile* 15/2 (2017), pp. 124–41.

[22] Cynthia Chambers and Erika Hasebe-Ludt with Dwayne Donald, Wanda Hurren, Carl Leggo, and Antoinette Oberg, 'Métissage: A

Research Praxis', in Gary Knowles and Ardra L. Cole (eds), *Handbook of the Arts in Qualitative Research: Perspectives, Methodologies, Examples, and Issues* (Thousand Oaks: SAGE Publications, 2007), pp. 141–53, at pp. 141–2.

23 Gary Lowen-Trudeau, 'Methodological Métissage: An Interpretive Indigenous Approach to Environmental Education Research', *Canadian Journal of Environmental Education* 17 (2012), pp. 113–30, at p. 125.

24 Chambers and Hasebe-Ludt et al., 'Métissage: A Research Praxis', pp. 141–2.

25 As Dwayne Donald explains, métissage is originally a French word 'loosely translated into English as "crossbreeding", that originally referred to racial mixing and procreation in derogatory terms'. In 'Indigenous Métissage: A Decolonizing Research Sensibility', *International Journal of Qualitative Studies in Education* 25/5 (2012), pp. 533–55, at p. 536.

26 Françoise Lionnet, *Autobiographical Voices: Race, Gender, and Self-Portraiture* (Cornell: Cornell University Press, 2018), p. 9.

27 Erika Hasebe-Ludt, Cynthia Chambers, and Carl Leggo, *Life Writing and Literary Métissage as an Ethos for Our Times* (New York: Peter Lang, 2009), p. 9.

28 Chambers and Hasebe-Ludt et al., 'Métissage: A Research Praxis', p. 142.

29 Métis refers to a Canadian Indigenous group of mixed European and Indigenous ancestry.

30 Lowan-Trudeau, 'Methodological Métissage', p. 114.

31 Quoted in Lowan-Trudeau, at p. 114.

32 Bernd Reiter, *Decolonizing the Social Sciences and the Humanities: An Anti-Elitism Manifesto* (New York: Routledge, 2021), at p. 21.

33 Dwayne Donald, at p. 535.

34 David Punter, *The Literature of Terror, Vol. I: The Gothic Tradition*, 2nd edn (London: Longman, 1996), p. 5.

35 Groom, 'Introduction', p. xiii.

36 Notably, Walpole's father, Robert Walpole, was First Minister of the Whig party from 1721–42. See Groom, p. xvi.

37 Giorgio Vasari qtd. in Groom, 'Introduction', p. xi.

38 Groom, 'Introduction', p. xix.

39 Horace Walpole, 'Preface to the Second Edition', *The Castle of Otranto and The Mysterious Mother*, ed. Frederick S. Frank (Peterborough: Broadview Press, 2011), p. 65.

40 Fred Botting, *Gothic*, 2nd edn (London and New York: Routledge, 2014), pp. 1–2.

41 Robert Miles, *Gothic Writing 1750–1820: A Genealogy*, 2nd edn (Manchester: Manchester University Press, 2002), p. 15.
42 Jodey Castricano, *Gothic Metaphysics: From Alchemy to the Anthropocene* (Cardiff: University of Wales Press, 2021), p. 6.
43 Castricano, *Gothic Metaphysics*, p. 14, p. 7, italics original.
44 Frank, 'Introduction', at p. 11.
45 Frank, 'Introduction', p. 17.
46 Frank, 'Introduction', p. 17, italics original.
47 Castricano, *Gothic Metaphysics*, p. 15, p. 21.
48 Cynthia Sugars and Gerry Turcotte, 'Canadian Literature and the Postcolonial Gothic', in C. Sugars and G. Turcotte (eds), *Unsettled Remains: Canadian Literature and the Postcolonial Gothic* (Waterloo: Wilfrid Laurier Press, 2009), pp. vii–xxvi.
49 Miles, *Gothic Writing*, p. 4.
50 Fred Botting, *Gothic*, vol. 1 (London and New York: Routledge, 1996), p. 12.
51 Castricano, *Gothic Metaphysics*, p. 14.
52 Miles, *Gothic Writing*, p. xi.
53 J. Halberstam, *Skin Shows: Gothic Horror and the Technology of Monstrosity* (Durham: Duke University Press, 1995), p. 2.
54 Miles, *Gothic Writing*, p. 2, p. 3.
55 Botting, *Gothic*, p. 2.
56 Botting, *Gothic*, 2nd edn, p. 1.
57 Roger Luckhurst, 'Introduction', in R. Luckhurst (ed.), *Late Victorian Gothic Tales* (Oxford and New York: Oxford University Press, 2005), pp. ix–xxxi, at p. ix.
58 Luckhurst, 'Introduction', p. xii.
59 Maggie Kilgour, *The Rise of the Gothic Novel* (London: Routledge, 1995), p. 4.
60 Jerrold E. Hogle, 'Introduction: The Gothic in Western Culture', in J. E. Hogle (ed.), *The Cambridge Companion to Gothic Fiction* (Cambridge: Cambridge University Press, 2002/2015), pp. 1–20, at p. 2.
61 Kilgour, *The Rise of the Gothic Novel*, p. 6, p. 1.
62 Kilgour, *The Rise of the Gothic Novel*, p. 2.
63 Miles, *Gothic Writing*, p. 17, p. 6.
64 Jerrold E. Hogle, 'The Gothic-Theory Conversation: An Introduction', in J. E. Hogle and R. Miles (eds), *The Gothic and Theory: An Edinburgh Companion* (Edinburgh: Edinburgh University Press), pp. 1–30, at p. 11.

65 Alexandra Warwick, 'Feeling Gothicky', *Gothic Studies* 9/1 (2007), pp. 5–15, at p. 6.

66 Julian Wolfreys, 'Victorian Gothic', in Anna Powell and Andrew Smith (eds), *Teaching the Gothic* (Basingstoke: Palgrave Macmillan, 2006), pp. 64–76, at p. 66.

67 Miles, *Gothic Writing*, p. 4.

68 Anne Williams, *Art of Darkness: A Poetics of Gothic* (Chicago: The University of Chicago Press, 1995), at p. 23.

69 Robert Mighall's definition of Gothic as a rhetoric has been especially influential. See *A Geography of Victorian Gothic Fiction* (Oxford: Oxford University Press, 1999).

70 Kilgour, *The Rise of the Gothic Novel*, p. 1.

71 John E. Smith, 'Time and Qualitative Time', *The Review of Metaphysics* 40/1 (1986), pp. 3–16 at p. 4, emphasis original.

72 Robert Leston, 'Unhinged: *Kairos* and the Invention of the Untimely', *Atlantic Journal of Communication* 21/1 (2013), pp. 29–50, at p. 47.

73 Thomas Rickert, 'In the House of Doing: Rhetoric and the Kairos of Ambience', *JAC* 24/4 (2004), pp. 901–27, at p. 904.

74 John E. Smith, 'Time and Qualitative Time', pp. 10–11.

75 Nathaniel A. Rivers, 'Deep Ambivalence and Wild Objects: Toward a Strange Environmental Rhetoric', *Rhetoric Society Quarterly* 45/5 (2015), pp. 420–40. See also Bruce Foltz, 'On Heidegger and the Interpretation of Environmental Crisis', *Environmental Ethics* 6 (1984), pp. 323–38.

76 Wilhelm Pauck and Marion Pauck, *Paul Tillich: His Life & Thought, Vol. 1: Life* (New York: Harper & Row, 1976), p. 73.

77 Castricano, *Gothic Metaphysics*, p. 2.

78 Andrew Smith, *Gothic Literature*, 2nd edn (Edinburgh: Edinburgh University Press, 2013), p. 88; Catherine Spooner, *Contemporary Gothic* (London, Reaktion Books, 2006), p. 69.

79 Debra Hawhee, *Bodily Arts: Rhetoric and Athletics in Ancient Greece* (Austin: University of Texas Press, 2004), at pp. 26–7. Agonism denotes the *agōn*, meaning struggle or contest and a 'gathering' or 'assembly', as well as agonist, a pharmaceutical or substance that binds to a receptor in or on a cell membrane. Hawhee, p. 15 and p. 26.

80 Cannon Schmitt, 'Notes Towards a Water Acknowledgement', plenary address at the North American Victorian Studies Association 2022 conference, online.

81 Paul J. Crutzen, 'The Geology of Mankind', *Nature* 415/6867 (2002), p. 23.

[82] For a helpful overview, see Simon L. Lewis and Mark A. Maslin, 'Defining the Anthropocene' *Nature* 519/7542 (2015), pp. 171–80.

[83] Wendy Parkins and Peter Adkins, 'Introduction: Victorian Ecology and the Anthropocene', *19: Interdisciplinary Studies in the Long Nineteenth Century* 26 (2018), pp. 1–15, at p. 2.

[84] Alexandra Warwick, 'Victorian Gothic', in Catherine Spooner and Emma McEvoy (eds), *The Routledge Companion to Gothic* (London and New York: Routledge, 2007), pp. 29–37, at p. 29.

[85] Julian Wolfreys, 'Victorian Gothic', at p. xv.

[86] Warwick, 'Victorian Gothic', p. 29.

[87] Luckhurst, 'Introduction', p. ix.

[88] Rosi Braidotti, *Posthuman Knowledge* (Cambridge: Polity Press, 2019), p. 69.

[89] Chambers, Hasebe-Ludt, and Leggo, *Life Writing*, p. 4.

[90] Braidotti, *Posthuman Knowledge*, p. 67.

[91] Simone Bignall and Rosi Braidotti, 'Posthuman Systems', in Rosi Braidotti and Simone Bignall (eds), *Posthuman Ecologies: Complexity and Process after Deleuze* (London: Rowman & Littlefield, 2019), pp. 1–16, at p. 4.

[92] Rosi Braidotti quoting Protagoras, 'Posthuman Critical Theory', in D. Banerji and M. R. Paranjape (eds), *Critical Posthumanism and Planetary Futures* (New Delhi: Springer, 2016), pp. 13–32, at p. 15.

[93] Bignall and Braidotti, 'Posthuman Systems', p. 4.

[94] Most simply, speculative realism challenges the Kantian distinction between the noumenal and the phenomenal along with the belief that philosophy can know the world only through the human. Graham Harman, *Towards Speculative Realism* (Winchester and Washington: Zero Books, 2010) and *Speculative Realism: An Introduction* (Cambridge: Polity Press, 2018).

[95] N. Katherine Hayles, *How We Became Posthuman* (Chicago: Chicago University Press, 1999), pp. 85–6.

[96] Graham Harman, *Tool-Being: Heidegger and the Metaphysics of Objects* (Chicago and La Salle: Open Court, 2002), p. 1.

[97] Jane Bennett, *Vibrant Matter: A Political Ecology of Things* (Durham: Duke University Press, 2010), p. xvi.

[98] Braidotti, *The Posthuman*, p. 5.

[99] Karen Barad, *Meeting the Universe Halfway: Quantum Physics and the Entanglement of Matter and Meaning* (Durham and London: Duke University Press, 2007), p. 136.

[100] Hayles, *How We Became Posthuman*, p. 84, p. 91.

101 Braidotti, 'Posthuman Critical Theory', p. 15.

102 Elizabeth Grosz, *Volatile Bodies: Toward a Corporeal Feminism* (Bloomington: Indiana University Press, 1994), p. ix.

103 Barad, *Meeting the Universe Halfway*, p. 139, p. 128.

104 Barad, *Meeting the Universe Halfway*, p. 33.

105 Barad, *Meeting the Universe Halfway*, p. 234, p. 153.

106 Stacy Alaimo, *Bodily Natures: Science, Environment, and the Material Self* (Bloomington: Indiana University Press, 2010), p. 20.

107 Barad, *Meeting the Universe Halfway*, p. 185, emphasis original.

108 Barad, *Meeting the Universe Halfway*, pp. 178–9., at p. 140.

109 Barad, *Meeting the Universe Halfway*, p. 394.

110 Anya Heise-von der Lippe, 'Introduction: Post/human/Gothic', in A. Heise-von der Lippe (ed.), *Posthuman Gothic* (Cardiff: University of Wales Press, 2017), pp. 1–18, at p. 3.

111 Castricano, *Gothic Metaphysics*, p. 15, p. 22.

112 Inspired by Elaine Graham's *Representations of the Post/Human: Monsters, Aliens and Others in Popular Culture* (Manchester: Rutgers University Press, 2002).

113 Anya Heise-von der Lippe, 'Techno-Terrors and the Emergence of Cyber-Gothic', in J. E. Hoggle and R. Miles (eds), *The Gothic and Theory: An Edinburgh Companion* (Edinburgh: Edinburgh University Press, 2019), pp. 182–202, at p. 182.

114 Graham, *Representations of the Post/Human*, p. 62.

115 Heise-von der Lippe, 'Introduction: Post/human/Gothic', p. 2.

116 Heise-von der Lippe, 'Introduction: 'Post/human/Gothic', p. 2.

117 Graham, *Representations of the Post/Human*, p. 221.

118 Hayles, *How We Became Posthuman*, p. 3.

119 Graham, *Representations of the Post/Human*, pp. 1–2.

120 J. Halberstam and Ira Livingston, 'Introduction: Posthuman Bodies', in J. Halberstam and I. Livingston (eds), *Posthuman Bodies* (Bloomington: Indiana University Press, 1995), pp. xv–xxxiii, at p. xxiv.

121 Gilles Deleuze and Félix Guattari, *A Thousand Plateaus: Capitalism and Schizophrenia*, trans. Brian Massumi (Minnesota: Minnesota University Press, 1987), p. 238, p. 273.

122 Halbertam and Livingston, 'Introduction', p. xxxii.

123 Deleuze and Guattari, *A Thousand Plateaus*, p. 238, p. 291.

124 Halberstam and Livingstone, 'Introduction', pp. xxii–xxiii, pp. xviii–xxiv.

125 Hayles, *How We Became Posthuman*, p. 283.

126 Cary Wolfe, *What is Posthumanism?* (Minneapolis: University of Minnesota Press, 2010), p. xv.

[127] Donna Haraway, *Simians, Cyborgs and Women: The Reinvention of Nature* (New York: Routledge, 1991), at p. 151.
[128] Halberstam and Livingstone, 'Introduction', pp. xviii–xxiv.
[129] Timothy Morton questions 'posthuman platitudes about malleable identity', *The Ecological Thought* (Cambridge, Mass.: Harvard University Press, 2010), p. 82.
[130] See Braidotti, *Posthuman Knowledge*, especially Chapter 2, 'Posthuman Subjects', pp. 40–74.
[131] Jeffrey Jerome Cohen, 'Monster Culture (Seven Theses)', in J. J. Cohen (ed.), *Monster Theory: Reading Culture* (Minneapolis: University of Minnesota Press, 1996), at p. 7.
[132] 'Monster' probably derives from the Latin, *monstrare*, meaning 'to demonstrate', and *monere*, 'to warn'.
[133] Cohen, 'Preface: In a Time of Monsters', in *Monster Theory*, pp. vii–xiii, at p. ix.
[134] Graham, *Representations of the Post/Human*, p. 12.
[135] Graham, *Representations of the Post/Human*, p. 11.
[136] Cohen, 'Monster Culture', p. 7.
[137] As per Hogle in Cohen, 'Monster Culture', p. 7.
[138] Victor Turner, *The Forest of Symbols: Aspects of Ndembu Ritual* (Ithaca: Cornell University Press, 1967), pp. 95–6.
[139] Turner, *The Forest of Symbols*, p. 110, p. 101, p. 97.
[140] Bart Kosko, *Fuzzy Thinking: The New Science of Fuzzy Logic* (New York: Hyperion, 1993).
[141] Braidotti, *Posthuman Knowledge*, p. 170.
[142] Kristin Pomykala, 'Snake(s)kin: The Intertwining *Mêtis* and Mythopoetics of Serpentine Rhetoric', *Rhetoric Society Quarterly* 47/3 (2017), pp. 264–74, at p. 266.
[143] Detienne and Vernant, *Cunning Intelligence in Greek Culture and Society*, p. 4.
[144] Detienne and Vernant, *Cunning Intelligence in Greek Culture and Society*, p. 3.
[145] De Certeau, *The Practice of Everyday Life*, p. 29, emphasis original.
[146] Raphals, *Knowing Words*, p. 196.
[147] Detienne and Vernant, *Cunning Intelligence in Greek Culture and Society*, p. 32.
[148] Detienne and Vernant, *Cunning Intelligence in Greek Culture and Society*, p. 2, pp. 3–4, p. 46.
[149] Detienne and Vernant's complex analysis covers several myths, rhetorical treatises and philosophical texts drawn from Classic Greece,

covering writing from Homer to Oppian (roughly ten centuries worth of materials), p. 12.

150 Detienne and Vernant, *Cunning Intelligence in Greek Culture and Society*, pp. 3–4.

151 Deteinne and Vernant, *Cunning Intelligence in Greek Culture and Society*, p. 5.

152 Hesiod, *Theogony* 920a, 886.

153 Apollodorus, *The Library* or *Bibliotheca* 1.2.1. (*c.* 101–200 CE), *https://www.theoi.com/Text/Apollodorus1.html*, accessed 1 June 2022.

154 Hesiod, *Theogony* 920a; 886.

155 Apollodorus, *Bibliotheca* 1.3.6

156 Jay Dolmage, 'Metis *Mētis*, Mestiza, Medusa: Rhetorical Bodies Across Rhetorical Traditions', *Rhetoric Review* 28/1 (2009), pp. 1–28, at p. 1.

157 Hawhee, *Bodily Arts*, p. 46.

158 Jay Dolmage, 'What is Metis?', *Disability Studies Quarterly* 40/1 (2020), np.

159 Detienne and Vernant, *Cunning Intelligence in Greek Culture and Society*, p. 272.

160 Detienne and Vernant, *Cunning Intelligence in Greek Culture and Society*, p. 3.

161 Hawhee, *Bodily Arts*, p. 48.

162 Dolmage, 'What is Metis?'.

163 Hawhee, *Bodily Arts*, p. 53.

164 Quoted in Detienne and Vernant, *Cunning Intelligence in Greek Culture and Society*, p. 35.

165 Detienne and Vernant, *Cunning Intelligence in Greek Culture and Society*, p. 35.

166 Detienne and Vernant, *Cunning Intelligence in Greek Culture and Society*, p. 36.

167 Detienne and Vernant, *Cunning Intelligence in Greek Culture and Society*, p. 134.

168 Stian Torjussen, 'Phanes and Dionysos in the Derveni Theogony', *Symbolae Osloenses* 80/1 (2005), pp. 7–22, at p. 11.

169 Detienne and Vernant, *Cunning Intelligence in Greek Culture and Society*, p. 133.

170 Detienne and Vernant, *Cunning Intelligence in Greek Culture and Society*, p. 137–8.

171 Torjussen, 'Phanes and Dionysos in the Derveni Theogony', p. 11.

172 'Shimmering' also resonates with Deborah Bird Rose's concept of 'shimmer' as 'an Aboriginal aesthetic that helps call us into . . .

multispecies worlds'. 'Shimmer: When All You Love Is Being Trashed', in A. Tsing, H. Swanson, E. Gan, and N. Bubandt (eds), *Arts of Living on a Damaged Planet* (Minneapolis: University of Minnesota Press, 2017), pp. G51–G63, at p. G53.

173 De Certeau, *The Practice of Everyday Life*, p. xi.

174 Detienne and Vernant, *Cunning Intelligence in Greek Culture and Society*, p. 20.

175 De Certeau, *The Practice of Everyday Life*, pp. xix–xx.

176 Detienne and Vernant, *Cunning Intelligence in Greek Culture and Society*, p. 317, emphasis original.

177 Detienne and Vernant, *Cunning Intelligence in Greek Culture and Society*, p. 3.

178 Raphals, *Knowing Words*, p. xii.

179 Detienne and Vernant, *Cunning Intelligence in Greek Culture and Society*, p. 4, p. 3.

180 Raphals is discussing Plato specifically here. *Knowing Words*, p. 228.

181 Sarah Kofman qtd. in Nandita Biswas Mellamphy, '(W)omen out/of Time: Metis, Medea, Mahakali', in K. Kolozova and E. A. Joy (eds), *After The 'Speculative Turn': Realism, Philosophy, and Feminism*, pp. 133–57, at p. 148.

182 Biswas Mellamphy, '(W)omen out/of Time', p. 148.

183 Biswas Mellamphy, '(W)omen out/of Time', p. 147.

184 Detienne and Vernant, *Cunning Intelligence in Greek Culture and Society*, p. 108.

185 De Certeau, *The Practice of Everyday Life*, p. xix.

186 Raphals, *Knowing Words*, p. xii.

187 Biswas Mellamphy notes that 'the French word *duplice* connotes both duplicity and duplication qua multiplicity', in '(W)omen out/of Time', pp. 147–8.

188 Detienne and Vernant, *Cunning Intelligence in Greek Culture and Society*, p. 46.

189 Yves Richez, *Corporate Talent Detection and Development* (Hoboken, NJ: Wiley, 2018), at p. 262, p. 250.

190 Nandita Biswas Mellamphy, 'Ghost in the Shell-Game: On the Mètic Mode of Existence, Inception & Innocence', *The Funambulist Papers, Volume Two* (2013), *https://thefunambulist.net/editorials/funambulist-papers-46-ghost-in-the-shell-game-on-the-metic-mode-of-existence-inception-and-innocence-by-nandita-biswas-mellamphy*, emphasis original.

191 A phrase and a practice inspired by Jay Dolmage's work; see for example 'Metis, *Mētis*, Mestiza, Medusa'.

[192] Also known as Critical Discourse Analysis or CDA.
[193] In weaving, the weft is the thread that passes horizontally through the warp threads to form the cloth.
[194] Discourse can be a convoluted term in CDS, denoting both topic-specific language and semiotic ways of construing worldviews.
[195] With this, I intend to evoke Fred Botting's list of common Gothic features, including transgression, negativity, darkness, uncanniness and alterity.
[196] Janus has been evoked by critics like Jerrold Hogle to describe the Gothic mode's double, divergent and dissonant nature. E.g., 'The Gothic-Theory Conversation'.
[197] My claim and approach are inspired by the work of Jay Dolmage.
[198] Dolmage, *Disability Rhetoric*, p. 200.
[199] Dolmage, *Disability Rhetoric*, p. 230.
[200] Hans Kellner qtd. in Dolmage, *Disability Rhetoric*, p. 230.
[201] Kelly Hurley, *The Gothic Body: Sexuality, Materialism, and Degeneration at the* fin de Siècle (Cambridge: Cambridge University Press, 1996).

Chapter 1

[1] Jack David Eller, 'The Trickster: Ancient Spirit, Modern Political Theology', *The Brink* (9 July 2022), *https://politicaltheology.com/the-trickster-ancient-spirit-modern-political-theology/*, accessed 3 May 2023.
[2] Some well-known and influential studies of the trickster are Joseph Campbell's *The Hero with a Thousand Faces* (Princeton: Princeton University Press, 1949) and *The Masks of God: Primitive Mythology* (New York: Penguin, 1976); Carl Jung's 'On the Psychology of the Trickster Figure', in P. Radin (ed.), *The Trickster: A Study in American Indian Mythology* (New York: Greenwood Press, 1956), pp. 195–211; and Paul Radin, *The World of Primitive Man* (New York: Dutton, 1971).
[3] A reference to Norse trickster, Loki, as a '"point of contact" between gods and giants'. Lewis Hyde qtd. in Árpád Szakolczai, *Post-Truth Society: A Political Anthropology of Trickster Logic* (London and New York: Routledge, 2022), p. 27.
[4] Helena Bassil-Morozow, *The Trickster and the System: Identity and Agency in Contemporary Society* (London and New York: Routledge, 2015), p. 11.
[5] In Apollodorus's version of the Metis myths, she is said to give Cronos a phármakon to vomit up his children.

6 Michel de Certeau, *The Practice of Everyday Life*, trans. Steven F. Rendall (Berkeley, Los Angeles, and London: University of California Press, 1984), p. xix.

7 John Roberts qtd. in Shane Phelan, 'Coyote Politics: Trickster Tales and Feminist Futures', *Hypatia* 11/3 (1996), pp. 130–49, at p. 135.

8 Nicholas Royle, *Veering: A Theory of Literature* (Edinburgh: Edinburgh University Press, 2001), p. 2.

9 Royle, *Veering*, p. 3.

10 Royle, *Veering*, p. 4, emphasis original.

11 Royle, *Veering*, p. 5.

12 The exact dates of the *fin de siècle* are debatable, but most critics focus on 1870–1914, especially the 1890s.

13 Michael Saler, 'Introduction', in M. Saler (ed.), *The Fin-de-Siècle World* (London and New York: Routledge, 2015), pp. 1–8, at p. 3 and Sally Ledger and Roger Luckhurst, *The Fin de Siècle: A Reader in Cultural History, c.1880–1900* (Oxford: Oxford UP, 2000), p. 1, p. 133.

14 Ledger and Luckhurst, *The Fin de Siècle*, pp. 133–35, at p. xvi.

15 Max Nordau, *Degeneration* (New York: D. Appleton and Company, 1895), p. 5.

16 Nordau, *Degeneration*, p. 6.

17 Nordau writes, 'Views that have hitherto governed minds are dead or driven hence like disenthroned kings'. *Degeneration*, p. 6.

18 Victoria Margree and Bryony Randall, '*Fin-de-Siècle* Gothic', in A. Smith and W. Hughes (eds), *The Victorian Gothic: An Edinburgh Companion* (Edinburgh: Edinburgh University Press, 2012), pp. 226–41, at p. 226.

19 Saler, 'Introduction', at p. 1.

20 Sally Ledger and Roger Luckhurst, 'Introduction: Reading the "Fin de Siècle"', in Sally Ledger and Roger Luckhurst (eds), *The Fin de Siècle: A Reader in Cultural History, c.1880–1900* (Oxford: Oxford UP, 2000), pp. xii–xxiii, at p. xiii.

21 Ledger and Luckhurst's 'Introduction: Reading the "Fin de Siècle"' offers a more robust overview of these 'constellation[s]' of newness. See xiii.

22 Ledger and Luckhurst, *The Fin de Siècle*, p. 97.

23 Ledger and Luckhurst, *The Fin de Siècle*, p. 98.

24 Saler, 'Introduction', p. 4.

25 Saler, 'Introduction', p. 4.

26 Nordau, *Degeneration*, at p. 6.

27 George Gissing in Elaine Showalter, *Sexual Anarchy: Gender and Culture at the Fin de Siècle* (New York: Viking, 1990).

[28] Roger Luckhurst, 'Introduction', in Rodger Luckhurst (ed.), *Late Victorian Gothic Tales* (Oxford and New York: Oxford University Press, 2005), pp. ix–xxxi, at p. xvi.
[29] Glennis Byron, 'Gothic in the 1890s', in D. Punter (ed.), *A New Companion to The Gothic* (Malden MA: Wiley Blackwell, 2015), pp. 186–96, at p. 187.
[30] See for example Kelly Hurley, *The Gothic Body: Sexuality, Materialism, and Degeneration at the* fin de siècle (Cambridge: Cambridge University Press, 1996).
[31] See Robert Mighall, *A Geography of Victorian Gothic Fiction* (Oxford, Oxford University Press, 1999) and Hurley, *The Gothic Body*.
[32] Bram Stoker, *Dracula* (Peterborough: Broadview Press, 2000), at p. 278, p. 279.
[33] See J. Halberstam, *Skin Shows: Gothic Horror and the Technology of Monstrosity* (Durham: Duke University Press, 1995).
[34] Hurley, *Gothic Body*, pp. 3–4.
[35] Halberstam, *Skin Shows*, p. 92.
[36] Natasha Rebry, 'Playing the Man: Mesmerism and Manliness in Richard Marsh's *The Beetle*', *Gothic Studies* 18/1 (2016), pp. 1–15.
[37] Richard Marsh, *The Beetle* (Peterborough: Broadview Press, 2004), at p. 322.
[38] Roger Luckhurst, 'Trance Gothic, 1882–97', in Julian Wolfreys (ed.), *Victorian Hauntings: Spectrality, Gothic, the Uncanny and Literature* (New York: Palgrave, 2002), pp. 148–167, at p. 106.
[39] Victoria Margree, '"Both in Men's Clothing": Gender, Sovereignty, and Insecurity in Richard Marsh's *The Beetle*', *Critical Survey* 19/2 (2007), pp. 63–81, at p. 69.
[40] The novels were published in the same year, and Marsh's novel was initially more popular than Stoker's.
[41] Byron, 'Gothic in the 1890s', pp. 132–41, at p. 133.
[42] Marsh, *The Beetle*, p. 223, p. 76, p. 263.
[43] Mesmerism or animal magnetism was an early precursor to hypnotism.
[44] Marsh, *The Beetle*, p. 79
[45] Marsh, *The Beetle*, p. 240, p. 245, p. 243.
[46] Marsh, *The Beetle*, p. 57, p. 52.
[47] Julian Wolfreys, 'Introduction' to Richard Marsh, *The Beetle* (Peterborough: Broadview Press, 2004), pp. 9–34, at p. 17.
[48] Marsh, *The Beetle*, p. 70, p. 82.
[49] Composing a narrative and automatic writing were common treatments for hysteria at the end of the nineteenth century, reflecting Pierre Janet's

influential theory that hysteria was a breakdown of self-composition that could be remedied by composing a linear autobiography.

50 Marsh, *The Beetle*, pp. 319–20.

51 Marsh, *The Beetle*, at p. 149, p. 112.

52 To be clear, my shifting pronouns are intentional to describe this amorphous creature.

53 Marsh, *The Beetle*, at p. 53.

54 Marsh, *The Beetle*, at p. 53.

55 Marsh, *The Beetle*, p. 140, pp. 9–34.

56 Hurley, *The Gothic Body*, p. 143.

57 For example, James Esdaile's work on mesmerism in India: *The Introduction of Mesmerism (With the Sanction of the Government) into the Public Hospitals of India* (London: W. Kent, 1856). See Alison Winter, *Mesmerized: Powers of Mind in Victorian Britain* (Chicago: University of Chicago Press, 1998).

58 Stefania Forlini, 'Introduction', in Arthur Machen, *The Three Impostors: Or the Transmutations* (Peterborough: Broadview Press, 2023), pp. 9–46, at p. 9.

59 Forlini, 'Introduction', pp. 10–11.

60 Arthur Machen, 'The Great God Pan', in *The Three Impostors and Other Stories: Vol. 1 of the Best Weird Tales of Arthur Machen*, ed. S. T. Joshi (Hayward: Chaosium Inc., 2007), pp. 1–50, at pp. 2–3.

61 Similarly, in 'The Inmost Light' (1894), Dr Black's occult neuroscientific experimentation involves drawing 'that essence which men call the soul' from his wife as he bridges the 'great abyss . . . the gulf between the world of consciousness and the world of matter'. Arthur Machen, 'The Inmost Light', in *The Three Impostors and Other Stories: Vol. 1 of the Best Weird Tales of Arthur Machen*, ed. S. T. Joshi (Hayward: Chaosium Inc., 2007), pp. 51–77, at p. 76, p. 75.

62 Machen, 'The Great God Pan', p. 2.

63 Machen, 'The Great God Pan', p. 6.

64 Machen, 'The Great God Pan', p. 27.

65 Machen, 'The Great God Pan', p. 15.

66 Machen, 'The Great God Pan', pp. 46–7.

67 Hurley, *The Gothic Body*, p. 13.

68 Halberstam, *Skin Shows*, p. 2.

69 Halberstam, *Skin Shows*, p. 23.

70 Machen, 'The Great God Pan', pp. 46–7.

71 Hurley, *The Gothic Body*, p. 13, p. 47, p. 46.

[72] Eve Kosofsky Sedgwick, *The Coherence of Gothic Conventions* (New York: Methuen, 1986).
[73] S. T. Joshi, 'Introduction', *The Three Impostors and Other Stories: Vol. 1 of the Best Weird Tales of Arthur* Machen, ed. S. T. Joshi (Hayward: Chaosium Inc., 2007), pp. xi–xix.
[74] As in *nouvelle*, a French term for a collection of short stories or tales. Forlini, 'Introduction', p. 36.
[75] Joshi, 'Introduction', p. xvi.
[76] Forlini, 'Introduction', pp. 18–19.
[77] Forlini, 'Introduction', pp. 9–10.
[78] Marcel Detienne and Jean-Pierre Vernant, *Cunning Intelligence in Greek Culture and Society*, trans. Janet Lloyd (New Jersey: Humanities Press, 1978), at p. 46.
[79] Vernon Lee, 'Prince Alberic and the Snake Lady', in *Hauntings and Other Fantastic Tales*, eds Catherine Maxwell and Patricia Pulham (Peterborough: Broadview, 2006), pp. 182–228, at p. 207.
[80] Lee, 'Prince Alberic and the Snake Lady', p. 183.
[81] Lee, 'Prince Alberic and the Snake Lady', p. 187, p. 184, p. 188.
[82] Mary Patricia Kane, 'The Uncanny Mother in Vernon Lee's "Prince Alberic and the Snake Lady"', *Victorian Review* 32/1 (2006), pp. 41–62, p. 44.
[83] Lee, 'Prince Alberic and the Snake Lady', p. 185.
[84] Lee, 'Prince Alberic and the Snake Lady', pp. 184–5.
[85] Significantly, the tale of a woman preyed upon by lascivious men. Catherine Maxwell and Patricia Pulham, in Vernon Lee, *Hauntings and Other Tales*, eds Catherine Maxwell and Patricia Pulham, n. 2, p. 184.
[86] Lee, 'Prince Alberic and the Snake Lady', p. 193.
[87] Lee, 'Prince Alberic and the Snake Lady', p. 191.
[88] Lee, 'Prince Alberic and the Snake Lady', p. 191, p. 192.
[89] Kane, 'The Uncanny Mother', p. 44.
[90] Kane, 'The Uncanny Mother', p. 47.
[91] Maxwell and Pulham, n. 2, p. 187. Other influences may have been the less predatory French Melusine, a female water spirit who is a serpent or fish from the waist down and able to transform into human form (see Maxwell and Pulham, n. 2, p. 187), and Italian folktales of cursed serpent-humans (Kane, 'The Uncanny Mother', pp. 46–7).
[92] Maxwell and Pulham, p. 187.
[93] Bram Dijkstra, *Idols of Perversity: Fantasies of Feminine Evil in Fin-de-siècle Culture* (Oxford: Oxford University Press, 1986).
[94] Lee, 'Prince Alberic and the Snake Lady', p. 183, p. 210.

[95] Lee, 'Prince Alberic and the Snake Lady', p. 184, p. 212.
[96] Kane, 'The Uncanny Mother', p. 48.
[97] Mary Aswell Doll qtd. in Kristin Pomykala, 'Snake(s)kin: The Intertwining *Mêtis* and Mythopoetics of Serpentine Rhetoric', *Rhetoric Society Quarterly* 47/3 (2017), pp. 264–74, at p. 266.
[98] Pomykala, 'Snake(s)kin', at p. 266, p. 267.
[99] Kane, 'The Uncanny Mother', p. 47.
[100] Detienne and Vernant, *Cunning Intelligence in Greek Culture and Society*, p. 37.
[101] Detienne and Vernant, *Cunning Intelligence in Greek Culture and Society*, p. 37.
[102] Pomykala, 'Snake(s)kin', p. 266.
[103] Pomykala, 'Snake(s)kin', p. 266.
[104] Three thousand water nymphs born to Oceanus and Tethys.
[105] J. G. Frazer (trans.), *Apollodorus, The Library Book 1, https://www.theoi.com/Text/Ap1a.html#18*, n. 54, accessed 1 July 2022.
[106] Detienne and Vernant, *Cunning Intelligence in Greek Culture and Society*, p. 134, p. 133.
[107] See Jay Dolmage, 'Metis, *Mêtis*, *Mestiza*, Medusa: Rhetorical Bodies across Rhetorical Traditions', *Rhetoric Review* 28/1 (2009), pp. 1–28, at p. 1.
[108] Metis's daughter Athena is also associated with androgyny.
[109] Ella Mershon, 'Pulpy Fiction', *Victorian Literature and Culture* 48/1 (2020), pp. 267–98, at p. 268.
[110] Christopher Long, 'The Daughters of Metis: Patriarchal Dominion and the Politics of the Between', *Graduate Faculty Philosophy Journal* 28/2 (2007), pp. 67–86, p. 70.
[111] Coatlalopeuh, or the renamed Virgin of Guadalupe, wears 'a skirt of twisted serpents' (Anzalduá, p. 27). Gloria Anzaldúa, *Borderlands/La Frontera: The New Mestiza* (San Francisco: Aunt Lute Books, 1987).
[112] Evelien Bracke, *Of Metis and Magic: The Conceptual Transformations of Circe and Medea in Ancient Greek Poetry* (PhD dissertation; Department of Ancient Classics, National University of Ireland, Maynooth, September 2009). *https://mural.maynoothuniversity.ie/2255/1/e_bracke_thesis.pdf*.
[113] Nandita Biswas Mellamphy, '(W)omen out/of Time: Metis, Medea, Mahakali', in K. Kolozova and E. A. Joy (eds), *After The 'Speculative Turn': Realism, Philosophy, and Feminism*, pp. 133–57, at p. 134.
[114] Dolmage, 'Metis, *Mêtis*, *Mestiza*, Medusa', p. 19.

115 Detienne and Vernant, *Cunning Intelligence in Greek Culture and Society*, p. 46.
116 Lisa Raphals, *Knowing Words: Wisdom and Cunning in the Classical Traditions of China and Greece* (Ithaca and London: Cornell University Press, 1992), p. 211.
117 Pomykala, 'Snake(s)kin', p. 266.
118 Royle, *Veering*, pp. 7–8.
119 Royle, *Veering*, p. 9, p. 8.
120 Detienne and Vernant, *Cunning Intelligence in Greek Culture and Society*, p. 137–8.
121 Detienne and Vernant, *Cunning Intelligence in Greek Culture and Society*, p. 157.
122 Long, 'The Daughters of Metis', p. 67.
123 I use 'witch' to connote Metis's place in a tradition of magical women whose cunning poses specific threats to patriarchal orders, such as Medea and Circe.
124 Long, 'The Daughters of Metis', p. 68.
125 Long, 'The Daughters of Metis', p. 81.
126 Biswas Mellamphy, '(W)omen out/of Time', p. 134, p. 136.
127 Bernd Reiter, *Decolonizing the Social Sciences and the Humanities* (New York: Routledge, 2021), p. 19.
128 Detienne and Vernant, *Cunning Intelligence in Greek Culture and Society*, p. 108.
129 De Certeau, *The Practice of Everyday Life*, p. xix.
130 Bassil-Morozow, *The Trickster and the System*, p. 7.
131 Patricia MacCormack, 'Lovecraft's Cosmic Ethics', in Carl H. Sederholm and Jeffrey Andrew Weinstock (eds), *The Age of Lovecraft* (Minnesota: University of Minnesota Press, 2016), pp. 199–214, at p. 213.
132 MacCormack, 'Lovecraft's Cosmic Ethics', p. 212.

Chapter 2

1 Arthur Machen, *The Three Impostors; or, The Transmutations*, *The Three Impostors and Other Stories: Vol. 1 of the Best Weird Tales of Arthur Machen*, ed. S. T. Joshi (Hayward: Chaosium Inc., 2007), pp. 101–234, at p. 173.
2 Eugene Thacker, *Tentacles Longer Than Night: Horror of Philosophy Vol. 3* (Alresford, Hants: Zero Books, 2015), p. 150.
3 Donna Haraway, *Staying with the Trouble: Making Kin in the Chthulucene* (Durham: Duke University Press, 2016), p. 32.

[4] Marcel Detienne and Jean-Pierre Vernant, *Cunning Intelligence in Greek Culture and Society*, trans. Janet Lloyd (New Jersey: Humanities Press, 1978), p. 37.

[5] Haraway, *Staying with the Trouble*, p. 32, p. 33, p. 31.

[6] Haraway *Staying with the Trouble*, p. 30.

[7] Haraway *Staying with the Trouble*, p. 31.

[8] Mary Louise Pratt, 'Arts of the Contact Zone', *Profession* 1 (1991), pp. 33–40.

[9] Tony Davies, *Humanism* (London: Routledge, 2008).

[10] Kelly Hurley, *The Gothic Body: Sexuality, Materialism, and Degeneration at the* fin de siècle (Cambridge: Cambridge University Press, 1996), p. 5.

[11] Martin A. Danahay, 'Introduction', Robert Louis Stevenson, *Strange Case of Dr Jekyll and Mr Hyde*, 3rd edn (Peterborough: Broadview, 2015), pp. 11–26, at p. 19.

[12] Danahay, 'Introduction', p. 19.

[13] Danahay, 'Introduction', p. 19.

[14] Charles Darwin, *The Descent of Man* (London: Penguin Books, 2004), p. 85, p. 86.

[15] Devin Griffiths and Deanna K. Kreisel, 'Introduction: Open Ecologies', *Victorian Literature and Culture* 48/1 (2020), pp. 1–28, at p. 3.

[16] Ernst Haeckel qtd. in Wendy Parkins and Peter Adkins, 'Introduction: Victorian Ecology and the Anthropocene', *19: Interdisciplinary Studies in the Long Nineteenth Century* (2018) 26, pp. 1–15, at p. 1.

[17] Parkins and Adkins, 'Introduction', p. 1.

[18] Griffiths and Kreisel, 'Open Ecologies', p. 3.

[19] Griffiths and Kreisel, 'Open Ecologies', p. 3, p. 7, p. 9.

[20] Griffiths and Kreisel, 'Open Ecologies', p. 3.

[21] Parkins and Adkins, 'Introduction', p. 1.

[22] Hurley, *The Gothic Body*, p. 5; Kelly Hurley, 'British Gothic Fiction, 1885–1930', in Jerrold E. Hogle (ed.), *The Cambridge Companion to Gothic Fiction* (Cambridge: Cambridge University Press, 2002), pp. 189–207, at p. 190.

[23] Machen, *The Three Impostors*, p. 209.

[24] Robert Miles, *Gothic Writing 1750–1820: A Genealogy*, 2nd edn (Manchester: Manchester University Press, 2002), p. 26.

[25] Elaine Showalter, *Sexual Anarchy: Gender and Culture at the* Fin de Siècle (London: Bloomsbury, 1990), p. 4.

[26] Victoria Margree and Bryony Randall, '*Fin-de-Siècle* Gothic', in A. Smith and W. Hughes (eds), *The Victorian Gothic: An Edinburgh*

Companion (Edinburgh: Edinburgh University Press, 2012), pp. 226–41, at p. 228.

27 Patricia MacCormack, 'Lovecraft's Cosmic Ethics', in Carl H. Sederholm and Jeffrey Andrew Weinstock (eds), *The Age of Lovecraft* (Minnesota: University of Minnesota Press, 2016), pp. 199–214, at p. 213.

28 Cary Wolfe, *What is Posthumanism?* (Minneapolis, University of Minnesota Press, 2010), pp. xv–xvi.

29 Margree and Randall, '*Fin-de-Siècle* Gothic', p. 227.

30 Robert M. Philmus and David Y. Hughes (eds), *H. G. Wells: Early Writings in Science and Science Fiction* (Berkeley, Los Angeles and London: University of California Press, 1975), p. 148.

31 Unfortunately, Wells has also been revealed to hold eugenicist views, complicating celebrations of his work.

32 H. G. Wells, 'The Man of the Year Million. A Scientific Forecast', *Pall Mall Gazette* 57/8931 (6 Nov. 1893), p. 3.

33 H. G. Wells, 'Zoological Retrogression', *Gentleman's Magazine* 271 (Sept. 1891), pp. 246–53, at p. 246.

34 H. G. Wells, 'Zoological Retrogression', p. 246, p. 253.

35 Martin A. Danahay, Appendix B, in H. G. Wells, *The War of the Worlds*, ed. Martin A. Danahay (Peterborough: Broadview, 2003), pp. 197–98.

36 Danahay, Appendix B, p. 207.

37 H. G. Wells, 'The Extinction of Man: Some Speculative Suggestions', *Pall Mall Gazette* 59 (25 Sept. 1894), p. 3.

38 Jacques Derrida, *The Animal That Therefore I Am*, trans. David Wills (New York: Fordham University Press, 2008). See also Matthew Calarco's study of Derrida's work in *Zoographies: The Question of the Animal from Heidegger to Derrida* (New York: Columbia University Press, 2008).

39 Matthew Calarco, 'Identity, Difference, Indistinction', *The New Centennial Review* 11/2 (2011), pp. 41–60, p. 53.

40 Sherryl Vint, *Animal Alterity: Science Fiction and the Question of the Animal* (Liverpool: Liverpool University Press, 2010), pp. 85–102, pp. 5–6.

41 Hurley, *The Gothic Body*, p. 58.

42 H. G. Wells, *The Time Machine: An Invention* (New York: The Modern Library, 1895/2002), p. 34.

43 Wells, *The Time Machine*, p. 59.

44 Title of Chapter 6 in *The Time Machine*.

45 H. G. Wells, *The War of the Worlds* (Peterborough: Broadview, 2003), p. 160.

[46] Peter Kemp, *H. G. Wells and the Culminating Ape: Biological Imperatives and Imaginative Obsessions* (Houndmills and London: Macmillan Press Ltd., 1996) p. 23.

[47] Wells, *The War of the Worlds*, p. 62.

[48] H. G. Wells, 'In the Abyss', in *The Complete Short Stories of H.G. Wells* (London: Benn, 1966), pp. 377–93, at p. 388.

[49] Wells, 'In the Abyss', p. 392.

[50] H. G. Wells, 'The Empire of the Ants', in *The Complete Short Stories of H.G. Wells* (London: Benn, 1966), pp. 92–108, at p. 93, p. 97.

[51] H. G. Wells, *The Island of Doctor Moreau* (Peterborough: Broadview, 2009), p. 133.

[52] Laura Otis, 'Monkey in the Mirror: The Science of Professor Higgins and Doctor Moreau', *Twentieth-Century Literature* 55/4 (2009), pp. 485–509, at p. 490.

[53] David Ferrier, *The Localisation of Cerebral Disease* (New York: G. P. Putnam's Sons, 1879), p. 21.

[54] Wells, *The Island of Doctor Moreau*, p. 94.

[55] Charles Darwin, *On the Origin of Species by Means of Natural Selection* (New York: Dover Publications, Inc., 2006), p. 272.

[56] Wells, *The Island of Doctor Moreau*, p. 88, p. 100.

[57] Wells, *The Island of Doctor Moreau*, p. 123.

[58] Michael Parrish Lee, 'Reading Meat in H. G. Wells', *Studies in the Novel* 42/3 (2010), pp. 249–68, p. 261.

[59] Wells, *The Island of Doctor Moreau*, p. 172, p. 165.

[60] Wells, *The Island of Doctor Moreau*, p. 113.

[61] Wells, *The Island of Doctor Moreau*, p. 114.

[62] Carrie Rohman, 'Burning Out the Animal: The Failure of Enlightenment Purification in H. G. Wells's *The Island of Dr. Moreau*', in Mary Sanders Pollock and Catherine Rainwater (eds), *Figuring Animals: Essays on Animal Images in Art, Literature, Philosophy and Popular Culture* (New York: Palgrave, 2005), pp. 121–34, at p. 129.

[63] Wells, *The Island of Doctor Moreau*, p. 173

[64] Wells, *The Island of Doctor Moreau*, p. 167, p. 129.

[65] Calarco, 'Identity, Difference, Indistinction', pp. 41–60.

[66] Wells, *The Island of Doctor Moreau*, p. 85.

[67] Hurley, *The Gothic Body*, p. 109.

[68] Wells, *The Island of Doctor Moreau*, p. 144.

[69] Wells, *The Island of Doctor Moreau*, p. 145.

70 Jacques Derrida and David Wills, 'The Animal That Therefore I Am (More to Follow)', *Critical Inquiry* 28/2 (2002), pp. 369–418, at pp. 380–81.

71 Mason Harris, 'Vivisection, the Culture of Science, and Intellectual Uncertainty in *The Island of Doctor Moreau*', *Gothic Studies* 4/2 (2003), pp. 99–115, at p. 104

72 Sherryl Vint, 'Animals and Animality from the Island of Moreau to the Uplift Universe', *The Yearbook of English Studies* 37/2 (2007), at p. 87.

73 Vint, 'Animals and Animality', p. 87.

74 Vint, 'Animals and Animality', p. 88.

75 Vint, *Animal Alterity*, p. 190.

76 Wells, *The Island of Doctor Moreau*, p. 130.

77 Vint, *Animal Alterity*, p. 8.

78 Wells, *The Island of Doctor Moreau*, pp. 173–4.

79 Keith Ansell Pearson, *Viroid Life: Perspectives on Nietzsche and the Transhuman Condition* (London: Routledge, 1997), p. 124, p. 5.

80 Scott F. Gilbert, Jan Sapp, and Alfred Tauber, 'A Symbiotic View of Life: We Have Never Been Individuals', *The Quarterly Review of Biology* 87/4 (2012), pp. 325–41, at p. 336.

81 Jane Bennett, *Vibrant Matter: A Political Ecology of Things* (Durham: Duke University Press, 2010), p. ix.

82 Stacy Alaimo, *Bodily Natures: Science, Environment, and the Material Self* (Bloomington: Indiana University Press, 2010), p. 2.

83 Karen Barad, *Meeting the Universe Halfway: Quantum Physics and the Entanglement of Matter and Meaning* (Durham and London: Duke University Press, 2007), p. 185, emphasis original.

84 Elizabeth Grosz, *Volatile Bodies: Toward a Corporeal Feminism* (Indiana University Press, 1994).

85 Barad, *Meeting the Universe Halfway*, pp. 178–9.

86 Jeanette Samyn, 'Intimate Ecologies: Symbioses in the Nineteenth Century', *Victorian Literature and Culture* 48/1 (2020), pp. 243–65, at p. 244.

87 Samyn, 'Intimate Ecologies', p. 243, p. 244.

88 Samyn, 'Intimate Ecologies', p. 245.

89 H. G. Wells, 'Ancient Experiments in Co-Operation', *Gentleman's Magazine* (Oct. 1892), pp. 418–22, p. 421.

90 Wells, 'Ancient Experiments', p. 420, p. 421.

91 Wells, 'Ancient Experiments', p. 421.

92 Wells, 'Ancient Experiments', pp. 421–2.

93 Wells, 'Ancient Experiments', p. 421.

[94] Haraway, *Staying with the Trouble*, p. 32, p. 33, p. 31.
[95] Haraway, *Staying with the Trouble*, p. 31–2.
[96] Haraway, *Staying with the Trouble*, p. 33, p. 30.
[97] Haraway, *Staying with the Trouble*, p. 2, 173n4.
[98] Haraway, *Staying with the Trouble*, p. 2.
[99] H. P. Lovecraft qtd. in S. T. Joshi, 'Introduction' to *The Call of Cthulhu and Other Weird Stories*, ed. S. T. Joshi (Penguin Books, 1999), pp. v–xvii, at p. xiii.
[100] Natasha Rebry Coulthard, 'Lovecraft's Viral Networks', in Antonio Alcala Gonzalez and Carl H. Sederholm (eds), *Lovecraft in the 21st Century: Dead, But Still Dreaming* (New York: Routledge, 2022), pp. 143–58.
[101] MacCormack, 'Lovecraft's Cosmic Ethics', p. 204, p. 206.
[102] Found in redwood forests in North Central California, the Pimoa cthulhu spider is named after Lovecraft.
[103] Haraway, *Staying with the Trouble*, p. 31, p. 52, p. 55; see also note on p. 173.
[104] Haraway, *Staying with the Trouble*, p. 33.
[105] Haraway, *Staying with the Trouble*, p. 53.
[106] Haraway, *Staying with the Trouble*, p. 33, p. 31.
[107] Haraway, *Staying with the Trouble*, p. 31, emphasis original.
[108] Kemp, *H. G. Wells and the Culminating Ape*, p. 27.
[109] Haraway, *Staying with the Trouble*, p. 43.
[110] Haraway, *Staying with the Trouble*, p. 55.
[111] Detienne and Vernant, *Cunning Intelligence*, p. 38.
[112] Meaning a cunning device, trick or ruse.
[113] Detienne and Vernant, *Cunning Intelligence*, p. 38.
[114] Detienne and Vernant, *Cunning Intelligence*, p. 46.
[115] Detienne and Vernant, *Cunning Intelligence*, p. 159, p. 37.
[116] Detienne and Vernant, *Cunning Intelligence*, p. 37.
[117] Jay Dolmage, 'Metis, *Mêtis*, *Mestiza*, Medusa: Rhetorical Bodies across Rhetorical Traditions', *Rhetoric Review* 28/1 (2009), pp. 1–28, p. 14.
[118] Nandita Biswas Mellamphy, '(W)omen out/of Time: Metis, Medea, Mahakali', in K. Kolozova and E. A. Joy (eds), *After The 'Speculative Turn': Realism, Philosophy, and Feminism*, pp. 133–57, at pp. 137–8, p. 139.
[119] Mellamphy, '(W)omen out/of Time', p. 137.
[120] Detienne and Vernant, *Cunning Intelligence*, p. 20.
[121] Margaret McFall-Ngai, 'Noticing Microbial Worlds: The Postmodern Synthesis in Biology', in A. Tsing, H. Swanson, E. Gan, and

N. Bubandt (eds), *Arts of Living on a Damaged Planet* (Minneapolis: University of Minnesota Press, 2017), pp. M51–M69, at p. M52.

122 Detienne and Vernant, *Cunning Intelligence*, p. 39.

123 Detienne and Vernant, *Cunning Intelligence*, p. 39

124 Detienne and Vernant, *Cunning Intelligence*, p. 39; Debra Hawhee *Bodily Arts: Rhetoric and Athletics in Ancient Greece* (Austin: University of Texas Press, 2004), pp. 26–7, p. 57.

125 Pindar qtd. in Hawhee, *Bodily Arts*, p. 56.

126 Qtd. in Hawhee, *Bodily Arts*, p. 56.

127 Hawhee, *Bodily Arts*, p. 56.

128 Detienne and Vernant, *Cunning Intelligence*, p. 37.

129 Hawhee, *Bodily Arts*, p. 56.

130 Detienne and Vernant, *Cunning Intelligence*, p. 159.

131 Haraway, *Staying with the Trouble*, p. 32, p. 33.

132 Haraway, *Staying with the Trouble*, p. 101.

133 MacCormack, 'Lovecraft's Cosmic Ethics', p. 204, p. 206.

134 H. G. Wells, 'The Future in America: A Search After Realities' (New York and London: Harper & Brothers Publishers, 1906), p. 4.

135 Haraway, *Staying with the Trouble*, p. 56.

136 A type of autoimmune cell with the ability to ingest things like bacteria, dust or dead cells.

137 Wells, 'Ancient Experiments in Co-Operation', p. 421.

138 Wells, 'Ancient Experiments in Co-Operation', p. 422.

139 H. G. Wells, *Mind at the End of its Tether* (London, Toronto: William Heinemann LTD, 1945), p. 18, p. 19.

140 Haraway, *Staying with the Trouble*, p. 31.

141 Samyn, 'Intimate Ecologies', p. 245.

142 J. Halberstam, *Skin Shows: Gothic Horror and the Technology of Monstrosity* (Durham: Duke University Press, 1995), p. 2.

143 Pascale McCullough Manning, 'The Hyde We Live in: Stevenson, Evolution, and the Anthropogenic Fog', *Victorian Literature and Culture* (2018), pp. 181–99, at p. 46.

144 Haraway, *Staying with the Trouble*, pp. 37–8.

145 Haraway, *Staying with the Trouble*, p. 2.

146 Frederick S. Frank, 'Introduction', in Horace Walpole *The Castle of Otranto and The Mysterious Mother*, ed. F. S. Frank (Peterborough: Broadview Press, 2011), pp. 11–34, at p. 11, p. 17, italics original.

147 Miles, *Gothic Writing*, p. 15.

Chapter 3

1 Robert Louis Stevenson, *Strange Case of Dr Jekyll and Mr Hyde*, 3rd edn, ed. Martin Danahay (Peterborough: Broadview, 2015), pp. 76–7.

2 R. L. Stevenson, qtd. in J. Halberstam, *Skin Shows: Gothic Horror and the Technology of Monsters* (Durham: Duke University Press, 1995), p. 54.

3 Stevenson, *Strange Case*, p. 76.

4 MPD first appears in the American Psychiatric Association's *Diagnostic and Statistical Manual of Mental Disorders* (DSM) III in 1980. The switch from the term multiple personality disorder to dissociative identity disorder occurred from the third to fourth edition of the DSM.

5 Mick Cooper, 'If you Can't be Jekyll be Hyde: An Existential-phenomenological Exploration of Lived-Plurality', in Mick Cooper and John Rowan (eds), *The Plural Self: Multiplicity in Everyday Life* (London: Sage, 1999), pp. 51–70.

6 Masao Miyoshi, *The Divided Self; a Perspective on the Literature of the Victorians* (New York: New York University Press, 1969), p. xiv; Matthew C. Brennan, *The Gothic Psyche: Disintegration and Growth in Nineteenth Century English Literature* (New York: Camden House, 1998), p. 9; Robert Miles, *Gothic Writing 1750–1820: A Genealogy*, 2nd edn (Manchester: Manchester University Press, 2002), p. 3.

7 Robert Miles, *Gothic Writing*, p. 2.

8 See also Cathryn Molloy, '"I Just Really Love My Spirit": A Rhetorical Inquiry into Dissociative Identity Disorder', *Rhetoric Review* 34/4 (2015), pp. 462–78.

9 Marcel Detienne and Jean-Pierre Vernant, *Cunning Intelligence in Greek Culture and Society*, trans. Janet Lloyd (New Jersey: Humanities Press, 1978), p. 18.

10 Debra Hawhee, *Bodily Arts: Rhetoric and Athletics in Ancient Greece* (Austin: University of Texas Press, 2004), p. 49.

11 I take ethos in the classic Aristotelian sense of character or a rhetorical appeal by character.

12 Donna Haraway, *Staying with the Trouble: Making Kin in the Chthulucene* (Durham: Duke University Press, 2016), p. 31.

13 More popularly known as 'mesmerism', a precursor to hypnotism.

14 M. Boor, 'The Multiple Personality Epidemic: Additional Cases and Inferences Regarding Diagnosis, Etiology, Dynamics, and Treatment', *Journal of Nervous and Mental Disorders* 170 (1982), pp. 302–4.

15 Ian Hacking, 'Multiple Personality Disorder and its Hosts', *History of the Human Sciences* 5/3 (1992), pp. 3–31.

16 Armand-Marie-Jacques de Chastenet, Marquis de Puységur, *Mémoires pour servir à l'histoiré et à l'établissement du magnétisme animal* (Paris: Dentu, 1784), p. 33, p. 35.

17 Puységur, *Mémoires*, p. 90.

18 Adam Crabtree, *From Mesmer to Freud: Magnetic Sleep and the Roots of Psychological Healing* (New Haven: Yale University Press, 1993), pp. 87–8.

19 John Herdman, *The Double in Nineteenth-Century Fiction* (London: Macmillan, 1990), p. 13.

20 Natasha Rebry, *Disintegrated Subjects: Gothic Fiction, Mental Science and the fin-de-siècle Discourse of Dissociation* (PhD Thesis, The University of British Columbia, Okanagan, 2013).

21 Eugène Azam had already published his opinions on the case in a series of articles that appeared in *Revue Scientifique* in the 1870s.

22 For example, Nancy K. Gish 'Jekyll and Hyde: The Psychology of Dissociation', *International Journal of Scottish Literature* 2/2 (2007), pp. 1–10; Jill Matus, *Shock, Memory and the Unconscious in Victorian Fiction* (Cambridge; New York: Cambridge University Press, 2009).

23 Morton Prince, *Dissociation of a Personality* (Oxford: Oxford University Press, 1905), p. 2.

24 Prince, *Dissociation of a Personality*, p. 1, p. 129, p. 410. Prince ascribes numbers to Clara's personalities; BIV is 'the one whom Miss Beauchamp look upon as her Mr. Hyde' (p. 410) while Sally, her 'devil', is the only one given a proper name as the most developed of Miss Beauchamp's personalities.

25 Ian Hacking, *Rewriting the Soul: Multiple Personality and the Sciences of Memory* (Princeton: Princeton University Press, 1995), pp. 232–3. Hacking cites the work of Gothic writers, such as E. T. A. Hoffmann, James Hogg, and, of course, Stevenson.

26 H. Merskey, 'The Manufacture of Personalities: The Production of Multiple Personality Disorder', *British Journal of Psychiatry* 160 (1992), pp. 327–40.

27 Ray Aldridge-Morris, *Multiple Personality: An Exercise in Deception* (Hillsdale: Lawrence Erlbaum Associates, Inc., 1989).

28 Robert W. Rieber, *The Bifurcation of the Self: The History and Theory of Dissociation and Its Disorders* (New York: Birkhäuser, 2006), p. 43.

29 Rieber, *The Bifurcation of the Self*, p. 43.

[30] Ian Hacking, 'Multiple Personality and its Hosts' *History of the Human Sciences* 5/3 (1992), pp. 3–31, at pp. 4–5.

[31] Hacking, *Rewriting the Soul*, p. 232.

[32] Jodey Castricano, 'Much Ado about Handwriting: Countersigning with the Other Hand in Stevenson's *The Strange Case of Dr. Jekyll and Mr. Hyde*', *Romanticism on the Net* 44 (2006), *https://erudit.org/en/journals/ron/2006-n44-ron1433/014001ar/*.

[33] Stevenson, *Strange Case of Dr Jekyll and Mr Hyde*, p. 76, emphasis added.

[34] Stevenson, *Strange Case of Dr Jekyll and Mr Hyde*, pp. 76–7.

[35] Stevenson, *Strange Case of Dr Jekyll and Mr Hyde*, p. 77, p. 83., p. 79, p. 77.

[36] Stevenson, *Strange Case of Dr Jekyll and Mr Hyde*, p. 78, p. 79.

[37] Peter K. Garrett, 'Cries and Voices: Reading Jekyll and Hyde', in William Veeder and Gordon Hirsch (eds), *Dr. Jekyll and Mr. Hyde: After One Hundred Years* (Chicago: University of Chicago Press, 1988), pp. 59–72, at p. 67. Garrett's point here is about the complete text rather than the statement.

[38] Martin A. Danahay, *A Community of One: Masculine Autobiography and Autonomy in Nineteenth-Century Britain* (Albany: State University of New York Press, 1993), p. 10.

[39] Stevenson, *Strange Case of Dr Jekyll and Mr Hyde*, p. 80, p. 81, p. 90.

[40] Stevenson, *Strange Case of Dr Jekyll and Mr Hyde*, p. 87.

[41] Stevenson, *Strange Case of Dr Jekyll and Mr Hyde*, p. 75.

[42] Pierre Janet, *Major Symptoms of Hysteria* (New York: Macmillan, 1907), p. 332, emphasis original.

[43] Prince, *Dissociation of a Personality*, p. 393.

[44] Janet believed that hysteria resulted from a traumatic experience left unassimilated from typical memories, leading to the development of unique memory clusters and ultimately separate personalities. He used distracted or automatic writing to tap into the subconscious aspects of personality and unite them.

[45] Molloy, '"I Just Really Love My Spirit"', p. 464.

[46] Laurence J. Kirmayer, 'Pacing the Void: Social and Cultural Dimensions of Dissociation', in David Spiegel (ed.), *Dissociation: Culture, Mind, and Body* (Washington: American Psychiatric Press, 1994), pp. 91–122, at p. 104, p. 107.

[47] Elizabeth F. Howell, *The Dissociative Mind* (New York: Routledge, 2008), p. 38, p. 47.

[48] Kirmayer, 'Pacing the Void', p. 110, p. 108.

[49] Kirmayer, 'Pacing the Void', pp. 106–07.

[50] Kirmayer, 'Pacing the Void', p. 104; Elizabeth F. Howell, *Understanding and Treating Dissociative Identity Disorder: A Relational Approach* (New York: Routledge, 2011), p. 2.

[51] Kirmayer, 'Pacing the Void', p. 113, p. 114.

[52] Kirmayer, 'Pacing the Void', p. 113.

[53] Amy Louise Miller, 'The Phenomenology of Self as Non-Local: Theoretical Consideration and Research Report', in Anna-Teresa Tymieniecka (ed.), *Logos of Phenomenology and Phenomenology of the Logos. Book 4. The Logos of Scientific Interrogation: Participating in Nature-Life-Sharing in Life* (New York: Springer, 2006), pp. 227–45, at p. 227.

[54] Stephen E. Braude, *First Person Plural: Multiple Personality and the Philosophy of Mind*, New York: Routledge, 1991), p. 66.

[55] Cooper, 'If you Can't be Jekyll be Hyde', p. 51, p. 62.

[56] Cooper, 'If you Can't be Jekyll be Hyde', p. 62.

[57] Cooper, 'If you Can't be Jekyll be Hyde', p. 69.

[58] Molloy, '"I Just Really Love My Spirit"', p. 463.

[59] Cooper, 'If you Can't be Jekyll be Hyde', p. 68.

[60] Kirmayer, 'Pacing the Void', p. 114.

[61] F. W. H. Myers, 'Multiplex Personality', *Proceedings of the Society for Psychical Research* 3 (1887), pp. 496–514, at p. 502. There is also overlap with Myers's descriptions of Vivet's 'monkey-like imprudence' and Stevenson's portrayal of Hyde's 'ape-like' (p. 46) behaviours.

[62] F. W. H. Myers qtd. in Matus, *Shock, Memory and the Unconscious*, p. 168. Ultimately, Myers questioned Stevenson's depictions of the shared memory and handwriting of Jekyll and Hyde.

[63] F. W. H. Myers, 'Obituary: Robert Louis Stevenson', *Journal of the Society for Psychical Research* 7 (January 1895), pp. 6–7, at pp. 6–7.

[64] F. W. H. Myers, *Human Personality and its Survival of Bodily Death*, vol. 1 (London: Longmans, Green & Co., 1903), p. 14; 'Multiplex Personality', p. 496

[65] Myers, *Human Personality*, vol. 2, p. 254.

[66] Myers, *Human Personality*, vol. 1, p. 34.

[67] Jack Hunter, 'Gothic Psychology, The Ecological Unconscious and the Re-Enchantment of Nature' (26 March 202), *https://gothicnaturejournal.com/gothic-psychology-the-ecological-unconscious/*.

[68] William James, 'Frederic Myers's Service to Psychology', *Popular Science Monthly* 59 (August 1901), pp. 380–89, at p. 383, p. 386.

[69] Myers, *Human Personality*, vol. 1, p. 15.

[70] Sonu Shamdasani, 'Encountering Hélène: Théodore Flournoy and the Genesis of Subliminal Psychology', in Théodore Flournoy, *From India*

to the Planet Mars: A Case of Multiple Personality with Imaginary Languages (Princeton: Princeton University Press, 1994), pp. xi–li, at p. xv.

71 F. W. H. Myers, 'To the Editor of the *Journal of the Society for Psychical Research*', *Journal of the Society for Psychical Research* IV/LX (May 1889), pp. 77–8, at p. 77.

72 Myers, *Human Personality*, vol. 1, p. 68.

73 Myers, 'Multiplex Personality', p. 503.

74 Myers, 'Multiplex Personality', p. 505, p. 514.

75 Myers, 'Multiplex Personality', p. 509.

76 F. W. H. Myers, 'Human personality in the light of hypnotic suggestion', *Proceedings of The Society for Psychical Research* 4 (1886–87), pp. 1–24, at p. 19.

77 Myers, *Human Personality*, vol. 1, p. 68.

78 Myers, 'Multiplex Personality', p. 503.

79 Myers, *Human Personality*, vol. 1, p. 9, p. 18.

80 James, 'Frederick Myers's Service to Psychology', p. 381.

81 Shamdasani, 'Encountering Hélène', p. xv.

82 Anne Stiles, *Popular Fiction and Brain Science in the Late Nineteenth Century* (Cambridge: Cambridge University Press, 2012), p. 14.

83 Stiles, *Popular Fiction and Brain Science*, p. 14.

84 James, 'Frederick Myers', p. 201.

85 The most recognisable and notable might be Freud's tripartite division of ego, id and superego, John Beahrs's theory of 'co-consciousness', and Kenneth Gergen's theory of masks.

86 Gary S. Gregg qtd. in Cooper, 'If you Can't be Jekyll be Hyde', p. 59.

87 Mick Cooper and John Rowan, 'Introduction: Self-Plurality – The One and the Many', in Mick Cooper and John Rowan (eds), *The Plural Self: Multiplicity in Everyday Life* (London: Sage, 1999), pp. 1–10, at pp. 2–3, emphasis original.

88 Daniel J. Siegel qtd. in Howell, *Understanding and Treating Dissociative Identity Disorder*, p. 7.

89 Rowan and Cooper, 'Introduction', p. 2.

90 Leon Rappoport, Steven Baumgardner and George Boone, 'Postmodern Culture and the Plural Self', in Mick Cooper and John Rowan (eds), *The Plural Self: Multiplicity in Everyday Life* (London: Sage, 1999), pp. 93–106; Cooper, 'If you Can't be Jekyll be Hyde', p. 68.

91 Rowan and Cooper, 'Introduction', p. 1, p. 5.

92 Cooper, 'If you Can't be Jekyll be Hyde', p. 67.

93 Cooper, 'If you Can't be Jekyll be Hyde', p. 68, p. 63.

94 Cooper, 'If you Can't be Jekyll be Hyde', p. 68, p. 65.

95 Cooper, 'If you Can't be Jekyll be Hyde', p. 60.
96 Detienne and Vernant, *Cunning Intelligence*, p. 18.
97 Detienne and Vernant, *Cunning Intelligence*, p. 32, pp. 39–40.
98 Many vulnerable or marginalised people have learned to disguise their difference to move freely through dangerous territory, to make do with available resources and ultimately to seize the opportunities of the elites.
99 Qtd. in Hawhee, *Bodily Arts*, p. 56.
100 Detienne and Vernant, *Cunning Intelligence*, p. 39.
101 Molloy, '"I Just Really Love My Spirit"', p. 473.
102 Molloy, '"I Just Really Love My Spirit"', p. 473, p. 474.
103 Molloy, '"I Just Really Love My Spirit"', p. 437.
104 Rosi Braidotti, *Posthuman Knowledge* (Cambridge: Polity Press, 2019), p. 40.
105 Stevenson, *Strange Case of Dr Jekyll and Mr Hyde*, p. 56.
106 Gilles Deleuze and Félix Guattari, *A Thousand Plateaus: Capitalism and Schizophrenia*, trans. Brian Massumi (Minnesota: Minnesota University Press, 1987), at p. 250.
107 Kirmayer, 'Pacing the Void', p. 115.
108 Molloy, '"I Just Really Love My Spirit"', p. 474, p. 468.
109 Molloy, '"I Just Really Love My Spirit"', pp. 463–4.
110 Stiles, *Popular Fiction and Brain Science*, p. 16.
111 Stiles, *Popular Fiction and Brain Science*, p. 13, p. 1, p. 16, p. 21.
112 Pascale McCullough Manning, 'The Hyde We Live in: Stevenson, Evolution, and the Anthropogenic Fog', *Victorian Literature and Culture* (2018), p. 46, pp. 181–99.
113 Hunter, 'Gothic Psychology'.
114 Frederick S. Frank, 'Introduction', in Horace Walpole *The Castle of Otranto and The Mysterious Mother*, ed. F. S. Frank (Peterborough: Broadview Press, 2011) pp. 11–34, at p. 17.
115 Barbara Eckman, 'Jung, Hegel, and the Subjective Universe', *Spring, An Annual of Archetypal Psychology and Jungian Thought* (1986), pp. 86–99, p. 94.

Chapter 4

1 Hesiod, *Theogony*, 929a (*c.* 730–700 BCE), *https://www.theoi.com/Text/HesiodTheogony.html*, accessed 1 June 2022.
2 Patrick J. Skerrett and W. Allan Walker, 'Say Hello to the Bugs in Your Gut', *Newsweek* 150/24 (10 Dec. 2007), p. 75.

[3] Lynn Margulis and René Fester are credited with coining the term. Scott F. Gilbert, 'Holobiont by Birth', in A. Tsing, H. Swanson, E. Gan, and N. Bubandt (eds), *Arts of Living on a Damaged Planet* (Minneapolis: University of Minnesota Press, 2017), pp. M73–M89, at p. 84.

[4] Gilbert, 'Holobiont by Birth', p. M75, p. M73.

[5] Gilbert, 'Holobiont by Birth', p. M75, p. M84.

[6] Margaret McFall-Ngai, 'Noticing Microbial Worlds: The Postmodern Synthesis in Biology', in A. Tsing, H. Swanson, E. Gan, and N. Bubandt (eds), *Arts of Living on a Damaged Planet* (Minneapolis: University of Minnesota Press, 2017), pp. M51–M69, at p. M52, p. M65.

[7] McFall-Ngai, 'Noticing Microbial Worlds', p. M52.

[8] Marcel Detienne and Jean-Pierre Vernant, *Cunning Intelligence in Greek Culture and Society*, trans. Janet Lloyd (New Jersey: Humanities Press, 1978), p. 159.

[9] Ed Yong, *I Contain Multitudes: The Microbes Within Us and a Grader View of Life* (New York HarperCollins, 2016), p. 5; see also Lynn Margulis and Dorion Sagan, 'The Beast with Five Genomes', *Natural History* 110/5 (June 2001), p. 38.

[10] Dorion Sagan, 'The Human is More than Human: Interspecies Communities and the New "Facts of Life"', Theorizing the Contemporary, *Fieldsights* (18 Nov. 2011), *https://culanth.org/fieldsights/the-human-is-more-than-human-interspecies-communities-and-the-new-facts-of-life*.

[11] Robert Miles, *Gothic Writing 1750–1820: A Genealogy*, 2nd edn (Manchester: Manchester University Press, 2002), p. 3.

[12] Nomination (naming), predication (qualification), argumentation (justification and questioning of claims), perspectivation (positioning or point of view) and intensification or mitigation (modifying the force of claims and status of utterances). Martin Reisigl and Ruth Wodak, 'The Discourse-Historical Approach (DHA)', in Ruth Wodak and Michael Meyer (eds), *Methods of Critical Discourse Studies*, 3rd edn (London: Sage, 2016), pp. 23–62, at p. 33.

[13] Ruth Wodak and Salomi Boukala, 'European Identities and the Revival of Nationalism in the European Union: A Discourse Historical Approach', *Journal of Language and Politics* 14/1 (2015), pp. 87–109, at p. 93.

[14] Wodak and Reisigl, 'The Discourse-Historical Approach (DHA)', p. 31, p. 25.

[15] Julia Kristeva, *Powers of Horror: An Essay on Abjection*, trans. Leon S. Roudiez (New York: Columbia University Press, 1982), p. 4.

[16] Luis P. Villarreal, 'Are Viruses Alive?', *Scientific American* 291/6 (2004), pp. 100–5, at p. 101.

[17] Traci Watson, 'The Trickster Microbes Shaking up the Tree of Life', *Nature* 569/16 (May 2019), pp. 322–4, at p. 322.

[18] Robert Hooke, *Micrographia: Or Some Physiological Descriptions of Minute Bodies Made by Magnifying Glasses with Observations and Inquiries Thereupon* (1665/2005), Project Gutenberg, *https://www.gutenberg.org/cache/epub/15491/pg15491-images.html*, accessed 6 July 2022, italics original.

[19] Antonie van Leeuwenhoek, qtd. in Nick Lane, 'The unseen world: reflections on Leeuwenhoek (1677) "Concerning little animals"', *Philosophical Transactions of the Royal Society B* (2015), *http://doi.org/10.1098/rstb.2014.0344.*

[20] Heather Paxson, 'Post-Pasteurian Cultures: The Microbiopolitics of Raw-Milk Cheese in the United States', *Cultural Anthropology* 23/1 (2008), pp. 15–47, at p. 28.

[21] Institute of Medicine (US) Forum on Microbial Threats, 'Ending the War Metaphor: The Changing Agenda for Unraveling the Host-Microbe Relationship: Workshop Summary' (2006), *https://www.ncbi.nlm.nih.gov/books/NBK57071/.*

[22] Elizabeth K. Costello, Keaton Stagaman, Les Dethlefsen, Brendan J. M. Bohannan, and David A. Relman, 'The Application of Ecological Theory Toward an Understanding of the Human Microbiome', *Science* 336/6086 (2012), pp. 1255–62, at p. 1260.

[23] Costello et al., 'The Application of Ecological Theory Toward an Understanding of the Human Microbiome', p. 1256, p. 1261.

[24] Penelope Ironstone, 'Me, My Self, and the Multitude: Microbiopolitics of the Human Microbiome', *European Journal of Social Theory* 22/3 (2019), pp. 325–41, at p. 334.

[25] Chen, Yijing, Jinying Xu and Yu Chen, 'Regulation of Neurotransmitters by the Gut Microbiota and Effects on Cognition in Neurological Disorders', *Nutrients* 13/6 (2021).

[26] Roman M. Stilling, Timothy G., and John F. Cryan, 'Microbial Genes, Brain & Behaviour – Epigenetic Regulation of the Gut-Brain Axis', *Genes, Brain and Behavior* 13/1 (2014), pp. 69–86.

[27] Carl Zimmer, 'The microbiome may be looking out for itself', *International New York Times* (14 Aug. 2014), *https://www.nytimes.com/2014/08/14/science/our-microbiome-may-be-looking-out-for-itself.html.*

[28] Joe Alcock, Carlo C. Maley, and C. Athena Aktipis, 'Is Eating Behaviour Manipulated by the Gastrointestinal Microbiota? Evolutionary

Pressures and Potential Mechanisms', *Bioessays* 36 (2014), pp. 940–9, at p. 943.

29 James Gallagher, 'More than half your body is not human', *BBC News* (10 April 2018), *https://www.bbc.com/news/health-43674270*; Yong, *I Contain Multitudes*, p. 88; Michael Pollan 'Some of My Best Friends are Germs', *The New York Times Magazine* (19 May 2013), *https://www.nytimes.com/2013/05/19/magazine/say-hello-to-the-100-trillion-bacteria-that-make-up-your-microbiome.html*.

30 Christopher Long, 'The Daughters of Metis: Patriarchal Dominion and the Politics of the Between', *Graduate Faculty Philosophy Journal* 28/2 (2007), pp. 67–86, p. 77.

31 Elizabeth A. Wilson, *Gut Feminism* (Durham and London: Duke University Press, 2015), p. 5.

32 van Leeuwenhoek qtd. in Lane, 'The unseen world'.

33 Stefan Helmreich, *Sounding the Limits of Life: Essays in the Anthropology of Biology and Beyond* (Princeton and Oxford: Princeton University Press, 2016), p. 62.

34 Scott F. Gilbert, Jan Sapp, and Alfred Tauber, 'A Symbiotic View of Life: We Have Never Been Individuals', *The Quarterly Review of Biology* 87/4 (2012), pp. 325–41, at p. 327, p. 336, p. 326.

35 Gilbert, 'Holobiont by Birth', p. M75.

36 Paxson, 'Post-Pasteurian Cultures', p. 18.

37 Jamie Lorimer, 'Gut Buddies: Multispecies Studies and the Microbiome', *Environmental Humanities* 8/1 (2016), pp. 57–76.

38 Ironstone, 'Me, My Self, and the Multitude', p. 329, p. 332.

39 Paxson, 'Post-Pasteurian Cultures', p. 19.

40 Anna Lowenhaupt Tsing, *The Mushroom at the End of the World: On the Possibility of Life in Capitalist Ruins* (Princeton: Princeton University Press, 2015).

41 Eben Kirksey, 'Queer Love, Gender Bending Bacteria, and Life after the Anthropocene', *Theory, Culture & Society* 36/6 (2019), pp. 197–219, at p. 199, p. 214.

42 Gilbert, 'Holobiont by Birth', p. M83.

43 Alexandra Warwick, 'Feeling Gothicky?', *Gothic Studies* 9/1 (2007), pp. 5–15.

44 Jodey Castricano, *Gothic Metaphysics: From Alchemy to the Anthropocene* (Cardiff: University of Wales Press, 2021), pp. 191–2.

45 Sara Mills, *Discourse* (The New Critical Idiom), 2nd edn (London: Routledge, 2004), p. 140.

46 Norman Fairclough, 'A Dialectical-Relational Approach to Critical Discourse Studies', in Ruth Wodak and Michael Meyer (eds), *Methods of Critical Discourse Studies*, 3rd edn (London: Sage, 2016), pp. 86–108, at p. 88.

47 Reisigl and Wodak, 'The Discourse-Historical Approach (DHA)', p. 33.

48 Reisigl and Wodak, 'The Discourse-Historical Approach (DHA)', p. 43

49 Reisigl and Wodak, 'The Discourse-Historical Approach (DHA)', p. 43

50 These materials were generally found online using general search terms like 'human microbiome' and represent a small sample.

51 Tina Hesman Saey, 'Inside job: teams of microbes pull strings in the human body', *Science News* 179/13 (18 June 2011), pp. 26–9, at p. 26, p. 27.

52 Gallagher, 'More than half your body is not human'.

53 Dara Moskowitz Grumdahl, 'Ghosts in Your Machine', *Experience Life* (Nov. 2012), *https://experiencelife.lifetime.life/article/ghosts-in-your-machine/*; Patrick J. Skerrett and W. Allan Walker, 'Say Hello to The Bugs in Your Gut', *Newsweek* 150/24 (10 Dec. 2007), p. 75.

54 Skerrett and Walker, 'Say Hello to The Bugs in Your Gut', p. 75.

55 'Microbes maketh man', *The Economist* 404/8798 (18 Aug. 2012).

56 Lizzie Buchen, 'The New Germ Theory', *Nature* 468/7323 (25 Nov. 2010), pp. 492–5.

57 Pollan, 'Some of My Best Friends are Germs', p. 36.

58 Skerrett and Walker, 'Say Hello to The Bugs in Your Gut', p. 75.

59 Virginia Hughes, 'Microbiome: Cultural Differences', *Nature* 492/7427 (2012), pp. S14–S15, at p. S14.

60 Costello et al., 'The Application of Ecological Theory Toward an Understanding of the Human Microbiome', p. 1256; Gallagher, 'More than half your body is not human'.

61 Zimmer, 'The microbiome may be looking out for itself'.

62 Hughes, 'Microbiome: Cultural Differences', p. S14; Margulis and Sagan, 'The Beast with Five Genomes', p. 38; Saey, 'Inside job'.

63 Moheb Costandi, 'Microbes Manipulate Your Mind', *Scientific American* (1 July 2012), *https://www.scientificamerican.com/article/microbes-manipulate-your-mind/*; *The Economist*, 'Microbes maketh man'.

64 Pollan, 'Some of My Best Friends are Germs'.

65 Buchen, 'The New Germ Theory', p. 492; Skerrett and Walker, 'Say Hello to The Bugs in Your Gut', p. 75.

[66] Pollan, 'Some of My Best Friends are Germs'; Zimmer, 'The microbiome may be looking out for itself'; Saey, 'Inside job'.
[67] Grumdahl, 'Ghosts in Your Machine'.
[68] Skerrett and Walker, 'Say Hello to The Bugs in Your Gut', p. 75.
[69] Clair Folsome in Sagan, 'The Human is More than Human'.
[70] Yong, *I Contain Multitudes*, p. 3.
[71] Saey, 'Inside job'.
[72] Maria Cohut, 'Human microbiota: The microorganisms that make us their home', *Medical News Today* (27 June 2020), *https://www.medicalnewstoday.com/articles/human-microbiota-the-microorganisms-that-make-us-their-home*.
[73] Grumdhal, 'Ghosts in Your Machine'.
[74] Gallagher, 'More than half your body is not human'.
[75] Skerrett and Walker, 'Say Hello to The Bugs in Your Gut', p. 75.
[76] Buchen, 'The New Germ Theory', p. 492.
[77] Folsome qtd. in Sagan, 'The Human is More than Human'.
[78] Saey, 'Inside Job'; Pollan, 'Some of My Best Friends are Germs'.
[79] *The Economist*, 'Microbes maketh man'.
[80] Saey, 'Inside Job'; Gallagher, 'More than half your body is not human'.
[81] *The Economist*, 'Microbes maketh man'; Sagan 'The Human is More than Human'; Gallagher, 'More than half your body is not human'; Pollan, 'Some of My Best Friends are Germs'; Saey 'Inside job'.
[82] Rob DeSalle and Susan Perkins qtd. in Ironstone, 'Me, My Self, and the Multitude', p. 329; Gallagher, 'More than half your body is not human'; Sagan, 'The Human is More than Human'.
[83] Pollan, 'Some of My Best Friends are Germs'; Tina Hesman Saey, 'Year in Review: Your Body Is Mostly Microbes', *Science News* (20 Dec. 2013), *https://www.sciencenews.org/article/year-review-your-body-mostly-microbes*.
[84] Alexander Kriss, 'The Microbiome and the Multiple Self', *The New School: Critical Psychology* (1 June 2013), *https://newschoolpsychology.blogspot.com/2013/06/the-microbiome-and-multiple-self.html?m=1*.
[85] Skerrett and Walker, 'Say Hello to The Bugs in Your Gut', p. 75.
[86] *The Economist*, 'Microbes maketh man'.
[87] Pollan, 'Some of My Best Friends are Germs'.
[88] Sarkis Mazmanian qtd. in Saey, 'Inside Job'.
[89] *The Economist*, 'Microbes maketh man'.
[90] Yong, *I Contain Multitudes*, p. 71.
[91] Yong, *I Contain Multitudes*, p. 71; Saey, 'Inside Job'.
[92] Zimmer, 'The microbiome may be looking out for itself'.

[93] Heidi Kong qtd. in Saey, 'Year in Review'.
[94] Costandi, 'Microbes Manipulate Your Mind'.
[95] Saey, 'Inside Job'.
[96] Dorion Sagan, 'Beautiful Monsters: Terra in the Cyanocene', in A. Tsing, H. Swanson, E. Gan, and N. Bubandt (eds), *Arts of Living on a Damaged Planet* (Minneapolis: University of Minnesota Press, 2017), pp. M169–M174.
[97] Lynn Margulis and Dorion Sagan, *Acquiring Genomes: A Theory of the Origins of Species* (New York: Basic Books, 2002), p. 205.
[98] Lynn Margulis and Dorion Sagan, *What is Life?* (Berkeley: California University Press, 1995) p. 194.
[99] Helmreich, *Sounding the Limits of Life*, p. 62, p. 64.
[100] Dorion Sagan, 'Biography', *https://dorionsagan.wordpress.com/cv/biography/*, accessed 12 July 2022.
[101] Dorion Sagan, *Cosmic Apprentice: Dispatches from the Edges of Science* (Minneapolis: University of Minnesota Press, 2013), p. 166.
[102] Dorion Sagan, 'Metametazoa: Biology and Multiplicity', in Jonathan Crary and Sanford Kwinter (eds), *Zone 6: Incorporations: Fragments for a History of the Human Body* (Princeton: Princeton University Press, 1992), pp. 362–85, at p. 363, p. 362.
[103] Sagan, 'Metametazoa', p. 368.
[104] Sagan, 'The Human is More than Human'.
[105] Sagan, 'The Human is More than Human'.
[106] Sagan, 'The Human is More than Human'.
[107] Sagan, 'Metametazoa,' p. 379.
[108] Margulis and Sagan, 2002, p. 20; Jessica Hope Whiteside and Dorion Sagan, 'Medical Symbiotics', in Lynn Margulis, Celeste A. Asikainen, and Wolfgang E. Krumbein (eds), *Chimeras and Consciousness: Evolution of the Sensory Self* (Cambridge, MA: The MIT Press, 2011), pp. 207–18, at p. 211.
[109] Sagan, 'Metametazoa,' p. 379.
[110] A predatory bacteria, *Bdellovibrio*.
[111] Sagan 'Metametazoa', p. 378. p. 367; *Cosmic Apprentice*, p. 172, p. 167.
[112] Whiteside and Sagan, 'Medical Symbiotics', at p. 209.
[113] Sagan, 'Metametazoa,' p. 379.
[114] Sagan, *Cosmic Apprentice*, p. 24; Jim MacAllister qtd. in Sagan, 'Beautiful Monsters', p. M172.
[115] Whiteside and Sagan, 'Medical Symbiotics', p. 214.
[116] Dorion Sagan, 'Thermodynamics and Thought', in Lynn Margulis, Celeste A. Asikainen, and Wolfgang E. Krumbein (eds), *Chimeras and*

Consciousness: Evolution of the Sensory Self (Cambridge, MA: The MIT Press, 2011), pp. 241–50, at p. 248.

117 Sagan, 'The Human is More than Human'.

118 Grumdahl, 'Ghosts in Your Machine'; Sagan, 'The Human is More than Human'.

119 Helmreich, *Sounding the Limits of Life*, p. 62.

120 Robert Louis Stevenson, *Strange Case of Dr Jekyll and Mr Hyde* (Peterborough: Broadview, 2005), at p. 78–9.

121 Pollan, 'Some of My Best Friends are Germs'.

122 Robert Louis Stevenson, *Strange Case of Dr Jekyll and Mr Hyde*, at p. 76.

123 Costandi, 'Microbes Manipulate Your Mind'.

124 Fred Botting, *Gothic*, vol. 1 (London and New York: Routledge, 1996), p. 12.

125 Miles, *Gothic Writing*, p. 3.

126 Yong, *I Contain Multitudes*, p. 71; Carl Zimmer, 'The microbiome may be looking out for itself'.

127 Lynn Margulis, *Symbiotic Planet: A New Look at Evolution* (New York: Basic Books, 1998), p. 21.

128 Kelly Hurley, *The Gothic Body: Sexuality, Materialism, and Degeneration at the fin de siècle* (Cambridge: Cambridge University Press, 1996), p. 6.

129 Margulis, *Symbiotic Planet*, p. 4.

130 Simply, lab-produced empty cells, or 'non-living'.

131 Slava S. Epstein, 'Microbial Awakenings', *Nature* 457/26 (2009), p. 1083.

132 See for example, Copan, 'The Spooky Microbe Monsters Among Us', *Microbiology Today* (28 Oct. 2019), *https://www.copanusa.com/the-spooky-microbe-monsters-among-us/*.

133 John R. Brannon and Matthew A. Mulvey, 'Jekyll and Hyde: Bugs with Double Personalities', *Journal of Molecular Biology*, 431/16 (July 2019).

134 Margulis also uses Jekyll and Hyde as a metaphor to describe 'Centrioles and kinetosomes', *Symbiotic Planet*, p. 46.

135 Collectively, this is the message of studies of human health and disease (especially discussions of modern human microbiomes compared to hunter-gather microbiomes) and studies of ecology.

136 Elaine Graham, *Representations of the Post/Human: Monsters, Aliens and Others in Popular Culture* (Manchester: Rutgers University Press, 2002), p. 53.

137 A. Tsing, H. Swanson, E. Gan, and N. Bubandt, 'Introduction: Bodies Tumbled into Bodies' in A. Tsing, H. Swanson, E. Gan, and N.

Bubandt (eds), *Arts of Living on a Damaged Planet* (Minneapolis: University of Minnesota Press, 2017), pp. M1–M12, at p. M2.

138 Sagan, 'Beautiful Monsters', p. M169, p. M170.

139 Tsing et al., 'Introduction: Bodies Tumbled into Bodies', p. M5.

140 Kristeva, *Powers of Horror*, p. 4.

141 Kristeva, *Powers of Horror*, p. 9.

142 Kristeva, *Powers of Horror*, p. 5, p. 4, emphasis original.

143 Kristeva, *Powers of Horror*, p. 4, emphasis mine.

144 Kristeva, *Powers of Horror*, p. 5, p. 11, emphasis original, pp. 12–13.

145 Kristeva, *Powers of Horror*, p. 10.

146 Julia Kristeva, *Strangers to Ourselves*, trans. Leon S. Roudiez (New York: Columbia University Press, 1982), p. 181, p. 183.

147 Sigmund Freud, 'The Uncanny', in *The Standard Edition of the Complete Psychological Works of Sigmund Freud, Volume XVII (1917–1919): An Infantile Neurosis and Other Works* (London: The Hogarth Press: The Institute of Psycho-Analysis, 1955), pp. 217–56, at p. 220, p. 225.

148 Nicholas Royle, *The Uncanny* (New York: Routledge, 2003), p. 6.

149 Royle, *The Uncanny*, p. 1.

150 Andrew Bennett and Nicholas Royle, *Introduction to Literature, Criticism and Theory* (Harlow: Pearson Longman, 2004), at p. 34.

151 Warwick, 'Feeling Gothicky?', p. 6.

152 See for example Arran Stibbe, 'An Ecolinguistic Approach to Critical Discourse Studies', *Critical Discourse Studies* 11/1 (2014), pp. 117–28; 'Positive Discourse Analysis: Re-thinking human ecological relationships', in A. Fill and H. Penz (eds), *The Routledge Handbook of Ecolinguistics* (London: Routledge, 2017).

153 A. Stibbe, 'Critical discourse analysis and ecology: the search for new stories to live by', in J. Flowerdew and J. Richardson (eds), *The Routledge Handbook of Critical Discourse Analysis* (London: Routledge, 2018), pp. 497–509, p. 497.

154 Timothy Morton, *The Ecological Thought* (Cambridge, MA: Harvard University Press, 2010), p. 54.

155 Morton, *The Ecological Thought*, p. 53.

156 Julia Kristeva, 'The subject in process', in P. French & R-F. Lack (eds), *The Tel Quel reader* (London: Routledge, 1998), pp. 133–78.

157 Marek Tesar and Sonja Arndt, 'Writing the Human "I": Liminal Spaces of Mundane Abjection', *Qualitative Inquiry* 26/8–9 (2020), pp. 1102–9.

158 Tesar and Arndt, 'Writing the Human "I", p. 1104.

159 Kristeva, *Strangers to Ourselves*.

[160] Tesar and Arndt, 'Writing the Human "I"', p. 1105.
[161] Tsing et al., 'Introduction: Bodies Tumbled into Bodies', p. M10.
[162] Tsing, *The Mushroom at the End of the World*, p. 3, p. 28.
[163] Tsing, *The Mushroom at the End of the World*, p. 27.
[164] Tsing, *The Mushroom at the End of the World*, p. 28, p. 29.
[165] Tsing, *The Mushroom at the End of the World*, p. 31.
[166] Jeanette Samyn, 'Intimate Ecologies: Symbioses in the Nineteenth Century', *Victorian Literature and Culture* 48/1 (2020), pp. 243–65, at p. 245, p. 261.
[167] Tsing, *The Mushroom at the End of the World*, p. 33.
[168] Tsing, *The Mushroom at the End of the World*, p. 34, p. 33.
[169] Samyn, 'Intimate Ecologies: Symbioses in the Nineteenth Century', p. 261.
[170] R. L. Rutsky, 'Mutation, History, and the Fantasy in the Posthuman', *Subject Matters: A Journal of Communication and the Self* 3/2–4/1 (2007), pp. 99–112, p. 111.
[171] N. Katherine Hayles, *How We Became Posthuman* (Chicago: Chicago University Press, 1999), p. 3.
[172] Gilles Deleuze and Félix Guattari, *A Thousand Plateaus: Capitalism and Schizophrenia*, trans. Brian Massumi (Minnesota: Minnesota University Press, 1987), p. 238, p. 273.
[173] Donna Haraway, *Staying with the Trouble: Making Kin in the Chthulucene* (Durham: Duke University Press, 2016), p. 4, p. 64.
[174] Tsing et al., 'Introduction: Bodies Tumbled into Bodies', p. M10.
[175] Tsing et al., 'Introduction: Bodies Tumbled into Bodies', p. M2.
[176] Tsing et al., 'Introduction: Bodies Tumbled into Bodies', pp. M5–M6.
[177] Patricia MacCormack, 'Lovecraft's Cosmic Ethics', in Carl H. Sederholm and Jeffrey Andrew Weinstock (eds), *The Age of Lovecraft* (Minneapolis: University of Minnesota Press, 2016), pp. 199–214, at p. 208, p. 211.
[178] Sagan, *Cosmic Apprentice*, p. 1.

Chapter 5

[1] Gilles Deleuze and Félix Guattari, *A Thousand Plateaus: Capitalism and Schizophrenia*, trans. Brian Massumi (Minnesota: Minnesota University Press, 1987), p. 24.
[2] Dorion Sagan, 'The Human is More than Human: Interspecies Communities and the New "Facts of Life"', Theorizing the Contemporary,

Fieldsights (18 Nov. 2011) *https://culanth.org/fieldsights/the-human-is-more-than-human-interspecies-communities-and-the-new-facts-of-life*.

3 R. T. Rolfe and F. W. Rolfe, *The Romance of the Fungus World: An Account of Fungus in Its Numerous Guises Both Real and Legendary* (Mineola, New York: Dover Publications, Inc. 1925/2014), p. 50.

4 Rolfe and Rolfe, *The Romance of the Fungus World*, p. 15.

5 Anna Lowenhaupt Tsing, *The Mushroom at the End of the World: On the Possibility of Life in Capitalist Ruins* (Princeton: Princeton University Press, 2015), p. 138.

6 Ben Woodard, *Slime Dynamics* (Winchester, Washington: Zero Books, 2012), p. 27.

7 Robert Macfarlane, 'The Secrets of The Wood Wide Web', *The New Yorker* (7 August 2016), *https://www.newyorker.com/tech/annals-of-technology/the-secrets-of-the-wood-wide-web*.

8 Paul Stamets, '6 Ways Mushrooms Can Save the World', TED Talk (March 2008), *https://www.ted.com/talks/paul_stamets_6_ways_mushrooms_can_save_the_world?subtitle=en*, accessed 4 January 2022.

9 Tsing, *The Mushroom at the End of the World*, p. 137.

10 Ella Mershon, 'Pulpy Fiction', *Victorian Literature and Culture* 48/1 (2020), pp. 267–98, at p. 268.

11 Tsing, *The Mushroom at the End of the World*, p. 139.

12 Tsing, *The Mushroom at the End of the World*, p. 137, p. 139.

13 Tsing, *The Mushroom at the End of the World*, p. 138.

14 Eugene Thacker, *In the Dust of this Planet: Horror of Philosophy Vol. 1* (Winchester, Washington: Zero Books, 2011), p. 5, emphasis original.

15 Marcel Detienne and Jean-Pierre Vernant, *Cunning Intelligence in Greek Culture and Society*, trans. Janet Lloyd (New Jersey: Humanities Press, 1978), p. 37.

16 Deleuze and Guattari, *A Thousand Plateaus*, p. 238, p. 273; Donna Haraway, *Staying with the Trouble: Making Kin in the Chthulucene* (Durham: Duke University Press, 2016), p. 21.

17 William C. Trapani and Chandra A. Maldonado, '*Kairos*: On the Limits to Our (Rhetorical) Situation', *Rhetoric Society Quarterly* 48/3 (2018), pp. 278–86.

18 Rolfe and Rolfe, *The Romance of the Fungus World*, pp. 16–17.

19 Rolfe and Rolfe, *The Romance of the Fungus World*, p. 15.

20 Rolfe and Rolfe, *The Romance of the Fungus World*, p. 50.

21 Woodard, *Slime Dynamics*, p. 26.

22 Hodgson's 'The Voice in the Night' (1907) 'may be *the* tale of fungal terror' as per Orrin Grey and Silvia Moreno-Garcia, 'Introduction',

in O. Grey and S. Moreno-Garcia (eds), *Fungi* (Vancouver: Innsmouth Free Press, 2012), p. 1, emphasis original.

23 Edgar Allan Poe, 'The Fall of the House of Usher', in *Edgar Allan Poe Complete Tales & Poems* (Edison, NJ: Castle Books, 2002), pp. 171–83, at pp. 172–3, p. 177.

24 Natasha Rebry Coulthard, 'Lovecraft's Viral Networks', in Antonio Alcala Gonzalez and Carl H. Sederholm (eds), *Lovecraft in the 21st Century: Dead, But Still Dreaming* (New York: Routledge, 2022), pp. 143–58.

25 H. P. Lovecraft, 'The Shunned House', in *The Dreams in the Witch House and Other Weird Stories*, ed. S. T. Joshi (New York: Penguin Books, 2004), pp. 90–115, at p. 93, p. 99.

26 Lovecraft, 'The Shunned House', p. 111.

27 Lovecraft, 'The Shunned House', p. 97, p. 109.

28 Lovecraft, 'The Shunned House', p. 113, p. 112.

29 Stacy Alaimo, *Bodily Natures: Science, Environment, and the Material Self* (Bloomington: Indiana University Press, 2010), p. 11.

30 Andrew Smith and William Hughes, 'Introduction: Defining the Eco-Gothic', in A. Smith and W. Hughes (eds), *EcoGothic* (Manchester: Manchester University Press), pp. 1–33, at p. 14.

31 *Ophiocordyceps unilateralis.*

32 Specifically known as endoparasitoids.

33 Stamets notes the fungal reign after the collapse of the dinosaurs and asserts his confidence that fungi will continue to reign long after our demise; '6 Ways that Mushrooms can Save the World', TED Talk.

34 Arthur Machen, *The Hill of Dreams*, in *The Great God Pan and The Hill of Dreams* (London: Dover, 2006), p. 157.

35 Arthur Machen, *The Three Impostors; or, The Transmutations*, in *The Three Impostors and Other Stories: Vol. 1 of the Best Weird Tales of Arthur Machen*, ed. in S. T. Joshi (Hayward: Chaosium Inc., 2007), pp. 101–234, at p. 209.

36 Karen Barad, *Meeting the Universe Halfway: Quantum Physics and the Entanglement of Matter and Meaning* (Durham and London: Duke University Press, 2007), p. 33.

37 We might consider his decision to focus on Pan, a nature spirit, significant to this end.

38 Arthur Machen, *Far Off Things* (London: Martin Secker, 1922), pp. 19–20.

39 Machen, *Far Off Things*, p. 23.

40 Machen, *Far Off Things*, p. 11, p. 8, p. 11.

[41] Machen, *Far Off Things*, p. 154.
[42] Arthur Machen, 'The Shining Pyramid', in *The Three Impostors and Other Stories: Vol. 1 of the Best Weird Tales of Machen*, ed. S. T. Joshi (Hayward: Chaosium Inc., 2007), pp. 78–99, at p. 99.
[43] Mershon, 'Pulpy Fiction', p. 274.
[44] Mark Valentine, *Arthur Machen* (Bridgend: WBC Book Manufacturers, 1995), p. 7.
[45] Arthur Machen, 'The Great God Pan', in *The Three Impostors and Other Stories: Vol. 1 of the Best Weird Tales of Arthur Machen*, ed. S. T. Joshi (Hayward: Chaosium Inc., 2007), pp. 1–50, at p. 46; *The Three Impostors*, p. 207.
[46] Machen, *The Hill of Dreams*, p. 195, p. 196.
[47] *The Hill of Dreams* was composed in 1895–7 but not published until 1907.
[48] Machen, *The Hill of Dreams*, p. 69.
[49] Machen writes of his struggle to distinguish his style from R. L. Stevenson's, in *The Hill of Dreams*, p. 71.
[50] Machen, *The Hill of Dreams*, pp. 72–3.
[51] A reference to Isca Silurum.
[52] Machen, *The Hill of Dreams*, p. 84.
[53] Machen, *The Hill of Dreams*, pp. 76–7.
[54] Machen, *The Hill of Dreams*, p. 85, emphasis added.
[55] Machen, *The Hill of Dreams*, p. 85, emphasis added.
[56] Machen, *The Hill of Dreams*, p. 84.
[57] Mershon, 'Pulpy Fiction', p. 268.
[58] Machen, *The Hill of Dreams*, pp. 85–6.
[59] Machen, *The Hill of Dreams*, p. 94, p. 97, p. 98.
[60] Mershon, 'Pulpy Fiction', p. 284.
[61] Machen, *The Hill of Dreams*, p. 107, pp. 138–9.
[62] Machen, *The Hill of Dreams*, p. 107.
[63] Machen, *The Hill of Dreams*, p. 101.
[64] Machen, *The Hill of Dreams*, p. 101.
[65] Machen, *The Hill of Dreams*, pp. 109–10, p. 98.
[66] Machen, *The Hill of Dreams*, p. 133.
[67] Machen, *The Hill of Dreams*, p. 133.
[68] Machen, *The Hill of Dreams*, p. 130.
[69] Mershon, 'Pulpy Fiction', p. 268.
[70] Machen, *The Hill of Dreams*, p. 169, p. 184, p. 187.
[71] Mershon, 'Pulpy Fiction', p. 269.
[72] Mershon, 'Pulpy Fiction', p. 68, p. 267.

[73] Dennis Denisoff, 'The Queer Ecology of Vernon Lee's Transient Affections', *Feminist Modernist Studies* 3/2 (2020), pp. 148–61, at p. 155.

[74] Grace van Deelen, 'What Is Queer Ecology?' (3 June 2023), *https://www.sierraclub.org/sierra/what-is-queer-ecology*, accessed 18 Nov. 2023.

[75] Catriona Sandilands, 'Queer Ecology', in *Keywords for Environmental Studies* (2016), *https://keywords.nyupress.org/environmental-studies/essay/queer-ecology/*, accessed 18 Nov. 2023.

[76] Patricia MacCormack, 'Lovecraft's Cosmic Ethics', in Carl H. Sederholm and Jeffrey Andrew Weinstock (eds), *The Age of Lovecraft* (Minnesota: University of Minnesota Press, 2016), pp. 199–214, at p. 213.

[77] Read with Jodey Castricano's *Gothic Metaphysics* in mind, such a story seems to represent the moment when alchemical knowledge and worldview were denigrated if not hunted down to be eradicated.

[78] There are two types: arbuscular mycorrhizal fungi, which colonize the host plant's roots intracellularly, and ectomycorrhizal fungi, which colonize roots extracellularly. See Christopher Rhodes, 'The Whispering World of Plants: "The Wood Wide Web"', *Science Progress* 100/3 (2017), pp. 331–7 and Ana Lucía Castro-Delgado, Stephanie Elizondo-Mesén, Yendri Valladares-Cruz, and William Rivera-Méndez, 'Wood Wide Web: Communication Through the Mycorrhizal Network,' *Tecnología en Marcha* 33–4 (2020), pp. 114–25.

[79] Tsing, *The Mushroom at the End of the World*, p. 139.

[80] Rhodes, 'The Whispering World of Plants', pp. 331–7, p. 333.

[81] Tsing, *The Mushroom at the End of the World*, p. 139.

[82] Castro-Delgado et al., 'Wood Wide Web', pp. 114–25, at p. 118.

[83] Rhodes, 'The Whispering World of Plants', p. 331.

[84] G. Kim, M. L. LeBlanc, E. K. Wafula, C. W. dePamphilis, J. H. Westwood, 'Genomic-scale exchange of mRNA between a parasitic plant and its hosts', *Science* 345/6198 (2014), pp. 808–11, p. 808. See also Rhodes, 'The Whispering World of Plants', p. 335.

[85] Rolfe and Rolfe, *The Romance of the Fungus World*, p. 25.

[86] Jaco Bouwer (dir.), *Gaia* (2021), 1:02:12.

[87] According to Hesiod, Gaia is also mother to the Cyclopes and the Hundred-Armed. Detienne and Vernant, *Cunning Intelligence in Greek Culture and Society*, pp. 62–3.

[88] Detienne and Vernant, *Cunning Intelligence in Greek Culture and Society*, p. 62.

[89] Lynn Margulis, *Symbiotic Planet: A New Look at Evolution* (New York: Basic Books, 1998), p. 2.

[90] Margulis, *Symbiotic Planet*, p. 2.
[91] Lynn Margulis, Celeste A. Asikainen, and Wolfgang E. Krumbein, 'Introduction', in Lynn Margulis, Celeste A. Asikainen, and Wolfgang E. Krumbein (eds), *Chimeras and Consciousness: Evolution of the Sensory Self* (Cambridge, MA: The MIT Press, 2011), pp. 6–7.
[92] Dorion Sagan, *Cosmic Apprentice: Dispatches from the Edges of Science* (Minneapolis: University of Minnesota Press, 2013) p. 167, p. 175, emphasis original.
[93] Sagan, *Cosmic Apprentice*, p. 176.
[94] Haraway, *Staying with the Trouble*, p. 51.
[95] Bruno Latour in Haraway, *Staying with the Trouble*, p. 41.
[96] Haraway, *Staying with the Trouble*, p. 43.
[97] Haraway, *Staying with the Trouble*, p. 44, p. 52.
[98] Bouwer, *Gaia*, 38:28–38:41, 38:48–50.
[99] Bouwer, *Gaia*, 1:59–2:10.
[100] Bouwer, *Gaia*, 21:05.
[101] Bouwer, *Gaia*, 1:00:05.
[102] Detienne and Vernant, *Cunning Intelligence in Greek Culture and Society*, p. 39.
[103] Detienne and Vernant, *Cunning Intelligence in Greek Culture and Society*, p. 29.
[104] Rolfe and Rolfe, *The Romance of the Fungus World*, p. 29, p. 31.
[105] Mershon, 'Pulpy Fiction', pp. 278–79.
[106] Detienne and Vernant, *Cunning Intelligence in Greek Culture and Society*, p. 46, p. 27.
[107] There is also Stefan's mother, who becomes an hybrid tree.
[108] Bouwer, *Gaia*, 1:19:39.
[109] Detienne and Vernant, *Cunning Intelligence in Greek Culture and Society*, p. 28.
[110] Janet Atwill, *Rhetoric Reclaimed: Aristotle and the Liberal Arts Tradition* (Ithaca and London: Cornell University Press, 2009), p. 56.
[111] See Michelle Ballif, *Seduction, Sophistry, and the Woman with the Rhetorical Figure* (Carbondale: Southern Illinois University Press, 2001); William C. Trapani and Chandra A. Maldonado, '*Kairos*: On the Limits to Our (Rhetorical) Situation', *Rhetoric Society Quarterly* 48/3 (2018), pp. 278–86.
[112] Kristin Pomykala, 'Snake(s)kin: The Intertwining *Mêtis* and Mythopoetics of Serpentine Rhetoric', *Rhetoric Society Quarterly* 47/3 (2017), pp. 264–74, p. 265; Shannon Walters, 'Animal Athena: The

Interspecies "Mētis" of Women Writers with Autism', *JAC* 30/3/4 (2010), pp. 683–711, at p. 690.

113 Atwill, *Rhetoric Reclaimed*, p. 7.

114 Atwill, *Rhetoric Reclaimed*, p. 53, p. 48.

115 Atwill, *Rhetoric Reclaimed*, p. 48.

116 According to MycoLyco, it is possible to listen to 'mushrooms talk'. See MycoLyco, 'Five Minutes of Blue Oyster Mushrooms Talking', *YouTube* (28 Nov. 2020), *https://www.youtube.com/watch?v=J-nIBA0V_No*). There is also a product called PlantWave designed to allow us to listen to plants and fungi.

117 Ben Wheatley (dir.), *In the Earth* (2021), 1:28:59–1:29:13–15.

118 Orrin Grey and Silvia Moreno-Garcia, 'Introduction', p. 1, p. 2.

119 Quoted in Jodey Castricano, *Gothic Metaphysics: From Alchemy to the Anthropocene* (Cardiff: University of Wales Press, 2021), p. 197.

120 Timothy Morton, *Humankind: Solidarity with Nonhuman People* (London, New York: Verso, 2019), pp. 3–4.

121 Castricano, *Gothic Metaphysics*, p. 175.

122 Dorion Sagan, 'Thermodynamics and Thought', in Lynn Margulis, Celeste A. Asikainen, and Wolfgang E. Krumbein (eds), *Chimeras and Consciousness: Evolution of the Sensory Self* (Cambridge, MA: The MIT Press, 2011), p. 248.

123 George A. Kennedy, 'A Hoot in the Dark: The Evolution of General Rhetoric', *Philosophy and Rhetoric* 25/1 (1992), pp. 1–21, at p. 10.

124 Kennedy, 'A Hoot in the Dark', p. 12.

125 Kennedy, 'A Hoot in the Dark', p. 12, p. 13.

126 Kennedy, 'A Hoot in the Dark', p. 13; Nathaniel A. Rivers, 'Deep Ambivalence and Wild Objects: Toward a Strange Environmental Rhetoric', *Rhetoric Society Quarterly* 45/5 (2015), 420–40, at p. 438.

127 Aristotle posited three main genres or types of rhetoric: epideictic, forensic and deliberative, relating to praise or blame, guilt or innocence and courses of action, respectively.

128 Kennedy, 'A Hoot in the Dark', p. 15

129 Machen, *Far Off Things*, pp. 155–56.

130 H. P. Lovecraft, 'The Colour out of Space', in *The Call of Cthulhu and Other Weird Stories*, ed. S. T. Joshi (New York: Penguin Books, 1999), pp. 170–99, at p. 181.

131 Kelly Hurley, *The Gothic Body: Sexuality, Materialism, and Degeneration at the fin de siècle* (Cambridge: Cambridge University Press, 1996), p. 153.

132 Adrian Tait, '"[A] Mystic, Ineffable Force and Energy": Arthur Machen and Theories of New Materialism', in Antonio Sanna (ed.),

Arthur Machen: Critical Essays (London: Lexington Books, 2021), pp. 193–208, at p. 198.

133 Michael T. Wilson, '"Absolute Reality" and the Role of the Ineffable in Shirley Jackson's *The Haunting of Hill House*', *The Journal of Popular Culture* 48/1 (2015), pp. 114–23, at p. 114, p. 115.

134 Wilson, '"Absolute Reality"', p. 114, p. 117.

135 Castricano, *Gothic Metaphysics*, p. 106.

136 Machen, *The Hill of Dreams*, p. 214, p. 213.

137 Colm McCarthy (dir.), *The Girl with All the Gifts* (2016), 1:41:25–6.

Chapter 6

1 Timothy Morton, *Humankind: Solidarity with Nonhuman People* (London, New York: Verso, 2019), p. 84.

2 Karen Barad, *Meeting the Universe Halfway: Quantum Physics and the Entanglement of Matter and Meaning* (Durham and London: Duke University Press, 2007).

3 Dennis Denisoff, 'The Queer Ecology of Vernon Lee's Transient Affections', *Feminist Modernist Studies* 3/2 (2020), pp. 148–61, at p. 150.

4 Vernon Lee, *Limbo and Other Essays* (London: Grant Richards, 1897), p. 45, p. 6.

5 Lee, *Limbo and Other Essays*, p. 61.

6 Lee, *Limbo and Other Essays*, p. 18.

7 Janet Atwill, *Rhetoric Reclaimed: Aristotle and the Liberal Arts Tradition* (Ithaca: Cornell University Press, 1998), p. 7, p. 48.

8 Dennis Denisoff, 'The Lie of the Land: Decadence, Ecology, and Arboreal Communications', *Victorian Literature and Culture* 49/4 (2021), pp. 621–41, at p. 627, p. 622. See also Dennis Denisoff, *Decadent Ecology in British Literature and Art, 1860–1910: Decay, Desire, and the Pagan Revival* (Cambridge: Cambridge University Press, 2022).

9 Denisoff, 'The Lie of the Land', p. 623, p. 624.

10 Lee, *Limbo and Other Essays*, p. 21.

11 Vernon Lee, *Hauntings and Other Fantastic Tales*, eds Catherine Maxwell and Patricia Pulham (Peterborough: Broadview, 2006), p. 40.

12 Vernon Lee, 'Faustus and Helena: Notes on the Supernatural in Art', in *Hauntings and Other Fantastic Tales*, eds Catherine Maxwell and Patricia Pulham (Peterborough: Broadview, 2006), pp. 291–319, at pp. 309–10.

13 Lee, 'Faustus and Helena', p. 299, p. 296.

[14] Lee, *Limbo and Other Essays*, p. 30.

[15] Lee, 'Faustus and Helena', pp. 312–13.

[16] Lee, *Limbo and Other Essays*, p. 21, emphasis original, p. 32.

[17] Vernon Lee, 'A Wicked Voice', in *Hauntings and Other Tales*, eds Catherine Maxwell and Patricia Pulham (Peterborough: Broadview, 2006), p. 179.

[18] Mary Patricia Kane, 'The Uncanny Mother in Vernon Lee's "Prince Alberic and the Snake Lady"', *Victorian Review* 32/1 (2006), pp. 41–62, at p. 41.

[19] Emma Liggins, 'Gendering the Spectral Encounter at the *Fin de Siècle*: Unspeakability in Vernon Lee's Supernatural Stories', *Gothic Studies* 15/2 (2013), pp. 37–52, at p. 37.

[20] Liggins, 'Gendering the Spectral Encounter at the *Fin de Siècle*', p. 40, p. 38.

[21] Liggins, 'Gendering the Spectral Encounter at the *Fin de Siècle*', p. 38

[22] Liggins, 'Gendering the Spectral Encounter at the *Fin de Siècle*', p. 41.

[23] Ruth Robbins, 'Apparitions Can Be Deceptive: Vernon Lee's Androgynous Spectres', in R. Robbins and J. Wolfreys (eds), *Victorian Gothic: Literary and Cultural Manifestations in the Nineteenth Century* (Basingstoke and New York: Palgrave, 2000), pp. 182–200.

[24] Vernon Lee, *The Enchanted Woods: And Other Essays on the Genius of Places* (London: John Lane, The Bodley Head, 1905), p. 3.

[25] Lee, *The Enchanted Woods*, p. 4.

[26] Lee, *The Enchanted Woods*, p. 5.

[27] Lee, *The Enchanted Woods*, p. 56, p. 62.

[28] Julian Wolfreys, *Victorian Hauntings: Spectrality, Gothic, the Uncanny and Literature* (Basingstoke: Palgrave, 2002), pp. x–xi.

[29] Andrew Bennett and Nicholas Royle, *Introduction to Literature, Criticism and Theory*, 3rd edn (Harlow: Pearson Longman, 2004), p. 133.

[30] Anna Lowenhaupt Tsing, *The Mushroom at the End of the World: On the Possibility of Life in Capitalist Ruins* (Princeton, Princeton University Press, 2015), p. 168.

[31] Leonie Wanitzek, '"The South! Something Exclaims within Me": Real and Imagined Spaces in Italy and the South in Vernon Lee's Travel Writing', *Cahiers Victoriens & Édouardiens* 83 (2016), pp. 2–10, at pp. 2–3.

[32] Wanitzek, '"The South! Something Exclaims within Me"', p. 2.

[33] Denisoff, 'The Queer Ecology of Vernon Lee's Transient Affections', p. 151.

[34] Lee, *The Enchanted Woods*, p. 318.

[35] 5 out of 7, according to Wanitzek, '"The South! Something Exclaims within Me"', p. 2.
[36] Vernon Lee, *Genius Loci: Notes on Places* (London: Grant Richards, 1899), p. 5.
[37] Lee, 'Introduction', *Genius Loci*, p. 3.
[38] Lee, *The Enchanted Woods*, p. 220.
[39] Lee, *Limbo and Other Essays*, p. 31.
[40] Lee, *The Enchanted Woods*, pp. 143–44.
[41] Lee, *Genius Loci*, p. 6, emphasis original.
[42] Lee, *Genius Loci*, p. 71, p. 63, p. 66.
[43] Lee, *Genius Loci*, p. 121. Notably, Lee is paraphrasing Psalm 114.
[44] Lee, *Genius Loci*, p. 121.
[45] Lee, *Genius Loci*, pp. 120–21.
[46] Lee, *Genius Loci*, p. 120.
[47] Lee, *Genius Loci*, pp. 3–4.
[48] Lee, *Limbo and Other Essays*, p. 48.
[49] Denisoff, 'The Queer Ecology of Vernon Lee's Transient Affections', p. 151, p. 152.
[50] Denisoff, 'The Queer Ecology of Vernon Lee's Transient Affections', p. 152.
[51] Lee, 'Faustus and Helena', p. 299, p. 296.
[52] Lee, *The Enchanted Woods*, p. 31.
[53] Debra Hawhee, *Rhetoric in Tooth and Claw: Animals, Language, Sensation* (Chicago: University of Chicago Press, 2017).
[54] George A. Kennedy, 'A Hoot in the Dark: The Evolution of General Rhetoric,' *Philosophy and Rhetoric* 25/1 (1992), pp. 1–21, at p. 2.
[55] Kennedy, 'A Hoot in the Dark', p. 2, p. 3.
[56] Hawhee, *Rhetoric in Tooth and Claw*, p. 5.
[57] Hawhee, *Rhetoric in Tooth and Claw*, p. 5.
[58] Hawhee, *Rhetoric in Tooth and Claw*, p. 11, p. 27, p. 7.
[59] Hawhee, *Rhetoric in Tooth and Claw*, pp. 6–7.
[60] Hawhee, *Rhetoric in Tooth and Claw*, pp. 34–5.
[61] David Abram, *The Spell of the Sensuous: Perception and Language in a More-Than-Human World* (New York: Vintage, 2017), p. 89.
[62] Abram, *The Spell of the Sensuous*, pp. 74–5.
[63] Abram, *The Spell of the Sensuous*, p. 74, p. 66.
[64] Abram, *The Spell of the Sensuous*, p. 67.
[65] Abram, *The Spell of the Sensuous*, p. 81.
[66] Abram, *The Spell of the Sensuous*, p. 66.
[67] Abram, *The Spell of the Sensuous*, p. 90.

[68] Barad, *Meeting the Universe Halfway*, p. 33.
[69] Lee, *The Enchanted Woods*, p. 165.
[70] Lee, *The Enchanted Woods*, p. 166.
[71] Lee, *The Enchanted Woods*, p. 166.
[72] Lee, *Limbo and Other Essays*, p. 61.
[73] Lee, *The Enchanted Woods*, p. 167, p. 168, p. 170.
[74] Lee, *Limbo and Other Essays*, p. 45, emphasis original.
[75] Lee, *Limbo and Other Essays*, p. 45.
[76] Lee, *Genius Loci*, pp. 3–4.
[77] Lee, *Limbo and Other Essays*, p. 61.
[78] Debra Hawhee, *Bodily Arts: Rhetoric and Athletics in Ancient Greece* (Austin: University of Texas Press, 2004), p. 56.
[79] Michelle Ballif, *Seduction, Sophistry, and the Woman with the Rhetorical Figure* (Carbondale: Southern Illinois University Press, 2001), p. 189.
[80] Atwill, *Rhetoric Reclaimed*, p. 56.
[81] Shannon Walters, 'Animal Athena: The Interspecies "Mētis" of Women Writers with Autism', *JAC* 30/3/4, (2010), pp. 683–711, at p. 689.
[82] Atwill, *Rhetoric Reclaimed*, p. 56.
[83] Walters, 'Animal Athena', p. 690, p. 706.
[84] Walters, 'Animal Athena', p. 689, p. 707.
[85] William C. Trapani and Chandra A. Maldonado, '*Kairos*: On the Limits to Our (Rhetorical) Situation', *Rhetoric Society Quarterly* 48/3 (2018), pp. 278–86, at pp. 282–3.
[86] Nathaniel A. Rivers, 'Deep Ambivalence and Wild Objects: Toward a Strange Environmental Rhetoric', *Rhetoric Society Quarterly* 45/5 (2015), pp. 420–40, at p. 437, p. 431, p. 438.
[87] Kristin Pomykala, 'Snake(s)kin: The Intertwining *Mêtis* and Mythopoetics of Serpentine Rhetoric', *Rhetoric Society Quarterly* 47/3 (2017), pp. 264–74, at p. 265.
[88] Barad, *Meeting the Universe Halfway*, p. 185, emphasis original.
[89] Jane Bennett, *Vibrant Matter: A Political Ecology of Things* (Durham: Duke University Press, 2010), p. 23, p. viii.
[90] Bennett, *Vibrant Matter*, p. 121.
[91] Rivers, 'Deep Ambivalence and Wild Objects', p. 431.
[92] Rivers, 'Deep Ambivalence and Wild Objects', p. 432, p. 435.
[93] Lee, *Genius Loci*, p. 8.
[94] Lee, *Genius Loci*, p. 8.
[95] Tsing discusses the art of noticing as a form of reading in *The Mushroom at the End of the World*, p. 160, p. 168.
[96] Rivers, 'Deep Ambivalence and Wild Objects', p. 438.

[97] Devin Griffiths and Deanna K. Kreisel, 'Introduction: Open Ecologies', *Victorian Literature and Culture* 48/1 (2020), pp. 1–28; Catriona Mortimer-Sandilands and Bruce Erickson (eds), *Queer Ecologies: Sex, Nature, Politics, Desire* (Bloomington and Indianapolis: Indiana University Press, 2010).

[98] A. Tsing, H. Swanson, E. Gan, and N. Bubandt, 'Introduction: Haunted Landscapes of the Anthropocene' in A. Tsing, H. Swanson, E. Gan, and N. Bubandt (eds), *Arts of Living on a Damaged Planet* (Minneapolis: University of Minnesota Press, 2017), pp. G1–G14, at p. G1.

[99] A. Tsing, H. Swanson, E. Gan and N. Bubandt, *Arts of Living on a Damaged Planet*, p. G65.

[100] Morton, *Humankind*, p. 77.

[101] Morton, *Humankind*, p. 54.

[102] Morton, *Humankind*, p. 129, p. 105.

[103] Morton, *Humankind*, p. 64, p. 55, p. 64, emphasis original.

[104] Morton, *Humankind*, p. 54–5, emphasis original.

[105] Morton, *Humankind*, p. 55, emphasis original.

[106] Morton, *Humankind*, p. 84.

[107] Tsing et al., 'Haunted Landscapes of the Anthropocene', p. G6.

[108] Tsing et al., 'Haunted Landscapes of the Anthropocene', p. G2, emphasis original.

[109] Tsing et al., 'Haunted Landscapes of the Anthropocene', p. G9.

[110] Lee, *Limbo and Other Essays*, p. 35.

[111] Lee, *Limbo and Other Essays*, p. 35.

[112] Tsing et al., 'Haunted Landscapes of the Anthropocene', p. G2.

[113] Joshua Ewalt, 'Points of Difference in the Study of More-than-Human Rhetorical Ontologies', *Rhetoric and Public Affairs* 21/3 (2018), pp. 523–38; Danielle Endres, 'Environmental Criticism', *Western Journal of Communication* 84/3, 2019, pp. 1–18; Scot Barnett and Casey Boyle (eds), *Rhetoric through Everyday Things* (Tuscaloosa, AL: University of Alabama Press, 2016).

[114] See for example Steven Schwarze, 'Environmental Melodrama', *Quarterly Journal of Speech* 92/3 (2006), pp. 239–61; Phaedra Pezzullo, *Toxic Tourism. Rhetorics of Pollution, Travel, and Environmental Justice* (Tuscaloosa, AL: University of Alabama Press, 2007); Stacy Alaimo, *Bodily Natures: Science, Environment, and the Material Self* (Bloomington: Indiana University Press, 2010); Jennifer A. Peeples, 'Toxic Sublime: Imaging Contaminated Landscapes', *Environmental Communication* 5/4 (2011), pp. 373–92; Timothy Morton, *Dark Ecology: For a Logic of Future Coexistence* (New York: Columbia University Press, 2016).

[115] Cynthia Sugars and Gerry Turcotte, 'Canadian Literature and the Postcolonial Gothic', in C. Sugars and G. Turcotte (eds), *Unsettled Remains: Canadian Literature and the Postcolonial Gothic* (Waterloo: Wilfrid Laurier Press, 2009), pp. vii–xxvi, at p. xv.

[116] Jeffrey Andrew Weinstock, 'Lovecraft's Things: Sinister Souvenirs from Other Worlds', in Carl H. Sederholm and Jeffrey Andrew Weinstock (eds), *The Age of Lovecraft* (Minnesota: University of Minnesota Press, 2016), pp. 62–78, at p. 63.

[117] Weinstock, 'Lovecraft's Things', p. 62.

[118] Endres, 'Environmental Criticism', at p. 3.

[119] Phaedra Pezzullo, 'Unearthing the Marvelous: Environmental Imprints on Rhetorical Criticism', *Review of Communication* 16/1 (2016), pp. 25–42, at p. 27, p. 25.

[120] Weinstock, 'Lovecraft's Things', p. 63.

[121] Sugars and Turcotte, 'Canadian Literature and the Postcolonial Gothic'.

[122] Catherine Spooner, *Contemporary Gothic* (London, Reaktion Books, 2006).

[123] Xavier Aldana Reyes, 'Gothic Affect: An Alternative Approach to Critical Models of the Contemporary Gothic', in Lorna Piatti-Farnell and Donna Lee Brien (eds), *New Directions in 21st Century Gothic: The Gothic Compass* (New York: Routledge, 2015), pp. 11–23, at p. 14.

[124] See Jeanne Fahnestock's 'Accommodating Science: The Rhetorical Life of Scientific Facts', *Written Communication* 15/3 (1998), pp. 330–50, for an example.

[125] A. Tsing, H. Swanson, E. Gan, and N. Bubandt, 'Introduction: Bodies Tumbled into Bodies', in A. Tsing, H. Swanson, E. Gan, and N. Bubandt (eds), *Arts of Living on a Damaged Planet* (Minneapolis: University of Minnesota Press, 2017), pp. M1–M12, at pp. M2–M3.

[126] E.g., Timothy Morton's *Dark Ecology*, *Humankind* and *The Ecological Thought* (Cambridge, Mass.: Harvard University Press, 2010).

[127] Norman Fairclough, 'A Dialectical-Relational Approach to Critical Discourse Analysis in Social Research', in Ruth Wodak and Michael Meyer (eds), *Methods of Critical Discourse Studies*, 3rd edn (London; Los Angeles: SAGE Publications, 2016), pp. 86–108, p. 89.

[128] Norman Fairclough, 'Critical Discourse Analysis', *Marges Linguistiques* 9 (2005), pp. 76–94.

[129] Tsing et al., 'Haunted Landscapes of the Anthropocene', p. G2, emphasis original.

[130] Robert Mighall, *A Geography of Victorian Gothic Fiction* (Oxford, Oxford University Press, 1999), p. xx.

[131] Gina Wisker, 'Imagining Beyond Extinctathon: Indigenous Knowledge, Survival, Speculation – Margaret Atwood's and Ann Patchett's Eco-Gothic', *Contemporary Women's Writing* 11/3 (2017), pp. 412–31.

[132] Gregory Cajete, *Native Science: Natural Laws of Interdependence* (Sante Fe: Clear Light Books, 2016); Nic Paget-Clarke, 'Science From A Native Perspective: How Do We Educate for A Sustainable Future' (an interview with Gregory Cajete), *In Motion Magazine* (12 March 2016), *https://inmotionmagazine.com/global/cajete/gregory-cajete-int2015.html.*

[133] Wen Shi et al., 'What Framework Promotes Saliency of Climate Change Issues on Online Public Agenda', *Sustainability* 11 (2019), pp. 1–24, at p. 19.

[134] Peeples, 'Toxic Sublime: Imaging Contaminated Landscapes', pp. 373–92; Schwarze, 'Environmental Melodrama', pp. 239–61.

[135] Morton, *Dark Ecology*, p. 12, emphasis original.

[136] Reyes, 'Gothic Affect', p. 17, p. 12.

[137] Morton, *Humankind*, p. 63.

[138] Patricia MacCormack, 'Lovecraft's Cosmic Ethics', in Carl H. Sederholm and Jeffrey Andrew Weinstock (eds), *The Age of Lovecraft* (Minnesota: University of Minnesota Press, 2016), p. 212.

[139] MacCormack, 'Lovecraft's Cosmic Ethics', p. 213.

[140] Patricia MacCormack, 'Lovecraft Through the Deleuzio-Guattarian Gates', *Postmodern Culture* 20/2 (2010).

[141] Jodey Castricano, *Gothic Metaphysics: From Alchemy to the Anthropocene* (Cardiff: University of Wales Press, 2021), p. 173.

[142] Kel Pero in Castricano, *Gothic Metaphysics*, pp. 191–2.

[143] Andrew Smith and William Hughes, 'Introduction: Defining the Eco-Gothic', in A. Smith and W. Hughes (eds), *EcoGothic* (Manchester: Manchester University Press, 2013), pp. 1–33, at p. 14, p. 18.

[144] David Del Principe, 'Introduction: The EcoGothic in the Long Nineteenth Century', *Gothic Studies* 16/1 (2014), pp. 1–8, at p. 1.

[145] Dawn Keetley and Matthew Sivils, 'Introduction: Approaches to the Ecogothic', in Dawn Keetley and Matthew Sivils (eds), *Ecogothic in Nineteenth-Century American Literature* (New York: Routledge, 2017), pp. 1–20, at p. 4, p. 1, p. 3.

[146] Smith and Hughes, 'Introduction', pp. 16–17.

[147] Eduardo Kohn, *How Forests Think: Toward an Anthropology Beyond the Human* (Berkeley: University of California Press, 2013), p. 8.

[148] Kohn, *How Forests Think*, p. 9.

[149] Kohn, *How Forests Think*, p. 16.

[150] Kohn, *How Forests Think*, p. 9.

151 Bruce Foltz, 'On Heidegger and the Interpretation of Environmental Crisis', *Environmental Ethics* 6 (1984), pp. 323–38, at p. 324.

152 Foltz, 'On Heidegger and the Interpretation of Environmental Crisis'; Rivers, 'Deep Ambivalence and Wild Objects'.

153 Rivers, 'Deep Ambivalence and Wild Objects', p. 431.

154 Castricano, *Gothic Metaphysics*, p. 126.

155 Pero in Castricano, *Gothic Metaphysics*, pp. 191–2.

156 Lee, *Limbo and Other Essays*, p. 45.

157 Lee, *Genius Loci*, pp. 3–4.

Postscript

1 Angela Carter, *Burning your Boats: Collected Short Stories* (London: Chatto and Windus, 1995), p. 460.

2 Max Nordau, *Degeneration* (New York: D. Appleton and Company, 1895), p. 5.

3 Nordau, *Degeneration*, p. 6.

4 Bram Stoker, *Dracula* (Peterborough: Broadview Press, 2000), p. 118.

5 Nordau, *Degeneration*, p. 6.

6 Patricia MacCormack, 'Lovecraft's Cosmic Ethics', in Carl H. Sederholm and Jeffrey Andrew Weinstock (eds), *The Age of Lovecraft* (Minnesota: University of Minnesota Press, 2016), pp. 199–214, at p. 213.

7 Marcel Detienne and Jean-Pierre Vernant, *Cunning Intelligence in Greek Culture and Society*, trans. Janet Lloyd (New Jersey: Humanities Press, 1978), p. 248.

8 Detienne and Vernant, *Cunning Intelligence in Greek Culture and Society*, p. 152.

9 Detienne and Vernant, *Cunning Intelligence in Greek Culture and Society*, p. 222.

10 As is common in Greek myth, Pontos and Poros are sometimes personified as the Salty Deep (Pontos) and a future-oriented cosmogenic power 'capable of making the most of every opportunity' (Poros). Detienne and Vernant, *Cunning Intelligence in Greek Culture and Society*, p. 127, n. 5.

11 Detienne and Vernant, *Cunning Intelligence in Greek Culture and Society*, p. 222.

12 Detienne and Vernant, *Cunning Intelligence in Greek Culture and Society*, p. 150.

13 Detienne and Vernant, *Cunning Intelligence in Greek Culture and Society*, p. 150.

14 Michelle Burnham, 'Is There an Indigenous Gothic?', in Charles L. Crow (ed.), *A Companion to American Gothic* (Malden, MA: John Wiley & Sons, Ltd, 2014), pp. 225–37, at p. 226.

15 Mary Louise Pratt, 'Arts of the Contact Zone', *Profession* 1 (1991), pp. 33–40, at p. 36, p. 34.

16 Bart Kosko, *Fuzzy Thinking: The New Science of Fuzzy Logic* (New York: Hyperion, 1993); Bernd Reiter, *Decolonizing The Social Sciences and Humanities: An Anti-Elitism Manifesto* (New York: Routledge, 2021).

17 *Son of a Trickster* (2017), *Trickster Drift* (2018), and *Return of the Trickster* (2021) were recently made into a CBC series.

18 See for example Jodey Castricano, *Gothic Metaphysics: From Alchemy to the Anthropocene* (Cardiff: University of Wales Press, 2021) and Michelle Burnham, 'Is There an Indigenous Gothic?' (2014). I was lucky enough to chat to Robinson once at the Lethbridge library, where she told me that she consciously includes Gothic and horror in her work; an avid Stephen King fan who grew up on Canadian pop culture, Robinson uses the materials that are familiar to her to craft her stories of modern Canadian Indigenous peoples, who have, for better or worse, found themselves imbricated in a multicultural space with pronounced English and French colonial legacies.

19 Burnham, 'Is There an Indigenous Gothic?', p. 226.

20 Betty Bastien, *Blackfoot Ways of Knowing: The Worldview of the Siksikaitsitapi* (Calgary: University of Calgary Press, 2004) p. 80.

21 Castricano, *Gothic Metaphysics*, p. 196.

22 Castricano, *Gothic Metaphysics*, p. 200.

23 Nic Paget-Clarke 'Science From A Native Perspective: How Do We Educate for A Sustainable Future' (an interview with Gregory Cajete), *In Motion Magazine* (12 March 2016), *https://inmotionmagazine.com/global/cajete/gregory-cajete-int2015.html.*

24 Barbora Půtová, 'Historical Changes of the Coyote: An Anthropological Reflection on the Trickster', in B. Půtová (ed.), *Identity, Tradition, and Revitalization of American Indian Cultures* (Prague: Karolinum Press, 2017), pp. 203–14, at pp. 203–4.

25 Shane Phelan highlights Coyote's gender-bending and shapeshifting as feminist properties in their article 'Coyote Politics: Trickster Tales and Feminist Futures', *Hypatia* 11/3 (1996), pp. 130–49.

[26] Donna Haraway, *Simians, Cyborgs and Women: The Reinvention of Nature* (New York: Routledge, 1991), p. 3, p. 201.

[27] Nathaniel A. Rivers, 'Deep Ambivalence and Wild Objects: Toward a Strange Environmental Rhetoric', *Rhetoric Society Quarterly* 45/5 (2015), pp. 420–40, at p. 431.

[28] Eden Robinson, *Monkey Beach* (Toronto: Vintage Books, 2000), p. 1.

[29] Robinson, *Monkey Beach*, p. 3, p. 17.

[30] Robinson, *Monkey Beach*, p. 367.

[31] Robinson, *Monkey Beach*, pp. 371–2.

[32] Robinson, *Monkey Beach*, p. 125.

[33] Robinson, *Monkey Beach*, p. 354.

[34] Robinson, *Monkey Beach*, p. 154.

[35] Robinson, *Monkey Beach*, p. 295.

[36] Raymond Pierotti, 'Learning about Extraordinary Beings', *Ethnobiology Letters* 11/2 (2020), pp. 44–51, at p. 46, emphasis original.

[37] Pierotti, 'Learning about Extraordinary Beings', p. 46.

[38] Betty Coon Wheelwright, 'A Storytelling of Ravens', *Jung Journal* 7/1 (2013), pp. 4–18, at pp. 8–9.

[39] Pierotti, 'Learning about Extraordinary Beings', p. 46.

[40] Wheelwright's article offers a helpful overview of these myths, stemming from Nordic, Gaelic and North American Indigenous cultures.

[41] Pierotti, 'Learning about Extraordinary Beings', p. 45.

[42] Diana Kwon, 'Crows Perform yet Another Skill Once Thought Distinctively Human', *Scientific American* (2 Nov. 2022), *https://www.scientificamerican.com/article/crows-perform-yet-another-skill-once-thought-distinctively-human/*.

[43] Wheelwright, 'A Storytelling of Ravens', p. 5, p. 6, p. 8.

[44] Wheelwright, 'A Storytelling of Ravens', p. 8, p. 5.

[45] Corvids have been associated with darkness and death in part through myths and in part through human conflicts, where battlegrounds have been frequent sources of food for these omnivorous birds. See Wheelwright.

[46] Edgar Allan Poe, 'The Raven', in *Edgar Allan Poe Complete Tales & Poems* (Edison, NJ: Castle Books, 2002), pp. 773–5, at p. 775, p. 774.

[47] Detienne and Vernant, *Cunning Intelligence in Greek Culture and Society*, p. 219, p. 218, p. 216.

[48] Detienne and Vernant, *Cunning Intelligence in Greek Culture and Society*, p. 216.

[49] Detienne and Vernant, *Cunning Intelligence in Greek Culture and Society*, p. 217.

[50] MacCormack, 'Lovecraft's Cosmic Ethics', p. 213.

[51] A. Tsing, H. Swanson, E. Gan, and N. Bubandt, 'Introduction: Haunted Landscapes of the Anthropocene' in A. Tsing, H. Swanson, E. Gan, and N. Bubandt (eds), *Arts of Living on a Damaged Planet* (Minneapolis: University of Minnesota Press, 2017), pp. G1–G14, at p. G9.

[52] See for example Gregory Cajete's *Native Science: Natural Laws of Interdependence* (Sante Fe: Clear Light Books, 2016), Peter Hanohano's 'The Spiritual Imperative of Native Epistemology: Restoring Harmony and Balance to education' *Canadian Journal of Native Education* 23/ 2 (1999), pp. 206–19, and Aleksandar Janca and Clothilde Bullen's 'The Aboriginal Concept of Time and its Mental Health Implications', *Australasian Psychiatry* 11/1 (2003), pp. S40–S44.

[53] Rosi Braidotti, *Posthuman Knowledge* (Cambridge: Polity Press, 2019), p. 67.

[54] David Punter, 'On the Threshold of Gothic: A Reflection', in Jerrold E. Hogle and Robert Miles (eds), *The Gothic and Theory: An Edinburgh Companion* (Edinburgh: Edinburgh University Press), pp. 301–19, at p. 307.

[55] Christopher P. Long, 'The Daughters of Metis: Patriarchal Dominion and the Politics of the Between', *Graduate Faculty Philosophy Journal* 28/2 (2007), pp. 67–86, p. 67.

[56] Long, 'The Daughters of Metis', p. 68.

[57] Long, 'The Daughters of Metis', pp. 71–2.

References

Abram, David, *The Spell of the Sensuous: Perception and Language in a More-Than-Human World* (New York: Vintage Books, 1997).

Alaimo, Stacy, *Bodily Natures: Science, Environment, and the Material Self* (Bloomington: Indiana University Press, 2010).

Alcock, Joe, Carlo C. Maley, and Athena Aktipis, 'Is Eating Behavior Manipulated by the Gastrointestinal Microbiota? Evolutionary Pressures and Potential Mechanisms', *Bioessays* 36 (2014), pp. 940–9.

Aldana Reyes, Xavier, 'Gothic Affect: An Alternative Approach to Critical Models of the Contemporary Gothic', in Lorna Piatta-Farnell and Donna Lee Brien (eds), *New Directions in 21st Century Gothic: The Gothic Compass* (New York: Routledge, 2015), pp. 11–23.

Aldridge-Morris, Ray, *Multiple Personality: An Exercise in Deception* (Hillsdale, New Jersey: Lawrence Erlbaum Associates, Inc., 1989).

Ansell Pearson, Keith, *Viroid Life: Perspectives on Nietzsche and the Transhuman Condition*, (London and New York: Routledge, 1997).

Anzaldúa, Gloria, *Borderlands/La Frontera: The New Mestiza* (San Francisco: Aunt Lute Books, 1987).

Apollodorus, *The Library* or *Bibliotheca* 1.2.1. (*c.* 101–200 CE), *https://www.theoi.com/Text/Apollodorus1.html*, accessed 1 June 2022.

Atwill, Janet, *Rhetoric Reclaimed: Aristotle and the Liberal Arts Tradition* (Ithaca: Cornell University Press, 1998).

Azam, Eugene, *Hypnotisme, double conscience et altérations de la personnalité: le cas Félida X* (Paris: Librarie J. B. Baillière et Fils, 1887).

Ballif, Michelle, *Seduction, Sophistry, and the Woman with the Rhetorical Figure* (Carbondale: Southern Illinois University Press, 2001).

Barad, Karen, *Meeting the Universe Halfway: Quantum Physics and the Entanglement of Matter and Meaning* (Durham & London: Duke University Press, 2007).

Barnett, Scot and Casey Boyle (eds), *Rhetoric through Everyday Things* (Tuscaloosa, AL: University of Alabama Press, 2016).

Bassil-Morozow, Helena, *The Trickster and the System: Identity and Agency in Contemporary Society* (London and New York: Routledge, 2015).

Bastien, Betty, *Blackfoot Ways of Knowing: The Worldview of the Siksikaitsitapi* (Calgary: University of Calgary Press, 2004).

Bennett, Andrew and Nicholas Royle, *Introduction to Literature, Criticism and Theory* (Harlow: Pearson Longman, 2004).

Bennett, Jane, *Vibrant Matter: A Political Ecology of Things* (Durham: Duke University Press, 2010).

Biswas Mellamphy, Nandita, 'Ghost in the Shell-Game: On the Mètic Mode of Existence, Inception and Innocence', *The Funambulist Papers*, Volume Two (2013).

Biswas Mellamphy, Nandita, '(W)omen out/of Time: Metis, Medea, Mahakali', in K. Kolozova and E. A. Joy (eds), *After the 'Speculative Turn': Realism, Philosophy, and Feminism* (Santa Barbara: Punctum Books, 2016), pp. 133–57.

Boor, M., 'The Multiple Personality Epidemic: Additional Cases and Inferences Regarding Diagnosis, Etiology, Dynamics, and Treatment', *Journal of Nervous and Mental Disorders* 170 (1982), pp. 302–04.

Botting, Fred, *Gothic* (London; New York: Routledge, 1996).

Botting, Fred, *Gothic*, 2nd edn (London; New York: Routledge, 2014).

Bouwer, Jaco, (dir.), *Gaia*, XYZ Films, (2021).

Bracke, Evelien, *Of Metis and Magic: The Conceptual Transformation of Circe and Medea in Ancient Greek Poetry* (unpublished PhD thesis, University of Maynooth, Maynooth, 2009).

Braidotti, Rosi, 'Posthuman Critical Theory', in D. Banerji and M. R. Paranjape (eds), *Critical Posthumanism and Planetary Futures* (New Delhi: Springer, 2016), pp. 13–32.

Braidotti, Rosi, *Posthuman Knowledge* (Cambridge: Polity Press, 2019).

Braidotti, Rosi, *The Posthuman* (Cambridge: Polity Press, 2013).

Braidotti, Rosi and Simone Bignall, 'Posthuman Systems', in Rosi Braidotti and Simone Bignall (eds), *Posthuman Ecologies: Complexity and Process after Deleuze* (London: Rowman & Littlefield, 2019), pp. 1–16.

Brannon, John R. and Matthew A. Mulvey, 'Jekyll and Hyde: Bugs with Double Personalities that Muddle the Distinction between Commensal and Pathogen', *Journal of Molecular Biology* 431/16 (July 2019), pp. 2911–13.

Braude, Stephen E. *First Person Plural: Multiple Personality and the Philosophy of Mind* (New York: Routledge, 1991).

Brennan, Matthew C., *The Gothic Psyche: Disintegration and Growth in Nineteenth-Century English Literature* (New York: Camden House, 1998).

Buchen, Lizzie, 'The New Germ Theory', *Nature* 468/7323 (25 Nov. 2010), pp. 492–5.

Burnham, Michelle, 'Is There an Indigenous Gothic?', in Charles L. Crow (ed.), *A Companion to American Gothic* (Malden, MA: John Wiley & Sons Ltd, 2014), pp. 225–37.

Byron, Glennis, 'Global Gothic,' in David Punter (ed.), *A New Companion to The Gothic* (Malden MA: Wiley Blackwell, 2015), pp. 369–78.

Byron, Glennis, 'Gothic in the 1890s', in David Punter (ed.), *A New Companion to The Gothic* (Malden MA: Wiley Blackwell, 2015), pp. 186–96.

Cajete, Gregory, *Native Science: Natural Laws of Interdependence* (Sante Fe: Clear Light Books, 2016).

Calarco, Matthew, 'Identity, Difference, Indistinction', *The New Centennial Review* 11/2 (2011), pp. 41–60.

Calarco, Matthew, *Zoographies: The Question of the Animal from Heidegger to Derrida* (New York: Columbia University Press, 2008).

Campbell, Joseph, *The Hero with a Thousand Faces* (Princeton: Princeton University Press, 1949).

Campbell, Joseph, *The Masks of God: Primitive Mythology* (New York: Penguin, 1976).

Carter, Angela, *Burning your Boats: Collected Short Stories* (London: Chatto and Windus, 1995).

Castricano, Jodey, *Gothic Metaphysics: From Alchemy to the Anthropocene* (Cardiff; Chicago: University of Wales Press, 2022).

Castricano, Jodey, 'Much Ado about Handwriting: Countersigning with the Other Hand in Stevenson's *The Strange Case of Dr. Jekyll and Mr. Hyde*', *Romanticism on the Net* 44 (2006), *https://erudit.org/en/journals/ron/2006-n44-ron1433/014001ar/*.

Castro-Delgado, Ana Lucía, Stephanie Elizondo-Mesén, Yendri Valladares-Cruz, and William Rivera-Méndez, 'Wood Wide Web: Communication Through the Mycorrhizal Network,' *Tecnología en Marcha* 33–4 (2020), pp. 114–25.

Certeau, Michel de, *The Practice of Everyday Life* (Berkeley: University of California Press, 1984).

Chambers, Cynthia and Erika Hasebe-Ludt with Dwayne Donald, Wanda Hurren, Carl Leggo, and Antoinette Oberg, 'Métissage: A Research Praxis', in J. Gary Knowles and Ardra L. Cole (eds), *Handbook of the Arts in Qualitative Research: Perspectives, Methodologies, Examples, and Issues* (Thousand Oaks, CA: SAGE Publications, 2007), pp. 141–53.

Chen, Yijing, Jinying Xu, and Yu Chen, 'Regulation of Neurotransmitters by the Gut Microbiota and Effects on Cognition in Neurological Disorders', *Nutrients* 13/6 (2021).

Cocker, Emma. 'Weaving Codes/Coding Weaves: Penelopean Mêtis and the Weaver-Coder's Kairos', *Textile* 15/2 (2017), pp. 124–41.

Cohen, Jeffrey Jerome, 'Preface: In a time of Monsters', in Jeffrey Jerome Cohen (ed.), *Monster Theory: Reading Culture* (Minneapolis: University of Minnesota Press, 1996), pp. vii– xiii.

Cohen, Jeffrey Jerome, 'Monster Culture (Seven Theses)', in Jeffrey Jerome Cohen (ed.), *Monster Theory: Reading Culture* (Minneapolis: University of Minnesota Press, 1996), pp. 3–25.

Cohut, Maria, 'Human microbiota: The microorganisms that make us their home', *Medical News Today* (27 June 2020), *https://www.*

medicalnewstoday.com/articles/human-microbiota-the-microorganisms-that-make-us-their-home.

Copan, 'The Spooky Microbe Monsters Among Us', *Microbiology Today* (28 Oct. 2019), *https://www.copanusa.com/the-spooky-microbe-monsters-among-us/.*

Cooper, Mick, 'If you Can't be Jekyll be Hyde: An Existential-Phenomenological Exploration of Lived-Plurality', in Mick Cooper and John Rowam (eds), *The Plural Self: Multiplicity in Everyday Life* (London: Sage, 1999), pp. 51–70.

Costandi, Moheb, 'Microbes Manipulate Your Mind', *Scientific American* (1 July 2012).

Costello, Elizabeth, Keaton Stagaman, Les Dethlefsen, Brendan J. M. Bohannan, and David A. Relman, 'The Application of Ecological Theory Toward an Understanding of the Human Microbiome', *Science* 336/8 (June 2012), pp. 1255–62.

Crabtree, Adam, *From Mesmer to Freud: Magnetic Sleep and the Roots of Psychological Healing* (New Haven: Yale University Press, 1993).

Crutzen, Paul J., 'The Geology of Mankind', *Nature* 415/6867 (2002), p. 23.

Danahay, Martin A., *A Community of One: Masculine Autobiography and Autonomy in Nineteenth-Century Britain* (Albany: State University of New York Press, 1993).

Darwin, Charles, *The Descent of Man* (London: Penguin Books, 2004).

Darwin, Charles, *On the Origin of Species by Means of Natural Selection* (New York: Dover Publications, Inc., 2006).

Davies, Tony, *Humanism* (London: Routledge, 2008).

Deleuze, Gilles and Félix Guattari, *A Thousand Plateaus: Capitalism and Schizophrenia*, trans. Brian Massumi (Minneapolis: Minnesota University Press, 1987).

Del Principe, David, 'Introduction: The EcoGothic in the Long Nineteenth Century', *Gothic Studies* 16/1 (2014), pp. 1–8.

Denisoff, Dennis, 'The Lie of the Land: Decadence, Ecology, and Arboreal Communications', *Victorian Literature and Culture* 49/4 (2021), pp. 621–41.

Denisoff, Dennis, 'The Queer Ecology of Vernon Lee's Transient Affections', *Feminist Modernist Studies* 3/2 (2020), pp. 148–61.

Derrida, Jacques and David Wills, 'The Animal That Therefore I Am (More to Follow)', *Critical Inquiry* 28/2 (2002), pp. 369–418.

Detienne, Marcel and Jean-Pierre Vernant, *Cunning Intelligence in Greek Culture and Society*, trans. Janet Lloyd (New Jersey: Humanities Press, 1978).

Dijkstra, Bram, *Idols of Perversity: Fantasies of Feminine Evil in Fin-de-siècle Culture* (Oxford: Oxford University Press, 1986).

Dolmage, Jay, *Disability Rhetoric* (Syracuse, NY: Syracuse University Press, 2014).

Dolmage, Jay, 'Metis, *Mētis*, Mestiza, Medusa: Rhetorical Bodies Across Rhetorical Traditions', *Rhetoric Review* 28 (2009), pp. 1–28.

Dolmage, Jay, 'What is *Metis*?', *Disability Studies Quarterly* 40/1 (2020), *https://dsq sds.org/index.php/dsq/article/view/7224.*

Donald, Dwayne, 'Indigenous Métissage: A Decolonizing Research Sensibility', *International Journal of Qualitative Studies in Education* 25/5 (2012), pp. 533–55.

Eckman, Barbara, 'Jung, Hegel, and the Subjective Universe', *Spring, An Annual of Archetypal Psychology and Jungian Thought* (1986), pp. 86–99.

The Economist, 'Microbes maketh man', 404/8798 (18 Aug. 2012).

Endres, Danielle, 'Environmental Criticism', *Western Journal of Communication* 84/3 (2019), pp. 1–18.

Eller, Jack David, 'The Trickster: Ancient Spirit, Modern Political Theology', *The Brink* (9 July 2022), *https://politicaltheology.com/the-trickster-ancient-spirit-modern-political-theology/.*

Epstein, Slava S., 'Microbial Awakenings', *Nature* 457 (2009), p. 1083.

Esdaile, James, *The Introduction of Mesmerism (With the Sanction of the Government) into the Public Hospitals of India* (London: W. Kent, 1856).

Ewalt, Joshua, 'Points of Difference in the Study of More-than-Human Rhetorical Ontologies', *Rhetoric and Public Affairs* 21/3 (2018), pp. 523–38.

Fahnestock, Jeanne, 'Accommodating Science: The Rhetorical Life of Scientific Facts', *Written Communication* 15/3 (1998), pp. 330–50.

Fairclough, Norman, 'A Dialectical-Relational Approach to Critical Discourse Analysis in Social Research', in Ruth Wodak and Michael Meyer (eds), *Methods of Critical Discourse Studies*, 3rd edn (London; Los Angeles: SAGE Publications, 2016), pp. 86–108.

Fairclough, Norman, 'Critical Discourse Analysis', *Marges Linguistiques* 9 (2005), pp. 76–94.

Ferrier, David, *The Localisation of Cerebral Disease* (New York: G.P. Putnam's Sons, 1879).

Forlini, Stefania, 'Introduction' to Arthur Machen *The Three Impostors* (Peterborough: Broadview, 2023), pp. 9–46.

Foucault, Michel, 'The Order of Discourse', in Robert Young (ed.), *Uniting the Text: A Post Structuralist Reader* (Boston, London and Henley: Routledge & Kegan Paul, 1981), pp. 51–78.

Freud, Sigmund, 'The Uncanny', in *The Standard Edition of the Complete Psychological Works of Sigmund Freud, Volume XVII (1917–1919): An Infantile Neurosis and Other Works* (London: The Hogarth Press: The Institute of Psycho-Analysis, 1955), pp. 217–56.

Gallagher, James, 'More than Half your Body is Not Human', *BBC News* (10 April 2018), *https://www.bbc.com/news/health-43674270.*

Garrett, Peter K., 'Cries and Voices: Reading Jekyll and Hyde,' in William Veeder and Gordon Hirsch (eds.), *Dr. Jekyll and Mr. Hyde: After One Hundred Years* (Chicago: University of Chicago Press, 1988), pp. 59–72.

Gilbert, Scott, 'Holobiont by Birth: Multilineage Individuals as the Conretion of Cooperative Processes', in A. Tsing, H. Swanson, E. Gan, and N. Bubandt (eds), *Arts of Living on a Damaged Planet* (Minneapolis: University of Minnesota Press, 2017), pp. M73–M89.

Gilbert, Scott F., Jan Sapp, and Alfred Tauber, 'A Symbiotic View of Life: We Have Never Been Individuals', *The Quarterly Review of Biology* 87/4 (2012), pp. 325–41.

Gish, Nancy K., 'Jekyll and Hyde: The Psychology of Dissociation', *International Journal of Scottish Literature* 2/2 (2007), pp. 1–10.

Graham, Elaine, *Representations of the Post/Human: Monsters, Aliens and Others in Popular Culture* (Manchester: Rutgers University Press, 2002).

Grey, Orrin and Silvia Moreno-Garcia (eds), *Fungi* (Vancouver: Innsmouth Free Press, 2012).

Griffiths, Devin and Deanna K. Kreisel, 'Introduction: Open Ecologies', *Victorian Literature and Culture* 48/1 (2020), pp. 1–28.

Groom, Nick, 'Introduction' to Horace Walpole, *The Castle of Otranto*, ed. N. Groom (Oxford and New York: Oxford University Press, 2014), pp. ix–xxxviii.

Grosz, Elizabeth, *Volatile Bodies: Toward a Corporeal Feminism* (Bloomington: Indiana University Press, 1994).

Grumdahl, Dara Moskowitz, 'Ghosts in Your Machine', *Experience Life* (Nov. 2012), *https://experiencelife.com/article/ghosts-in-your-machine/*.

Hacking, Ian, 'Multiple Personality Disorder and its Hosts', *History of the Human Sciences* 5/3 (1992), pp. 3–31.

Hacking, Ian, *Rewriting the Soul: Multiple Personality and the Sciences of Memory* (Princeton: Princeton University Press, 1995).

Halberstam, J., *Skin Shows: Gothic Horror and the Technology of Monstrosity* (Durham: Duke University Press, 1995).

Halberstam, J. and Ira Livingston, 'Introduction: Posthuman Bodies', in J. Halberstam and Ira Livingston (eds), *Posthuman Bodies* (Bloomington: Indiana University Press, 1995), pp. 1–20.

Hanohano, Peter, 'The Spiritual Imperative of Native Epistemology: Restoring Harmony and Balance to Education', *Canadian Journal of Native Education* 23/2 (1999), pp. 206–19.

Haraway, Donna J., *Staying with the Trouble: Making Kin in the Chthulucene* (Durham: Duke University Press, 2016).

Harman, Graham, *Towards Speculative Realism* (Winchester and Washington: Zero Books, 2010).

Harman, Graham, *Speculative Realism: An Introduction* (Cambridge: Polity Press, 2018).

Harman, Graham, *Tool-Being: Heidegger and the Metaphysics of Objects* (Chicago and La Salle: Open Court, 2002).

Harris, Mason, 'Vivisection, the Culture of Science, and Intellectual Uncertainty in *The Island of Doctor Moreau*', *Gothic Studies* 4/2 (2002), pp. 99–115.

Hasebe-Ludt, Erika, Cynthia Chambers, and Carl Leggo, *Life Writing and Literary Métissage as an Ethos for Our Times* (New York: Peter Lang, 2009).

Hawhee, Debra, *Bodily Arts: Rhetoric and Athletics in Ancient Greece* (Austin: University of Texas Press, 2004).

Hawhee, Debra, *Rhetoric in Tooth and Claw: Animals, Language, Sensation* (Chicago: University of Chicago Press, 2017).

Hayles, N. Katherine, *How We Became Posthuman: Virtual Bodies in Cybernetics, Literature, and Informatics* (Chicago: Chicago University Press, 1999).

Heise-von der Lippe, Anya, 'Introduction: Post/human/Gothic', in A. Heise-von der Lippe (ed.), *Posthuman Gothic* (Cardiff: University of Wales Press, 2017), pp. 1–18.

Heise-von der Lippe, Anya, 'Techno-Terrors and the Emergence of Cyber-Gothic', in J. E. Hogle and R. Miles (eds), *The Gothic and Theory: An Edinburgh Companion* (Edinburgh: Edinburgh University Press, 2019), pp. 182–202.

Helmreich, Stefan, *Sounding the Limits of Life: Essays in the Anthropology of Biology and Beyond* (Princeton and Oxford: Princeton University Press, 2016).

Herdman, John, *The Double in Nineteenth-Century Fiction* (London: MacMillan, 1990).

Hesiod, *Theogony*, 929a (c. 730–700 BCE), *https://www.theoi.com/Text/HesiodTheogony.html*, accessed 1 June 2022.

Hogle, Jerrold E., 'Introduction: The Gothic in Western Culture', in Jerrold E. Hogle (ed.), *The Cambridge Companion to Gothic Fiction* (Cambridge University Press, 2002/2015), pp. 1–20.

Hogle, Jerrold E., 'The Gothic-Theory Conversation: An Introduction', in Jerrold E. Hogle and Robert Miles (eds), *The Gothic and Theory: An Edinburgh Companion* (Edinburgh: Edinburgh University Press, 2019), pp. 1–30.

Hooke, Robert, *Micrographia: Or Some Physiological Descriptions of Minute Bodies Made by Magnifying Glasses with Observations and Inquiries Thereupon* (1665/2005), Project Gutenberg, *https://www.gutenberg.org/cache/epub/15491/pg15491-images.html*, accessed 6 July 2022.

Howell, Elizabeth F., *The Dissociative Mind* (New York: Routledge, 2008).

Howell, Elizabeth F., *Understanding and Treating Dissociative Identity Disorder: A Relational Approach* (New York: Routledge, 2011).

Hughes, Virginia, 'Microbiome: Cultural Differences', *Nature* 492/7427 (2012), pp. S14–S15.

Hunter, Jack, 'Gothic Psychology, The Ecological Unconscious and the Re-Enchantment of Nature' (26 March 202), *https://gothicnaturejournal.com/gothic-psychology-the-ecological-unconscious/.*

Hurley, Kelly, *The Gothic Body: Sexuality, Materialism, and Degeneration at the* fin de siècle, (Cambridge: Cambridge University Press, 1996).

Hurley, Kelly, 'British Gothic Fiction, 1885–1930', in Jerrold E. Hogle (ed.), *The Cambridge Companion to Gothic Fiction* (Cambridge: Cambridge University Press, 2002), pp. 189–207.

Institute of Medicine (US) Forum on Microbial Threats, 'Ending the War Metaphor: The Changing Agenda for Unraveling the Host-Microbe Relationship: Workshop Summary' (2006), *https://www.ncbi.nlm.nih.gov/books/NBK57071/.*

Ironstone, Penelope, 'Me, My Self, and the Multitude: Microbiopolitics of the Human Microbiome', *European Journal of Social Theory* 22/3 (2019), pp. 325–41.

James, William, 'Frederick Myers's Service to Psychology 1901', *The Works of William James: Essays in Psychical Research* (Cambridge, Mass.: Harvard University Press, 1986), pp. 192–202.

Janca, Aleksandar and Clothilde Bullen, 'The Aboriginal Concept of Time and its Mental Health Implications', *Australasian Psychiatry* 11/1 (2003), pp. S40–S44.

Janet, Pierre, *The Major Symptoms of Hysteria* (New York: Macmillan, 1907).

Joshi, S. T. 'Introduction', in *The Three Impostors and Other Stories: Vol. 1 of the Best Weird Tales of Arthur Machen,* ed. S. T. Joshi (Hayward: Chaosium Inc., 2007), pp. xi–xix.

Jung, Carl, 'On the Psychology of the Trickster Figure', in P. Radin (ed.), *The Trickster: A Study in American Indian Mythology* (New York: Greenwood Press, 1956), pp. 195–211.

Kane, Mary Patricia, 'The Uncanny Mother in Vernon Lee's "Prince Alberic and the Snake Lady"', *Victorian Review* 32/1 (2006), pp. 41–62.

Kemp, Peter, *H. G. Wells and the Culminating Ape: Biological Imperatives and Imaginative Obsessions* (Houndmills and London: Macmillan Press Ltd., 1996).

Kennedy, George A., 'A Hoot in the Dark: The Evolution of General Rhetoric', *Philosophy and Rhetoric* 25/1 (1992), pp. 1–21.

Keetley, Dawn and Matthew Sivils, 'Introduction: Approaches to the Ecogothic', in Dawn Keetley and Matthew Sivils (eds), *Ecogothic in Nineteenth-Century American Literature* (New York: Routledge, 2017), pp. 1–20.

Kilgour, Maggie, *The Rise of the Gothic Novel* (London: Routledge, 1995).

Kim, G., M. L. LeBlanc, E. K. Wafula, C. W. dePamphilis, and J. H. Westwood, 'Genomic-scale exchange of mRNA between a parasitic plant and its hosts', *Science* 345/6198 (2014), pp. 808–11.

Kirksey, Eben, 'Queer Love, Gender Bending Bacteria, and Life after the Anthropocene', *Theory, Culture & Society* 36/6 (2019), pp. 197–219.

Kirmayer, Laurence J., 'Pacing the Void: Social and Cultural Dimensions of Dissociation', in David Spiegel (ed.), *Dissociation: Culture, Mind, and Body* (Washington: American Psychiatric Press, 1994), pp. 91–122.

Kohn, Eduardo, *How Forest Think: Toward an Anthropology Beyond the Human* (Berkeley: University of California Press, 2013).

Kosko, Bart, *Fuzzy Thinking: The New Science of Fuzzy Logic* (New York: Hyperion, 1993).

Kriss, Alexander, 'The Microbiome and the Multiple Self' (1 June 2013), *https://newschoolpsychology.blogspot.com/*.

Kristeva, Julia, *Powers of Horror: An Essay on Abjection*, trans. Leon S. Roudiez (New York: Columbia University Press, 1982).

Kristeva, Julia, *Strangers to Ourselves*, trans. Leon R. Roudiez (New York: Columbia University Press, 1991).

Kristeva, Julia, 'The Subject in Process', in P. French & R-F. Lack (eds), *The Tel Quel reader* (London, England: Routledge, 1998), pp. 133–178.

Kwon, Diana, 'Crows Perform yet Another Skill Once Thought Distinctively Human', *Scientific American* (2 Nov. 2022), *https://www.scientificamerican.com/article/crows-perform-yet-another-skill-once-thought-distinctively-human/*.

Lane, Nick, 'The unseen world: reflections on Leeuwenhoek (1677) "Concerning little animals"', *Philosophical Transactions of the Royal Society B* (2015), *http://doi.org/10.1098/rstb.2014.0344*.

Ledger, Sally and Roger Luckhurst (eds), *The Fin de Siècle: A Reader in Cultural History, c. 1880–1900* (Oxford: Oxford University Press, 2000).

Lee, Michael Parrish, 'Reading Meat in H. G. Wells', *Studies in the Novel* 42/3 (2010), pp. 249–68.

Lee, Vernon, *The Enchanted Woods: and Other Essays on the Genius of Places* (London: John Lane, The Bodley Head, 1905).

Lee, Vernon, *Genius Loci: Notes on Places* (London: John Lane, 1907).

Lee, Vernon, *Hauntings and Other Fantastic Tales*, eds Catherine Maxwell and Patricia Pulham (Peterborough: Broadview Press, 2006).

Lee, Vernon, *Limbo, and Other Essays* (London: Grant Richard, 1897).

Leston, Robert, 'Unhinged: *Kairos* and the Invention of the Untimely', *Atlantic Journal of Communication* 21/1 (2013), pp. 29–50.

Lewis, Simon L. and Mark A. Maslin, 'Defining the Anthropocene', *Nature* 519/7542 (2015), pp. 171–80.

Lifton, Robert Jay, *The Protean Self: Human Resilience in an Age of Fragmentation* (Chicago: University of Chicago Press, 1993).

Liggins, Emma, 'Gendering the Spectral Encounter at the *Fin de Siècle*: Unspeakability in Vernon Lee's Supernatural Stories', *Gothic Studies* 15/2 (2013), pp. 37–52.

Lionnet, Françoise, *Autobiographical Voices: Race, Gender, and Self-Portraiture* (Ithaca, NY: Cornell University Press, 1989).

Long, Christopher, 'The Daughters of Metis: Patriarchal Dominion and the Politics of the Between', *Graduate Faculty Philosophy Journal* 28/2 (2007), pp. 67–86.

Lorimer, Jaime, 'Gut Buddies: Multispecies Studies and the Microbiome', *Environmental Humanities* 8/1 (2016), pp. 57–76.

Lovecraft, H. P., *The Call of Cthulhu and Other Weird Stories*, ed. S. T. Joshi (New York: Penguin Books, 1999).

Lovecraft, H. P., *The Dreams in the Witch House and Other Weird Stories*, ed. S. T. Joshi (Penguin Books, 2004).

Lowan-Trudeau, Gary, 'Methodological Métissage: An Interpretive Indigenous Approach to Environmental Education Research',

Canadian Journal of Environmental Education 17 (2012), pp. 114–15.

Luckhurst, Roger, *Late Victorian Gothic Tales* (Oxford and New York: Oxford University Press, 2005).

Luckhurst, Roger, 'Trance Gothic, 1882–97', in Julian Wolfreys (ed.), *Victorian Hauntings: Spectrality, Gothic, the Uncanny and Literature* (New York: Palgrave, 2002), pp. 148–167.

MacCormack, Patricia, 'Lovecraft's Cosmic Ethics', in Carl H. Sederholm and Jeffrey Andrew Weinstock (eds), *The Age of Lovecraft* (Minneapolis: University of Minnesota Press, 2016), pp. 199–214.

MacCormack, Patricia, 'Lovecraft Through the Deleuzio-Guattarian Gates', *Postmodern Culture* 20/2 (2010), *doi:10.1353/pmc.2010.0008*.

Macfarlane, Robert, 'The Secrets of The Wood Wide Web', *The New Yorker* (7 August 2016), *https://www.newyorker.com/tech/annals-of-technology/the-secrets-of-the-wood-wide-web*.

Machen, Arthur, *Far Off Things* (London: Martin Secker, 1922).

Machen, Arthur, *The Three Impostors and Other Stories: Vol. 1 of the Best Weird Tales of Arthur Machen*, ed. S. T. Joshi (Hayward: Chaosium Inc., 2007).

Machen, Arthur, 'The Hill of Dreams', in *The Great God Pan and The Hill of Dreams* (Mineola NY: Dover Publications, 2006), pp. 67–236.

Manning, Pascale McCullough, 'The Hyde We Live in: Stevenson, Evolution, and the Anthropogenic Fog', *Victorian Literature and Culture* 46 (2018), pp. 181–99.

Margree, Victoria and Bryony Randall, '*Fin-de-Siècle* Gothic', in A. Smith and W. Hughes (eds), *The Victorian Gothic: An Edinburgh Companion* (Edinburgh: Edinburgh University Press, 2012), pp. 217–32.

Margree, Victoria, '"Both in Men's Clothing": Gender, Sovereignty, and Insecurity in Richard Marsh's *The Beetle*', *Critical Survey* 19/2 (2007), pp. 63–81.

Margulis, Lynn, *Symbiotic Planet: A New Look at Evolution* (New York: Basic Books, 1998).

Margulis, Lynn, Celeste A. Asikainen, and Wolfgang E. Krumbein, 'Introduction: Life's Sensibilities', in Lynn Margulis, Celeste

A. Asikainen, and Wolfgang E. Krumbein (eds), *Chimeras and Consciousness: Evolution of the Sensory Self* (Cambridge, MA: The MIT Press, 2011), pp. 1–13.

Margulis, Lynn and Dorion Sagan, *Acquiring Genomes: A Theory of the Origins of Species* (New York: Basic Books, 2002).

Margulis, Lynn and Dorian Sagan, 'The Beast with Five Genomes', *Natural History* 110/5 (2001), p. 38.

Margulis, Lynn and Dorian Sagan, *What is Life?* (Berkeley, CA: California University Press, 1995).

Marsh, Richard, *The Beetle*, ed. Julian Wolfreys (Peterborough: Broadview Press, 2004).

Matus, Jill, *Shock, Memory and the Unconscious in Victorian Fiction* (Cambridge; New York: Cambridge University Press, 2009).

Maudsley, Henry, 'The Double Brain', in *The Strange Case of Dr Jekyll and Mr Hyde*, 2nd edn, ed. Martin Danahay (Peterborough: Broadview Press, 2005), pp. 193–8.

Maxwell, Catherine and Patricia Pulham, 'Introduction', *Hauntings and Other Fantastic Tales* by Vernon Lee, eds. Catherine Maxwell and Patricia Pulham (Peterborough: Broadview Editions, 2006), pp. 9–27.

McCarthy, Colm, (dir), *The Girl with All the Gifts*, Warner Bros., (2016).

McDermott, Lydia, 'Birthing Rhetorical Monsters: How Mary Shelley Infuses *Mêtis* with the Maternal in Her 1831 Introduction to *Frankenstein*', *Rhetoric Review* 34/1 (2015), pp. 1–18.

McFall-Ngai, Margaret, 'Noticing Microbial Worlds: The Postmodern Synthesis in Biology', in A. Tsing, H. Swanson, E. Gan, and N. Bubandt (eds), *Arts of Living on a Damaged Planet* (Minneapolis: University of Minnesota Press, 2017), pp. M51–M69.

Merskey, H., 'The Manufacture of Personalities: The Production of Multiple Personality Disorder', *British Journal of Psychiatry* 160 (1992), pp. 327–40.

Mershon, Ella, 'Pulpy Fiction' *Victorian Literature and Culture* 48/1 (2020), pp. 267–98.

Mighall, Robert, *A Geography of Victorian Gothic Fiction* (Oxford, Oxford University Press, 1999).

Miles, Robert, *Gothic Writing 1750–1820: A Genealogy*, 2nd edn (Manchester: Manchester University Press, 2002).

Miller, Amy Louise, 'The Phenomenology of Self as Non-Local: Theoretical Consideration and Research Report', in Anna-Teresa Tymieniecka (ed.), *Logos of Phenomenology and Phenomenology of the Logos* Book 4 *The Logos of Scientific Interrogation: Participating in Nature-Life-Sharing in Life* (New York: Springer, 2006), pp. 227–45.

Mills, Sarah, *Discourse* (The New Critical Idiom), 2nd edn (New York, Routledge, 2004).

Miyoshi, Masao, *The Divided Self; a Perspective on the Literature of the Victorians* (New York: New York University Press, 1969).

Molloy, Cathryn, '"I Just Really Love My Spirit": A Rhetorical Inquiry into Dissociative Identity Disorder', *Rhetoric Review* 34/4 (2015), pp. 462–78.

Mortimer-Sandilands, Catriona and Bruce Erickson (eds), *Queer Ecologies: Sex, Nature, Politics, Desire* (Bloomington and Indianapolis: Indiana University Press, 2010).

Morton, Timothy, *Dark Ecology: For a Logic of Future Coexistence* (New York: Columbia University Press, 2016).

Morton, Timothy, *Humankind: Solidarity with Nonhuman People* (London, New York: Verso, 2019).

Morton, Timothy, *The Ecological Thought* (Cambridge, Mass.: Harvard University Press, 2010).

MycoLyco, 'Five Minutes of Blue Oyster Mushrooms Talking', *YouTube* (28 Nov. 2020), *https://www.youtube.com/watch?v=J-nIBA0V_No*.

Myers, F. W. H., *Human Personality and its Survival of Bodily Death* (London: Longmans, Green & Co., 1903).

Myers, F. W. H., 'Human personality in the light of hypnotic suggestion', *Proceedings of The Society for Psychical Research* 4 (1886–87), pp. 1–24.

Myers, F. W. H., 'Multiplex Personality', *Proceedings of the Society for Psychical Research* 3 (1887), pp. 496–514.

Myers, F. W. H., 'Obituary: Robert Louis Stevenson', *Journal of the Society for Psychical Research* 7 (Jan. 1895), pp. 6–7.

Myers, F. W. H., 'To the Editor of the *Journal of the Society for Psychical Research*', *Journal of the Society for Psychical Research* IV/LX (May 1889), pp. 77–8.

Nordau, Max, *Degeneration* (New York: D. Appleton and Company, 1895).

Otis, Laura, 'Monkey in the Mirror: The Science of Professor Higgins and Doctor Moreau', *Twentieth-Century Literature* 55/4 (2009), pp. 485–509.

Paget-Clarke, Nic, 'Science From A Native Perspective: How Do We Educate for A Sustainable Future' (and interview with Gregory Cajete), *In Motion Magazine* (12 March 2016), *https://inmotionmagazine.com/global/cajete/gregory-cajete-int2015.html.*

Parkins, Wendy and Peter Adkins, 'Introduction: Victorian Ecology and the Anthropocene', *19: Interdisciplinary Studies in the Long Nineteenth Century* 26 (2018), pp. 1–15.

Pauck, Wilhelm and Marion Pauck, *Paul Tillich: His Life & Thought, Vol. 1: Life* (New York: Harper & Row, 1976).

Paxson, Heather, 'Post-Pasteurian Cultures: The Microbiopolitics of Raw-Milk Cheese in the United States', *Cultural Anthropology* 23/1 (2008), pp. 15–47.

Paxson, Heather and Stefan Helmreich, 'The Perils and Promises of Microbial Abundance: Novel Natures and Model Ecosystems, From Artisanal Cheese to Alien Seas', *Social Studies of Science* 44/2 (2014), pp. 165–93.

Peeples, Jennifer A., 'Toxic Sublime: Imaging Contaminated Landscapes', *Environmental Communication* 5/4 (2011), pp. 373–92.

Pezzullo, Phaedra, *Toxic Tourism. Rhetorics of Pollution, Travel, and Environmental Justice* (Tuscaloosa, AL: University of Alabama Press, 2007).

Pezzullo, Phaedra, 'Unearthing the Marvelous: Environmental Imprints on Rhetorical Criticism', *Review of Communication* 16/1 (2016), pp. 25–42.

Phelan, Shane, 'Coyote Politics: Trickster Tales and Feminist Futures', *Hypatia* 11/3 (1996), pp. 130–49.

Philmus, Robert M. and David Y. Hughes (eds), *H. G. Wells: Early Writings in Science and Science Fiction* (Berkeley, Los Angeles and London: University of California Press, 1975).

Pierotti, Raymond, 'Learning about Extraordinary Beings', *Ethnobiology Letters* 11/2 (2020), pp. 44–51.

Poe, Edgar Allan, *Edgar Allan Poe Complete Tales & Poems* (Edison, NJ: Castle Books, 2002).

Pollan, Michael, 'Some of my Best Friends are Germs', *The New York Times* (15 May 2013) *https://nyti.ms/YTN1m3*.

Pomykala, Kristin, 'Snake(s)kin: The Intertwining Mêtis and Mythopoetics of Serpentine Rhetoric', *Rhetoric Society Quarterly* 47/3 (2017), pp. 264–74.

Pratt, Mary Louise, 'Arts of the Contact Zone', *Profession* 1 (1991), pp. 33–40.

Prince, Morton, *Dissociation of a Personality* (Oxford: Oxford University Press, 1905).

Punter, David, 'On the Threshold of Gothic: A Reflection', in Jerrold E. Hogle and Robert Miles (eds), *The Gothic and Theory: An Edinburgh Companion* (Edinburgh: Edinburgh University Press, 2019), pp. 301–19.

Punter, David, *The Literature of Terror, Vol. I: The Gothic Tradition*, 2nd edn (London: Longman, 1996).

Půtová, Barbora, 'Historical Changes of the Coyote: An Anthropological Reflection on the Trickster', in B. Půtová (ed.), *Identity, Tradition, and Revitalization of American Indian Cultures* (Prague: Karolinum Press, 2017), pp. 203–14.

Puységur, Armand-Marie-Jacques de Chastenet, Marquis de, *Mémoires pour servir à l'histoiré et à l'établissement du magnétisme animal* (Paris: Dentu, 1784).

Radin, Paul, *The World of Primitive Man* (New York: Dutton, 1971).

Raphals, Lisa, *Knowing Words: Wisdom and Cunning in the Classical Traditions of China and Greece* (Ithica, NY: Cornell University Press, 2018).

Rappoport, Leon, Steven Baumgardner, and George Boone. 'Postmodern Culture and the Plural Self', in Mick Cooper and John Rowan (eds), *The Plural Self: Multiplicity in Everyday Life* (London: Sage, 1999), pp. 93–106.

Rebry Coulthard, Natasha, 'Lovecraft's Viral Networks: A Contaminated Ethics for the Chthulucene', in Antonio Alcala Gonzalez and Carl H. Sederholm (eds), *Lovecraft in the 21st Century: Dead, But Still Dreaming* (New York: Routledge, 2022), pp. 143–58.

Rebry, Natasha, 'Disintegrated Subjects: Gothic Fiction, Mental Science and the *fin-de-siècle* Discourse of Dissociation' (PhD Thesis, The University of British Columbia, Okanagan, 2013), *https://open.library.ubc.ca/cIRcle/collections/ubctheses/24/items/1.0073632.*

Rebry, Natasha, 'Playing the Man: Mesmerism and Manliness in Richard Marsh's *The Beetle*', *Gothic Studies* 18/1 (2016), pp. 1–15.

Rees, Tobias, Thomas Bosch, and Angela E. Douglas, 'How the microbiome challenges our concept of self', *PLOS Biology* 16/2 (2018), *P. e2005358.*

Reiter, Bernd, *Decolonizing the Social Sciences and Humanities: An Anti-Elitism Manifesto* (New York: Routledge, 2021).

Rhodes, Christopher J., 'The Whispering World of Plants: "The Wood Wide Web"', *Science Progress* 100/3 (2017), pp. 331–7.

Rieber, Robert W., *The Bifurcation of the Self: The History and Theory of Dissociation And Its Disorders* (New York: Birkhäuser, 2006).

Rickert, Thomas, 'In the House of Doing: Rhetoric and the Kairos of Ambience', *JAC* 24/4 (2004), pp. 901–27.

Richez, Yves, *Corporate Talent Detection and Development* (London: John Wiley & Sons, 2018).

Rivers, Nathaniel A., 'Deep Ambivalence and Wild Objects: Toward a Strange Environmental Rhetoric', *Rhetoric Society Quarterly* 45/5 (2015), pp. 420–40.

Robbins, Ruth, 'Apparitions Can Be Deceptive: Vernon Lee's Androgynous Spectres', in R. Robbins and J. Wolfreys (eds), *Victorian Gothic: Literary and Cultural Manifestations in the Nineteenth Century* (Basingstoke and New York: Palgrave, 2000), pp. 182–200.

Robinson, Eden, *Monkey Beach* (Toronto: Vintage Canada, 2001).

Rohman, Carrie, 'Burning Out the Animal: The Failure of Enlightenment Purification in H. G. Wells's *The Island of Dr. Moreau*', in Mary Sanders Pollock and Catherine Rainwater (eds), *Figuring Animals: Essays on Animal Images in Art, Literature, Philosophy and Popular Culture* (New York: Palgrave, 2005), pp. 121–34.

Rolfe, R. T. and F. W. Rolfe, *The Romance of the Fungus World: An Account of Fungus in Its Numerous Guises Both Real and Legendary* (Mineola, New York: Dover Publications, Inc. 1925/2014).

Rose, Deborah Bird, 'Shimmer: When All You Love Is Being Trashed', in A. Tsing, H. Swanson, E. Gan, and N. Bubandt (eds), *Arts of Living on a Damaged Planet* (Minneapolis: University of Minnesota Press, 2017), pp. G51–G63.

Rowan, John, *Subpersonalities: The People Inside Us* (New York: Routledge, 1990).

Rowan, John and Mick Cooper (eds), *The Plural Self: Multiplicity in Everyday Life* (London: Sage, 1999).

Royle, Nicholas, *The Uncanny* (New York: Routledge, 2003).

Royle, Nicholas, *Veering: A Theory of Literature* (Edinburgh: Edinburgh University Press, 2001).

Rutsky, R. L., 'Mutation, History, and the Fantasy in the Posthuman', *Subject Matters: A Journal of Communication and the Self* 3/2–4/1 (2007), pp. 99–112.

Saey, Tina Hesman, 'Inside job: teams of microbes pull strings in the human body', *Science News*, 179/13 (18 June 2011).

Saey, Tina Hesman, 'Year in Review: Your Body Is Mostly Microbes', *Science News* (20 Dec. 2013).

Sagan, Dorion, 'Beautiful Monsters: Terra in the Cyanocene', in A. Tsing, H. Swanson, E. Gan, and N. Bubandt (eds), *Arts of Living on a Damaged Planet* (Minneapolis: University of Minnesota Press, 2017), pp. M169–M174.

Sagan, Dorion, 'Biography', *https://dorionsagan.wordpress.com/cv/biography/*, accessed 12 July 2022.

Sagan, Dorion, *Cosmic Apprentice: Dispatches from the Edges of Science* (Minneapolis: University of Minnesota Press, 2013).

Sagan, Dorion, 'The Human is More than Human: Interspecies Communities and the New "Facts of Life"', *Society for Cultural Anthropology* (18 Nov. 2011), *https://culanth.org/fieldsights/the-human-is-more-than-human-interspecies-communities-and-the-new-facts-of-life*.

Sagan, Dorion, 'Metametazoa: Biology and Multiplicity', in Jonathan Crary and Sanford Kwinter (eds), *Zone 6: Incorporations: Fragments for a History of the Human Body* (Princeton: Princeton University Press, 1992), pp. 362–85.

Sagan, Dorion, 'Thermodynamics and Thought', in Lynn Margulis, Celeste A. Asikainen, and Wolfgang E. Krumbein (eds), *Chimeras and Consciousness: Evolution of the Sensory Self* (Cambridge, MA: The MIT Press, 2011), pp. 241–50.

Saler, Michael, 'Introduction', in M. Saler (ed.), *The Fin-de-Siècle World* (London and New York: Routledge, 2015), pp. 1–8.

Samyn, Jeanette, 'Intimate Ecologies: Symbioses in the Nineteenth Century', *Victorian Literature and Culture* 48/1 (2020), pp. 243–65.

Sandilands, Catriona, 'Queer Ecology', in *Keywords for Environmental Studies* (2016), *https://keywords.nyupress.org/environmental-studies/essay/queer-ecology/*, accessed 18 Nov. 2023.

Schmitt, Cannon, 'Notes Towards a Water Acknowledgement', plenary address at the North American Victorian Studies Association 2022 conference, online.

Schwarze, Steven, 'Environmental Melodrama', *Quarterly Journal of Speech* 92/3 (2006), pp. 239–61.

Sedgwick, Eve Kosofsky, *The Coherence of Gothic Conventions* (New York: Methuen, 1986).

Shamdasani, Sonu, 'Encountering Hélène: Théodore Flournoy and the Genesis of Subliminal Psychology', in Théodore Flournoy *From India to the Planet Mars: A Case of Multiple Personality with Imaginary Languages*, ed. Sonu Shamdasani (Princeton: Princeton University Press, 1994), pp. xi–li.

Shelley, Mary, *Frankenstein; or, The Modern Prometheus*, eds. D. L. Macdonald and Kathleen Scherf (Peterborough: Broadview Press, 1994).

Shi, Wen, et al., 'What Framework Promotes Saliency of Climate Change Issues on Online Public Agenda', *Sustainability* 11 (2019), pp. 1–24.

Showalter, Elaine, *Sexual Anarchy: Gender and Culture at the* Fin de Siècle (London: Bloomsbury, 1990).

Smith, Andrew, *Gothic Literature*, 2nd edn (Edinburgh: Edinburgh University Press, 2013).

Smith, Andrew and William Hughes (eds), *EcoGothic* (Manchester: Manchester University Press, 2013).

Smith, John E., 'Time and Qualitative Time', *The Review of Metaphysics* 40/1 (1986), pp. 3–16.

Spooner, Catherine, *Contemporary Gothic* (London, Reaktion Books, 2006).

Stamets, Paul, '6 Ways Mushrooms Can Save the World', *TED Talk* (March 2008), *https://www.ted.com/talks/*

paul_stamets_6_ways_mushrooms_can_save_the_world?subtitle=en, accessed 4 January 2022.

Stibbe, Arran, 'An Ecolinguistic Approach to Critical Discourse Studies', *Critical Discourse Studies* 11/1 (2014), pp. 117–28.

Stibbe, Arran, 'Positive Discourse Analysis: Re-thinking human ecological relationships', in A. Fill and H. Penz (eds), *The Routledge Handbook of Ecolinguistics* (London: Routledge, 2017).

Stibbe, Arran, 'Critical discourse analysis and ecology: The search for new stories to live by', in J. Richardson and J. Flowerdew (eds), *The Routledge Handbook of Critical Discourse Analysis* (London: Routledge, 2018), pp. 497–509.

Stiles, Anne, *Popular Fiction and Brain Science in the Late Nineteenth Century* (Cambridge: Cambridge University Press, 2012).

Stevenson, Robert Louis Stevenson, *Strange Case of Dr Jekyll and Mr Hyde*, 3rd edn, ed. Martin Danahay (Peterborough: Broadview Press, 2015).

Stilling, Roman M., Timothy G. Dinan, and John F. Cryan, 'Microbial Genes, Brain & Behaviour – Epigenetic Regulation of the Gut-Brain Axis', *Genes, Brain and Behavior*, 13/1 (2014), pp. 69–86.

Stoker, Bram, *Dracula* (Peterborough: Broadview Press, 2000).

Sugars, Cynthia and Gerry Turcotte, 'Canadian Literature and the Postcolonial Gothic', in Cynthia Sugars and Gerry Turcotte (eds), *Unsettled Remains: Canadian Literature and the Postcolonial Gothic* (Waterloo: Wilfrid Laurier Press, 2009), pp. vii–xxvi.

Szakolczai, Árpád, *Post-Truth Society: A Political Anthropology of Trickster Logic* (London and New York: Routledge, 2022).

Tait, Adrian, '"[A] Mystic, Ineffable Force and Energy": Arthur Machen and Theories of New Materialism', in Antonio Sanna (ed.), *Arthur Machen: Critical Essays* (London: Lexington Books, 2021), pp. 193–208.

Tesar, Marek and Sonja Arndt, 'Writing the Human "I": Liminal Spaces of Mundane Abjection', *Qualitative Inquiry* 26/8–9 (2020), pp. 1102–9.

Thacker, Eugene, *In the Dust of this Planet: Horror of Philosophy Vol. 1* (Winchester, Washington: Zero Books, 2011).

Thacker, Eugene, *Tentacles Longer than Night: Horror of Philosophy Vol. 3* (Winchester, Washington: Zero Books, 2015).

Torjussen, Stian, 'Phanes and Dionysos in the Derveni Theogony', *Symbolae Osloenses* 80/1 (2005), pp. 7–22.

Trapani, William C. and Chandra A. Maldonado, '*Kairos*: On the Limits to Our (Rhetorical) Situation', *Rhetoric Society Quarterly* 48/3 (2018), pp. 278–86.

Tsing, Anna Lowenhaupt, *The Mushroom at the End of the World: On the Possibility of Life in Capitalist Ruins* (Princeton: Princeton University Press, 2015).

Tsing, Anna, Heather Swanson, Elaine Gan, and Nils Bubandt (eds), *Arts of Living on a Damaged Planet* (Minneapolis: University of Minnesota Press, 2017).

Turner, Victor, *The Forest of Symbols: Aspects of Ndembu Ritual* (Ithaca: Cornell University Press, 1967).

Valentine, Mark, *Arthur Machen* (Bridgend: WBC Book Manufacturers, 1995).

van Deelen, Grace, 'What Is Queer Ecology?' (3 June 2023), *https://www.sierraclub.org/sierra/what-is-queer-ecology*.

Villarreal, Luis P., 'Are Viruses Alive?', *Scientific American* 291/6 (2004), pp. 100–05.

Vint, Sherryl, *Animal Alterity: Science Fiction and the Question of the Animal* (Liverpool: Liverpool University Press, 2010).

Vint, Sherryl, 'Animals and Animality from the Island of Moreau to the Uplift Universe', *The Yearbook of English Studies* 37/2 (2007), pp. 85–102.

Walker, Patrick J. Skerrett, and W. Allan, 'Say Hello To The Bugs In Your Gut', *Newsweek*, 150/24 (10 Dec. 2007), p. 75.

Walpole, Horace, *The Castle of Otranto and The Mysterious Mother*, ed. F. S. Frank (Peterborough: Broadview Press, 2011).

Walters, Shannon, 'Animal Athena: The Interspecies "Mētis" of Women Writers with Autism', *JAC* 30/3/4, (2010), pp. 683–711.

Wanitzek, Leonie, '"The South! Something Exclaims within Me": Real and Imagined Spaces in Italy and the South in Vernon Lee's Travel Writing', *Cahiers victoriens et éduardienes* 83 (2016).

Warwick, Alexandra, 'Feeling Gothicky', *Gothic Studies* 9/1 (2007), pp. 5–15.

Warwick, Alexandra, 'Victorian Gothic', in Catherine Spooner and Emma McEvoy (eds), *The Routledge Companion to Gothic* (London and New York: Routledge, 2007), pp. 29–37.

Watson, Traci, 'The Trickster Microbes Shaking up the Tree of Life', *Nature* 569/16 (May 2019), pp. 322–4.

Weinstock, Jeffrey Andrew, 'Lovecraft's Things: Sinister Souvenirs from Other Worlds', in Carl H. Sederholm and Jeffrey Andrew Weinstock (eds), *The Age of Lovecraft* (Minneapolis: University of Minnesota Press, 2016), pp. 62–78.

Wells, H. G., 'Ancient Experiments in Co-Operation', *Gentleman's Magazine* (Oct. 1892), pp. 418–22.

Wells, H. G., *Mind at the End of its Tether* (London, Toronto: William Heinemann LTD, 1945).

Wells, H. G., *The Complete Short Stories of H.G. Wells* (London: Benn, 1966).

Wells, H. G., 'The Extinction of Man: Some Speculative Suggestions', *Pall Mall Gazette* 59 (25 September 1894), p. 3.

Wells, H. G., 'The Future in America: A Search After Realities' (New York and London: Harper & Brothers Publishers, 1906).

Wells, H. G., *The Island of Doctor Moreau*, ed. Mason Harris (Peterborough: Broadview Press, 2009).

Wells, H. G., 'The Man of the Year Million. A Scientific Forecast', *Pall Mall Gazette* 57/8931 (6 Nov. 1893), p. 3.

Wells, H. G., *The Time Machine: An Invention* (New York: The Modern Library, 2002).

Wells, H. G., *The War of the Worlds*, ed. Martin A. Danahay (Peterborough: Broadview, 2003).

Wells, H. G., 'Zoological Retrogression', *Gentleman's Magazine* 271 (Sept. 1891), pp. 246–53.

Wheatley, Ben, (dir.), *In the Earth*, Rock Films, (2021).

Wheelwright, Betty Coon, 'A Storytelling of Ravens', *Jung Journal* 7/1 (2013), pp. 4–18.

Whiteside, Jessica Hope and Dorion Sagan, 'Medical Symbiotics', in Lynn Margulis, Celeste A. Asikainen, and Wolfgang E. Krumbein (eds), *Chimeras and Consciousness: Evolution of the Sensory Self* (Cambridge, MA: The MIT Press, 2011), pp. 207–18.

Williams, Anne, *Art of Darkness: A Poetics of Gothic* (Chicago: The University of Chicago Press, 1995).

Wilson, Elizabeth A., *Gut Feminism* (Durham and London: Duke University Press, 2015).

Wilson, Michael T., '"Absolute Reality" and the Role of the Ineffable in Shirley Jackson's *The Haunting of Hill House*', *The Journal of Popular Culture* 548/1 (2015), pp. 114–23.

Winter, Alison, *Mesmerized: Powers of Mind in Victorian Britain* (Chicago: University of Chicago Press, 1998).

Wisker, Gina, 'Imagining Beyond Extinctathon: Indigenous Knowledge, Survival, Speculation – Margaret Atwood's and Ann Patchett's Eco-Gothic', *Contemporary Women's Writing*, 11/3 (2017), pp. 412–31.

Wodak, Ruth and Salomi Boukala, 'European Identities and the Revival of Nationalism in the European Union: A Discourse Historical Approach', *Journal of Language and Politics* 14/1 (2015), pp. 87–109.

Wodak, Ruth and Martin Reisigl, 'The Discourse-Historical Approach (DHA)', in Ruth Wodak and Michael Meyer (eds), *Methods of Critical Discourse Studies*, 3rd edn (London; Los Angeles: SAGE Publications, 2016), pp. 23–61.

Woodard, Ben, *Slime Dynamics* (Winchester, Washington: Zero Books, 2012).

Wolfe, Cary, *What is Posthumanism?* (Minneapolis: University of Minnesota Press, 2010).

Wolfreys, Julian, 'Victorian Gothic', in Anna Powell and Andrew Smith (eds), *Teaching the Gothic* (Basingstoke: Palgrave Macmillan, 2006), pp. 64–76.

Wolfreys, Julian, *Victorian Hauntings: Spectrality, Gothic, the Uncanny and Literature* (New York: Palgrave, 2002).

Yong, Ed, *I Contain Multitudes: The Microbes Within Us and a Grander View of Life* (New York: HarperCollins, 2016).

Zigarovich, Jolene, 'The Trans Legacy of *Frankenstein*', *Science Fiction Studies* 45/2 (2018), pp. 260–72.

Zimmer, Carl, 'Our Microbiome May Be Looking Out for Itself', *The New York Times* (14 Aug. 2014), *https://www.nytimes.com/2014/08/14/science/our-microbiome-may-be-looking-out-for-itself.html*.

Index